THE MAID MARRIED TO THE BILLIONAIRE

LYNNE GRAHAM

UNVEILED AS THE ITALIAN'S BRIDE

CATHY WILLIAMS

MILLS & BOON

First published in Great Britain 2023
by Mills & Boon, an imprint of HarperCollins*Publishers* Ltd,
1 London Bridge Street, London, SE1 9GF

www.harpercollins.co.uk

HarperCollins*Publishers*, Macken House, 39/40 Mayor Street Upper,
Dublin 1, D01 C9W8, Ireland

The Maid Married to the Billionaire © 2023 Lynne Graham

Unveiled as the Italian's Bride © 2023 Cathy Williams

ISBN: 978-0-263-30684-2

07/23

MIX
Paper | Supporting
responsible forestry
FSC™ C007454

This book is produced from independently certified FSC™ paper
to ensure responsible forest management.
For more information visit: www.harpercollins.co.uk/green.

Printed and Bound in the UK using 100% Renewable Electricity
at CPI Group (UK) Ltd, Croydon, CR0 4YY

THE MAID MARRIED TO THE BILLIONAIRE

LYNNE GRAHAM

MILLS & BOON

CHAPTER ONE

A LARGE AND expensive four-by-four awaited Lorenzo
Durante when he arrived in his private jet at Norwich
airport.

It had been a long time since he had driven himself.
Limousines were more Enzo's style. He gritted his teeth.
He didn't whine about stuff, and he wasn't a kid any
more. He had got himself into his current predicament
and he would get himself out of it again. That he was unlikely to enjoy the experience of relinquishing his afflu-
ent way of life went without saying but then wasn't that
part of the punishment?

His grandfather, Eduardo Martelli, had, however, insisted that the challenge he had set *wasn't* a punishment.
Eduardo had preached at length about the need for Enzo
to *grow up*. Just remembering that demeaning phrase
made Enzo seethe, his quick, hot temper ready to spark.
He compressed his lips, his lean, darkly handsome features taut. He was twenty-seven years old and aside from
his university studies and spells as an intern, he had never
worked a day in his life. Why would he have? Orphaned
as a baby, he had inherited billions from his late father,
Narciso.

His maternal grandparents were nowhere near as wealthy as his paternal grandparents had been, yet they had fought them for custody and, probably because they were younger and healthier than their opponents, had won the case. In court they had promised to raise their grandson in what they had termed an *ordinary* life. Sadly, they had had their work cut out on that front, Enzo acknowledged ruefully, thinking of the legion of Durante relations and hangers-on who had constantly invaded his childhood with their visits and invitations, their ridiculously lavish gifts and their eagerness to tempt him into the supremely privileged permissive lifestyle his late father had enjoyed.

Somewhere around his twenty-third birthday, after he had completed his education in the business world, he mused grimly, the seduction had begun to work. Fresh from university and nursing a broken heart, Enzo had been vulnerable to the temptation of the playboy lifestyle. That was where it had started, the slow steady sink into a self-indulgent decadence that had appalled the grandparents who in every way had truly been his parents.

And a few years on, the inevitable had happened: his two lifestyles had collided and fatally clashed. The scandalous headlines their grandson attracted had been studiously ignored by Eduardo and Sophie Martelli. But after he had made the fatal mistake of attending a social occasion drunk with an equally drunken partner, the balloon had gone up on forgiveness. He still broke out in a cold sweat when he recalled that evening. The next day he had attempted to apologise. Eduardo Martelli had refused to listen while his wife had simply sobbed in embarrassment and heartbreak because her husband seemed determined to disown the grandson she adored.

That had been the shocking moment when Enzo had realised that it didn't matter how much money he had, how many friends or what exciting opportunities to enjoy himself still shone on his horizon. He had finally appreciated how much more his family meant to him and his loving grandmother's distress had shamed him. And coming to England, taking charge of a small company recently acquired by his grandfather and striving to live a more *useful*, normal life was the price of reconciliation. Only there was nothing normal about it, Enzo conceded in exasperation, not on *his* terms.

He drew up at the house he was to use. It was in the back of beyond, a couple of miles from the nearest town and larger than he had expected. He was accustomed to spacious accommodation, but a serviced apartment would have suited him better than an old country house with a turret. He hoped it looked better inside than it did from the outside. Minutes later, Enzo contemplated the fresh horror of an antique furnished décor and an empty kitchen, when he was starving. How the hell was he supposed to manage alone when he couldn't cook? First world problem, he lamented wryly, and probably the opening to a long line of such jarring wake-up calls. He would manage, of course he would.

An hour later, the takeaway pizza he had ordered thrust into the bin in disgust, Enzo drove into the town to find a restaurant. He couldn't find one. He located a twenty-four-hour supermarket but drove past it, deciding that he could do without eating for one night. Instead, he went to check out the business he would be dragging into the twenty-first century. The office block beside the factory he had to overhaul was substantial. He would be as popular as poison when he arrived in the morning as the new CEO. It had been a family business and there would be redundancies, restructuring, all the changes necessary to make the firm viable again.

On his drive back to the house he drove past a car parked by the side of the road, a young woman standing by its bonnet. A woman on her own in the dark with a broken-down car. A groan of frustration escaped him. He didn't want to get involved. Nobody would ever accuse Enzo of being a good Samaritan, but he was too well brought up to ignore the dangers threatening a woman in such a situation. Biting back a curse of irritation, he turned the car and drove back, buzzing down the window to lean out…

One hour earlier

Skye lay where she fell after Ritchie threw her viciously away from him. She was so terrified she couldn't breathe, wasn't even sure a breath could manage to squeeze past her agonisingly sore throat. He had semi-strangled her but only after he had first punched her in the face and the stomach to bring her down, glaring down at her like a madman as though he hated her, and then kicking her. She felt as if she was broken inside, as though the world had stopped suddenly and flung her off at a height and she was still falling. Shock was roaring through her because Ritchie had never hit her before. He had shouted but there had never been any violence.

Ritchie was still ranting, crashing about the bedroom, slamming doors, shouting abuse back at her. She stayed still, eyes shut tight, afraid he would notice her again, *hurt* her again. Or worse, get so mad at her lack of response that he hurt the children. Brodie, the poor little mite, having seen the attack, had rushed in front of her in a pathetic toddler attempt to protect her but she had managed to get between him and Ritchie and get Brodie into the safety of his bedroom. Her frantic intervention had only made Ritchie angrier than ever. She needed to get herself and the kids out of the apartment fast but Ritchie would never willingly let her leave him. She stayed on the floor, quiet as a mouse, her heart thumping at an insane rate as she played dead.

'You stupid cow! I'm going down to the off-licence!' Ritchie spat down at her.

A moment later, the front door slammed and she was up, trying to move at speed but then staggering in pain, groaning helplessly at the burning agony of her battered ribs. She stumbled straight into the kids' room, found her little brother, Brodie, sobbing and frightened on his bed, and she reached for him first.

'We're going out,' she told him soothingly, smoothing his tumbled blond curls. 'But you have to be quiet.'

She scooped her sleeping sister, Shona, straight out of her cot, snatching up a cot blanket to keep the baby extra warm. Her feet were bare and she looked in vain for her shoes. Brodie was clingy and anxious, which was hardly surprising after what he had witnessed. It was bad enough that Ritchie had attacked her but unimaginable that she could have allowed him to hurt a two-year-old in his ungovernable rage.

It was *her* fault, she thought in an agony of guilt. After all, she had chosen to move in with Ritchie. She was the fool who had put her innocent siblings into contact with such a man and put them at risk. But she hadn't known, hadn't dreamt what Ritchie might be capable of in a temper. And now that she knew, now that she had learned her mistake, she was leaving. But there was no time to pack. There was too big a risk of Ritchie coming back before she could get away. She could return for their stuff later when everything had calmed down and he was hopefully at work.

Hands all clumsy fingers and thumbs, she strapped the kids into their car seats and collapsed into the driver's seat, saying a momentary prayer to the god of ancient motor vehicles that Mavis would start for her because Mavis, her late mother's elderly car, could be very temperamental. When the engine burst into noisy life, she heaved a sigh of relief and moved off, hunched over the wheel while she worried about where on earth she would go. A homeless shelter? A women's refuge? Hopefully there would be somewhere in the town that would take them in. If not, they would have to spend the night in the car. Escaping Ritchie would be only the first step on a stony road, she conceded unhappily, guilt pulling at her afresh.

Enzo leant out of the window of his car.

'Do you need help?'

'Do you know anything about cars?' Skye asked hopefully.

Suppressing a sigh, Enzo climbed out. He had spent his teens tinkering with engines. Unfortunately, one glance under the rusted bonnet was sufficient to tell him that it had been at least a decade since even basic maintenance had been carried out on the old banger. 'It could be any one of a number of problems,' he pointed out wryly. 'Have you called anyone? Do you belong to a motoring organisation?'

'I'm afraid not and I haven't called anyone, but I don't have anyone I can call, right now,' she framed awkwardly, stepping back from him because he was very tall and broad and somehow elegantly intimidating, beautifully dressed as he was in a business suit.

Enzo looked at her for the first time. She had blonde corkscrew curls that fluffed round her triangular features like a tousled lion's mane *and*...there was something wrong with her face. If she would just move out of the shadows into the brightness of his headlights, he could get a better look at her.

'There must be someone,' Enzo told her confidently. 'Friends? A family member?'

'No, at this time of night there's really no one,' she insisted uncomfortably, stepping off one foot onto the other.

Enzo stilled and scrutinised her bare feet in disbelief. 'Why do you have no shoes on? It's freezing tonight!'

'I left home in a hurry.' She tried to laugh but the effort seemed to choke her. Her hand flew up to her face and she winced in obvious pain.

'You're hurt,' Enzo registered in consternation. 'Was there an accident? Should I call the police?'

'No, please don't get the police,' she urged with a shiver of dismay.

'Then what can I do to help you?'

'Just drive on. You did the kind thing and stopped but I'm not really in a position to *be* helped, unless you can fix the car,' she muttered shakily.

'I can't leave you out here on your own,' Enzo objected, peering down at her as she shifted position. She was very small, possibly about five feet tall and probably only about a hundred pounds soaking wet as well as being pretty young. 'Surely I can drop you off somewhere?'

As she moved forward, he saw her swollen face, the partially closed eye and the ring of dark bluish bruising circling her throat like a macabre necklace. '*Madonna mia*, you've been attacked and you're hurt! Is that why you left home in such a hurry?'

'Yeah, we're running away, just not doing a very efficient job of it,' she mumbled shakily.

'I'll ring a breakdown company,' Enzo informed her, digging out his phone, only vaguely wondering why she had referred to 'we' when she was alone.

'I'm not sure I can afford one.'

'Then let it be at my expense,' Enzo urged, searching for the nearest breakdown service on his phone, keen to find a solution and move them on. 'But let me take you to the nearest hospital now. You need medical attention.'

'Do I look that bad?' she asked baldly.

'You look like someone tried to strangle you and you got punched in the face,' Enzo bit out in a taut undertone, for although he knew that some men beat up women he had never come across it in his own life and he was very much shocked by the state she was in. 'A doctor should look at you, but I still believe that the police would be the best option as a first port of call.'

'I *can't* go to the police.'

Enzo lowered his phone with a frown of irritation. 'Your car can't be picked up until tomorrow. I'll drive you into town.'

'I don't know you... I can't get into a car with you!' Skye gasped.

'My name is Lorenzo Durante. My friends call me Enzo. And you are...?'

'Skye Davison,' she provided reluctantly.

'If I leave you here,' Enzo murmured drily, 'I'll be informing the police of your location and the condition I found you in.'

'Why on earth would you do that?' Skye gasped.

'In case something happens to you, or the driver of one of the cars that have already been past assumes that I'm responsible for your condition!' he completed grimly.

'Oh, for goodness' sake!' Skye exclaimed, out of all patience.

'I have a solution. One of my employees is a qualified paramedic,' he told her. 'If you were agreeable, Paola could check you out at my home but, firstly, let's get you some shoes.'

'Paola...is that a woman's name?'

Enzo nodded confirmation and saw some of her tension evaporate because she found the mention of another woman reassuring.

'But first we'll get you a pair of shoes,' he repeated stubbornly, evidently finding her shoeless state intolerable.

Skye caved in. 'I'll have to move the car seats over... and I hope you don't mind dogs.'

Enzo frowned in bewilderment as she moved round to open the passenger door. 'Car seats? You have a dog?'

Over her shoulder inside the dim interior of the old car, he glimpsed a baby covered to the chin by a blanket and beyond her a dozing toddler. Something small and wriggly bounced out of the passenger seat foot well to dance round his feet.

'That's Sparky,' she said hoarsely, detaching the straps holding the baby and lifting the baby to settle her down in the foot well while she removed the car seat.

As another's car's headlights lit up the night, Enzo bent down and scooped up the little dachshund and put him straight into his car before he could streak off and become roadkill. As Skye struggled to lift the baby's car seat, he lifted it out of her arms and settled it into the back seat. Registering that she was in too much pain to bend and do what had to be done, he reached in and took care of it, reaching out for the baby and tucking it into the cosy carrier to snap the belt closed again.

'Thanks,' she said in surprise that he should have done that for her, for Ritchie had never helped with the children.

The little boy started crying the minute he saw Enzo. 'It's not your fault.' Skye sighed. 'He's just a bit scared of men after what he saw tonight—'

'The assault happened in front of him?' Enzo exclaimed as she lifted out the toddler, leaving him free to remove the second car seat.

'I'm afraid so. I feel so guilty about it,' she whispered.

'You don't have anything to feel guilty about,' Enzo told her squarely. 'It's not your fault that you were attacked.'

Enzo attached the second seat and helped her to stow the little boy into it. All that finally accomplished, he closed the door on his unexpected cargo. Two children and a dog, he was thinking in sheer wonderment. But what else could he do but help? It was an emergency.

The transfer complete, Skye clambered painfully and slowly up into the front passenger seat. 'I'm so sorry about all this,' she mumbled. 'I'm sure you don't need the hassle.'

'Takes my mind off my own problems,' he countered calmly. 'I'll ring Paola while you're in the supermarket buying some shoes.'

His complete calm and assurance were wonderfully soothing to her raw nerves.

'Will you stay in the car with the children?' she heard herself ask daringly.

'I'm not going to abandon them and we don't want to move them again at this time of night,' he pointed out.

A few minutes later, he drew up in the car park and said, 'Would you like me to go in first and get shoes for you?'

Skye shook her head and that hurt too. She didn't think there was a single part of her body free from aches and pains. 'No, I'll be fine.'

Relieved she had brought her bag, she went into the shop, receiving barely a glance from the security guard on the door. She grabbed a basket and selected a pair of canvas shoes from the display, hurrying round to the baby section to pick up nappies, baby milk and a bottle and a few other necessities for her siblings, grateful that she had enough money from a recent tax refund to cover her purchases and keeping her head down to avoid notice.

When she returned to the car, Enzo was on the phone talking in another language. He had rung Paola at the hotel his security team were using and asked the older woman to meet him at the house. She complained vehemently about the fact he had gone out again without his bodyguards. In return, he told her about Skye and the children. She wanted to know why Skye wasn't willing to go to the police. Enzo admitted that he had no idea and had hesitated to push lest she took fright. He had thought it was more important to help her than demand answers about what was, strictly speaking, none of his business.

'Paola will meet us at my home,' he advanced, finishing the call. 'If you can give me ten minutes I'll go and buy coffee and a few essentials because there's no food in the house.'

'Why not?' she asked as he swung out and the lights from the shop illuminated him.

Her breath caught in her throat as she saw him clearly for the first time. He was exceptionally handsome with sculpted cheekbones, a strong hard jawline and dark deep-set eyes set below straight ebony brows. His hair was black and thick, cropped short. His whole vibe was stylish and classy from his haircut to the fashionable cut of his fancy suit.

'I only arrived at the house this evening. I haven't had time to get anything in.'

'I can do without coffee,' she told him.

Enzo raised a perfect dark brow. 'I *can't*.'

And then he was gone, the stranger who was being kind to her when the man she had believed she loved and who loved her had almost killed her. There was a lesson there somewhere and inevitably the inescapable fact that she needed to cut Ritchie out of her life. Not that she had any doubts about doing that, especially not after what he had done to her.

Enzo returned with a couple of carrier bags and drove off again. 'The house isn't far. Paola will tell you if she thinks you need to go to hospital.'

'How could I go to a hospital with the kids in tow?' she asked ruefully.

'You must have been very young when you had them,' Enzo remarked.

'They're not mine. They're my brother and sister,' she confided. 'My mother and stepfather died in a train de-railment almost a year ago. Shona was only a month old.'

The strangest pang of relief that the baby and the tod-dler were not hers trickled through Enzo and he ques-tioned it, wondering why he should even have an opinion about such a thing. 'I'm sorry for your loss.'

'Thank you but, in an odd way, the kids saved my younger sister Alana and I from falling apart at the seams. We had to keep going for their sake.'

'Were you running away from a husband tonight?' he asked flatly.

'No, a boyfriend. Luckily, we're not married,' she whispered. 'And although splitting up poses some chal-lenges, we don't own property together or anything else.'

Enzo filtered the car off the road and down a drive-way lined with tall laurel hedges.

Her jaw dropped when she saw the big Victorian house with the spectacular tower attached to one end. '*This* is where you live?' she queried.

'As of this evening, yes,' Enzo confirmed without en-thusiasm. 'Paola is already here. I suppose we'll have to bring the kids and the dog indoors too.'

'Yes. You wouldn't want to see what Brodie could get up to left in a car by himself.'

His head of security awaited them in the front porch. Her eyes widened into a fixed stare when she saw Enzo with Brodie in his arms. The toddler was grizzling and cross and wriggling like a snake in a sack.

'Let's get inside first,' he suggested as Paola led the way into the gracious hall.

'I'll check Skye over in the sitting room,' Paola an-nounced, her first-aid bag firmly gripped in her hand. 'Are you able to look after the children?'

Brodie sobbed into his shoulder and tried to struggle free. 'I'll manage,' Enzo intoned with determination.

As he set the toddler down on his own feet rather than risk dropping him, Skye handed him the baby. 'Try not to wake her up,' she advised.

Enzo walked into the kitchen and sat down, heaving a sigh. Rescuing women was exhausting and frustrat-ing and he lacked the appropriate skill set required for tending to children, but he knew that he still would have helped Skye even had he known that she had children and a dog in the car with her.

'Who you?' Brodie demanded tearfully, stopping dead

in front of Enzo, stretching up, striving to look bigger than he was.

'I'm Enzo.'

'I'm hungry,' Brodie announced. 'And I have to go potty.'

Enzo almost groaned out loud, suddenly grateful that he had noticed where the downstairs cloakroom was and leading the little boy there.

'I need help,' Brodie told him.

Clutching the baby under one arm and thinking that it was really a remarkably accommodating baby, Enzo crouched down to help Brodie with his clothes. That accomplished, he turned on the tap for the toddler to wash his hands. He couldn't believe what a production it was to take care of so simple a task.

'The boss doesn't know anything about children.' Paola was chuckling as she attended to Skye in the elegant drawing room. 'It'll be an education for him.'

'He's been very kind to us,' Syke said ruefully. 'But when he saw the kids and the dog I think he was tempted to run. Don't tell him I said that but his face was a study. Is he single?'

'Very much so, not the settling-down type,' the older woman confirmed calmly. 'I think your ribs are bruised rather than cracked so you'll just have to nurse them along until they heal. Your throat, try not to talk too much and rest it. That's more serious and I still think you should have let the boss take you to hospital.'

'The nearest hospital is miles away and the children have gone through enough tonight.'

'You need to go to the police and report the assault.'

Skye looked away uncomfortably. 'I *can't*.'

'Why not? He might do this again and you might not survive the next time.'

Skye paled and winced. 'He's in the police. How could I report him where he works? They might not even believe me and he's bound to have friends there and then he would find out where I am. I think he has a tracker app on my phone.'

Paola studied her, appalled. 'He's a policeman? You *still* have to report him. As for the app, give me your phone now and I'll check it. If there's an app, I'll remove it.'

Skye walked back out into the hall and saw Enzo with Brodie at his feet and a still slumbering Shona draped over one broad shoulder. She hovered uncomfortably while Paola took her leave and departed through the front door, having returned her phone to her.

'I should get going as well,' Skye remarked.

'That would be crazy this late at night when I have at least six bedrooms empty here,' Enzo contended. 'Pick your own rooms upstairs.'

Skye winced. 'That's very generous of you *but*—'

Enzo surveyed her lazily. Without the bruising and swelling that marred her delicate features, he surmised, she would be very pretty. 'No, I'm being practical and you need to try and see the bigger picture here. You and the children are *safe* under this roof. I have twenty-four-seven security. You can also lock yourself into your room. You will not be disturbed, I assure you. You are totally free to leave the house any time you wish.'

Skye reddened and checked the time, lifting Shona off his shoulder with an exhausted sigh of surrender. He crouched down to lift Brodie, who was mumbling in a semi-doze. 'I'll show you upstairs. I'll be leaving early in the morning for work. If you want a lift into town, let me know.'

One of the bedrooms had a cot as well as a bed and Skye immediately opted for that room because she could share the bed with Brodie. Mercifully the bed was already made up and she lowered the side of the cot to slide her little sister in, covering her with her blanket.

'If you hadn't run into me, where were you planning to go tonight?' Enzo asked from the doorway.

'There's a homeless shelter in town but that would involve social services and I'm worried that they would take the kids into care.'

'Are you their legal guardian?'

'Yes, but when that was agreed, I was living with my sister and working as a teacher. My life was…stable. Now everything's changed.'

'A teacher? What age group?'

'Kindergarten but my first job was only temporary, and when my sister got a live-in job at the hotel, I couldn't afford the rent of our apartment on my own. Ritchie asked me to move in with him and agreeing has to be the worst decision I ever made. For a start he didn't want me to find another job. I should have smelt a rat then,' she confided tightly. 'And now here I am, homeless, unemployed and practically penniless.'

'You'll get through,' Enzo assured her. 'Now let's both get some sleep.'

'Thanks for everything,' she muttered as he turned away.

'Think of it as my good deed for the day,' Enzo commented lightly. 'And I haven't done so many that I deserve your gratitude. I'm a selfish bastard at the best of times.'

'You weren't tonight when it mattered,' Skye responded.

Closing the door, she turned the key in the lock. Yes, she felt better in a securely locked room now, she conceded uncomfortably. It would be a long time, if ever, before she relaxed around a man again.

She undressed her little brother and tucked him into bed, walking through to the old-fashioned bathroom to stare in horror at her reflection. Paola had given her painkillers and if she didn't try to move too fast the pain was now a dulled ache but, unfortunately, she was aching all over, in fact even her face ached. Tomorrow she would have a multicoloured black eye.

And she still had to get their possessions collected. How was she supposed to do that without a car? She probably didn't even have the money to pay for the necessary repairs to get her car back! Recognising that her worries were rising in an ever-increasing spiral of woe, she calmed herself. She would deal with each problem as it came up and resolve it. She had to be strong and steady, only dealing with one problem at a time.

It was painful to recall how much she had trusted Ritchie. He had asked her to marry him and, secure in that proposal of his, she had surrendered pretty much all her freedom, believing that he would offer her and her siblings a better life. So, she had ignored his lack of enthusiasm for the amount of time she spent with her siblings, his jealous and sulky behaviour if another man so much as looked at her, his eagerness to determine where she went and who she spoke to, not to mention his need to know where she was virtually every hour of the day. Yes, she had ignored, overlooked or forgiven far too much, believing that he loved her and was simply insecure.

Alana, on the other hand, had never liked Ritchie, deeming him too possessive. Skye had believed she loved him, although now she knew it hadn't been real love because she was painfully aware that she didn't ever want to lay eyes on him again. But she had loved him for accepting the children with her, loved him for seemingly seeing her as special when nobody had ever seen her in that light before. And it had all been an illusion, wishful thinking more than fact, because she had thought he loved her too.

After a shower, Enzo slid into bed and made plans. He would offer Skye a job as his housekeeper. He wouldn't be at the house much because he would be working long hours but, when he was here, he wanted to be comfortable. And he wouldn't be comfortable if he had to worry about shopping and learning to cook and all that jazz. That short supermarket visit, the first of his entire life, had been an unnerving experience. Surprisingly he didn't really mind the kids once he had got used to their unpredictability, although that baby would sleep through a riot, he conceded in admiration. In any case, it was a big enough house to lose two kids and a dog in, he reflected thankfully.

It had never occurred to him that he might actually like

children. After his disastrous experience of love at university had taught him how little some women could be trusted, he had assumed that he would never marry and never have children of his own. Only now did it strike him that he shouldn't allow that experience to dictate the rest of his life.

Skye woke up as usual when Shona let out a hungry wail. She felt like wailing too because she was also hungry and thirsty. Her sudden movement to get out of bed reminded her sharply of her condition. A jagged moan of pain was wrenched from her and Brodie sat up with a start.

'Bekfast,' he said cheerfully, unconcerned by their unfamiliar surroundings.

She had a quick shower in the bathroom, took care of her siblings and was about to go downstairs with them when a knock sounded on the door. She undid the lock and peered out through the gap.

'I heard the children and thought you might appreciate a change of clothes.' Enzo extended a pile of clothing. 'It's not much and we're a hopeless mismatch in size but it's better than nothing.'

'Thank you,' Skye said. 'That was thoughtful of you.'

Brodie squeezed past her. 'Enzo!' her little brother carolled in delight as though Enzo were his best pal.

'I'll be down in two minutes,' she called, shaking out a T-shirt and a pair of sweats.

She shed her jeans and sweater, dispensed with her underwear and pulled on the T-shirt. She rolled up the legs on the sweat pants and pulled the ties at the waist tight

to keep them up on her slender frame. She looked ridiculous but feeling clean made her feel immensely better.

Enzo took her breath away in his conservative navy
pinstripe suit teamed with a dark shirt and red silk tie.
He was standing with the microwave oven open.

'S'not a toaster,' Brodie was saying authoritatively.

'It may have a toasting mechanism,' Enzo told the little boy very seriously.

'I'll take care of the toast,' Skye said with amusement,
Shona clasped under one arm while she filled the ket-
tle to make a bottle for the baby. 'I need the baby stuff
I left behind.'

'I'll send you over with a car and a driver today and
you can collect it all. I also have a proposition to make,'
Enzo announced. 'I need a housekeeper. You need a job
and a roof over your head. Interested?'

CHAPTER TWO

SKYE FROWNED IN surprise and then nodded as she filled the bottle and mixed it before plunging it into cold water to cool. 'I could be. Where's Sparky?'

'Out in the back garden. I'm afraid we've no food for him,' Enzo reminded her.

'Sparky hungie… Brodie hungie,' her little brother complained.

'Hungry,' she corrected as she slotted bread into the toaster. 'The toast is on now and I bought some cereal last night.'

Housekeeping, she reflected absently. It would give them a safe place to live and allow her to continue looking after the children. Taking care of one man's household requirements didn't sound too onerous either and, best of all, while she was earning she would be free to search out another teaching job, temporary or otherwise. Allowing Ritchie to clip her employment wings and keep her at home had been a mistake but at the time she had been glad of the opportunity to spend time with her newly bereaved little brother and sister. It had been a period of terrible upheaval for all of them, she conceded belatedly. Maybe grief for the loving parents she had lost had played a part in her decision to move in with Ritchie.

'Let me take the baby,' Enzo offered, reaching out to cradle Shona and sit down by the kitchen table.

'Exactly what would the job entail?' Skye asked.

'It would only be for a couple of months because I won't be in England much beyond Christmas,' Enzo warned. 'You look after the house and the shopping and the cooking and I'll be happy. I only need a late evening meal. I'll be working most of the time.'

Skye tested the milk from the bottle on her wrist. 'It sounds good. I could do with some breathing space to get myself back together before I make a fresh start somewhere. What would you pay me?'

Enzo quoted a sum.

'That's far too much!' she told him instantly, shocked by the amount of money he was offering her.

'You'll be doing everything here and I suspect that you could do with the money,' Enzo pointed out calmly. 'As soon as your car is back on the road, you'll have your independence back.'

'I'll take it. What's the address of this place? I need to let my sister know where we are.'

Taking note of the address, she gathered Shona back into her arms, and gave her the bottle, which she drank happily, big blue eyes firmly locked on Skye's face.

'If you can get the coffee machine to produce a decent coffee, there'll be a bonus,' Enzo informed her wryly.

'It's not rocket science.'

'Might as well be.' Enzo sighed, watching her pour cereal for Brodie and seat him at the table before starting to butter toast. 'You're good at multi-tasking.'

'You have to be with kids. Do you want any toast?' she asked.

Her slight frame was really tiny in his clothes and there was something oddly sexy about knowing she was wearing something of his against her skin. He didn't know what it was, didn't wish to dwell on that angle. Such considerations were out of bounds now that she was an employee. In any case, he was very aware of how vulnerable she was right now; she'd clearly been in an abusive relationship and he felt a responsibility towards her. He would need to be careful to make her feel safe and not give her any reason to be nervous around him.

Her movements were very stiff and he noticed that she was avoiding bending or twisting as best she could, not an easy challenge with young children to look after, he reflected grimly. One eye was encircled with multicoloured bruising but nothing could hide her delicate bone structure, her pale-as-alabaster, perfect skin or the soft fullness of her pink lips.

'Enzo? *Toast?*' she queried when he failed to respond.

Enzo shook his handsome dark head a little as though to clear his thoughts. 'No, thanks. I like fruit, coffee and a croissant in the morning.'

'OK, you've got yourself a housekeeper,' Skye told him. 'I'll get our stuff picked up today and go shopping.'

He set a black credit card down on the table.

'What's my budget?'

'There isn't one.'

'What do you like to eat?' Skye enquired as she dug a small notebook out of her bag and flashed a pen. 'And what do you *not* like?'

Those details acquired, Enzo stood up. 'We have to exchange phone numbers. I'm sending two men with you to collect your belongings just in case your ex is there and causes trouble. You need to be protected and you will have the kids with you, which is enough of a challenge.'

'Thanks. I'm very grateful. Could you take the car seats out of your car before you leave?' Skye reminded him as she took his number and shot a text to him.

In truth, she was dreading that moment that she would have to enter the apartment, unsure as to Ritchie's whereabouts. Stalwart male company would be a very welcome support.

As it was still early, she decided to ring her sister and hope to catch her before she went to bed. Alana worked a permanent night shift at the hotel where she worked and lived and usually slept in the mornings but there would have been no point in calling Alana the night before because she didn't have a car, she had a bicycle, and, in any case, would have been at work. Skye still needed Alana's help though and she had to tell her what had happened and that Ritchie was out of her life now. Her sibling often spent the afternoons with her and the children and she wanted Alana to know that she was no longer at the apartment. The last thing she wanted to risk was her sister running into Ritchie without knowing how volatile the situation with him was.

Alana came on the phone on a bright, breezy note. 'It's my day off...well, at least until I report for duty tonight again. My co-worker called in sick.' She sighed before she listened in disgust to what her sister had to tell her and she immediately offered to take care of the children while Skye removed her possessions from Ritchie's apartment.

Skye had dressed the kids, fed poor Sparky some toast and cleaned up the kitchen by the time the two men, Matteo and Antonio, arrived. Alana arrived soon after them.

'Oh, my word, your face!' Alana gasped in horror when she saw her sibling's black eye.

Alana was the taller, curvier version of Skye with blonde hair, gloriously *straight* blonde hair that Skye envied, down to her waist. 'I should kill Ritchie for what he's done to you!' her kid sister swore fiercely.

Skye calmed her down and left her with the children, grateful for her sister's support. She felt like a tramp in Enzo's overly large clothes with the ugly bruises marring her face and decided she would live in her sunglasses for the next week. Her nervous tension climbed as the car was parked outside the small apartment block.

The apartment was mercifully empty. Feeling as though she were in some television competition for speed or a supermarket trolley rush, Skye clasped a roll of bin-bags and went into the children's room first.

In the midst of dismantling Shona's cot and recalling that there were a baby buggy, a high chair and various other bulky equipment as well, she noticed Antonio was on the phone. 'We'll need a van to move all of it,' he explained as Skye rammed clothes into a bag. 'But Matteo will arrange one for us.'

'I should've said there was so much large stuff before we came.' Skye sighed guiltily while Antonio bagged toys for her, leaving her free to go into the bedroom she had briefly shared with Ritchie.

She grimaced as she glanced at the bed, averting her gaze from a place she had begun to dread. No, she didn't like sex. Contrary to every article she read, she hadn't enjoyed it. That might put her in a minority but that was just how she was and, now that Ritchie was out of her life again, she could be honest about the fact. All that faking and pretending an enjoyment she didn't feel to keep Ritchie happy had drained her, made her feel dishonest and, what was more, a little on the odd side because she evidently didn't like what other women liked. Well, that was done and dusted now, she reminded herself. A man-free future stretched in front of her.

Skye had had such great hopes when she'd moved in with Ritchie and it hurt her pride to remember her trusting naivety. She lifted the photograph of her mother and stepfather from the bedside cabinet and tears of grief stung her eyes. Their loving happiness together had become her ideal and it seemed laughable now to recall that she had actually hoped to build the same kind of relationship with Ritchie. After all, her stepfather had taken on two little girls that weren't his own and treated them as though they were his own flesh and blood.

Ritchie's readiness to accept that she came as a package with Brodie and Shona had encouraged her to believe that he was a man similar to her stepfather. But once she had moved in with Ritchie, he had had little time to spare for her siblings and he had complained bitterly that the children were always underfoot. He had also accused her of always putting her siblings first.

In reality, she had done the opposite and she was ashamed of that fact. She had put herself first. She had grabbed at that whole fantasy dream of a supportive, caring partner who would lighten her load and make her feel less alone, but family life had been too restrictive and domestic for Ritchie. For all his talk of marriage, he hadn't been ready to settle down. He might've wanted her, but the children had just been unfortunate baggage that came along with her.

She finished putting her clothes and shoes into bags and hauled them out to the lounge, ready for the van that was coming. She pounced with relief on her sunglasses and put them on.

The two men concentrated on getting her belongings down in the lift and packing the car. While she was helping them move the baby equipment down to the ground floor, the van arrived and, with it, another man, who made short work of loading everything. She was smiling as she walked out of the apartment block and was totally disconcerted to find herself unexpectedly confronted by Ritchie.

'Where the hell have you been?' he demanded wrathfully as he strode up onto the pavement. 'You were out all night and you didn't phone. I was worried sick about you!'

Skye froze where she stood. Surprisingly, Ritchie looked the same as always. Blond hair, an aggressively square jaw, pale blue eyes, an angry flush on his cheeks. He wasn't in uniform, clearly wasn't working and she realised with an inner shiver that they had been very lucky that he hadn't come home while they were still in the apartment. At least she had got all their stuff out without any hassle, although she had left behind kitchen equipment and china she had brought from her own home because she couldn't afford storage costs and could hardly clutter up Enzo's imposing house with her household goods.

'I asked you a question!' Ritchie reminded her, towering over her menacingly and glowering at Antonio. 'And who is this man?'

'I'm moving out, Ritchie,' Skye framed tautly. 'This is the last time you'll see me.'

'Back away,' Antonio told Ritchie, stretching a protective arm out in front of Skye. 'You're getting too close.'

'What the hell are you playing at, Skye?' Ritchie demanded furiously. 'Why would you move out? So, we had a little fallout...'

Syke whipped off her sunglasses. 'You call this a little fallout? You beat me up!'

Ritchie averted his gaze from her bruised face. 'You fell. Don't blame me for it. Let's talk about this like adults in private.'

'No, thanks. I don't want anything more to do with you,' Skye countered, backing away and heading for the car.

Ritchie made a sudden lurch in her direction in an effort to cut off her escape, only to be hauled back by Antonio. He twisted free again and swung round to punch the other man but Antonio was too quick on his feet. Moving out of reach, Antonio quickly climbed into the car, which pulled away as soon as he closed the door. Breathless and shaken by Ritchie's continuing aggression, Skye was very relieved that Alana was looking after the children and that Brodie hadn't been subjected to another violent scene. Tears stung her eyes while Antonio and Matteo talked in their own language.

'He's following us,' Antonio informed her.

Skye suppressed a groan. She hadn't wanted Ritchie to find out where she was staying. She resisted the urge to twist round in her seat and look.

'Whatever you want. We're on call. The boss doesn't want us leaving you alone anywhere,' Matteo explained. 'And after what I just witnessed, that's definitely the right decision.'

Her mobile phone buzzed. 'How are you?' Enzo asked huskily.

'A bit shaken up. Very grateful I wasn't on my own,' she confided, thinking that he had the most beautiful voice, dark and deep, edged with his purring accent. 'I'm sorry I'm being such a nuisance.'

'That's not what I think, *piccolo mio*. Just make sure you keep my men with you.'

Enzo finished the call as the firm's head of marketing hovered, a languorous light in her appreciative gaze as the sinuous brunette studied him with naked longing. He had had a difficult first day. Stripping out the top-heavy management layer in the company would gain him no friends. As for the new ideas he had brought with him, they were no more welcome except to the few who'd had the foresight to see a more prosperous future for the firm.

'My girlfriend,' Enzo lied smoothly.

Martina had spent the day trying to flirt with him, brush against him, catch his attention. He wanted her to back off and the pretence that he already had a woman in his life was the easiest cure for what ailed her. Regrettably, Enzo was all too well accustomed to women who threw themselves at him. He was rich, young and single and such pronounced attention went with the territory. Being hunted and propositioned didn't turn him on and he did not want that complication in the workplace.

'I thought you were in England alone, Mr Durante,' Martina remarked.

Enzo cursed the notoriety of his name. Of course, the staff knew who he was: Lorenzo Durante, dubbed the Playboy Prince by the Italian media, a moniker he had inherited from his late father, whose legendary exploits with women had destroyed his marriage soon after Enzo was born. He and his wife had been in the throes of their last attempt at reconciliation when they had died together.

'I'm not.' He murmured the untruth without hesitation and found himself thinking with helpless longing of Skye, who had no notion of flirting with him or jumping his bones. It was a new experience for him to be treated as an adult man, rather than a fabulously rich asset to be acquired. It was also oddly restful.

Alana was an invaluable help when their possessions were loaded willy-nilly into the hall. 'It's truly over with Ritchie?' she prompted hopefully as she set the high chair into the kitchen. 'You know he'll come after you and apologise and maybe even grovel and promise that it won't ever happen again.'

'It doesn't matter. It's over for ever and ever,' Skye confirmed. 'I don't ever want to see him again. He saw us leaving and he was still in a temper.'

Alana frowned. 'Tell me about the businessman who owns this place,' she urged.

Skye made coffee for everyone and allowed Brodie to take his trike out into the back garden with Sparky because it was fully enclosed by a fence.

While helping to feed Shona in her high chair, Skye filled in the details about what had happened the night before.

'And there's nothing icky about this guy Enzo?' Alana pressed suspiciously.

'No, definitely no ick factor there. To be honest, he's gorgeous but I don't have any worries in that direction. I imagine he goes for much more glamorous types than me.'

'I'm worried because I honestly don't think Ritchie is going to leave you alone. He's more likely to act like a stalker, always wanting to know your business,' Alana murmured anxiously. 'I think you need to report him to the police. What if he finds you on your own and attacks you again?'

Skye mulled that thorny question over while Alana helped her get unpacked and persuaded her to choose the bedroom next door to hers for the children, because there was more space and storage. There were *six* bedrooms in total and she could always double up with the children if Enzo was entertaining and needed an extra room. The unpacking achieved, Skye mustered her shopping list and rang Antonio to tell him that she was ready to go into town. Alana offered to accompany her to help her with the kids.

As they left the supermarket laden with shopping, Alana took the children straight to her car and Paola took the trolley from Skye. 'You shouldn't be pushing that,' she told Skye firmly.

As the older woman returned to the car to unload the trolley, Ritchie stepped into view between two cars and grabbed Skye's arm. 'Who are those people you are with?' he demanded angrily. 'Who owns that house you're staying in?'

'Let me go!'

As he leant down to her, she smelt the alcohol on him and grimaced. 'It's over, Ritchie. Let go of my arm.'

'Let go of my sister!' Alana seethed, running up to intervene and aiming a kick at the blond man.

In a fury, Ritchie swung round as Skye finally broke free of him, and found Antonio in his path. But it was Paola who surged forward, seemingly out of nowhere, and took Ritchie down with a martial arts move, dragged his hands behind his back and, with a remarkable lack of drama, handed him over to the security guard approaching them.

'Now you know why you have to go to the police,' Paola said quietly as Skye, white-faced and trembling, accompanied her sister back to her car. 'That man is going to continue coming after you. He's angry and stubborn.'

'I'll do it this evening,' she promised shakily.

Skye started dinner. But before she even got halfway through her preparations, Enzo strode into the kitchen. 'Your sister has agreed to stay with your siblings. I'm here to take you to the police station before you lose your nerve.'

Skye tensed. 'But—'

'You have no choice,' he reminded her.

No, she had had no choices while she was living with

Ritchie, Skye conceded, thinking of all the times she had given way to Ritchie to placate him. But now she was supposed to be leading her life again and making her own choices. Even so, it seemed that reclaiming her freedom required more from her than simply walking away from Ritchie: it meant she had to *fight*. Not go apologetically about her business, certainly not depend on Enzo's employees to protect her. She had to fight and stand on her own two feet.

'Okay. Maybe I should get changed first,' she said, smoothing damp palms down her slender thighs, feeling that her jeans and long-sleeved T-shirt might be too casual.

'You'll do fine as you are,' Enzo asserted as she went into the cloakroom to retrieve her padded jacket, wincing as she slid her arms into the sleeves.

He's gorgeous! Alana mouthed at her in wonderment when she glanced into the sitting room where her sister was now sitting with the children. Skye went pink and glanced uneasily at Enzo. He needed a shave. His strong jawline was shadowed by blue-black stubble. He also looked a little weary and her heart smote her without warning. He should have been coming home to relax and eat.

'I was planning such a good meal for dinner,' she confided guiltily.

'It'll keep until later.'

'But you must be hungry,' she protested as he led her outside into the cold crisp air.

'Take the sunshades off,' he urged.

Skye lowered them to blink at him. Her bruised eye

was opening again and now he saw the unusual colour of them in the artificial light. A violet blue so light and soft it reminded him of lilac blossom in the spring. His lush black lashes came down low over his eyes and he turned his head away, irritated by that momentary distraction. 'Let's go,' he urged.

Skye climbed awkwardly into the passenger seat. There was no avoiding the step up into the car, no way that every movement of her body could fail to jar her ribs. She grimaced, wondering about that strange moment when Enzo had stared down at her. He had wanted to see how she looked and the news was nothing good. The bruises round her eye had turned all the colours of the rainbow and had only deepened overnight, but at least her eye was opening again.

The instant they arrived at the police station, Enzo requested a senior officer, his quiet confidence patent. Shown into an interview room, Enzo explained why they had asked for a senior officer. A female officer was called and Skye was shown into another interview room, this time without Enzo by her side, where she explained what had happened with Ritchie. After she had made a statement, she had to wait for a police doctor to arrive and undergo an examination and have her injuries photographed. Not once did anyone refer to the fact that her assailant was a policeman who worked under the same roof as them. That professional attitude eased Skye's surging tension.

By the time she saw Enzo again, she was exhausted and her throat was sore from all the talking she'd had to do. He escorted her back out to the car. 'Paola and the rest of her team are witnesses and will go in tomorrow to make statements,' he explained. 'I also think you need to ask for a non-molestation order to be placed on your ex. I've arranged for you to consult a solicitor about that tomorrow.'

'You've had to go to an enormous amount of trouble on my behalf.' Skye groaned in embarrassment. 'Why did you bother?'

'First of all, now that you're working for me, your safety is my responsibility. Second, your ex cannot be allowed to get away with hurting and threatening you, nor can he be permitted to continue working in a position of trust. Thirdly, the children must be assured of a safe environment.'

'You only met me yesterday,' Skye reminded him. 'Don't you wish you had simply driven on past?'

Enzo shrugged a broad shoulder and filtered the car back down the driveway. 'Here we are, home to the haunted house.'

'Why do you call it that?'

'That's what it reminds me of…the era and the décor. If we don't have a ghost, I'll feel short-changed.'

'So, you don't own this place?'

'No, I assume it's rented. My grandfather made the arrangements for my stay. By the way, your sister had to leave to go to work. Paola took over as babysitter.'

There she went again, Skye thought in embarrassment. She was one big problem. Employing her when she came with two children was more hassle than any job she could do would be worth.

'I had no work to do. Your sister put the children to

bed before she left,' Paola told her soothingly. 'Do you feel better now that you've reported him?'

'Yes,' Skye fibbed because, in truth, she felt worse and more scared than ever because Ritchie would be enraged that she had gone to the police to report the assault.

As Paola departed, Skye went into the kitchen to start the meal she had planned. Enzo appeared in the doorway. 'You can cook tomorrow night. I've ordered a meal from the hotel your sister works for to be delivered for both of us. It's late and you're exhausted.'

'Cooking is supposed to be my job,' Skye reminded him stubbornly.

'And tonight, you're having a night off.'

She wanted to argue with him but there was a hard edge to his fabulous bone structure that persuaded her to accept his wishes. 'You're tired too,' she conceded. 'What was your first day like?'

'Bloody,' he confided with a feeling grimace.

Skye went into the dining room to set the table for the meal. She put the electric fire on to make it less gloomy and lit the lamp on the corner table. Enzo had gone upstairs and when he reappeared, his hair was still damp from the shower and he was clad in faded jeans that fitted him like a glove and a grey sweater. For a split second she found herself staring and she quickly caught herself and moved past him to fill a jug with cold water and bring glasses.

For goodness' sake, she worked for the guy. Agreed, he was breathtakingly handsome and her heart had skipped a beat as he'd walked into the room, but she had to bury those kinds of female responses and pay no heed to such

promptings. Fortunately for her, she was not the most ravishing woman on the planet so he was highly unlikely to
look at her in the same way.

'What made it a bloody day?' she asked quietly.

'Redundancies, but if business goes the way I hope
we'll be hiring more people in the near future,' he pointed
out. 'That's how it goes.'

'Is it Mackies, the packaging factory in the industrial
estate that was bought out?' Skye asked. 'Mackies is the
main employer around here.'

Enzo nodded as the doorbell chimed.

Skye went to answer the door and stepped back as a
heated trolley was trundled in complete with waiter.

'In here…' Enzo instructed. 'Sit down, Skye.'

Awkwardly she took a seat at the table when she had
planned to take her plate through to the kitchen.

'We'll serve ourselves,' Enzo decreed.

'I'll do it,' Skye offered, registering that there was an
entire three-course meal awaiting them and utterly taken
aback by the lavish quality of the food.

The salad starter was set out first and the desserts laid
on the sideboard.

'This is lovely,' Skye said warmly. 'I wasn't expecting such a spread.'

She shook out her napkin and began to eat with appetite.

Enzo told her that the company was to begin selling
biodegradable packaging, which was currently much in
demand. To enable that switch, new machinery would
be installed in the factory and there was already a large

contract in the pipeline. 'I think my *nonno*…my grand-father tailored this job for my benefit.'

'How?'

'I own one of the largest companies that provide pack-aging of that kind in the world,' he admitted with the utmost casualness. 'My grandfather hoped that I would have a personal interest in setting up a new business in that field.'

The main course was served while Enzo talked. Al-though she had never thought about packaging much, she was a keen recycler. When the waiter departed with the trolley, leaving them to attend to the desserts, she was relieved not to have anyone else listening to their conver-sation, although she had noticed that that silent third pres-ence had not inhibited Enzo in the slightest. Every minute in his company, she was learning something new about him. Seemingly, Lorenzo Durante was much richer than she had assumed. The largest company…*in the world*? She should have checked him out on the Internet, she thought wryly. Clearly, he was accustomed to having people wait on him.

'Did you have an argument with your ex?' Enzo in-toned quietly, once they were alone. 'Is that what started the assault?'

'No, there was no argument. He came home from work in a foul mood,' Skye explained heavily. 'He had found out that he had failed the exam he needs to pass to go for promotion. It was the third time he'd failed and he blamed us for it.'

'How?'

'He blew up in a rage, shouting that it was impossible

for him to study with the kids around,' Skye proffered, her soft mouth compressing. 'I made the mistake of trying to reason with him. I didn't remind him that he had failed the exam twice before we moved in or that I only saw him trying to study *once*. I just said that the next time I would take the children out and that's when he went over the edge because, apparently, he can't sit the exam again until next year. He punched me and called me stuff and when I fell, he went for my throat. I honestly thought he was going to kill me…'

Enzo swore in Italian under his breath. 'I'm sorry I brought it up again.'

'It happened.' Skye lifted and dropped a shoulder and then stood up to fetch the desserts from the sideboard. 'But he'd never hit me before. I wouldn't have stayed with him if he had.'

'How long were you with him?'

For an instant, Skye focused on his eyes, amber gold in the low light, enhanced by spiky black lashes, and her mouth ran dry.

'Skye?'

'Oh, you asked me a question,' she recalled belatedly, her face burning with discomfiture because she had zoned out just looking at his eyes. 'We were together four months, not very long really. But it wasn't working for me. He was controlling, possessive, suspicious of every move I made. He didn't want me to have friends, he didn't even like me seeing Alana. It's a challenge to act normally with someone like that and, more and more, I felt like a cat on hot bricks around him. If it hadn't been for the children and my reluctance to disrupt their lives again, I wouldn't have stayed as long as I did with him.'

'Will you go back into teaching?'

'If I can find a job that doesn't entail moving miles away from my sister, yes. Did you get any word about my car?'

'Yes.' Enzo sighed. 'There's so much wrong with it, you'd be wiser letting it go to the scrapyard.'

'No!' Skye cut in, her dismay obvious. 'Mavis was my mum's car and she's irreplaceable.'

Enzo studied her in disbelief. 'Mavis? You actually *named* that hunk of junk?'

'Mum did.' Skye stood up. 'I'll go and fetch the coffee. I got the machine working. I even ground the beans.'

'The car has sentimental value?'

'Yes. Mavis comes with a carload of childhood happy memories.'

'At least you *knew* your mother. Mine died with my father when I was six weeks old,' Enzo admitted. 'A car accident. My grandparents raised me.'

'Photographs aren't much of a comfort, are they?' Skye quipped as she hovered beside him on her way out of the door to the kitchen. Without thought, she squeezed his shoulder in consolation. 'At least you have grandparents. Mine were long gone by the time my mother and stepfather passed away.'

Enzo blinked in shock at that affectionate shoulder squeeze. The only person who had ever touched him like that was his grandmother. Outside the bedroom door, Enzo was unaccustomed to such gestures, and in the bedroom he usually avoided that kind of intimacy because it was likely to give women the wrong message. After almost marrying the wrong woman at university, flings had become much more Enzo's style with the opposite sex. There were no misunderstandings or future expectations that way.

A cup of coffee was slid in front of him.

Skye watched him sip and smile with pleasure and she began to clear away the dishes.

'No, sit down and join me,' Enzo urged. 'I have a proposition to put to you.'

Her brow furrowed, her violet eyes widened and flashed with curiosity and he smiled. 'You look like a kitten when you do that.'

Skye pursed her lips. 'Think panther or tiger, definitely *not* kitten.'

And Enzo burst out laughing at that advice. 'I don't think that's likely to work for me, *piccolo mio*. How do you feel about acting as my fake girlfriend at a party next week?' he extended, the laughter still lending a buoyant afterglow to his lean, darkly attractive features. He had charm in spades, she conceded abstractedly, struggling to concentrate.

CHAPTER THREE

'FAKE GIRLFRIEND?' SKYE repeated uncertainly. 'What's a fake girlfriend?'

'A pretend relationship. No sex involved nor, indeed, anything else you might reasonably object to,' Enzo clarified smoothly. 'I have several women coming on to me at work and there's a staff party next week. I would like a platonic girlfriend on my arm to ensure that nobody thinks I'm available. I'm afraid my reputation as a womaniser goes before me but I have no intention of getting involved with anyone while I'm here.'

Skye wasn't surprised that women were making advances to him. He was exceedingly well built and extraordinarily gorgeous. Any single woman would look twice and hang out a welcome sign, but she was shocked that he could so lightly refer to having a reputation as a womaniser. 'A womaniser?' she queried with a wrinkled nose of distaste.

'Believe it or not, that attracts some women. Right now, however, I'm living the celibate life,' Enzo quipped with a wry curve of his lips. 'And I intend to continue to do so while I'm here.'

'Good to know,' Skye countered, feeling her cheeks

burn. 'So, you want a fake girlfriend to keep you safe from temptation.'

'*Sì*... No affairs, no one-nighters and no entanglements of any kind,' he spelt out.

'But nobody would credit me in a role like that. I'm not stylish enough for someone like you,' she said ruefully.

'Your bruises will have faded by the end of next week and clever make-up will take care of any marks that linger. I will naturally cover the expense of an outfit for the occasion as I doubt you have anything suitable.'

'I'll think about it. I suppose I could do it as a favour in return for all that you've done for me,' Skye conceded quietly.

'I'm not a fan of favours. I'll *pay* you for doing it.'

'No. The party will be my thank you for you helping us last night and for coming to the police station with me this evening,' Skye countered with quiet dignity. 'I'm not a hired escort. I'll do it for free, so please don't offer me money again.'

Enzo's dark as night eyes positively shimmered. 'Is that a warning?'

'Yes,' Skye confirmed, rising to start clearing the table. 'Will you be wanting anything else tonight? I was thinking of having an early night.'

'Go to bed. I'll see you in the morning.'

Skye paused at the door and then turned back, unable to resist saying, 'Isn't it crazy that we've only known each other for twenty-four hours?'

Enzo thought about that and he was equally taken aback by the reminder. It was rare for him to feel so comfortable with a woman and yet, in reality, he barely knew Skye. Perhaps that was because he knew nothing could happen between them, he reasoned thoughtfully. Perhaps he relaxed more with her as a result of that awareness. And possibly she was comfortable with him for the exact same reason. In any case it would take her a while to get over the abusive creep she had been living with. In addition, posing as his fake girlfriend might give her an extra layer of protection against her ex, he reflected wryly.

His grandmother called him to catch up and he told her at length about finding Skye and her siblings and the dog by the side of the road.

'You're not getting involved with this young woman?' she questioned worriedly. 'I'm proud that you helped her, but I wouldn't want you hurting her by taking too much of an interest in her.'

'No, there's nothing of that nature between us. She's totally safe with me. The kids are quite cute, though,' he remarked, something of his surprise at that discovery clear in his voice.

A womaniser? Skye lay in bed and played with her phone, slotting his name into a search engine and then reading results. It took a couple of attempts to spell his name correctly and then a cascade of results tumbled onto the screen. She saw a photo of him half naked in shorts on a yacht with a gaggle of blonde tanned beauties surrounding him. Suddenly feeling like a disrespectful snoop, she closed the site and put her phone down. Enzo's personal life was none of her business and he was entitled to his privacy.

* * *

Skye rose early and had the children fed and dressed before Enzo even got downstairs. There was no reason to subject him to the early morning chaos of life with young children, she reasoned. 'I planned to serve your breakfast in the dining room,' she remarked when he strode into the kitchen.

As usual, at first glimpse, Enzo knocked the breath right out of her lungs. Sheathed in a light grey, exquisitely tailored suit that lovingly outlined his broad shoulders, lean hips and long powerful legs, he looked amazing. Everything he wore fitted him to perfection. She wondered how many suits he owned because she had yet to see him in the same one twice.

'I'm happy enough to eat in here... *Dio mio!*' he exclaimed in apparent astonishment as Shona crawled across the floor towards him. 'She moves on her own!'

Helplessly amused by his fascination, Skye watched her sister claw her way upright by dint of clutching Enzo's legs. 'I'll put her out in the hall,' she said abruptly.

'No need. She's not doing any harm,' Enzo declared as Brodie, hungry for his attention, brought him a toy car to examine. 'What age are they?'

'Brodie is almost three and Shona's thirteen months.' Skye ferried coffee to him and plucked Shona from his knees to give him some peace. She remained convinced that he should be sitting in the dining room where she had laid the table for him. She would never forget his conviction that the microwave would make his toast for him. She suspected that Enzo was woefully unacquainted with kitchens and with eating his meals against such a

humble backdrop. Furthermore, he was only making do
with her as a housekeeper because she had already been
on his doorstep and an easily available option.

Enzo ate only part of the supermarket croissant, his
aristocratic nose wrinkling a tad, and she resolved to
try the bakery in town for a substitute. Instinct warned
her that Enzo was accustomed to only the very best. He
didn't like the house and was certainly not impressed by
it, yet it was large and warm and had been sensitively
renovated with modern utilities while retaining all the
features that gave it character. There were probably many
things in life that Enzo Durante took entirely for granted,
she decided ruefully.

'You are looking very serious,' Enzo commented.

'I was just thinking that you don't really appreciate
this house,' she heard herself admit. 'And yet it's very
comfortable and in excellent order.'

'You sound like my conscience speaking,' Enzo retali-
ated with a groan as he sliced an apple into slim segments.
'I agree that it's functional, but I prefer a contemporary
style. My grandparents live in an old ancestral house and
that is probably why he chose this place for me.'

'You're spoiled,' Skye responded before she could bite
back the words.

A slanting grin slashed Enzo's lean, hard-boned face,
unhidden amusement glittering in his very dark eyes.
'Probably,' he agreed equably.

'I'm sorry. I shouldn't have said that.' Skye's cheeks
were wreathed in pink and embarrassment engulfed her.
Who was she to criticise him? His laid-back manner had

momentarily betrayed her into forgetting that he was her employer.

'I don't take offence easily,' Enzo riposted, enjoying the way the blush made her eyes look lighter in hue and enthralled by the habit she had of looking down, her feathery lashes drooping when she was embarrassed while her teeth plucked at the edge of her full lower lip. 'I have many choices others don't enjoy and I should be more aware of that. I also like an honest woman, who isn't out to impress me and watching her every word.'

'But I should be watching every word,' Skye replied. 'I *should* be behaving professionally.'

'But your profession isn't housekeeping and we're alone in this house, so obviously we can't ignore each other,' Enzo pronounced with an air of finality as he vaulted upright. 'I'll text you with the time of your appointment with the solicitor.'

'I can take care of that for myself.'

'It's halfway to being organised already,' Enzo told her as he turned away.

'Thanks, then,' Skye said awkwardly, grabbing Brodie as he tried to follow Enzo out into the hall.

The interview with the solicitor later that morning was a sobering experience because it brought up everything she had crammed down to the very bottom of her memory. She didn't want to remember what Ritchie had done to her because the recollection of how she had lain on the floor pretending to be unconscious to avoid further injury still made her cringe. It wasn't an image she wanted to have of herself and she knew that she would never again put herself in such a position with the children.

Her thoughts, however, were slowly becoming less negative and self-critical. It wasn't her fault that Ritchie had turned out to be violent and nasty. There had been no warning of his explosion of rage and subsequent attack. But possibly, if she hadn't feared moving the children and disrupting their lives all over again, she would have told him sooner that the relationship wasn't working for her.

That evening, Enzo found himself dining in the solitary splendour of the dining room and he felt ridiculously lonely. Skye had informed him that she had already eaten and she was bathing the kids upstairs. From somewhere above, he could hear the sound of Brodie's giggles. Boundaries, he thought. Skye was carefully marking boundaries, reminding him that she worked for him and making it clear that she would stick to the rules…even though he hadn't laid down *any* rules.

In defiance, he climbed the stairs and followed the noise. Brodie was capering around the main bathroom half dressed in dinosaur pyjama bottoms while Skye endeavoured to insert a squirming Shona into what he believed was known as a onesie. Flushed and very damp, her tee clinging to her slight curves, Skye looked harassed and as Brodie charged at him in welcome, Enzo picked up the discarded pyjama top and corralled Brodie to put it on him. The little boy startled him by winding his arms round his neck and forcing Enzo to lift him.

'Thanks. Sorry we were so noisy,' Skye muttered. 'They both sort of wind up at bedtime.'

'They're in the room next door to you?' Enzo checked.

'I'll put him in there. How did the meeting go with the solicitor?'

'He was very efficient and the police phoned me. Ritchie has been suspended from duty pending investigation.'

Enzo lowered Brodie to the bed and watched him snatch up a scruffy rabbit soft toy, pressing it to his chest and turning over, all liveliness draining away as evidently the day's activities caught up with him. Shaking loose the duvet to cover him, Enzo straightened as Skye settled her sister into the cot.

'The solicitor thinks there's sufficient evidence for Ritchie to be arrested and charged,' she told him quietly, something of her mental turmoil showing in her troubled gaze. 'I can't get past the fact that I thought he loved me and yet he did *that* to me.'

Enzo lounged in the doorway, his big frame lithe and sleek and relaxed as she switched out the light. 'I thought a woman loved me once but it went badly wrong, although she didn't assault me,' he remarked with graveyard humour, brooding dark eyes glinting beneath lush black lashes. 'Now I steer clear of the love thing…'

His blunt candour disconcerted her and as he stepped back to allow her to partially close the door of the children's room, she winced and sighed. 'As will I in the future.'

CHAPTER FOUR

'IT'S LIKE BEING a princess for the day!' Alana carolled. 'I'm so envious I'm ashamed of myself!'

'Alana…' Skye felt guilty and rather vain for being equally thrilled by her elegant, groomed appearance in the mirror.

It was so very long since she had seen herself polished up to her best. The last time had been for a formal dance at college in her final year. A visit to the beauty salon at the exclusive hotel where her sister worked had transformed her hair and the professional but subtle make-up covered her fading bruises to perfection. Her rebellious curls had been tamed into glossy honey-blonde ringlets that tumbled artfully down to her slim shoulders. The dress, in the palest shade of lilac, was fashioned in a glistening fabric that caught the light and came to mid-thigh, short enough to be fashionable, long enough not to be daring. Her arms were bare, and an unusual toning collar of artificial pearls contrived to conceal the marks on her neck. The stylist, whom Enzo had organised to come to the house, had brought a selection of cocktail dresses for her to choose from. She slid her feet into the delicate high heels and lifted the beaded purse and shawl that completed the outfit.

'Well, when did either of us last have any fun?' Her sister sighed. 'We lost Mum and Dad and it was one long struggle to survive afterwards. There was no time and no money for girly stuff and remembering that we were still young.'

And that was true, horribly true, Skye conceded with regret. In the midst of their shock and grief, she and Alana had made the decision to step into their late parents' shoes for Brodie and Shona's sake and that had entailed serious sacrifices. Initially, it had been a long, dreary haul, working hard to meet the bills, find employment and somewhere affordable to live. Alana had insisted on dropping out of university, as determined as Skye to do the very best she could for their younger siblings.

Skye turned back to her sister. 'I promise that you and I will have a night out some time soon and relive exactly what it is like to *be* young.'

Alana's eyes lit up and then fell again. 'We'll need a babysitter.'

'We'll find one,' Skye declared and hugged the younger woman. 'We'll look for somewhere where we can live together after Christmas, when Enzo leaves.'

'I *have* to live in at the hotel,' Alana reminded her with a frown. 'Even if I get this assistant night-shift manager promotion, I'll still have to live in.'

'We'll cope, but maybe get to spend more time together, make it more about us than about the kids,' Skye proposed. 'The little ones do get star billing all the time!'

'But that's what makes you a great second mum,' the blonde told her a little chokily, her eyes filming with tears.

Skye was a little misty-eyed and touched by her sister's faith in her. Enzo strode out of the sitting room. Over the past ten days, she had seen surprisingly little of him and her attention locked onto him as though he were a magnet and she an iron filing. He was working long hours, leaving very early in the morning and rarely coming back before nine in the evening. Sparky was on his heels as usual. Sparky, their late parents' pet, had always preferred men and had once been her stepfather's shadow. Now Sparky was like a horse out of the starting gate the instant he heard Enzo's car pulling up.

He wore yet another different suit, but this one had a designer hip edge of fashion that could have come straight off a Paris catwalk, and the man within that beautiful light grey suit teamed with a dark roll neck was as sleekly, smoothly and smoulderingly sexy as a movie star. That very thought shook her. She didn't look at men and think…hmm, he's sexy, but Enzo was in a class all of his own and very good at knocking her off balance. Not a thought she should be having about him, absolutely not, she censured herself and wiped her mind blank of all such embarrassing stuff.

Enzo stared intently as Skye approached him. 'You look amazing,' he murmured sincerely, rather taken aback by just how beautiful she looked, his gleaming dark gaze flaming to gold and his appraisal lingering. There was a lightness in her shy smile and a glow in her face. As he had hoped, she had enjoyed a day of pampering, a day unshaded by the turmoil her ex-boyfriend had plunged her into.

Her curls framed her heart-shaped face, brushing against her fine flushed cheekbones, and the make-up had been applied brilliantly to cover the dark shadowing that still marred her eye. The colour of that dress, that particular shade of lavender, lit up her eyes like stars. The bespoke fit enhanced her diminutive frame, only hinting at her slender curves while putting a pair of award-winning legs and dainty ankles on display. The hardening at his groin was as familiar as it was forbidden, and Enzo breathed in slow and deep to steady himself. She trusted him and he would not betray that trust.

He was well aware that he was attracted to her and that he shouldn't be. He grasped her hand in his. 'You're cold.' He swept the light shawl from her loose hold, shook it out and draped it deftly round her.

'Thanks,' Skye murmured, suddenly unsure of him and the weirdly tense intimacy of the moment. She lowered her eyes to avoid his clear dark golden gaze. He was so polite, so protective and concerned for her comfort. She wasn't used to those qualities in a man. Ritchie had been hewn from a much rougher rock and she had told herself that that was his tough upbringing, not any lack in him. She supposed that that had been her making excuses for him, overlooking his flaws, refusing to see the bigger picture and that she had picked a man who had *no* caring, respectful side to his character.

As she parted from her sister, Alana bent her head and whispered, 'Enzo is so *hot* for you.'

'No way!' Skye laughed, lest Enzo guess that her sister had been talking about him because Alana had never been a good dissembler and Enzo was as observant as he was quick on the uptake. He was also, she had discovered that very day, chaotically untidy.

'Why didn't you tell me that you were still living out of suitcases and garment bags?' she asked in reproach as she joined him in his car. 'I only found out when I went into your room to change the bed this morning.'

'*Sì*...you've got me all sorted out now. I intended to thank you. At least I can see the floor now,' he remarked with amusement.

Skye gritted her teeth on a tart response. 'Are you aware that all your shirts are dry-clean only?' she continued.

'On the domestic front I am...pretty useless,' Enzo conceded after a moment's pause. 'But I shine in other fields.'

'I put the shirts into the dry-cleaners in town. Which other fields?'

'I'm good at dealing with people...as long as I'm sober,' he qualified, thinking back darkly a couple of months to the dinner party that he had unwisely attended at his grandparents' home. 'I'm innovative in business and courteous. I was very well raised. I've also discovered to my surprise that I can work very hard when I'm challenged and that my concentration is stellar.'

'You're used to maids picking up after you though, aren't you?'

'I would prefer not to answer that question on the grounds that I suspect that some kind of moral judgement is likely to come my way,' Enzo replied.

'Any other fields in which you shine?' she prompted, ready to change the subject because it wasn't her place to nag when he was paying her to take care of everything on the domestic front.

'I speak several languages fluently. I'm good at negotiation. I'm supposed to be terrific in bed but then women will always tell you that, if you're rich,' he quipped wryly, shocking her with his candour. 'Am I allowed to ask if you shine there as well?'

Skye had grown very tense. She knew that he had recognised that she was nervous of the evening ahead and that he was trying to distract her to get her to relax. It was just unfortunate that he had stumbled on that particular subject. 'I don't…shine, I mean,' she told him tightly. 'In fact, I have it on recent authority that I'm rubbish in that line. And I really don't care if it's true or not. I don't like sex. It does nothing for me.'

Having stopped at the traffic lights, Enzo flicked her a frowning glance. 'He *was* a charmer, wasn't he? He was putting you down. He seems to have been the sort of guy who likes to keep a woman down. Don't pay any heed to his opinion.'

'I'm not. I was just being frank, possibly *too* frank,' she muttered uneasily, her cheeks belatedly burning like fire in the dimness of the car. 'Shouldn't we be talking about this evening? Who am I supposed to be?'

'Yourself, of course. My girlfriend. Teacher, currently too busy with me and your siblings to work.'

'Girlfriend?'

'You're living with me. I have no intention of telling anyone that you're my housekeeper.'

'Ashamed?'

'*Dio mio*…it's simpler for us both if we pretend to be together this evening,' Enzo responded. 'I could have called half a dozen women in London to come up here and act the part but there would've been strings and expectations attached, and I didn't want that complication. You're doing me a huge favour and I appreciate it.'

'It's costing you enough…the trip to the Blackthorn Hotel beauty spa and the outfit I'm wearing did not, I suppose, come cheap,' Skye reminded him. 'And really…? *Half a dozen* women would have been willing to drop everything and come up here on short notice just to please you?'

'It's the wealth I inherited that's the draw, not me as an individual,' he breathed with sardonic bite.

'Maybe for some of them but I doubt it's the driving motivation for *all* of them,' Skye told him mildly. 'I mean, stop being such a cynic. Some of those ladies may just like you.'

'Do you?' he asked her unexpectedly.

Skye shot him an unexpectedly sunny smile. 'Yes, I do. You have a great deal of charm, which I'm sure you're well aware of, and you've been kind to the kids. If you're kind to my siblings, I become a big fan. Oh…random question here. Why were all the frocks the stylist brought some shade of purple? Is it your favourite colour?'

Enzo laughed. 'No, your eyes are the colour of lilacs, and I thought a similar shade would suit you.'

Skye shot him an unimpressed glance. 'They're not lilac. My goodness, I only wish they were! Lilac sounds exotic. Actually, they're a greyish light blue,' she told him informatively.

'Lilac,' Enzo repeated stubbornly as he turned down the road to the Blackthorn Hotel where her sister worked and the Mackies executive dinner was being held.

'Oh, my goodness, so where are we supposed to have met?'

'Your car broke down. Always best to stick as close to the truth as possible. Of course, the car breakdown happened months ago,' Enzo mocked. 'I'm not the sort of crazy guy who would invite a woman I've only known a few hours to live with me.'

'Aren't you?' Skye sent him a winging look of amusement. 'It's my bet that you can be impulsive and that you pride yourself on your ability to judge character.'

Enzo shot her an arrested glance, for that surmise had struck a little too close to home for comfort. 'Do you think you could act keen and clingy at this event for my benefit?'

Skye heaved a long-suffering sigh. 'If I worked at it. I'm not the clingy type and I imagine that you hate clingers.'

'I do,' Enzo confirmed, closing an arm round her for show and walking her towards the hotel entrance. 'But I'm fed up with the ambitious sex bombs at Mackies coming on to me and a clingy girlfriend will tell them that they're wasting their time.'

'I won't let you out of my sight,' Skye promised with amusement.

As drinks were served in an anteroom, Skye was conscious of being the cynosure of curious eyes. Enzo introduced her to the executives, including three very attractive brunettes, garbed in dresses that were very short and harboured strategic cut-outs that played up their ample bosoms and curvy behinds.

'You're sisters,' she guessed, having registered that they all had the same surname. 'And the daughters of the Mackie family, who originally owned the firm?'

'Your boyfriend hasn't made the same connection,' Martina, the head of marketing, informed her rather smugly.

'I would doubt that,' Skye countered gently, well aware that she enjoyed access through Enzo to confidential information and she knew that he believed that the firm had been ruined by placing highly paid family members in executive positions, even though they had few qualifications and little experience. 'He doesn't miss much.'

'You're a little petite to be a model,' Martina remarked. 'I was so sure you would be a model. Lorenzo has a long track record of dating models.'

Skye didn't bat an eyelash at that tactless reference to Enzo's past. She simply smiled and mentioned that she was a teacher, not currently employed.

'What do you think attracted him to you?' one of the sisters asked her with deadly seriousness.

'Skye's a fabulous cook,' Enzo drawled from behind her, tugging her back against him with easy intimacy. 'And the only woman I know who would dare to serve a pasta dish to a native-born Italian!'

'You *liked* it!' Skye reminded him, content to act the couple for the benefit of their audience. 'Most men like mac and cheese. It's a comfort food.'

'But it's not Italian,' Enzo told her, dark eyes glinting, determined to have the last word.

'I don't know how to cook in the Italian style,' Skye admitted calmly as he led her off to join another group.

'Were the Mackie daughters pleasant?'

'Martina was very surprised that I wasn't a model. Apparently, you have an impressive record of dating models,' Skye teased.

'The past is the past and we're leaving it there,' Enzo murmured sibilantly. 'But I haven't *dated* anyone since university.'

'So, you really don't do serious? Is that because you got burned?'

'I like to think I'm a little more mature than that.' Enzo's strong profile tautened. 'Maybe I'm just not ready to settle down yet.'

'Or maybe you missed your *one* by treating her like all her predecessors, like she was just a hook-up and nothing special,' Skye suggested with a wry smile.

Enzo swung back to her as though she had jabbed him with a knife, dark eyes glittering as though he were under attack. 'We have the most extraordinary conversations. Have you noticed that?'

'Not really,' Skye fibbed, not wanting him to appreciate that the way she relaxed with him was exceptional for her in male company, particularly after her ordeal with Ritchie, with whom an unguarded word could induce a surly silent mood that could last for hours. Yet on instinct she trusted Enzo, she registered in surprise. He wasn't given to moods and she suspected that even if she annoyed him, he would be blunt and straightforward about setting her straight.

'You're insidious.' Enzo gazed down at her with hooded dark eyes that glinted in the low light. 'You make sneaky little comments that stay with me.'

Her lilac eyes gleamed, and she bobbed a mock curtsy as if she were a maid being rebuked by the master of the house while her generous mouth curled into a mischievous grin. 'I'm sorry, sir. I'll try to mind my words better.'

'Like I believe that!' Enzo mocked back, his smile matching her own as he closed an arm round her to guide her into the private dining room.

'What's your secret?' the woman next to her whispered over the soup.

'Excuse me? Sorry, I didn't quite catch what you—'

'You have a notorious international playboy hanging on your every word like a puppy,' the blonde whispered. 'What's your secret? There are women at this table who would kill you and walk over your body to find out.'

Skye flushed. 'Enzo and I are…well, first and foremost, friends,' she selected awkwardly but with quiet sincerity. Friends without benefits, that was what they were, she reasoned, and Enzo was not in any way like a puppy. Puppies were innocent and there was nothing innocent about Enzo. If he seemed to be hanging onto her every word, it was just part of the whole pretence that she was his girlfriend.

'Keep it up. You're breaking the hearts of Macbeth's witches!' The other woman laughed and Skye glanced up to encounter the grim spiteful looks coming her way from the brunette bombshell trio Enzo had warned her about.

'The Witches. That's what they're called at work. I believe you're a teacher...'

With relief, Skye relaxed into an uncontroversial topic and another young mother began to talk to her about childhood development. Before she knew where she was, Enzo was tugging her up out of her seat with a rueful look. 'Time to go home,' he chided. 'We promised Alana we wouldn't be late.'

As it wasn't anywhere near late, Skye could only assume that Enzo had had enough of glad-handing and polite conversation. 'Well, you went down well with everyone,' he commented with satisfaction as he tucked her into the car.

'Apparently they call the Mackie daughters Macbeth's witches at work...'

Enzo laughed out loud as he drove off. 'Yes, one can imagine them toiling over a cauldron plotting and making spells.'

'If you turn left just down there, it's a shortcut back into town,' Skye informed him, indicating the country road.

'I haven't been along here before,' Enzo admitted as buildings appeared, marking the outskirts of the town.

'I know it well. I grew up around here,' Skye confided, peering out of the windows and smiling at the familiarity of the street. 'Oh, Enzo, if you're not in a hurry, turn down there. There used to be an ice-cream shop I was last in as a teenager. I bet it's long gone.' She sighed apologetically.

But the ice-cream shop had turned into a small café

and Skye beamed. 'I wonder if they still do home-made ice cream.'

'I have the feeling we're about to find out.'

'Do you like ice cream?' she asked him on the pavement, enthusiasm already moving her ahead of him.

He watched her break into an animated chat with the woman behind the counter, who turned out to be the daughter of the original owners. She tasted three different flavours and picked the fudge one, groaning out loud as she savoured it. 'That is *so* good!' she carolled.

Enzo picked vanilla with a lot less animation.

'You're not very adventurous,' she scolded as they got back in the car. 'Gosh, that place brings back so many memories of my parents. It was our local shop back then and on Saturdays, we got ice cream.'

'You must have been a very easily pleased teenager.'

'I'm talking about when I was younger, like still a kid.'

'Are you? You're what…twenty-two or twenty-three? And you seem equally enthusiastic now.' Tawny eyes rested on her with gentle mockery. 'I've given women diamonds and received less appreciation. Give you an ice-cream cone *and*…?'

Skye giggled. 'No, you'd have to give me more than an ice-cream cone,' she warned him, digging into her cone with gusto, little pink tongue swirling round the sweet confection, soft pink lips savouring.

'You've got it on your face now,' Enzo complained, digging a tissue out to wipe the tip of her gently tilted nose clean, the pulse at his groin downright painful. 'Take your time.'

'You've got to eat it quickly or it melts all over your

hands.' As she licked her pink lips clean she encountered Enzo's scorching golden gaze. *'What?'* she prompted.

'Throw out the cone and lick me instead,' Enzo stunned her by suggesting.

'Enzo!' she exclaimed in stark reproof.

Then she stilled as she collided with smouldering dark golden eyes. Her heart jumped inside her chest, her mouth running dry as a bone. Little tingles of awareness unlike anything she had ever felt travelled through her slender and now very tense frame.

'Your ice cream is melting,' Enzo warned her as she sat there frozen and staring back at him with wide lilac eyes. 'I didn't intend to bring you to an emergency stop. If you mess up the upholstery, I'll throw a fit!'

'You took me by surprise...you shocked me,' she muttered unevenly, struggling to catch her breath, thoroughly unnerved by the sensations that had shimmied up through her taut body and then down again to a place that had ignited with a burst of warmth that mortified her to the very bone.

Enzo released his breath on a measured hiss. 'Relax. For a moment, I was tempted. But nothing is going to happen unless you want it to. I'm attracted to you. I know I shouldn't be but I'm not perfect, in fact it seems I'm all too human. But you are completely safe with me, *piccolo mio.*'

'Maybe I don't need to be safe...with you,' Skye muttered uncertainly. 'You make me feel things I didn't expect to feel. You make me curious. I know, like you said, I shouldn't be in these circumstances. But the truth is, I am and I'm attracted too.'

Literally trembling from her own daring in being that candid, Skye swallowed convulsively and dropped her head, ashamed of the sheer power of his draw for her. She had barely escaped alive from her last entanglement and wouldn't dream of embarking on another. *But*... There was definitely a *huge* 'but' enmeshed in all her thoughts about Enzo, as if he belonged in a category all of his own. Would one kiss hurt? Men and women kissed all the time. It would hardly be a major event.

'So...' Enzo breathed a touch raggedly, his breathing audible. 'What do you want to do about this?'

'We...we could try a kiss...just *one*,' she stressed, evidently fearful that more than one kiss might push him past all restraint. 'Just to satisfy our curiosity, and we'll probably find out it's not worth our while.'

'Not worth our while,' Enzo repeated thickly, afraid that if he didn't speak, he would laugh out loud at her naivety. One kiss. *One kiss.* Even as a teenager, girls had offered him a great deal more than that. And one kiss wasn't going to do anything to tackle his raging arousal, was it? But then, he reminded himself, it wasn't about what he wanted, it was about what *she* wanted and all she could apparently envisage was a very brief, controlled experiment. It was ridiculous. He knew it was. And yet... and yet, he was as fascinated and as aroused as if she'd ripped off her clothes and propositioned him.

'Agreed. One kiss,' he asserted not quite levelly. 'It won't give me any expectations either, in case you're worried about that possibility. I won't be demanding anything more. But we'll experiment somewhere else, somewhere we're not in full view of my security team.'

'Why do you have so much security?' Skye asked, relaxing a little again now that touching was no longer imminent. Yet it was an effort to speak, to even think rationally because Enzo tied her up in knots to the extent that she barely recognised herself in his company. She said things to Enzo she had never dreamt of saying to any man. He blew through her defensive barriers as though they didn't exist.

'My father was kidnapped when he was younger than I am now. The kidnappers demanded a ransom. My father's father refused to pay and he was tortured…for weeks,' he completed flatly. 'Ultimately, he was rescued but the experience broke something in him and he was never the same afterwards.'

'Oh, my word,' she whispered sickly.

'That's the only reason I have protection. I have to accept that with my wealth I will always be a target. I have my grandparents equally well protected,' he admitted steadily. 'Security being around all the time, however, is occasionally a pain.'

'But necessary. I get it.' She nodded, shaken by what he had revealed.

'Well, that took me out of the moment,' he confided in a roughened undertone, switching on the engine. 'I'll take you back home now.'

'No…*wait*!' Skye exclaimed, grabbing him by his jacket and practically lurching across the car to cover his mouth with her own. She was driven by something she didn't understand but it was still something stronger than she was, something capable of suppressing her essential lack of confidence in that field. The need to connect with Enzo at that instant was more powerful than almost any urge she had ever experienced, indeed almost on a par with her desperate need to escape Ritchie that awful night when he had attacked her. And now here she was attacking Enzo instead, she reflected in disbelief.

'No, not like that.' Predictably, Enzo took charge, ramming back his seat to the furthest to gain more space, lifting her right down on top of him so that her clumsy, uncomfortable stretching lean towards him was no longer necessary. 'Relax, take your time,' he urged.

'But we're in full view of your security team,' she reminded him, face red as fire.

'I don't care. A kiss is no big deal.'

He brushed his lips gently across hers and she stopped breathing, her heart a racing thud in her eardrums. 'No big deal,' he repeated, lifting his handsome dark head again to look down at her where she trembled on his lap. 'There's no need to be scared—'

'I'm *not* scared!' Skye snapped, hands closing into the lapels of his jacket to yank him back to her with an aggression she had never ever felt before. 'If it's one kiss, you do it properly!'

'Is that so?' Enzo regrouped because he had never been forcibly grabbed before and he finally appreciated that she wasn't in the least afraid of him. 'What would madam find acceptable?'

'Oh, stop it!' she scolded him feverishly, stretching up as she had to do even on his lap to find his wickedly attractive mouth for herself. Her palms framed his hard cheekbones and smoothed down to his stubbled jawline, her fingers enjoying the roughness of that dark shadow.

In fact, Enzo gave her a feast of different sensations to revel in. There was the wildly enticing smell of him that close, a sort of spicy, musky cologne-tinged masculinity that called to every sense. There were the fingers gently smoothing over her back and the sheer burning, sizzling excitement of his firm lips moving on hers.

It would have been fair to say that a single kiss had never lit a fire in Enzo before but the slight weight of Skye on top of him when he was already hard enough to pound nails was more than sufficient, especially when added to the little throaty sounds she emitted while she squirmed and pressed closer. In fact, a bushfire could not have been hotter. His tongue delved deep and she shuddered, hands on his shoulders now, her fingers digging into him making him think of other things he could be doing to feed that much-to-be-encouraged enthusiasm. Enzo was on a total high.

A trio of teenage boys stopped on the pavement to catcall and make obscene gestures. The sound of their voices broke the spell. Skye tore her swollen lips from his, as shocked as a nun waking up to an orgy, and removed herself so fast from his lap that she was in danger of whiplash. 'What on earth were we thinking of?' she exclaimed sharply.

Enzo forced a laugh when he didn't feel like laughing. He felt more like getting uncharacteristically violent with the teenagers who had wrecked the most erotic encounter he had had in years. That *had* to be his imagination, he told himself straight away. 'We weren't thinking,' he pointed out drily.

'I can't believe I did that!' Skye erupted in sheer embarrassment.

'It's not like we were having sex,' Enzo shot back at her, pulling the car away from the kerb. 'It was just a stupid kiss. Don't overreact!'

Skye's mortification still threatened to swallow her alive. She had told him that she didn't like sex and then snatched at him like an oversexed maneater! Just a *stupid* kiss. Well, she supposed it was stupid on playboy terms. He probably hadn't done anything that innocent in the last ten years or been greeted with any greater female fervour!

'So what went wrong?' Alana asked Skye as she passed her a cup of tea.

'Why do you think there's anything wrong?' Skye asked, struggling to seem cool and unconcerned.

'*He* came in the door like a tornado and went straight upstairs. You came in all pink and stiff. Obviously, something happened,' her wily sibling pointed out and then frowned anxiously. 'Did he make a pass at you?'

'No, I made a pass at him,' Skye corrected. 'But I don't want to talk about it.'

Alana startled her by grinning and then mock-zipping her mouth before grasping her tea and telling her about Brodie's high jinks at bedtime.

The next morning, Skye decided that Enzo lacked the sensitive gene. She set his breakfast at the dining-room table and he carried it through into the kitchen to sit down opposite her when she was feeling as though if she saw him before the end of the century, it would be too soon.

'Do you always make a major event out of little mole-hills?' Enzo enquired lazily.

'Don't be smart—'

'One of us has to be.'

Skye's cheeks flamed and she dealt him a speaking look.

It was those lilac eyes, Enzo thought in frustration, they got to him in some weird annoying way and made him feel guilty even when she was thoroughly exasperating him.

'I suppose this is not the optimum time to tell you that Mavis is being delivered back to you today.'

'Seriously?' she gasped in disconcertion.

'Roadworthy this time,' Enzo added a tad smugly. 'Your car was in a dangerous condition.'

'Mum was a care assistant. She didn't earn enough to keep Mavis maintained. Keeping her *on* the road was a big enough challenge.'

'I want another favour from you,' Enzo said bluntly. 'But I know you're not in the mood to hear it, right now.'

CHAPTER FIVE

'I'M NOT A moody person!' Skye proclaimed defensively.

'Either that or you're a little puritanical,' Enzo retorted. 'We shared a single kiss, nothing more.'

'I'm sorry,' Skye framed shakily, reaching for her morning coffee only to meet Enzo's hand instead. Long brown fingers enclosed hers in silence.

Regrettably that silence thrummed like a drumbeat inside her and she dropped her eyes to the table top as her insides liquefied at even that minor physical contact. She felt as if she were burning up and the ache between her legs appalled her. It was exactly that same feeling that had made her want to throw herself at him the night before. No guy had ever made her feel like that, certainly not her ex. It was as terrifying as it was thrilling and it was her problem, *not* his.

'What's the favour?'

'It's a big one this time but, as I own the Blackthorn Hotel, you *could* accommodate me, if you chose to do so, because I can free up your sister to take care of the kids while we're away.'

'You *own* the Blackthorn Hotel?' Skye studied him, eyes wide. 'I thought your family business was related to packaging?'

'Companies diversify.' Enzo shrugged. 'I own hotel chains, property, all sorts of stuff in different fields. The Blackthorn belongs to one of the luxury chains.'

'Oh...' Skye said, shattered by the thought of any one man owning so many businesses because it made the extent of his wealth much more obvious and real to her. And you don't like that, do you? She scolded herself with a mentally curled lip of scorn. After all, the richer Enzo was, the more out of her league he was. As if he weren't already out of her league! With his devastating good looks and charisma and even hotter kisses, never mind the playboy reputation that would enhance him in the eyes of some women.

'This favour?'

Enzo let go of her fingers to make an uncharacteristically jerky gesture and frowned. 'I refuse to go into any details but, two months ago, I went to a dinner party drunk with a drunk and not very ladylike partner and something very embarrassing happened. I was in disgrace with my family. *Madre di Dio*... I made my grandmother *cry*...'

'Everyone makes mistakes, Enzo.' Skye recaptured his hand to smooth the back of it gently, recognising that the recollection still filled him with regret.

'You're very tactile...' Enzo breathed.

Skye reddened and immediately let go of his hand, clasping her hands together on her lap to keep them from temptation. 'It's the kids. I'm always touching them, and it gets to be a habit. Sorry.'

Enzo didn't know how to tell her that he liked her easy way of touching him because if he did admit that he would be giving her the wrong impression, wouldn't he? Creating complications he didn't need, possibly hurting her as well, not a risk he should take, he acknowledged grimly.

'Look, I have to go up to Glasgow to see this old guy who is a silent partner in Mackies with my grandfather. He's entitled to a personal report on the firm. But Robinson Davies was at that ghastly dinner party in Italy with his wife and everyone present was very shocked by what happened. I could do with some company to get through lunch with the couple.'

'What happened?'

'I already said that I'm not going to give you the details. Not even thumbscrews would get that confession out of me,' he stated with a sardonic twist of his beautiful stubborn mouth. 'But will you accompany me to Glasgow if your sister is able to stay here to take care of the kids?'

Skye thought about it in the space of a moment. She knew she should say no. She knew that further extended exposure to Lorenzo Durante was bad for her and that she would be wiser to avoid him to the best of her ability. But she also knew how much she owed him for their current safety and stability.

Besides, it wasn't his fault that she was absolutely fascinated with him. Around Enzo, she was starting to feel like a teenager with an outsized crush she couldn't handle. As he had reminded her, she was no longer a teenager and she knew that she *should* have better control of her feelings. Especially so soon after her misjudgement of Ritchie's character, she affixed with regret. But perhaps, she thought, with Enzo it was literally a pure sexual attraction sort of a thing and hitting her all the harder because she had never experienced reactions that powerful with anyone else. It was even possible that that was why everything in the bedroom had been a disaster with Ritchie, because she hadn't been sufficiently attracted to her ex from the start. Whichever, she knew she wanted to know and running away from that attraction was foolish when she had still to live in the same house with Enzo.

'I'll do it. Glasgow?'

'We're flying up. I have a business meeting with Robinson first and then I'll pick you up at the hotel and we'll go to lunch at their home the next day.'

'I can wear the same dress I wore last night.'

'No, you can't. They're a very traditional couple and they don't do anything flash. If you have a reasonable outfit of your own, it will do fine,' he advanced.

'That's a relief,' Skye told him cheerfully. 'I didn't want you to have to buy me anything more.'

'You really need to be greedier around me,' Enzo complained. 'I'm used to buying stuff for women.'

'Well, you're not buying stuff for me. It's...just uncomfortable,' she explained with a wry shake of her blonde curly head as Shona clasped her knees and she lifted her baby sister onto her lap. 'You can't mix as equals when one person is doing all the giving.'

'It hasn't bothered any other woman in my life.'

'You've been involved with the wrong kind of women, then.'

Enzo didn't know a polite way of telling her that she sounded like his grandmother, and there was no polite way of saying that casual sex in return for his expected generosity went with the same territory even though no-body was crude enough to state the fact. So, he said noth-ing, merely watched her steadily from beneath long black curling eyelashes, dark eyes flashing gold as the morn-ing sunlight lit them.

Now she wanted to kill him for the length and lush-ness of his eyelashes, Skye conceded, wondering in some desperation when she would return to sanity and calm again. In Enzo's presence she was all of a twitter like some stage maiden aunt.

'So, when's this trip taking place?' she prompted.

'We'll fly up Friday and be back by Saturday evening.' With that casual conclusion, Enzo vaulted upright. 'I'll see you tonight.'

'If Mavis comes in back in time, I'll be able to go shop-ping on my own,' Skye said with relief. 'I won't need to bother your security team.'

'No, they must still accompany you.' Enzo had stilled in the doorway, his lean, darkly handsome features taut. 'Unless your ex is in police custody, you're not safe. Paola spotted him sitting in a car in a layby just up the road yesterday. He's persistent and I don't want you taking any unnecessary risks until he's off the streets.'

Skye paled at the news that Ritchie had been spotted nearby and swallowed the thickness in her throat. The prospect of the complete freedom she longed to reclaim shrank again because, even though she didn't want to admit it, she *was* scared of Ritchie. A shiver ran down her spine at the confirmation that he knew where she was living and that the day before he could have been *that* close to them.

'I'll see you later.' Enzo's firm footsteps sounded in the hall.

'Enzo going?' Brodie prompted in his little voice.

'I'll be home later,' Enzo repeated for her little brother's benefit.

She had only finished cleaning up the kitchen when the bell went. A delivery man handed her a big bouquet of flowers. 'Who's it for?' she asked.

'Skye Davison.'

She retreated indoors with the red roses and looked for a vase in the kitchen. Who on earth would send her flowers? Enzo?

Without hesitation she phoned him because she had to know one way or another. 'Did you send me flowers?' she queried as soon as she heard his deep voice.

At his end of the phone, Enzo frowned reflectively. With the sole exception of his grandmother, he had never sent a woman flowers in his life. 'No. I'm not really a flower-giving sort of guy with women,' he admitted, feeling strangely uncomfortable at making that statement while wondering who the hell had sent her a bouquet.

'Then that means Ritchie sent them. You see, there was no card with them,' she responded tensely. 'Sorry for disturbing you at work.'

And she was gone before he could muster his thoughts into a better response. He groaned out loud. Her beast of an ex was sending her flowers. What a creep the guy was! Later he could not comprehend what he did next because he summoned his PA and ordered flowers for Skye. One of those extravagant wildflower-type arrangements, he described vaguely, instinctively shying away from the romantic intent inherent in sending roses and the like.

Two hours later, Ritchie's roses dispatched to the bin because the sight of them made her flesh crawl, Skye had a second delivery. A magnificent artistic bouquet was brought in by Paola, who was wreathed in unexpected smiles.

'From the boss,' she announced with deep satisfaction, as if Enzo had trekked through the Amazon jungle to acquire them in some great praiseworthy feat.

Skye texted him.

Enzo, you shouldn't have, but the flowers are really beautiful, thank you.

And Enzo smiled. Well, he had only done it to take her mind off the creep's stratagems, he assured himself, and Skye was far too sensible and practical not to appreciate that there was nothing romantic about the gesture.

The post came in the afternoon. A letter tumbled out of the usual pile of brochures, addressed to some previous occupant of the property, and her heart almost stopped dead when she saw the envelope and her own name because she recognised Ritchie's very distinctive copperplate handwriting immediately and turned pale as milk.

'What is it?' Alana asked.

'A letter from Ritchie,' Skye told her, dropping it on the kitchen table for the younger woman to see.

'Bin it,' her more outspoken sister advised.

'No, I can't do that. I have to open it and if there's threats in it, I'll have to take it to the police and hand it over and tell the solicitor.' Skye collapsed down on a chair.

'It would be really dumb of him to write down threats. Is he that stupid?'

'I don't want to open it,' Skye admitted dully. 'It just rakes it all up again and plunges me back into what a pathetic mistake I made with him.'

'Ask Paola to check it first. She's a really tough lady,' Alana said admiringly. 'I've signed up for a martial arts class starting after Christmas purely from seeing her in action in that car park with Ritchie. It was so cool.'

'Involving Paola would be gutless. This is *my* responsibility,' Skye declared, lifting a knife off the table where they had had their lunch to slit open the envelope.

She read Ritchie's letter with a sinking heart and a growing sense of disbelief. There was no expression of regret, no admission of fault beyond a reference to her 'fall' and his apparent hope that she had recovered and *calmed down*. It infuriated her almost as much as it intimidated her and when she read to the end and realised that he was trying to get her to meet up with him, her tummy turned over queasily at even the suggestion.

She tossed the letter over to her sister. 'He's trying to get me to agree to see him.'

'Of course, he is. He'll be wanting you to drop those assault charges. He's going to lose his job and may well go to prison,' Alana pointed out. 'Have you "calmed down"?'

'Not in the slightest. I'll never forget or forgive what he did to me.'

'So, will you agree to tell Enzo I'm in for that assistant

night-shift manager promotion at the Blackthorn?' Her sister was returning to an earlier conversation.

'I don't think it would be fair,' Skye parried a second time.

Alana grimaced. 'He owns the blasted place! It would mean nothing to him!'

'He's done me enough favours,' Skye countered.

Alana rolled her eyes. 'You're the one doing *him* favours. Fake girlfriend? Trip to Glasgow?'

'Alana, look at what he's had done to Mavis. She's transformed,' Skye argued. 'He must've spent hundreds of pounds on that car.'

'I reckon thousands,' her sister opined. 'It didn't even look that good when Mum bought it ten years ago.'

Enzo arrived home to an empty house and was greeted rapturously only by Sparky.

'Skye and her sister went out shopping,' Paola reported. 'Antonio and Matteo are with them.'

Enzo reheated the meal left for him in the microwave and wondered if Skye really thought he was stupid enough to need the step-by-step instructions she had left for him, but, on another level, he was telling himself that he should be relieved that Skye was absent. Their relationship—and even the word threatened a man who didn't have relationships—had a weird lack of boundaries and he *had* sent her those showy flowers on prominent display in the hall. She *worked* for him, he reminded himself fiercely. She was an employee even if she didn't feel like one, any more than the kids and the dog felt like an employee's dependants. He had got too close to her, become too involved. Intelligence warned him that he should pull back. Having eaten, he went into the room he was using as an office and stubbornly ignored the sounds of Skye and her siblings returning home.

Skye couldn't sleep that night. She had wanted to see Enzo and she hadn't seen him and then had warned herself that she had no need to see him either. The *clingy* housekeeper, knocking on the door with an offer of supper? No, that was not a label she sought. She grimaced.

Around one in the morning, weary of tossing and turning, she went down to the kitchen to have a cup of tea and dug Ritchie's letter out of her bag to have another look at it. She refused to be scared of him or of anything he had written. Unhappily, all those nasty little jabs about how overly emotional she could be, how she jumped to conclusions, how she always thought the worst in situations and dramatised herself washed over her afresh and knocked her flat. Rereading the letter had not been a good idea, she acknowledged. Even mulling over his criticisms of her after he had violently assaulted her was crazy.

Enzo heard Skye heading downstairs and worried that something was amiss. He climbed out of bed and tugged on a pair of jeans, deeming a T-shirt unnecessary. Barefoot, he descended the stairs without a sound and saw Skye sitting at the kitchen table, her head buried in her folded arms, her narrow shoulders shaking.

'What's wrong?' Enzo demanded, striding over to her, registering that she was quietly crying.

'Go away,' she told him hoarsely. 'I'm having a mini breakdown and I don't need an audience!'

'What's this?' Enzo lifted the letter off the table. 'He had the nerve to write you a *letter* after what he did?' he bit out incredulously.

Enzo read it and rolled his eyes, tossing it back down on the table while Skye mopped her eyes and struggled to regain control. 'You can tell he's abusive simply by the stuff he writes. He beat you up and he's finding fault with you!'

'I know. How could I have been foolish enough to move in with a man like that?' she gasped, stricken, and leapt out of her chair to rush over and put on the kettle. 'Do you want something to drink?'

'Water will do me.'

Enzo breathed in deep and slow, hating that sense of being out of his depth, but there was no use pretending that he was experienced at comforting distressed women when he had always avoided distressed women like the plague. As he followed her across the spacious kitchen, he rested both hands on her slender shoulders in an effort to ground her.

'You didn't know what he was like until you moved in with him. People don't wear their secrets, flaws and kinks like badges. They keep up a front to lure you in until you trust them. But you're not to blame. He's a weirdo and I'm dropping that letter into the police tomorrow morning.'

'Thanks,' she muttered. 'But I'm just so angry with myself.'

'Try being angry with *him*! How dare he send you flowers and write to you after assaulting you?' Enzo framed in a raw undertone. 'Call your solicitor and update him about this. I'm quite sure that the police will have warned your ex to stay well away from you and now he's harassing you.'

Skye spun round with a moisture-beaded glass of water for him. He set it down on the counter behind her and stared down at her with intense dark golden eyes. 'You shouldn't be crying about that bastard, you should be celebrating the fact that you escaped him!'

'That letter upset me. I'll get over it. And I wasn't crying about *him*, I was crying about how stupid I was to trust him and now the kids have had all this upheaval…'

'Your siblings are perfectly happy here.'

'Enzo…working here is only a staging post because it's temporary. I have to think of the future and we'll be moving on *again*.'

His hands slid down from her shoulders to her hands. 'Take a deep breath and give yourself time to recover from what happened to you first. It's much too soon for you to be freaking out about the future.'

'I wish it was, but I've already been here two weeks and in another six weeks you may be gone,' she pointed out, frantically striving not to look at his bare chest.

Half naked, there was so much of him, an expanse of bronzed hair-roughened muscular flesh that any woman would have gawped at. He towered over her with his taut abs, well-developed biceps and a flat stomach framed by that fabled vee of lean muscle leading down to his hips. Perspiration broke out on her short upper lip as she looked up at him, connecting with stormy dark-as-night eyes, beautiful eyes, changeable according to mood, she had long since learned. The tension in the atmosphere was stifling her ability to breathe. She sucked in air a little desperately.

Enzo ran a long finger along the lower line of her lips, feeling that soft pillowy mouth he wanted under his and fighting that instinct with all his might. Holding her breath tight, in a spirit of unfamiliar daring, Skye lifted her hand and shakily traced the waistband of his jeans. He was as aroused as she was. The prominent bulge below the denim assured her of that and it made her feel almost light-headed with satisfaction, vindicating the feminine power that Ritchie had assured her she didn't have. One of the many insults he had hurled while she'd lain on that floor in terror had been that she was sexless and frigid, useless to any normal man.

'You don't want this,' Enzo told her hoarsely.

'What I don't want,' she whispered unevenly, 'is another man making *my* choices for me.'

'I'm trying to protect you,' Enzo gritted between clenched teeth, because with every breath she drew her small breasts stirred beneath the thin pyjama top she wore, the peaks of her nipples indenting the cloth, and he wanted to grab her, ravish her, do everything his raging libido demanded that he do. His lean hands clenched into knotted fists by his side.

'I can protect myself,' Skye argued, spinning round to walk away, chin lifted against rejection, determined not to betray that another ego-squashing wound had been inflicted.

Enzo ground something out in explosive Italian and then lifted her up against him to set her down on the table edge, standing back again, deliberately not crowding her. 'You need a friend right now, *not* a lover.'

The ease with which he lifted her off her feet and set her down again struck her as ridiculously sexy. He was strong but he didn't use that strength against her. 'There's nothing wrong with a friend with benefits,' Skye heard herself say.

And that declaration disagreed with every moral tenet and ideal Skye had ever cherished and she knew it did. But she wanted Enzo, and she was willing to fib because she knew that it would only ever be a passing thing with him and that there was no other way of being with him. Either she accepted that, or she didn't. But right now, after her life had fallen in round her ears with every hope and expectation destroyed, she was struggling to find her feet in a new world and somehow being desired by Enzo made her feel better, so much better she couldn't believe it.

'I'm not sure I can believe that you mean that,' Enzo murmured, searching dark golden eyes compelling hers. 'I was very sure you were a white-picket-fence girl with a church at the end of the drive.'

Skye flushed to the very roots of her hair because Enzo had already had her labelled and he was entirely correct with his estimate. She had wanted love, she had wanted a wedding, she had wanted everything perfect, only to discover that life was not perfect any more than men were or even she was. And now she was in a new place, ready to try something different, something more, something much bolder than her usual choices.

'I'm changing my outlook.'

Enzo rested his mesmeric dark golden eyes on her

hot face. 'But I don't want you doing that just for me. I don't want to hurt you. With me, it's sex and a good time. There's nothing else on offer,' he spelt out curtly.

Skye gulped because that sounded so harsh and hurtful and risky and she wasn't a risk-taker, never had been. It sounded like a devil's bargain for a young woman who believed in love, who was already getting more attached than she should be to the man in front of her. She swallowed hard, her hands gripping the edge of the table as she sat there. 'I understand.'

'I don't think I'd be much good at anything deeper,' Enzo breathed in a roughened undertone.

But he had a huge heart even though he hid it to the very best of his ability, Skye reflected, confused by him and by all the conflicting messages he gave her. His actions with her had taught her to trust in that heart of his even though he was not emotionally available to her. He could be warm and gentle one moment, then cold and hard the next. He was unfathomable, unpredictable, everything she had once avoided in a man. Her brain screamed that she would be making a mistake but thought had no control over instinct and every instinct she possessed drew her to Enzo.

'You deserve a much nicer guy,' Enzo added, still stubbornly holding back.

Skye looked up at him and laughed because she couldn't help it. She stretched out her arms to tug him closer, hands travelling up his taut spine to his shoulders and even sitting on the table it was a stretch for her. 'Shut up, Enzo…please stop talking and just kiss me…'

CHAPTER SIX

ENZO LOOKED DOWN into those entrancing lilac eyes of hers and all his disciplined restraint evaporated in the same moment. His hands rose of their own volition to cup her triangular face, long fingers slowly spearing into her soft mop of curls.

Her face was already so familiar to him that he wondered sometimes if she reminded him of someone, but she was too individual to be a copy of anyone else. The only woman he had ever known who had breakfast with him without make-up on. The only woman who finished a phone call even faster than he did. The only woman, who seemed to see him for who he was rather than what he possessed and who treated him accordingly, just as if he was the same as everyone else. And best of all, Skye had not a clue how special it was for someone like him to be treated as though he was no one special either. In much the same way, he registered, he had not a clue why he found that so appealing a trait.

'Enzo...' Skye urged, every fibre of her being tensely awaiting the slow descent of his lips onto hers, his lips brushing back and forth over hers, so gentle, so stimulating as he gathered her up off the table like a doll and literally welded her to every muscular line of his long, hard body. Every sensitive spot she possessed squirmed with delight at that full contact and she gasped. It was like the kiss in the car, like sticking her finger in an electric socket, like a tidal wave engulfing her. Excitement rolled through her in a heady surge and made her wonder if she could be quite normal in such an overreaction.

When she surfaced, she was in Enzo's bedroom with no recollection of the journey upstairs. 'You *carried* me up here?' she exclaimed as he settled her down on the tumbled bed.

'You don't weigh much more than your little brother. It was hardly an extraordinary feat.' Enzo laughed.

And now here they were in the bedroom where the bonfire of her best hopes had previously burned into dreary ash. Apprehension leapt through her. 'There's just one thing I don't like…the choking thing,' she muttered uncomfortably, needing to put that out there but cringing at the necessity of saying it.

Comprehension gripped Enzo and he mentally cursed the male who had put that nervous, anxious look on her flushed face. 'I'm not into that sort of stuff. In fact, I'm pretty vanilla in my tastes. Nothing to frighten the horses, as my grandmother would say.'

'That's a very English saying,' she remarked, relief filling her to overflowing.

'My grandmother *is* English. Nonno…my grandfather…met her when she was a chalet girl at a ski lodge when they were both very young. Against everybody's wishes, they married and they're still together.'

'That's why your English is so good.'

'Probably.' Enzo could see the nerves infiltrating her

again, her skin taut across her cheekbones, eyes downcast. 'Do you mind me asking if your ex was your first lover?'

Skye nodded silent confirmation.

'So, practically a virgin on my terms,' Enzo teased as he unzipped his jeans and kicked them aside to come down beside her on the rucked bed. 'I may not be able to offer you for ever, but I can show you pleasure and, hopefully, a little fun.'

He didn't have a shy bone in his body. Why would he have? she asked herself, scanning his near godlike physical perfection. He was all bronzed, hair-roughened vitality and virility. He was also primed for action and there was definitely more of him than she was accustomed to dealing with. She lay back on the bed, trying not to feel like a human sacrifice, wondering for a moment what insanity had persuaded her that she ought to try again to see if intimacy was any different with Enzo.

'Look on the bright side,' Enzo whispered, leaning over her with unvarnished cool. 'If you don't like it with me either, you don't ever have to do it again.'

'I suppose that's a good point,' she said, a little breathless at him being that close.

She sat up again, almost knocking him back, nervous tension making her jerky and indecisive. She peeled her pyjama top over her head, snaked her hips free of the shorts, flung them on the floor, lay back down again and found Enzo staring down at her with wondering amusement brimming in his gaze.

'What?' she said flatly.

'You're so obviously in this "let's get this over as fast

as possible" mode,' he proffered. 'And that's not how I operate.'

Skye ignored him to slide beneath the duvet, too self-conscious about her lack of sexy curves to stay naked on top of the bedding.

'Do you think it's possible for you to switch off your brain and relax for a moment?'

'Doubt it.'

'You're not allowed to bail on me as soon as it's over, either,' Enzo warned her, although a quick departure had never bothered him with any other woman because he never stayed the whole night with anyone. But he already knew that it would be different with Skye, that he had *one* chance and he had to go for it and make the most he could out of it.

'Why not?'

'Because that's not what I want...perfunctory sex, brief and superficial.'

'I thought that's what you specialised in. Isn't that what womanisers do?'

'What would you know about womanisers?' Enzo enquired as he slid in beside her, sudden heat burning down her right side, making her shiver in reaction.

'Nothing,' she admitted.

'Well, there you are. It's not all about scoring for me, at least not with you.'

'I'm sure you say that to all your women,' Skye told him huffily. 'I don't need that sort of reassurance. I'm perfectly happy just to be here...for *one* night.'

'And all the more precious for it,' Enzo husked, claiming her parted lips with his warm, hungry mouth, stealing the very breath from her lungs as honeyed warmth spread through her lower body, driving off the chill of nerves that had been spreading through her.

'Enzo… I—'

'Shush,' he hummed against her parted lips. 'I'm not going to do anything you don't want to do and the minute you say stop, I *stop*. You can trust me.'

Skye drew in a quivering breath, feeling reassured. 'All right.'

'It will be better than all right; it will be fantastic because we have explosive chemistry.'

'Is that so?'

'*Sì*…that means yes.'

'I know that! You're always spluttering Italian when you're not thinking about it,' she told him.

And Enzo laughed and thought how unusual it was for him to laugh with a woman in bed, never mind have a conversation. He lifted his dark tousled head and stared down at her in the lamplight and used a long finger to trace her fine brows, her delicate cheekbones and the soft pink cushion of her swollen lips. 'You're beautiful.'

And she almost argued with him but bit it back, assuming it was standard for him to say that sort of thing, but that didn't mean that she had to be clumsy about receiving a compliment, did it? As far as she was concerned the only beautiful individual in the room was Enzo with his classic bone structure, dark deep-set eyes and that particular rare smile on his lips that hinted that he didn't have a care in the world.

'You're so warm,' she told him with a grin. 'As good as an electric blanket.'

'Livelier, I hope, *piccolo mio.*'

Still smiling, Enzo shaped a dainty breast with a hunger he was fiercely striving to restrain. He brushed away the bedding only to discover that she was inadvertently holding onto it. He detached her from the duvet like a man making the first move to open a box containing a fascinating puzzle. He bent over her, the apprehension in her wide eyes clenching something painful inside his broad chest. In all his life no woman had ever looked at him with that degree of anxiety and so he kissed her and he kissed her for a very, very long time, sliding against her, dipping his tongue in the tender interior of her mouth with a little flick and a promise that began to ignite something low in her pelvis that Skye had never felt before.

All sorts of unfamiliar sensations began to shimmy through Skye and demolish her tension to replace it with a tension of a different type. She grew less worried about Enzo hurting or embarrassing her and more concerned with what he would do next, which, she dimly registered, was a lot healthier an attitude. Her fingers crept up over his stubbled jaw into his luxuriant black hair. It felt so good to finally touch him again and so strange to realise that she who had come to detest physical contact with one man could be so different with another.

Enzo stroked a taut pink nipple while toying with its twin. He captured the swollen peak with his mouth and dallied there, teasing and sucking and tasting until the burst of warmth being created in Skye's pelvis rose into a flame, making her push her hips down into the mattress and writhe, unable to lie still.

'I want us both to enjoy this, *piccolo mio,*' Enzo intoned when Skye sent him a winging glance of impatience. 'It's not likely to be over in five minutes.'

'I didn't say a word!' she protested shakily.

But Skye was stubborn for all her diminutive size, Enzo reckoned. It shone out of her character. She was the woman who had taken on her vulnerable siblings in spite of the reality that that weight and size of responsibility had made her life much more difficult. She was the woman irritated with him for paying for all the food in the kitchen even while she was staying there with her little brother and sister. She was used to independence and hated relying on other people. Her hand ran down over his chest to skim a long, powerful thigh and his mind went momentarily blank.

He returned her hand concisely to the mattress. 'Tonight, it's my show.'

'You're a control freak.'

'No, I know I'm on trial and I need a clear head,' Enzo countered smooth as glass.

'I did not say you were on trial.'

'But we both know I am,' he replied unanswerably.

As Skye compressed her lips, still struggling to control herself and her responses, Enzo kissed her again with passionate urgency and why it was so important to hold the line then escaped her. Enzo was very good at kissing, so good that before he could regroup and address his attention elsewhere, she grabbed him back to her, her own hunger for his mouth coming out of nowhere at her and startling her.

'I'm doing okay,' Enzo drawled thickly, all confidence

and unshakeable control, as he kissed a haphazard trail down over her midriff.

'Did I say that?'

'In bed your body speaks for you,' Enzo purred, entirely preoccupied by her smooth satiny soft skin and every tiny revealing twitch of her slender hips.

'Enzo…' she gasped on a long, broken sigh as he traced the heart of her with his fingers and his tongue.

Skye had never indulged in that particular pursuit before and her body's fiery reaction took her very much by surprise. Enzo was discovering sensitivities even she had not known she possessed. When he ran the tip of his tongue along the line of her inner thigh, she almost spontaneously combusted at the surge of heat that began to warm her up from the inside out. Indeed, being in bed with Enzo, it was almost impossible for her to think with any clarity. She would start a thought and then he would do something that tore her every expectation up and shook her from head to toe.

He traced her, he stroked her, he explored her. And little tremors of response began to run through Skye like a river threatening to burst its banks and overflow. He had trapped her because she could no more have persuaded herself to get out of that bed than she could have stopped breathing. And it was a revelation to her that sex could feel so intense and so powerful that it suppressed every other response.

The clenching low in her pelvis led to an inner tightness like a knot low in her tummy and she couldn't stay still then, she became insanely conscious of Enzo's big hands clamped to her hips. She twisted and squirmed and suddenly that ball of heat inside her just mushroomed up out of her in an earth-shaking climax that left her quivering and in shock in the aftermath.

'Did you like that?' Enzo whispered.

And that fast, she wanted to slap him for his nerve. 'It was okay,' she told him unevenly.

Skye watched him don a condom, all of an unexpected quiver inside herself because she was wanting something she had learned not to want and it unnerved her. He slid over her, all male, hot and demanding and, for a moment, she simply tuned him out, refused to think, refused to feel.

Enzo claimed her lips in a long, drugging kiss. 'There you are again, *piccolo mio*,' he remarked, dark eyes gleaming gold, and she reddened, registering that he had noted her withdrawal.

Comparisons were utterly distasteful to her but it was different, everything was different from past experience. Enzo sank into the slippery welcome of her and sent a jolt of arousal travelling through her lower body. From there, and to her astonishment, it only became more riveting in the most delicious of ways. In fact, she responded with all the enthusiasm of a new convert, eager to learn and progress. Every movement of his body into hers delivered a jolt of arousal beyond anything she had experienced. Her ability to reason was interrupted by the sheer intensity of excitement that began to grip her. The clench of her internal muscles meshed with growing heat and a powerful wave of renewed response engulfed her before she was flung breathless and gasping into a second climax that absolutely wiped her out.

'Was I a hero or a zero?' Enzo enquired with a flippancy that set her teeth on edge.

Skye sat up. 'I think you know.'

He grabbed her arm. 'Where are you going?'

'Back to my room. I'm sure your one-nighters,' she commented with a flippancy to match his own lack of tact, 'don't stay either—'

'The difference is that I *want* you to stay,' Enzo cut in, tugging her down to him again.

Disconcerted, Skye lay back down as he brought her close and wrapped both arms round her. In truth she was very tired. Her days were always long and started early, as was the norm with young children to care for. She was mentally listing all the reasons why she should return to her own bed when she fell asleep.

Enzo woke to find a two-year-old kneeling beside him.

'Dood morning,' Brodie said with a huge grin. 'You dot Skye wif you?'

Enzo laughed and nudged Skye awake because he couldn't get up naked. Of course, she was naked too, he realised, and he leant out of bed to reach for the PJs she had discarded the night before and shoved them in her general direction. Quicker than him, Skye made herself presentable, sliding out of bed to gather up Brodie, who was full of beans and chattering away as she took him out of the bedroom.

Enzo was downstairs, showered, shaved and fully clothed in one of his business suits in record time, only to discover his breakfast had been laid once again in the dining room. He suppressed a groan, feeling as though he had been sent into exile. Once more, Skye was imposing distance between them and he didn't like it. After all, they had had a great time together. Why would she now start treating him as though nothing had changed?

Skye bashed around the kitchen, working fast on the breakfast clean-up because she had signed Brodie up to a new, more convenient playgroup and she would drop him off and then go shopping with Shona.

'Zozo…' Shona framed brightly, pausing in her greeting crawl to the doorway where Enzo hovered.

Skye turned red as fire even before she turned around to face him as she had hoped to avoid doing. What was she playing at? She had had her first ever and probably *last* ever one-night stand. That wasn't her and would probably never be her but the benefit was, she told herself, that she was now free of the fears Ritchie had cursed her with. She had had a fabulous time with Enzo but in truth she was somewhat ashamed of having taken that freedom to share a bed with him. Her book of rules had no room for uncommitted sex and now she was free of her ex, she had no plans to change her value system.

'You're not speaking to me,' Enzo gathered as he bent down and swept up Shona, who was now clinging hopefully to his legs. 'But *you* are, aren't you? Even if I have to be called Zozo!' he teased, swinging her high up into the air so that the little girl laughed in delight.

'Of course, I'm speaking to you,' Skye responded in a rattled undertone. 'I hope I'm not that childish.'

'But you're avoiding me as if we did something shameful,' he pointed out.

Skye burned so hot she was surprised she didn't flame under her skin because that particular adjective made her think about some timeless dark space of the night when he had turned to her, or she had turned to him—she didn't honestly know which of them had been responsible—and once again they had made love with a passion that still mortified her. In fact, she hadn't been able to get enough of him and that awareness *did* make it a huge challenge to treat Enzo as an employer.

'I work for you,' she reminded him chokily.

'Don't hold *that* against me. Not much I can do about it,' he traded levelly. 'Keep it separate.'

'I *can't*,' Skye framed woodenly.

Lean, darkly handsome features taut, Enzo murmured, 'Are you still accompanying me to Glasgow?'

'I promised. Yes.'

Enzo nodded in silence and then laid Shona gently down on the floor again. She looked up at him with disappointed eyes. 'I'll see you later,' he told her.

Skye breathed in deep and slow as the front door slammed shut on Enzo's departure. She was doing the right thing…she was doing the right thing, she told herself urgently. Step away, pull back, don't bounce into another relationship straight after the hard lesson that had been Ritchie, especially when the very word 'relationship' might bring Enzo out in a cold sweat. But she should not even be thinking of him. She had to be stable and sensible for the children's sake and for the foreseeable future that meant no men.

CHAPTER SEVEN

A FEW DAYS LATER, Skye rested back in a reclining white leather seat of incredible opulence on Enzo's private jet.

For all the attention Enzo was paying her, though, she might as well not have been onboard. Attention had, nevertheless, been showered on Enzo by the glamorous blonde beauty acting as stewardess. In fact, so noticeable was the blonde's interest in her boss that Skye was embarrassed witnessing her sultry smiles and her habit of bending over to serve him with rather too many shirt buttons undone. To give him his due, however, Enzo had ignored the display and the underwritten invitation.

And why was she thinking about it anyway? Enzo had been working on his laptop throughout the journey, brief though the flight to Glasgow was to be. Skye had no grounds for complaint: nobody was more conscious of that fact. She had reminded him of the boundaries of their working relationship, and he had stuck scrupulously to those limits ever since. He had still, nonetheless, continued to play with the kids and acknowledge the dog.

Skye? Only Skye was now out in the cold. She got the occasional murmured thanks when she put a plate in front of him and absolutely no personal chat. Be careful what you wish for, she reflected ruefully, because you might just get it and discover that you didn't like it the smallest bit.

Alana had suggested that she was acting like an idiot. She had even hinted that she thought that Skye *could* be punishing Enzo for Ritchie's sins...*as if*! But then Lorenzo Durante had no bigger fan than her sister, who believed the sun rose and set on him because he had come to her family's rescue that night by the side of the road.

Alana had been very much looking forward to an evening with her little brother and sister in the comfort of the old house. In a sudden passion of regret and confusion over her troubled state of mind, Skye wished she were with her sister, but as soon as she glanced across the aisle at Enzo, she knew she was lying to herself to save face.

Enzo looked amazing in a dark pinstripe suit teamed with a fashionable royal-blue shirt and paler silk tie and it was a challenge for her to keep her eyes off him. What right had she to resent the stewardess trying to flirt with him? No right whatsoever, when she had directly warned him off. It was little wonder though that Enzo Durante had a reputation with women. He drew her sex like bees to a honeypot. With his height, athletic build and lean bronzed classic features, he was extravagantly good-looking. Even his voice, that husky purr he used in bed, had made her very toes curl! Wreathed in blushes and mortified heat at that last, far too intimate recollection, Skye lifted the magazine on her lap and attempted to read it.

Skye definitely didn't like the stewardess flirting with him, Enzo ruminated. Was that a dog-in-the-manger attitude? And why did he care anyway? For several years he had had the vague suspicion that *all* the women he met were totally interchangeable in looks, clothing and personality, but Skye stood out from the crowd for him and had from the outset, though he still had to work out why. It wasn't healthy to be brooding over one of the very few rejections he had ever received. It was done and dusted, *over*. As always, he remained free as a bird and that had always been his preference. So, what if it had been an incredible night? His preoccupation, his ongoing interest in her, was beginning to exasperate him.

They passed through the busy airport where Enzo attracted a good deal of fascinated feminine scrutiny. A luxurious limousine awaited them outside and Skye slid into it, feeling like a stranger in a foreign land and, much as she had felt on the luxury private jet, poorly dressed for such surroundings and out of place. The hotel, however, was even more intimidating from the moment they were greeted by name by their personal concierge in the echoing marble foyer, which contained various groups of clearly wealthy people, the women with perfect hair, clad in the subtle gleam of expensive jewellery and the latest fashions. Into the lift they went and then they were shown into a vast suite with sleek modern furniture and an elegant décor, other doors leading off to bedrooms.

While Skye was packing her small case, she had actually wondered if Enzo would somehow inveigle her into sharing a room with him, but evidently that was *not* a scenario she needed to worry about. It was impossible to explain why Enzo choosing to go to the opposite extreme and proving that he was honourable should make her feel slightly depressed. Her face flushed, she went into the room designated as hers by the concierge and began to unpack. Beyond the doorway she could hear Enzo talking on the phone in Italian, the lyrical rise and fall of his dark drawl, the syllables sliding softly against each other striking her as outrageously sensual. So, you still have a bad case of the hots for your employer, Skye conceded. Stop it, just *stop it*.

'I'm afraid there's been a change in our itinerary,' Enzo announced from the doorway. 'Robinson has asked me to view a company he's thinking of buying and, because it's close to his home, he has invited us to stay there and dine with them tonight instead. And I may have underestimated Robinson's lifestyle because, apparently, he lives in a *castle*.'

'Oh, my goodness.' Skye grimaced, thinking of the plain trousers and sweater she had decided would do for the non-fancy lunch date. 'My outfit won't pass muster at dinner in a castle!'

Enzo shrugged a broad shoulder. 'Relax. I'll get that sorted now.'

'How?' Skye immediately bristled, her small figure going rigid. 'I don't want you spending any more money on me, Enzo!'

Enzo raised a perfectly shaped ebony brow at her raised tone of voice. 'We're only talking about a few props to aid the fake-girlfriend charade,' he said very drily, as if she were making a fuss about nothing.

'It's not that simple,' Skye protested.

'It's exactly that simple but, by all means, give away anything I buy you to a charity shop afterwards, if it makes you feel better,' Enzo countered in the same flat, laconic tone. 'Is that it?'

In frustration, Skye whirled away from him and stationed herself beside the window. Her teeth were gritted. 'You don't understand.'

'Try me.' Enzo heaved a sigh, while striving not to notice how shapely her legs were below the skirt she had worn to travel in. A memory of sliding between those slender thighs did not help and he frowned, the throb at his groin offending him. Where was his self-discipline? He was furious with himself, furious with her for making what he deemed to be a fuss about inconsequential stuff. What the hell did what she wore and who paid for it have to do with anything? How could that be important?

'You buying me clothes, it makes me uncomfortable because Ritchie controlled what I wore while I was with him,' she explained reluctantly. 'It made me feel like he owned me.'

'I'm not your ex. I know I don't own you. I have no influence over what you do or where you go and you know it. We're in companion territory, *not* relationship territory,' he reminded her with strong emphasis. 'Even so, if you want to wear your own clothes and risk feeling underdressed this evening, that is your choice to make.'

Inwardly, Skye cringed at the prospect of being underdressed at a *castle*. 'Possibly I was a bit hasty in my objections,' she muttered grudgingly.

'I thought you would see it that way,' Enzo parried smoothly, relieved that common sense was once again in control of her. 'Now let's get this show on the road.'

Suitable outfits, she learned, would be brought to the hotel suite for her viewing while she could use the hotel beauty spa for any grooming requirements she felt necessary. And with that casual conclusion, Enzo apologised for the change of plan that their host's new itinerary had forced on them and departed with his luggage. She would not see him again until she arrived at the castle and she didn't much fancy arriving at a castle alone without Enzo to hide behind.

Enzo left the hotel feeling thoroughly dissatisfied and not quite sure why that should be the case. He was being sensible, he assured himself fiercely. He had got badly hurt in his one and only relationship and he refused to do anything like that to Skye. The more distance there was between them, the safer she would be.

The stylist and her assistant with a rail of glamorous clothes and bags of accessories arrived with Skye within the hour. She supposed that someone like Enzo always got top service of that nature and he took it for granted in a way she never would because he had, it seemed, grown up accustomed to such advantages.

Having picked a dress, she noted that nothing had a price tag attached and, wondering if that omission was at Enzo's instigation, she also selected shoes with a heel because she had only brought flats. That achieved, she booked a late afternoon appointment for her hair at the hotel spa and was wondering what to do next when Paola arrived to inform her that she and a car were at her disposal.

'I'm starting to feel like an overnight princess,' she joked with the older woman.

'Nothing wrong with that,' Paola told her with a smile. 'Have you any idea what you would like to do with the rest of the day?'

And Skye had a very good idea. She had watched a

programme on television about the famous stately home, Dumfries House, saved for the public by the King's intervention before his ascension to the throne. True, it was a winter day, but it was sunny and dry, and she knew that she would still enjoy the house and gardens.

As the estate was only forty miles from Glasgow, she and Paola decided to enjoy lunch there at the Coach House Café. They were just walking out of the house with its fabulous Chippendale collection of furniture into the gardens when she rang Alana to ask if she was comfortable staying at the house with the children.

Alana sighed. 'Yes, but I've been too angry after Ritchie's visit to relax.'

Skye froze in dismay. 'Ritchie came to the *house*?'

'This morning Yes, I should think your application for that non-molestation order will be easily granted now. I'm surprised Paola didn't tell you about it,' her sister rattled on. 'She was marvellous and called the police and he was arrested. Apparently, he'd been suspended and he was trying to blame you for it. He's also very worked up about you living in Enzo's home. I was grateful you weren't here. He's put you through enough.'

When Skye came off her phone, Paola gave her a rueful smile of understanding. 'The boss asked me not to tell you. He didn't want you to be upset.'

Skye nodded acceptance of the older woman's loyalty to her employer and resolved to tackle Enzo on her own. Of course, there was nothing she could have done to protect her sister from that visit and clearly Alana had been safe with Paola present. 'So, you only flew up to Scotland this morning?' she said to the other woman.

'Yes.'

'I was incredibly lucky to meet Enzo that night on the road.' Perhaps that was a rather belated appreciation, Skye reflected guiltily. Enzo had gone above and beyond to protect her and the children from Ritchie's confrontations. And in her ignorance, she had rather taken it all for granted, not even considering the costs or inconveniences caused by that level of protection.

'Keeping security on the house and me while Enzo was at work must have left you short-staffed,' Skye surmised lightly.

'The boss brought in more guards from home.'

Determined not to betray how much that information embarrassed her, Skye asked, 'Where in Italy is home?'

'The boss's grandparents live in Tuscany but he's mainly based at an apartment in Rome, although he owns other properties round the world,' Paola told her. 'He inherited some of them from his father.'

'How long have you worked for Enzo?'

'I left the police, trained as a paramedic and became a bodyguard when he was a little boy and I worked for his grandfather. I'm older than I look.' Paola chuckled as Skye glanced at her in surprise.

They passed a very pleasant afternoon wandering round the beautiful gardens before returning to the hotel where Skye went to the spa and then returned to the suite to dress.

Garbed in a dark purple sheath dress worn with toning heels, Skye climbed into the waiting car and found a package on the seat beside her with her name on it. She opened it up and tugged out a jewel case in some dismay to reveal a delicate gold necklace with a glittering diamond-studded star pendant. It was gorgeous. She was supposed to be Enzo's girlfriend. The necklace was only a prop and not something she would be keeping, she told herself as she attached it to her throat.

When the car drove down a long, wooded driveway an hour later and the massive castle with its twin circular towers was revealed, Skye was enormously relieved to see Enzo standing outside the front door with an older man, obviously waiting there in readiness to greet her. Her nerves evaporated and she fairly surged out of the car as he strode across the gravel towards her.

The slender beauty of her in the plain but elegant dress made Enzo smile, particularly when he saw the diamond star twinkling in the lights. He had hoped she would wear it because she ought to have more pretty things, he reasoned absently. From what he had witnessed, he reckoned the little ones got first bite of every financial apple and that she rarely spent on herself. He had not seen her wear a single new item since they had met and, being highly observant, Enzo noticed the fact.

'My word…the castle is huge,' she whispered.

'Sì…talk about an underestimation,' Enzo conceded with the slanting easy grin that illuminated his lean, darkly handsome face and her heart jumped inside her, refusing to settle except to a fast pitter-patter as he dropped an arm round her to guide her back towards their host.

Skye discovered that she wanted to nestle into that sheltering arm and it unnerved her. The scent of the cologne he used flared her nostrils, intimate memories tugging at her composure as she was introduced to Robinson

Davies, slightly stooped with age but still a hearty man with grey hair and twinkling blue eyes. A step indoors, she met his wife, Alyson, who took over to show Skye to her room.

'You could have brought the children with you,' the tall dark-haired woman told her. 'We had no idea you had a family until Enzo told us. I love children. My grand-children are teenagers now and it's difficult to organise visits when they're studying at school.'

'Perhaps if we visit again, we'll bring the children.' Skye smiled as warmly as she could, wanting to respond to that friendly hospitality while knowing that she was extremely unlikely ever to meet the woman a second time because, after all, for all her impressive props, she remained only a fake, not a genuine girlfriend.

She was shown into a gorgeous circular bedroom in one of the towers where a fire already burned in the im-posing stone fireplace. She adored it and asked all sorts of questions about the history of the building.

'Sadly, it's getting too big for us now and we're think-ing of looking for a more manageable retirement home. It was different when we had four children running round the place.'

'Times change,' Skye acknowledged as Alyson de-parted again.

It was only then that she noticed that Enzo's luggage was in the room as well and she frowned. She was will-ing to bet that Enzo had not foreseen that development.

Twenty minutes later, he joined her. '*Sì*, we're shar-ing,' he conceded wryly. 'That surprised me. They're very close with my grandparents and my grandparents would never put an unmarried couple in the same room.'

'I think that could be seen as quite old-fashioned these days…but I'm not criticising your family. Their home, their rules,' Skye hastened to assure him. 'I'm sure we can manage for one night.'

'I'll use the sofa.'

Skye glanced at the majestic wood-framed antique by the wall and laughed in disagreement because, while an impressive piece, it looked as though it would offer all the comfort of a bed of nails. 'No need for such dramatic gestures, Enzo. It's a huge bed. We can share it.'

Some of the tension left Enzo's taut features at her relaxed acceptance. He yanked up a case and opened it to extract a suit bag. 'Do you mind if I use the bathroom first?'

'No. I'm already dressed for the evening.'

He took his change of clothing into the bathroom but before doing so, he made a rather endearing effort to tidy up the tumbled case. 'I'll fix it,' she told him with amusement.

Pre-dinner drinks were served in a comfortable sitting room. Skye settled down with Alyson Davies and the two women discussed her visit to Dumfries House and the gardens there.

'Do you have a garden of your own?'

'No. I've never had a garden.'

'Never?' Enzo broke into their dialogue to query. 'How did you get interested in the great outdoors, then?'

'We always lived in an apartment, but my stepfather had an allotment where he grew all our vegetables,' Skye told them with a smile. 'He allowed me to have a little patch to grow annual flowers every summer.'

'If you don't mind me asking,' Alyson murmured, 'what happened to your real father?'

'Oh, that's a very long story,' Skye declared lightly. 'And not one I'm comfortable sharing outside the family.'

A potentially awkward moment was smoothed over by Skye's warm and ready smile. She was good with people, Enzo acknowledged, would be an asset at business socialising because she didn't have a rude, unkind or pretentious bone in her body. He was starting to see why Skye had more effect on him than other women had. She truly *was* different. And he watched her, even while he talked to his host, noting the pink plumpness of her lower lip, the light glow of her beautiful eyes, the slender shapely legs crossing, one dainty ankle dangling, and his hunger for her mounted, making him tense.

Having promised to allow Alyson and Robinson the chance to give her a grand tour of their walled garden after breakfast the next day, Skye and Enzo headed upstairs to bed.

'Am I allowed to ask about your birth father?' he enquired. 'Feel free to tell me to mind my own business if it's painful.'

'No, it's not painful, just a little too personal to unpack in company. Mum got pregnant with me when she was at school. My father and her were sixteen and some people tend to be judgemental about that,' she explained with a grimace. 'Her parents threw her out and *his* parents took her in. That lasted for about two years, long enough for

Mum to conceive Alana, and then my father took off for a job on the oil rigs and never came back.'

'Never?'

'No, never. He didn't stay in touch either. Once or twice, he sent money to help Mum out but nothing regular and by the time I was four, it stopped altogether. Mum had a rough time raising us.' Skye sat down on the hard sofa by the wall while Enzo crouched down by the fire and fed it more fuel.

'So, what did your mother do?'

'She worked two jobs to get us out of his parents' house because she didn't feel she should be staying there, not when my father was sending photos of his new girlfriend and talking about making a visit.'

'*Dio mio*…where did he think your mother and his children were going to go?'

'As my grandparents then actually pointed out, their son wasn't married to Mum and they had both been kids when they brought me and Alana into the world. I can see their point too and he was the son that they loved,' Skye admitted, wanting to be fair to all parties involved at the time. 'But it was very hard on Mum because she had no other family to fall back on.'

'Certainly that must've been a challenge.' Enzo suppressed his outrage on her behalf, recognising that when Skye didn't make a drama out of her difficult childhood, he had even less right. Even so, it went against the grain when he looked back at his own idyllic years of development, cocooned in love and security and appreciation, even his awful little pictures put on display as though they were works of art when he had never had even the smallest ounce of talent in that department. It had never before occurred to Enzo to think of how lucky he had been to have such grandparents, who had given him a decent, loving home.

'Mum got us into an apartment and kept on working and Steve, my stepfather, came along when I was about eight. It took him six years to persuade her to marry him because she didn't trust men, but he was the best thing that ever happened for all of us. He adopted Alana and me and gave us his name. He was the best dad imaginable,' she said sadly, her eyes misting over. 'He was just an ordinary man, a taxi driver, but he was a lovely person.'

'Rather like you…' Enzo reached down to close her tiny hands into his and raised her, wiping the dampness from her cheeks with his thumb. 'I can understand now why your mother started a second family.'

'Brodie and Shona were their world…and they were *so* happy together,' she said chokily.

'I haven't even got that consolation. My parents' marriage was a disaster. My grandparents were frank with me. My father was continually unfaithful, the sort of person who made promises and kept on breaking them. There were several separations and reconciliations. I was conceived during the last of those. I doubt their marriage would have lasted even had they lived,' Enzo stated wryly. 'Did you ever meet your father?'

'No, and it doesn't bother Alana and me,' Skye confessed very quietly. 'Actions speak louder than words and we knew how he treated Mum. Her life would have been so much easier if he had paid support for us but, even though we know that he was earning very well, he never

once spared a thought for us and he didn't treat his own
parents any better. When they fell ill, it was my mum
who helped them out. He was a deadbeat dad, a heart-
less son and no loss.'

'Sometimes, you're much tougher and less sentimental than I expect.'

'Down to earth,' she corrected with a rueful smile,
lilac eyes soft and still a little misty from the tears that
had overcome her when she had talked about her stepfather. 'I learned to be, growing up.'

And it made him respect her, Enzo registered in surprise, suddenly aware that he had never respected a
woman that way, at least not since his university days
when he had learned that he had awarded his love and respect to the wrong woman. Her lies, the calculated treach-
ery enacted by her and his best friend, had wrecked his
faith in his fellow humans and he had shut down hard
on his emotions, determined never to leave himself that
vulnerable ever again.

Skye gazed up, her head tilted back, into Enzo's glittering dark eyes, semi-shielded by his glorious lush black
lashes, and her heart was racing and her breath was trip-
ping in her throat. She knew in that moment just how
much she had kidded herself when she had believed that
she could step back, turn away, *forget* about him. Hardly
a realistic possibility of that when she was obsessed with
him, when she barely stopped thinking about him even
when he was away from her, when in bed at night he was
all she could think about. And here he was, already so
much more interested in her than Ritchie had ever been,
already so much more caring.

As he began to step back from her, an almost imperceptible flush accentuating his spectacular cheekbones, she shifted closer. 'Just kiss me,' she urged.

Enzo studied her as if she were insane. 'I can't...you said—'

'What I said a few days ago doesn't matter any more,' she muttered in a rush. 'It doesn't matter that this is only a stupid rebound fling, it's only what we feel that should count.'

'When I tried to tell you that, you wouldn't listen.'

'I'm stubborn and I thought I was doing what I *should* do. Now I know that's not important compared to what I feel,' she told him almost frantically. 'I just want you—'

'And you already know how much I want you, *piccolo mio*,' Enzo groaned, leaning down to her, claiming her parted lips in a passionate assault that sent the very blood rushing through her veins in ecstasy.

He lifted her up against him with gentle hands and her body turned fluid with longing as though he had pressed a button that only he knew how to access. Long fingers trailed up her thigh beneath the skirt of her dress and the ache at the heart of her felt like spontaneous combustion, burning her up from the inside out. Never in her life had she imagined that a man could make her feel like that, but Enzo was teaching her new lessons. Unzipped, her dress fell round her shoulders and he settled her on the side of the bed while he took it off, lifting her up at one point, and every action was so smooth it made her laugh.

'You really are such a womaniser, Enzo.'

'That's not what I want to hear from you.'

'Sorry, I—'

'No, what you think of me isn't crucial, but while I don't deny that there have been a lot of women, I never lied to any of them or cheated on them. I do have standards,' he proclaimed somewhat defensively.

Meeting those unguarded dark eyes of his, Skye registered in shock that she had hurt him and she paled, shaken that she could have been so tactless, so certain he would be more flattered than offended to be labelled as the paparazzi had categorised him. 'I know you have,' she said softly, hoping to redeem herself.

'Particularly where you're concerned, because if you're about to wake up tomorrow morning and tell me to go cold turkey again, I don't want to do this,' he told her bluntly.

'I promise you I won't do that,' Skye declared unevenly, shaken by that challenge, which she had not been prepared to meet. Yet there was some justification on his part for that cold-turkey comment. She had encouraged him, wanted him, become intimate with him and then slammed the door on their relationship. Of course, Enzo didn't want a relationship, did he? Earlier that day he had reminded her that they were in companion territory, as he had called it then, only that was about to change *again*. Maybe right now his head was spinning a little, as hers was.

'Stop overthinking this, stop worrying,' Enzo urged, crouching down at her feet to flip off her shoes and then the stay-up lace-edged dark stockings that he lingered over with unhidden male appreciation. 'You are such a worrier.'

'How do you know that about me?'

'By watching you. Brodie goes out on his trike round the garden and you hover by the back door like a mother hen even though there's nothing out there that could hurt him. Shona crawls into the hall and you follow her.'

'Possibly I worry too much about keeping them safe.'

'You had good cause but I will not harm you...*ever*,' Enzo swore, ripping off his jacket and embarking on his shirt.

Skye slid off the bed in her lingerie and covered his impatient hands with her own to take over the buttons with a confidence she had never felt in male company before. 'I know that,' she said truthfully, parting the edges of his shirt to splay her fingers across his warm, hard pectoral muscles, heat spearing up inside her, magnifying every sensation. 'I want you so much.'

Oh, no, I didn't say that out loud, she assured herself, but the sudden brilliance of Enzo's dark golden scrutiny warned her that she *had*.

'Feels like months since we were together.'

'It's only been days.' She sighed. 'You're all drama, Enzo.'

'And you're *not*? Banging about the kitchen just because you want me? Treating me like the invisible man?'

Skye reddened at that telling comeback as he tipped her back on the bed, spreading her slender limbs out, narrowed dark eyes glittering with a predator's hunger while he took in her petite curves, cupped in plain white deeply unsexy cotton. 'I love your body,' he confided in a roughened undertone as he removed the rest of his clothing, flung an intimidating handful of condoms on the bedside cabinet and got on the bed to join her.

'Us…we don't make sense.'

'We don't need to make sense,' Enzo told her robustly, strong jawline hard with resolve. 'And I am *not* a rebound fling, stupid or otherwise. I refuse to be a rebound following such a drastic embarrassment as Ritchie the stalker.'

Unexpectedly, Skye found herself grinning, lifting wondering fingers to trace the full line of his soft full lower lip, the pads on her fingers softly tracing through the black shadow of stubble surrounding his sculpted mouth. 'Is that so?'

'I have much more experience than you. You were too naïve to make a major choice like moving in with your first lover.'

'Agreed. Happy now?' Skye asked.

'Won't be happy until I wake up tomorrow and you're still in my arms.'

He detached the light bra, let his lips tease a pink nipple while his fingers moulded her straining flesh and her whole body went haywire with instant response, the tug of his mouth awakening a tightening sensation in her pelvis. Her hips squirmed as his hands ran over her, smoothing, awakening, sending taut little trickles of arousal travelling along her sensitised skin. Fingers sinking into his tousled black hair, she tugged him up to kiss her. And excitement thrummed through her like bolts of white lightning and made her sizzle from head to toe.

'Slow down,' Enzo urged.

'No,' she exclaimed, wrenching at the zip in his trousers, fingers splaying across the hot, hard thrust of him beneath the fine material, her impatience, her need at a level of hunger she had not known she could feel.

'I don't want to hurt you.'

'You're not going to hurt me.'

As long fingers established the slick welcome at the heart of her, Enzo groaned and freed himself in frantic haste from the rest of his clothing. He tipped her back and rose over her with an urgency that finally reflected her own and plunged into her. Sensual shock rippled through her lower body, her inner walls stretching and contracting on his wonderfully effective invasion while little tremors of pleasure gathered and intensified.

'At last,' Enzo framed hoarsely, shifting lithely over her, lean hips circling to settle into a steady rhythm that sent every nerve ending flying and speeded up her heart rate.

Pleasure laced with feverish excitement engulfed her. She moved with him, far more a participant than she had been their first time together, but then she wasn't, she recognised dimly, the same woman she had been even a few weeks earlier. With Enzo, she felt free, equal, safe. As the throbbing beat of desire and need in her pelvis increased, she clung to him, her fingers digging into his shoulders, head thrown back, lips parted and then her climax hit her like a battering ram, throwing her up and tossing her down again with such strength that she cried out and then gasped as the convulsions of delight and satiation followed.

Enzo pulled free of her and flopped back on the bed next to her. *'Dio,'* he husked, out of breath. 'I needed that…and in a few minutes I'm going to need it again.'

Skye laughed, wishing she didn't want him to come back to her and hold her close.

Enzo widened his rich dark golden gaze and looked back at her. *'What?'*

'You're so full of yourself. I bet you were like that in the cradle.' And she stared back at him, heart lurching at the image of a little Enzo throwing his rattle away, expecting it to magically come back and very possibly receiving that amount of attention from a grandmother who, she suspected, from his occasional references, adored him. And why wouldn't she? Enzo had likely exuded that same charisma from a very young age.

He reclined on the bed, naked and unashamed, every inch of his beautiful bronzed body on display. Men weren't supposed to be beautiful, but Lorenzo Durante was lean, muscular and magnificent, a glorious arrangement of bone and flesh that she found impossible to resist. When had that happened? she wondered. When had her last defences gone down and left her so vulnerable? When she'd tried to walk away in spirit if not in body? It hadn't worked, none of her failsafe plans to protect herself had worked. Enzo had also contrived to draw her in without promises. Nothing she had with him was stable or offered her a future and that terrified her because she already knew that she was falling in love with him and falling deeper and harder than she had ever dreamt possible…and in only a few more weeks, he would probably be returning to Italy.

'What's wrong?'

Skye veiled her eyes, wondering just how Enzo had become so attuned to her every change of mood. 'There's nothing wrong.'

'There had better not be, *piccolo mio*.' Enzo tugged

her across the mattress and clamped an arm to her hip. 'We're together now.'

Skye wondered what that meant. How together? As a couple in a relationship? Or as lovers enjoying a brief fling? She reckoned, however, that, bearing in mind Enzo's sensitivities, it was far too soon to be asking for any clarification on that score.

The next morning, Enzo was in a terrific mood and it showed. Although he had as much interest in trees and plants as Skye had in big business, he accompanied Skye and their hosts on the tour of their wintry garden. Throughout that chilly expedition, he kept a hand or an arm anchored to some part of Skye and his attentive display surprised her because she had assumed that in front of his grandparents' friends, he would treat her more casually.

From the castle they travelled straight to the airport and boarded the jet. Skye's mind was untethered, still wandering dizzily through the passionate night they had shared, marvelling at her lack of control and the sheer joy of letting go of her inner critic. Yes, it would hurt when Enzo moved on, as he surely would, but she was strong, she told herself sternly, and she would move on as well when the time came. After all, hadn't she already moved on and past Ritchie?

'Why didn't you tell me about Ritchie turning up at the house yesterday?' she asked Enzo abruptly, marvelling that she had actually forgotten that fact in the excitement of the night that had passed.

He sprang upright, leaning down over her to snap loose

her belt, and without the smallest warning he scooped her up out of her seat into his arms.

'*Enzo!*' she shrieked as he sank down with her still anchored in his arms on the other side of the aisle.

'You were too far away,' he pointed out just as the stewardess appeared, clearly having heard Skye cry out, and her eyes widened at the sight of them together.

Enzo angled his head to smoothly dismiss her again.

Her face hot, her bare feet draped on the arm rest, a muffled giggle escaped Skye as she finally recognised that his shameless spontaneity was one of the things she liked most about him. 'You still haven't answered my question.'

'But you already know the answer.'

Her lilac eyes widened and softened as she looked up at his lean, strong face. He bent his dark head and circled her parted lips with his. Her heart pounded as an electrifying wave of sexual awareness claimed her and she tipped back her head, licking experimentally into his mouth. He responded, sucking her tongue, sending a ripple of sensation through her tautening length. Inner muscles flexed and tightened. She fought to stay in control, embarrassed by the ease with which he overwhelmed her. He ran a long, soothing finger gently down over her cheek.

'You didn't want to bother me,' she said for him.

'You deserved a break from all that. I didn't want you worrying and feeling guilty. Alana was angrier about his visit than she was upset and you must stop blaming yourself for *his* behaviour.'

He claimed her soft, swollen mouth with urgent hunger and she trembled, hopelessly sensitised by the night she had spent in his arms and insanely aware of how much she still wanted him. Slowly he rose and settled her down in the seat opposite him. 'Later,' he murmured with anticipation glittering in his dark golden gaze as the jet powered into landing.

A couple of hours after that, engulfed in the noisy welcome of the children at the house, Skye gathered Shona up and straightened to approach her sister. 'No problems...apart from Ritchie?' she queried.

'I almost forgot. Miss Tomkins, the social worker, called by in the afternoon to check on the kids,' Alana imparted. 'She said she would call in again soon.'

'I wonder how she knew to come here.'

'Apparently, Ritchie gave her the address.'

Skye lost colour, stressed by that information as she wondered what her ex-boyfriend would have said in such circumstances. About her, about the children, about her current living situation. It was an unnerving thought.

CHAPTER EIGHT

'WHY WOULD A social worker be calling on you?' Enzo enquired with a frown.

'I foster Brodie and Shona in a kinship agreement because we're related by blood. Obviously, there's occasional checks to ensure I'm taking proper care of them,' Skye pointed out absently as she helped her sister gather up her coat and bag and saw her to the front door.

When Skye emerged from her sister's hug and closed the front door again, Enzo was still frowning at her. 'I thought you had adopted them?'

'That's the ultimate goal, and I've applied to adopt them, but currently I'm fostering my little brother and sister under the supervision of the social services,' Skye explained ruefully. 'Worst-case scenario, if the authorities are not satisfied by how I'm caring for them, I could lose them.'

'*Lose* them?' Enzo repeated in evident disbelief.

'Yes, my siblings could be taken from me and placed elsewhere with strangers, even put up for adoption.' Pale and taut at even voicing that frightening possibility, Skye swallowed the sudden thickness in her throat and found her voice again. 'So, naturally I'm worried when I find out that Ritchie directed the social worker here because what else may he have said or insinuated? And I'm already in the wrong for not having immediately contacted the authorities to inform them of our change of address. I intended to but I hung back because I didn't know what best to say about us living here.'

Enzo paced the hall floor, swinging back to shoot her a troubled glance. 'I didn't fully understand your situation. You should have filled me in on these facts sooner.'

'And what difference would that have made? I'll have to admit what happened with Ritchie.' Skye sighed with compressed lips. 'Honesty is always the best policy.'

Skye went through to the kitchen and began to empty the dishwasher. The table and the counters and even the sink were full of dirty dishes. Alana was great with their siblings but not so keen on cleaning up. Skye smiled. She cut her sister a lot of slack on that score because she was aware that Alana dealt daily with some rich, horrendously entitled and arrogant guests in her job at the hotel and was often treated badly in her role.

Enzo retreated to his office to work, flipping open his laptop. His quick and clever brain was already assessing the likely official response to Ritchie's violence and Skye's current plight. Here she was in temporary employment, intimately involved with her employer and protected everywhere she went by Enzo's security staff because of her unhinged ex-boyfriend. He gritted his teeth and suppressed a groan. None of those facts would look good for her on paper. He knew much more about such official decisions than most people in his age group. A couple of years earlier he had studied his own custody case papers, keen to understand the legal hoops and obstacles his grandparents had traversed to adopt him. When he found it impossible to suppress his concern on the children's behalf and still work effectively, he surrendered and pondered the problem some more before deciding to consult his British lawyer.

Regrettably, that long and frustrating phone conversation told Enzo nothing he wanted to hear. His belief that he could magically sort out Skye's situation died an immediate death when he was very politely informed that his reputation as a notorious playboy would only exacerbate her problems.

'You could only help her by marrying her!' His lawyer chuckled, clearly considering that possibility so farfetched as to be hilarious. 'Officials involved in care and custody cases look for stable relationships and financial security as a baseline.'

'I'm not thinking of marriage,' Enzo asserted immediately, while his agile intellect pounced on the concept and played with it, turning it round until he could come up with a more acceptable solution. The advantages of such a move piled up even quicker in his brain.

Brodie was in the bath and Skye was towelling dry Shona's hair when Enzo strolled into the bathroom. He had already changed out of his suit into faded jeans and a dark shirt. He rolled up his sleeves, already experienced enough in the bed-and-bath routine to know that Brodie would get him wet.

'I thought you were working. Were we making too much noise?'

'It only gets noisy when I'm here,' Enzo reminded her without embarrassment.

'Enzo,' Brodie proclaimed with a beaming smile and an attitude of deep satisfaction.

'No splashing Enzo,' Skye warned her little brother without much hope because Enzo was as much a fan of splashing games as the toddler.

'No splash,' Brodie promised obediently.

'We'll take them to the zoo on Saturday,' Enzo told her cheerfully.

'It's a very long drive.'

'We'll go by helicopter then.'

Skye heaved a sigh at that careless suggestion but said nothing, striving not to criticise or seem ungrateful for the lifestyle that Enzo enjoyed. For now, they were together, she reasoned, and the children were young enough that they would not remember much about him in a few months' time. She wondered ruefully if she would be able to say the same thing on her own behalf and prayed for a short memory. Right at that moment though, even glancing at Enzo's bronzed profile as he grinned wickedly and capsized one of Brodie's plastic boats, she felt as though she were riding hell for leather for a terribly steep fall. Enzo lit her up like a firework just by being in the same room.

Once the children were fed and in bed, Skye set up the dining room for dinner. She had prepared a casserole for their evening meal, striving to behave as though nothing had changed between her and Enzo when, in truth, everything had changed and she was trying to make little adjustments and avoid making a fuss. A *fuss*? Like asking him where they were going as a couple when obviously they weren't going anywhere, and Enzo's fast-approaching departure would conclude whatever they did have. In short, she was trying to be sensible, not being the woman who hoped against hope for some fairy-tale ending to suddenly pop up in front of her.

'I've had an idea,' Enzo announced over the meal.

Skye pushed her plate away and endeavoured to smother the yawn creeping up on her. Sometimes Enzo's boundless energy was a challenge for her. He strode full tilt into every new day and attacked it like an obstacle course. He didn't slow down as the day progressed. He didn't seem to suffer from her insecurities and if he had worries, he either rose above them or solved them. And even more to the point, the previous night spent in his arms had exhausted her right down to the marrow of her bones.

'You look tired,' Enzo remarked, ebony brows pleating as he scanned the faint purple shadows below her beautiful eyes and the downward curve of her lips.

'I was thinking of an early night…without the usual connotations,' she added in haste as Enzo's dark glittering gaze literally smouldered.

Enzo laughed with considerable amusement. 'As long as you're in my bed.'

'Actually, I was thinking—'

'*My* bed,' Enzo incised without hesitation. 'We don't sleep apart. When I'm back at work I won't see much of you otherwise and we need to make the most of the time we have.'

Disconcerted by that speech and the assurance with which he spoke, Skye felt her cheeks burn even while her heart turned over at the news that he wanted to spend more time with her. 'You said that you'd had an idea?'

'I'm not sure you're ready to hear it yet. When you explained that you were under supervision with the social services, I realised that I had put you in a rather dodgy position. If you were simply working for me, it might be all right, but we're having an affair and some people would view that as a matter of concern, particularly when I'm said to have a…questionable reputation with women,' he framed between compressed lips.

At last he had put a label on what they shared. An affair? It sounded rather racier than Skye felt herself to be, but she couldn't think of any other word to cover their new togetherness. Colour fluctuating, she went off to fetch the coffee. He had seen the same writing on the wall that she had foreseen. Her standing in his life was far from ideal. She was no longer merely a live-in housekeeper, not since they had become much more personally involved. She would look like a foolish, undisciplined woman who had tumbled carelessly out of one disastrous relationship with a man into another that could prove almost as damaging from her siblings' point of view.

Enzo accepted his coffee. 'No comment?'

Skye compressed her lips. 'What you said was true and the children are already attached to you, which is not a good idea when you're leaving.'

'I have a solution to all of it and I would be happy to make the sacrifice.'

'Sacrifice?' Skye interrupted in dismay. 'What on earth are you talking about?'

'You're so good at being a fake girlfriend I think you would be a blast as a fake wife.'

Lilac eyes as wide as they would open stared back at him in disbelief. 'Enzo…are you crazy?'

'I want you to consider the idea. I've become fond of the children and I would pretty much do anything to ensure that you get to keep them with you,' Enzo admitted. 'I consulted my British lawyer for advice—'

'I bet he didn't tell you to marry your penniless housekeeper to help her!' Skye exclaimed, wreathed in mortification as she understood the meaning of that word 'sacrifice' as pertaining to her and the children.

'I'm completely free to marry anyone I want and if I can put you in a better position to adopt your siblings, I'm willing to do it.'

'Well, thank you very much but I'm not willing to accept you as a *sacrifice*!' Skye shot back at him with burning cheeks, thrusting back the dining chair to stand up.

'We have to talk about this.'

'No, we *don't*! We definitely don't!'

'Skye?' Enzo swore under his breath as he watched her pile up dishes to clear the table. 'Sit down and have your coffee.'

She raised a brow. 'Is that an order, sir?'

Enzo dealt her a quelling appraisal. 'It is. But let's take the coffee across the hall and be a little more relaxed.'

'I can't be relaxed when you're talking about marrying me purely to do the kids and me a favour,' she argued.

Ignoring that statement, Enzo swept up the coffee and strode across the hall into the sitting room where she had already lit the corner lamps. He proceeded to seek the controls that would ignite the gas fire because the room was chilly and, while he was still searching, Skye nudged him gently out of the way and took care of it.

'I was planning to start putting up the Christmas decorations tomorrow. Is that all right with you?' she asked brightly, faking it as best she could, keen to change the subject when what he had suggested was sheer insanity.

'You'll have to buy it all new for this place.' Enzo pulled out a credit card and extended it to her as she sank down on the edge of a plush sectional unit. She grasped it with reluctant fingers. 'And stop trying to change the subject.'

'But what you said…about marriage…was ridiculous,' Skye told him tautly. 'You can't say stuff like that.'

'Why not?' Enzo sent her a questioning look, refusing to be either uncomfortable or knocked off topic. 'I'm prepared to deliver on my suggestion. Right now, you need me.'

Skye flipped upright again in frustration and embarrassment. 'I *don't* need you!'

'No?' Enzo stalked closer, dark eyes as hot and golden as the heart of a fire. 'You need me. Without realising what I was doing, I placed you in a difficult position here and then I exacerbated the situation by having sex with you. I wasn't aware that you were in a situation with the children that entailed official scrutiny but I am conscious that my reputation won't do you any favours. Why shouldn't I choose the one option that could sort this mess out?'

'Well, for a start, I can sort out my own problems. You talking nonsense about us getting married is sheer folly!'

Black-lashed eyes of gold shimmered. 'I'm a very good

catch,' Enzo quipped with an infuriating grin, lean dark features illuminated by his unholy amusement. 'Well worth the investment of time required and a lot of women would be willing to take the risk on me. I like kids and animals but, most of all, I appreciate very small, slightly built women with curly hair.'

'Enzo…' Skye groaned, her face heating as she recognised herself in that description. 'Stop it.'

'We would only have to stay married until the children are safely and legally yours by adoption. Then we would both take our freedom back and I would ensure that when we separated you, at least, had a decent home for you and your siblings. Once I was gone, you would be able to make a completely fresh start,' Enzo pointed out convincingly.

Once I was gone…

That single phrase reverberated inside Skye like a death knell and ran chills down her spine, making her skin break out in goosebumps. 'It's a very generous offer—' Only not quite the offer that could have thrilled rather than chilled, she recognised guiltily. He meant fake, indeed could only have faced the idea of a marriage that would be a fake. It wouldn't be real, but she would know that from the start. She would also know that it would hurt like hell when she was no longer flavour of the month and he walked away. Her heart sank.

'It's the practical solution to all your worries and it allows us to continue our current arrangement for as long as we choose.'

Skye emitted a second groan. 'Enzo, you wouldn't even be with me if you were living your normal playboy life,' she protested. 'You're only with me now because there isn't much choice in this locality and I'm convenient.'

Enzo reached down to grasp her hand and tugged her upright. '*Madre di Dio*, what did that cowardly little rat do to your self-esteem?' he demanded fiercely. 'Do you truly believe that I suffer from a lack of choice with women? Or that I would simply settle for *convenient*?'

'No, I was trying to explain—'

'I could have called any number of women that I know and invited them to keep me company here. But I met you... I wanted *you...you* in particular, *you especially*,' he emphasised in lethal continuance. 'Absolutely no other woman would have done or could have taken your place.'

His stunning eyes were smouldering gold, luxuriant black lashes low over his intense gaze, his conviction undeniable. Her tummy flipped, her breath catching in her throat, every inch of her pulled taut with tension. 'I shouldn't have said that,' she mumbled, embarrassed now.

'Particularly when it wasn't the truth,' Enzo cut in, one lean hand travelling from her taut shoulder, through the soft, silky fluff of her curls and down to the taut line of her spine. 'You and I are together.'

'In a *relationship*?' she stressed in astonishment.

'We've always been in a relationship,' Enzo countered with unblemished cool, convinced that it was safe to use that word when he was not emotionally invested in it. 'It was never a question of just one night. The moment I had you, I wanted you again and it's still that way.'

'Does that bother you?' she whispered, more seriously this time.

'If you wanted your own bed, it would,' he confided huskily.

As he eased her slight body up against his and he shifted lithely against her, she felt the hard, unashamed promise of his arousal and she trembled, filled to over-flowing with sensual awareness. 'So, you're prepared to ask me to marry you on the basis of sex.'

'It's not that basic. Do we really need to go into detail about this attraction?'

Skye stared up at him in silence because that same at-traction, that crazy explosive chemical reaction, was tear-ing her in two. He was talking about marriage and she wasn't stupid, she was intelligent enough to appreciate that a wealthy husband would be an advantage in official terms while a legendary playboy would be a dangerous drawback as a lover, their relationship viewed as inse-cure and temporary. But Enzo could still offer her and the children a safe future where she could not. As yet, she had neither a permanent home nor reliable employ-ment to offer in her own favour.

And more than anything she yearned for the security of knowing that the young brother and sister she loved to distraction would remain in her care. The fear of losing custody of Brodie and Shona haunted her and made her seriously regret the choice she had made when she had agreed to move in with Ritchie. Of course, Ritchie had talked of marriage as well but there had been no further mention of it once he'd had her within his power.

At least, Enzo was truthful about what he was offering and what he wanted from such an arrangement. A wife who was a wife only on paper. A wife who would agree to a divorce the minute he got bored. He wasn't pretending to love her, he wasn't acting as though he wanted her by his side for ever and wasn't there something to be said about that honesty, wounding as it was? With Enzo, she would know where she stood from the outset, what she could expect from him as well as the terrible truth that a parting was inevitable. The status of a wife was, even so, a lot stronger and safer than that of a casual lover.

'I'll think about it... Have you ever been in love?' she asked weakly.

Enzo grimaced. 'Once was enough. I was young and stupid. I'm not young and stupid any more.'

'Who was she?'

'I don't talk about that. It was years ago!'

'I would still like to know,' she admitted, avoiding his gaze.

'Then you are doomed to disappointment.'

'Did you think of marrying her?'

'Yes, but soon after that I discovered that she had been lying to me and cheating on me. I had a lucky escape.

'Are you thinking about marrying me?' Enzo murmured huskily, the dark timbre of his deep voice making an intimate part of her clench tight with awareness. 'I believe all your worries would be over if you were with me.'

'Of course, I'm thinking about it,' Skye muttered ruefully. 'You're gorgeous and sexy and incredible in bed and I've found you very reliable, in spite of your reputation.'

Enzo stretched out a hand and switched off the fire. 'Leave the cleaning up for the morning. *Incredible?*' he husked.

Skye went red as fire. 'You know you are!'

Enzo closed long fingers round hers to lead her upstairs. Skye pulled free long enough to run around and douse the lights that had been left on.

'You're so responsible,' Enzo told her appreciatively as she joined him on the landing where he awaited her.

'And you don't think about stuff like that because you've never had to worry about bills,' she guessed and then sealed her mouth closed again because sniping at him about his privileged status in life was pointless.

He gathered her into his arms and ravished her parted lips with feverish hunger and then pulled back. 'Sorry, early night *without* interference… I forgot.'

Skye laughed. 'Enzo, you chased my early night right out of my head when you mentioned your idea.'

'You *are* thinking about my suggestion, aren't you?'

'Of course, I am.' But even more, she was wondering about the identity of the woman he had once thought of marrying when he'd deemed himself to be 'young and stupid' and whether that romance had turned him off love and commitment for ever. Evidently the episode still rankled enough that, even now, he didn't want to talk about it.

His room had become their room, although her clothes were still across the corridor in her original room and she wouldn't be moving them any time soon because the wardrobes in Enzo's room were packed to the gills with fancy suits and shirts. Having fetched her cleansing stuff, she removed her make-up while Enzo watched her from the doorway.

'I never saw a woman without make-up until I met you,' he confided.

'And I shouldn't have let you sneak up on me.' Skye pushed him out of the doorway and closed the door in his face while she cleaned her teeth.

'I checked on the kids,' he told her when she reappeared and jumped into bed.

'Some day you'll make a great father,' she whispered as he undressed, although her tummy turned over when she reflected that if she did marry him, she would not be the wife he chose to have a family with. Their marriage would only be temporary.

She tried to close her eyes but the temptation of watching Enzo strip was too great and too strong. Lean, flexing muscle sheathed in golden skin began to emerge and her mouth ran dry and her breathing became audible.

'I feel objectified,' Enzo lamented with dancing dark golden eyes. 'But I love feeling your eyes on me. When are you planning to rip off your clothes for my benefit?'

'That would be...never,' Skye warned him.

Enzo strolled lazily out of the bathroom. 'Never say never around me. Are you thinking about it yet? Has a guy ever received a less enthusiastic response to a marriage proposal?'

'Has ever a woman been told that the prospective bridegroom would be sacrificing himself?'

Enzo vaulted into bed beside her. 'That wasn't diplomatic. It wouldn't be a sacrifice. I have never wanted any woman the way I want you. No matter where you are, what you're doing, what you're wearing.'

'You're just oversexed,' Skye told him, snuggling up to him, one small hand smoothing down over his abs.

'I'm not going to lay a finger on you tonight,' he swore, heavy-lidded dark eyes scanning her face. 'You're tired.'

'Not *that* tired,' Skye teased, allowing that admiring hand to travel south, listening to his groan of startled pleasure with deep satisfaction.

'Possibly I'm off limits until you decide on the proposal.'

'We both know I'm going to say yes because you will keep on and on and on about it until I do.' Skye sighed.

'Now you're talking my language, *piccolo mio*.' Enzo turned over and pulled her close, running his hands down over her slender back and pulling her slight body over his. 'And we can celebrate.'

'Sacrifices don't celebrate unless they're martyrs.'

Undeterred, he laughed and extracted a long, drugging kiss. A wave of intoxicated happiness washed over Skye. She had said yes to the insanity. But from her point of view, it would be a sensible move as the authorities would much prefer a couple to adopt the children. She would be fine, she told herself urgently, she would live in the moment and look neither forward nor back. Life was too short for regrets and far too colourless without Enzo.

An hour later, just as she was drifting on the edge of sleep, Enzo sprang out of bed, pulled on a pair of jeans and stabbed a number into his phone.

'Who on earth are you calling this late?' she mumbled, watching the unbuttoned jeans slide down to his hip bones, leaving her to look at a flat hard stomach traversed by a dark furrow of hair.

'Chiara, a friend of mine, and it's not too late an hour for a party girl and the best wedding planner in Italy,' he explained, switching to liquid Italian and settling into a very long and animated conversation while Skye slowly wakened, galvanised into the act by those magic words, 'wedding planner'.

'Wedding planner?' she queried as he set his phone aside with an air of satisfaction.

'Yes, she'll fly over here tomorrow. We're thinking the Maldives. We could do with a bit of sunshine.'

'The *Maldives*?' she exclaimed.

'It's the right time of year and then we'll be home here for Christmas.'

'Enzo, I would need permission from the authorities to take the children out of the country!'

'Then get it organised. Set up a meeting for us, whatever...' Enzo spread an eloquent brown hand to underscore his urgency. 'We have to get this show on the road and there's some stuff I can't do for you. I'll ring my grandparents and tell them what's happening at breakfast time. You should put Alana on alert. I assume you want her at the wedding? And we ought to consider a nanny for the occasion as well.'

Now fully awake as that detailed list of instructions penetrated, Skye sat up in bed and stared back at him, her eyes huge. He was overflowing with raw energy, dark eyes glittering, vitality and impatience splintering from every inch of his long, lean body. 'It's one in the morning, Enzo. What on earth are you planning to tell your grandparents about us?'

'The truth, only the truth. It wouldn't be fair to let them believe that we were a real for-ever couple, but that won't stop them dreaming the dream and hoping we fall for each other regardless of what I've said.' Enzo frowned. 'They'll be disappointed but there's not much I can do about that.'

Skye tried and failed to come up with a conversational response. He had silenced her. 'We could get married here,' she pointed out weakly.

'Not very festive. It's dull and damp and wet. I like sunshine.'

Skye nodded slowly. 'I'll contact our case worker when the office opens.'

'My legal team will take care of any legalities involved.'

'So, it seems we are definitely getting married,' she commented shakily.

'And all you need to worry about is what you wear,' Enzo asserted with satisfaction.

He would make her happy, he reasoned. He would stay married to her until she had her life and her future plans sorted out. He reckoned that that would take at least a year to achieve. A year was no time at all. It would be a practical arrangement that met both their needs. And he needed her, he needed her very much at present, although he was certain that that driving need to be with her would fade as time moved on.

CHAPTER NINE

'I LIKE THE tree and the traditional colours,' Enzo declared from the kitchen doorway a week later as Brodie whooped at his arrival and Shona began to fast-crawl towards him.

Skye gazed back at him for a split second, drinking him in like a dangerous drug. His tie was loose at his throat, stubble roughening his bronzed skin in denial of that sleek sophisticated elegance that was the norm for him. Instead, he simply looked all male and dangerously, smoulderingly sexy, particularly when he watched her through narrowed dark eyes framed with lashes so dense they doubled as eyeliner. Something clenched low in her tummy and she struggled to put her thoughts together again.

'Dinner's almost ready. Alana was here all afternoon and she helped me with the Christmas decorations. Keeping Shona away from the tree is a challenge but I put some soft things on the low branches, so that even if she pulls them, she can't do much damage,' Skye explained. 'We've got another meeting with the case worker tomorrow. There are forms to fill in and they want to meet you again. That's at ten. Can you make it?'

'Yes.' As she reached out to open the oven and check on dinner, Enzo stepped between her and the door and lightly grasped her wrist to deftly ease a ring onto her wedding finger.

Skye froze in surprise.

'An engagement ring? I wasn't expecting *that*,' she confessed with a frown of discomfiture, holding her hand up so that the light from the window illuminated the large oval stone that glittered and sent rainbow facets dancing across the tiled floor. 'A sapphire?'

'It's a very rare blue diamond,' Enzo told her casually. 'But don't get excited about it. It's only window dressing.'

In receipt of that statement, the thrill factor dropped to zero for Skye, although she still could not help staring fixedly at the ring because the jewel was magnificent. Enzo had deliberately chosen to give her the ring in the kitchen and without ceremony, bluntly emphasising how far removed both the ring and their relationship were from real romance. 'It's beautiful. I won't say thanks because I won't be keeping it but I'm sure I'll enjoy wearing it.'

'An update on the wedding plans,' Enzo continued. 'My legal team tells me that a marriage in the Maldives wouldn't be lawful, and my grandmother tells me that if I don't get married in my childhood church she will be heartbroken. Therefore, we will get married in Italy, have the reception there and then fly on to the Maldives for a couple of nights.'

'Yes, your grandmother has already phoned me to explain.' Skye was amused to see that Enzo was disconcerted by that news. 'Apparently your PA had my phone number and she passed it on. I spoke to your grandmother this afternoon. She may have forgotten to ask my shoe size but she got everything else there is to know about me in triplicate.'

'Nonna doesn't miss a trick,' Enzo quipped. 'I'm sorry.'

'No, no need to apologise. Your family don't know me and all of a sudden, you're marrying me. Your grandmother was warm, friendly and delightful. I have no complaints.'

'They wanted to fly over and meet you and the children before the wedding even though they're aware that the wedding is more a paper event than a real one,' he confided. 'I told them that we'd be too busy getting all our ducks in a row in time for the wedding and requesting permission for the children to accompany us. You'll have to go shopping and you'll need swimwear et cetera for the Maldives, as well as all the bridal stuff.'

'I don't even know where to start.'

'Chiara will make arrangements for the bridal end of things. She's a seasoned operator.'

'And a friend, you said?'

'I've known her since I was a teenager.'

They had eaten and Skye had got the children to bed when the doorbell sounded.

'It's Chiara... Paola texted me that she had arrived. She's staying at the Blackthorn Hotel. She asked if she could stay here but we need our privacy. Of course, she'll be curious about you.'

'I suppose,' Skye conceded nervously on her path to the front door, turning her head, her voice dropping as she glanced back at Enzo with a troubled expression. 'Before we go any further, you *are* sure about marrying me, aren't you?'

'Nobody ever made me do anything I didn't want to do…aside from my grandfather. Stop worrying,' he urged.

The sleek sports car parked outside and the woman on the doorstep were not at all what Skye had expected. Chiara was almost six feet tall and towered over her. She was built like a leggy supermodel with long blonde hair halfway to her waist and a perfect face. She was also clad head to toe in skin-tight midnight-blue leather leggings and a fitted jacket. Breezing past Skye without even looking at her, she headed straight for Enzo and a flood of Italian broke from her in a wave.

'Use your English, Chiara. Come and meet Skye.' Enzo closed his hand to Skye's to bring her forward and introduce her. 'Skye is your client and the bride-to-be.'

Chiara surveyed Skye in literal wonderment, much as though a worn hall rug had stood up and tried to trip her. 'Skye…how lovely to meet you. I hope you're free for the next forty-eight hours at least. I need to know your taste in *everything* before we can get organised.'

Enzo smiled at both women. 'I'll be working.'

Skye showed the blonde into the sitting room and offered her refreshments.

'I'd prefer a drink to coffee,' Chiara told her.

'I'll open one of Enzo's bottles of wine.'

When Skye returned with a glass of wine for both of

them, the blonde opened a sleek tablet and proceeded to ask for preferences in colours and styles. 'It's a shame Enzo's grandparents are so determined to get heavily involved. It'll have to be a modest traditional dress to please them, which cuts your options down.'

'I suspect that I'll choose something fairly traditional anyway.'

Chiara was very efficient but she shot in loads of personal questions, which Skye carefully sidestepped, assuming that the information that their marriage would be a paper sham had been disclosed only to Enzo's grandparents.

'It sounds like it was love at first sight,' Chiara remarked after Skye had admitted meeting Enzo by the side of the road, although Skye had not mentioned that she had been fleeing an assault by her former boyfriend. 'That doesn't fit Enzo's profile. He prefers a challenge, and you being here and available on site—'

'Is just what I enjoy most,' Enzo chipped in from the doorway.

Chiara raised a brow. 'If you say so, but, let me tell you, none of your friends are likely to believe this caper is for real.'

'I think, if that is your attitude,' Skye interposed tautly, 'you should leave me to organise our wedding.'

'Perfectly said, *piccolo mio*.' Enzo studied the blonde, who had flushed. 'I know you can be nice if you want to be nice, Chiara. What's it to be?'

'I will mind my own business and say nothing more,' Chiara responded tightly. 'I *want* to do this wedding. It will be the society event of the year and I want it on my résumé to impress my other clients.'

Amused by that candour, Skye stood up to fetch another glass and poured wine for Enzo.

'You look after him. *Dio mio*, no wonder he's in seventh heaven!' Chiara exclaimed. 'Enzo, if that secret had got out sooner, you'd have had a queue of happy housewives at your door years ago.'

Ironically, Skye had some sympathy for that tart aside. Enzo *did* enjoy being looked after and she didn't mind doing it because he was always appreciative and he didn't take advantage. Clearly, Chiara had never wished to take care of any man but then every relationship was different and what was right for her might not be right for someone else.

'Skye is not a housewife. She's a teacher.'

'But surely you won't be working?'

'We'll have to see,' Skye said equably, knowing very well that in the not so distant future she would be looking for another teaching position, keeping up her own life and independence to lay the basis for the time when she would be living alone again.

Chiara sighed like someone in pain when she saw the engagement ring and raved about it. By the time she departed, Skye was heartily bored with discussing wedding finery but she was looking forward to seeing the gowns that were to be brought to the house for her.

'Chiara has an acid tongue,' she remarked thoughtfully once they were alone again.

'Her parents went through a very nasty divorce when

she was a teenager, and she developed that edge after-wards.'

'She's kind of possessive of you,' Skye continued dog-gedly. 'Did you date her at one stage?'

'No, but I slept with her when I was fifteen. She was my first. It was casual, friendly, nothing either of us viewed as important at the time.'

'I knew it.' Skye groaned. 'It was the way she looked at you. I didn't like it, but I can ignore it. Your grand-mother did say she's very good at her job.'

'I love your practicality,' Enzo confided, tucking her face into his chest, where she drowsily breathed in the scent of him like an unrepentant addict as they climbed the stairs.

Skye pulled her head back. 'I have to go to court to-morrow afternoon for the non-molestation order to be granted against Ritchie.'

'I know. Your solicitor advised me. I'll accompany you.'

'No, I don't want that. You shouldn't get involved,' Skye told him anxiously. 'Ritchie will be there as well and I don't want you associated with me for his benefit. He's dangerous.'

'Associated? We're getting married!' Enzo countered squarely.

'Stay out of it. It's my mess and I will deal with the consequences. Imagine what the press could do with it if you were recognised and we'd both be embarrassed if his attack on me came out in public.'

Enzo frowned. 'You'll have a protection team with you tomorrow.'

'Of course.'

Enzo compressed his lips. 'I'd prefer to be there in person to support you.'

'I know you would, but some things are mine to handle.'

In the midst of the very busy two weeks that followed the children came down with chickenpox and Skye ended up sleeping in their room every night to be within easy reach when they woke up crying from feverish dreams and needing soothing. The non-molestation order was granted and Ritchie was no longer allowed to contact or approach Skye.

That had been a relief but the sight of Ritchie, bitter, flat-eyed and threatening in the courtroom, had unnerved her. She marvelled that she had ever believed he loved her or that she had loved him. His expressions in court had shown his nastiness and she shuddered, thinking of how close he had come to killing her. No matter how hard she had stood tall on the outside, on the inside she had still felt sick and scared at being that close to him again.

The night before their Italian wedding and within hours of their flight to Italy, however, disaster struck. Enzo's mobile rang while they were eating and he sprang out of his chair, his voice rising in volume as he demanded repetition and clarification. Pocketing his phone, his face stamped with tension and urgency, he strode to the door.

'What's happened?' Skye jumped up out of her seat, registering that there was some sort of crisis afoot.

'The factory's on fire!' Enzo bit out rawly. 'The security guard has been taken to hospital. Someone knocked him out.'

'Good heavens...what do you want me to do?' It was almost their wedding day, she thought in dismay.

'It's doubtful that I'll be able to fly out with you now. I'll join you as soon as I can. Don't worry... I'll make it,' Enzo promised grittily.

Skye swallowed a groan and raced out to the hall after him. 'Enzo!'

If the factory had gone up in flames, it would be very hard for him to leave the UK. 'Maybe we should postpone the wedding,' she suggested reluctantly as he swung back from the front door.

Enzo angled his tousled dark head back to her, his dark eyes unusually grave. 'No way, not when we've finally got everything ready to go.'

Skye couldn't sleep and got up early, creeping around, keen to avoid waking up the children. She reckoned she would be flying out to Italy alone without Enzo and meeting his grandparents without him present to ease the introduction. At the same time though, she would have Alana, Isabel, the bright and cheery young nanny Enzo had hired, and Shona and Brodie with her. She would manage, she told herself, she always did.

The afternoon of that same day in the privacy of the bedroom set aside for her to dress in his grandparents' home, Skye recalled that brief exchange and wondered what would happen if Enzo didn't arrive in Italy on time, because he was cutting it fine. What if he jilted her at the altar? Her tummy gave a sick lurch. No, Enzo would never leave it to the very last moment, nor would he ever seek to humiliate her.

As the owner of the packaging business, Eduardo Martelli, Enzo's grandfather, had been in constant touch with the authorities and Enzo. Skye was already aware that arson was suspected. The fire was out but a great deal of damage had been done and the professionals were currently trying to decide whether a total rebuild of the factory or a restoration and an extension to the building would work the best.

Alana, vibrant in an emerald-green bridesmaid dress, literally burst through the door. 'Enzo's arrived! He wanted to come up and see you but his grandmother won't allow it because she says it's bad luck for the groom to see the bride before the church!' she gabbled and then she stopped to stare at her older sister. 'My goodness, Skye...you look magical in that gown.'

Enzo was finally, safely under the same roof. Much of Skye's anxiety drained away and a smile stole the tension from her generous mouth. She studied her reflection in the wardrobe mirror. Her dress was made of lace that sparkled when the crystal beads caught the light. It had long tight sleeves, a fitted bodice, a sweetheart neckline and a narrow skirt. Chiara had complained that it was dull but Skye didn't like frills or too much embellishment. There was only a very small removable train and her veil was short and attached to the beautiful pearl tiara that Sophie Martelli had insisted on loaning her. The beauty of the gown lay in the exquisite lace from which it was fashioned and its classic design.

As she descended the imposing staircase with Alana at her heels, she passed by a framed photograph of Enzo as a teenager, an Enzo who, by the wicked sparkle in his eyes, was often up to no good. Enzo had never been an angel, she reckoned, but he had a surprisingly serious side to his nature. He had been devastated by the fire at Mackies, particularly when everything had been going so well there and now business was at a standstill. He intended to stay longer in the UK to supervise the rebuild. Once he committed to something, he stayed committed.

He had grown up in an old, gracious family house where he had been very much loved. Yet somewhere along the line his faith in other people had sunk without trace, filling him with restlessness and distrust. Had that change been caused by that long ago relationship that had gone wrong for him at university? Or was it simply the influence of the Durante wealth that he had not been allowed to escape? Sophie, who had asked Skye to call her Nonna, had shown her photo albums. Enzo was the very image of his late father, whose life had stumbled from one disaster to the next, and his grandparents had done everything within their power to ensure that Enzo enjoyed a different outcome.

He had come to *her* rescue, Skye conceded as she climbed with care into the beribboned wedding car with her sister and Eduardo Martelli, who, in the absence of any male relative on her side, had offered to walk her down the aisle. Enzo had so many positives going for him. He had been marvellous with her and the children, in spite of the fact that he was not a domesticated male, eager to settle down with one woman.

Enzo desired her but what was that worth at the end of the day when there was nothing surer than the fact that eventually another woman would come along whom he desired even more? Their marriage had an agreed end date and she needed to keep that in mind. She had signed a prenup, packed with cold, hard financial facts. She knew the score. She shouldn't be continually thinking about Enzo, missing him or worrying about him. She had got in too deep, far too deep, she scolded herself, her fingers tightening round her bouquet.

'You're nervous. I wasn't expecting that,' Alana confided as they entered the big church in the village.

At first glance Skye felt as though she were standing in a field of flowers because every surface seemed to be decorated with beautiful blooms and ribbons and the candles were lit, illuminating the man at the altar. Enzo wore a dove-grey morning suit and he stood there, tall and strong and incredibly masculine from his broad shoulders to his long, powerful legs. He didn't look remotely nervous, he looked cool as ice and confident, possibly even a little impatient for the ceremony to begin, and she smiled because that complete innate assurance was so Enzo.

There was something incredibly appealing about Skye's smile, Enzo reflected calmly. He could see how nervous she was and it tightened something in his chest. The small quick wedding he had envisaged had turned into a massive elaborate event to which everyone who was anyone was invited, both the elite of society and the business world. The church was packed and his bride had done him proud. She was the picture of elegance, her slender delicacy encased in lace that somehow sparkled, just as her personality did. His grandparents loved her and the children, had already mentioned how much natural class she had and how admirable was her devotion and loyalty to her siblings. She was a hell of a girl and, for the first time, he found himself acknowledging that it was a great shame that their marriage would be fake.

That very thought shook him inside out and he paled, hands clenching into fists. So, he had grown fond of her and the children, even the stupid dog, well, that was no crime and hardly surprising in the circumstances, he told himself. He strove to ignore Shona, sitting on his grand-mother's lap and stretching out hopeful arms to him while Brodie sulked on Isabel, the nanny's knee, having already made a break for freedom several times and been thwarted. He knew they would be lucky to get through the ceremony without the toddler throwing a tantrum.

He had got attached to them all and when they split up, he would keep on visiting them. At least until Skye met someone else. His teeth gritted fiercely at that idea, but he knew that she was far too lovely to be left on any shelf as a single parent. She was beautiful, intelligent and unfailingly loyal and honest. She would be a major catch for any man, just not him.

As they knelt before the priest, Skye noticed that Enzo seemed to have become very tense and she linked her fingers with his and squeezed and he sent her a gleam-ing glance of amusement. The elderly priest talked while

Enzo quietly translated the gist of the ceremony. Before she knew where she was, Enzo was sliding the ring onto her finger and snatching her close for a kiss.

'Enzo!' she scolded and saw his grandmother laughing.

And then her lips shifted beneath the soft firmness of his and she quivered, heat sparking at the heart of her and stirring an ache that reminded her of just how long it had been since they had made love. The chickenpox had been as effective as a vote of celibacy and had kept her firmly clamped to the children and by the time they had recovered, she had been exhausted and stressed out and Enzo had told her to catch up on her beauty sleep.

A blaze of cameras awaited them outside the church and it was a relief to escape into the limousine and be ferried off to the hotel where the reception would take place. 'I didn't realise there would be so many guests,' she confided.

'There will be many more joining us at the hotel. The church wasn't big enough to take everyone. I suspect children I played with in kindergarten may even have been included. Nonna wanted everyone I ever knew to have the opportunity to attend.'

Skye blinked, wondering if his former love from university had been included and asking before she could think better of the question.

Enzo slung her a stunned appraisal. 'Of course not! Why would she be invited?'

Skye ignored the anger flaring in his dark golden eyes. 'So, you didn't stay friends,' she gathered.

'Why are you so curious?' he demanded impatiently.

Skye widened her eyes. 'You tell me that you've only been in love once in your life and you expect me *not* to be curious?'

Enzo shrugged a broad shoulder. 'I don't discuss it.'

'Even though you know every good, bad and ugly thing there is to know about me?' Skye questioned, lilac eyes bright with challenge. 'And what's more, *expect* to know it?'

'Even though,' he confirmed, determined to close the topic.

Total silence fell.

'I didn't even get to tell you how gorgeous you look in that dress.'

'And that compliment is not exactly falling on fertile ground now,' Skye pointed out without apology.

They arrived at the hotel to be engulfed by a flood of guests. The introductions seemed to go on for ever. Skye's mouth ached from smiling and she flexed fingers stiff from handshakes. The instant she was free from the line-up she went off to reunite with her smallest siblings. Shona sat in her arms saying, 'Zozo? Want Zozo.'

'Enzo... *Enz*o,' Brodie sounded out importantly for his little sister's benefit.

'I suppose we've had our first row,' Skye remarked when she took her seat by his side at the bridal table.

'Merely a difference of opinion,' Enzo contradicted.

'The next time you want to know something about me, I'll do a brick-wall shutdown on you.' While Skye knew that their sexual chemistry was amazing, Enzo's ongoing refusal to confide in her merely emphasised the fact that their marriage wasn't a real one, she conceded ruefully.

An unexpected chuckle fell from Enzo's lips. 'I will give you a hint. The stories I refuse to tell you are the ones that make me feel like a fool.'

'Like the dinner-party disaster,' Skye guessed, in more charity with him after that admission.

'My grandparents and Alana have offered to look after the kids while we're in the Maldives,' Enzo imparted. 'Nonna pointed out that a twelve-hour flight for such young children wasn't the best idea and we are only going to be there for forty-eight hours.'

'I thought Alana was coming with us.'

'She told me that she doesn't much fancy being a third in a party for two. We'll be spending our wedding night on the jet. I'd prefer to take Brodie and Shona away when we have more time to spend with them.'

It was a sensible suggestion and Skye simply ensured that she enjoyed time with the children that afternoon, freeing Alana up to chat to other guests and dance. It was wonderful to see her sister relax and have a good time for a change. Alana had changed so much after the death of their parents, focusing only on work and how much she could earn, where once she had been focused purely on art and money hadn't seemed to matter to her. Now she worked endless overtime in a menial job. Their sudden responsibility for their younger brother and sister had forced them both to grow up faster than was comfortable and much of the fun had gone out of their lives, Skye acknowledged ruefully.

It was a lively celebration, powered by catchy music, dancing and laughter. Italians, Enzo told her with pride, knew how to party. Skye's throat ached with talking and she had to dig deep for the energy to stay on the dance floor and keep up with Enzo. When it was time to leave, she went upstairs with her sister to remove her wedding dress and change into a comfortable outfit in which to travel.

'That was a very long day and you are very tired,' Enzo commented in the limo on the way to the airport as she flopped back in the corner.

'But it's our wedding night.' As soon as she said it, her cheeks burned an almost painful red because once again she felt as though she was parading too many feelings that he did not share. It was a sham marriage and they were lovers but not in the romantic everlasting sense. Enzo could live without her. Enzo *would* move on to other women. The promises they had exchanged at the altar were meaningless.

'All you'll be doing on the flight is sleeping. You're dead on your feet,' Enzo said drily. 'Tomorrow we'll wake up to sunshine and blue skies.'

'Yes,' she conceded sleepily, smiling.

He took her hand as they walked into the airport flanked by his security team. 'Her name was Allegra—the name of the woman I loved,' he told her in a driven undertone.

'Tell me about her…if you want?' Skye tacked on that last qualifier on a questioning note at his unexpected willingness to talk.

'I don't want to, but I shouldn't have secrets from you,' Enzo conceded tautly as they boarded the jet. 'You have kept none from me.'

Warmed by that belated concession, Skye sank down into a seat in the opulent cabin.

'Allegra's cousin, Niccolò, was my best friend at university. We were both equally into sport and I met Allegra through him. They were cousins who grew up together in close families. Their fathers were twin brothers who'd married sisters and they all lived in the same town. They even looked like siblings.'

'What was she like?' Skye interrupted, surprised that he was choosing to tell her so much about his former girlfriend's background.

'A vivacious brunette who loved to dance, the life and soul of every party. I fell for her very quickly and I was with her over two years before I asked her to marry me. We planned to marry after our graduation.'

'What went wrong?' Skye asked when he fell silent.

'I went home for the weekend to tell my grandparents. I got a mixed reaction. Nonno had no objections, but my grandmother thought Allegra was what she termed *secretive* and that I shouldn't rush into setting a date. That night I drove over to the apartment Allegra shared with her cousin and as I was parking my car, I saw a silhouette behind the blinds of a couple kissing. They often had friends in, so I thought nothing of it,' he admitted.

A sinking suspicion infiltrated Skye and she stiffened in dismay.

'They weren't expecting me. They had no guests either. I just looked at them together…and I *knew* but I couldn't understand *why* they were pretending that their relationship was only familial. Everything else fitted in. Allegra had refused to move in with me, insisting that her parents wouldn't like it. Although I spent the night with her there occasionally, she never gave me a key. Behind closed doors they were free to do as they liked.'

'What did you do?' Skye whispered sickly.

'I confronted them. Ironically it was Niccolò who came clean first. I think he'd been so jealous, he almost enjoyed telling me. Allegra, however, lied to the bitter end. Apparently, they fell for each other as teenagers and their families were horrified. Although being with a cousin is not illegal, their parents believed that they were too genetically close to ever be a couple, so their relationship went underground but it never stopped. They had continued having sex the whole time I was with her. That turned my stomach,' Enzo admitted with a grimace.

'I'm not surprised,' Skye commented, feeling a little queasy too at the extent of the deception that had been practised on him.

'I was shattered. I had fallen in love with a girl who didn't exist. She had picked me out and told him to become my friend. She needed a boyfriend to keep her family in the dark. Being with me and Niccolò being my friend gave them endless excuses to be together without rousing any suspicions. She was planning to go the whole way and marry me. I doubt if any children we might have had would have been mine.'

'What happened next?'

'I never spoke to either of them again. I didn't tell anyone what had happened. I felt like such a stupid, gullible idiot for not suspecting them sooner,' he bit out ruefully. 'I told my grandparents that I had caught her cheating on me. The rest of it was too sordid for their ears. Allegra and Niccolò set out to use me and succeeded for over two years. I've never forgotten that.'

Skye could only begin to imagine how humiliated Enzo must have felt once he knew the truth. They had lied to him and deceived him without shame in a calculated betrayal of trust. 'Nothing that they did to you was excusable. They should've stood up to their families and gone for testing to see if there was any medical reason why they couldn't be together.'

'Agreed, but Allegra is why I don't do love,' Enzo confided as he buckled in and the jet engines fired up. 'It blinds you, makes you vulnerable. You can have a very good time with a woman without handing over your soul.'

'I'm so sorry that happened to you,' Skye told him and as soon as a light meal had been served, she fell into the bed in the sleeping compartment like a rock dropped from a height.

Skye woke the following morning to dappled sunlight playing across an unfamiliar wooden ceiling, rays and shadows playing over the muslin drapes on the bed and screening the windows. She had a guilty recollection of being roused by Enzo to leave the plane, then stumbling through a busy airport and into transport. She remembered him helping her to undress and sliding into bed and she now felt wonderfully rested for the first time in weeks. There was a dent in the pillow beside hers, telling her that Enzo had slept beside her.

She showered and dug into her case for a bright red bikini. Tugging back the screen doors, she walked out onto the wooden pier outside. The sea, almost as clear as glass, rippled only inches beneath her. She could see pebbles, tiny colourful fish and shells and above her the sky was a deep strong cobalt blue. The sunshine poured down on her and she lifted her face dreamily into that golden heat, soaking up the warmth on her skin.

'Morning, sleepyhead. I ordered breakfast for us when I heard you in the shower,' Enzo murmured, and she jerked round to focus on him.

Clad only in a pair of swim shorts, he stood by one of the pier struts, his long, lean, bronzed length gleaming wetly. He had clearly just climbed out of the water and every single strong line of his powerful body, from his wide shoulders to his hard abdomen and narrow waist, was delineated in the sunshine. She watched a water bead slowly trickle down over his muscular torso. Her nipples pinched taut inside her bra and her tummy clenched. As always, he looked magnificent. Clothed or unclothed, Enzo was gorgeous. And she was married to him now. No, don't get carried away with that knowledge, she scolded herself. Remember it's not real, it's just a short-term marriage.

'I don't remember seeing a resort last night, but then I don't remember much of anything.' She sighed with a guilty wince.

'The resort is out of view to the right at the end of the pier. This island we're on is totally private,' he told her. 'Only the staff have access. I'm looking forward to skinny dipping at midnight.'

'Breakfast is on its way,' she noted, strolling down to the table set in the shade, glancing across at the island, which was covered with lush palm trees running down to a white sand beach. 'This is idyllic. My apologies for sleeping like Rip van Winkle.'

An appetite-tempting array was delivered to the table. 'Gosh, I'm starving!' Skye confided, reaching for a piece of tropical fruit and then a pancake. 'I was too stressed to eat much yesterday.'

Coffee and tea were poured. Enzo stretched back in his chair, dark golden eyes locked to her as he ate a croissant. 'Sleepy or not, I still fancy the pants off you, Signora Durante. And I'm appreciating the downtime here. We needed a break.'

Eating her fruit, she rested back feeling gloriously relaxed. 'Any news about the fire?'

His lean, darkly handsome features tensed. 'The arson has been confirmed. An accelerant was used and they have the evidence. The stores went up like a bonfire and spread to the factory. The security man saw nothing. Someone came at him from behind. The surveillance cameras may show something but one of them was offline.'

He discussed his plans for the rebuild, confessed that the architect had already sent him some rough sketches and then he laughed. 'I got up at six and touched base with everyone. Twelve months ago, I never saw the dawn.

I was partying half the night but I was incredibly bored. I much prefer work to boredom and I like a routine. I will hate admitting it to my grandfather but blackmail works on me.'

Her smooth brow indented. *'Blackmail?'*

Without fanfare, Enzo explained the agreement he had made with the older man following what he referred to as 'the dinner-party episode'. 'And the irony is that I'm much happier working than when I was chasing the next big thrill.'

'I can't comment because I didn't know you before.'

'You wouldn't have liked me. I was a case of arrested development. I think I've finally finished growing up.'

'You still haven't told me about the dinner-party thing,' she reminded him, amusement dancing in her bright eyes.

Enzo grimaced. 'My companion got under the table and tried to unzip me.'

'No?' Skye framed in disbelief.

Enzo winced. 'In the middle of the meal because she was bored stiff. I then had an embarrassing struggle with her to get her back into her seat, but it was more my fault than hers. Neither of us were sober and she had no idea how to behave in company.'

Skye groaned. 'What were you thinking of?'

Enzo sprang upright, stalked round the table and bent down to scoop her bodily out of her seat. 'I think much more efficiently around you,' he told her as she laughed. 'And I have learned to appreciate common sense.'

'Common sense isn't sexy.' Skye wrinkled her nose.

'It is when you see the opposite in action. And you

come out here in a minuscule scarlet bikini and say you're *not* sexy?' Thrusting open the screen doors, Enzo tumbled her down on the bed.

'It's not minuscule. It's just that I don't have a lot to put in it,' she lamented.

'More than enough for me.' Enzo crushed her lush mouth hungrily beneath his and groaned, stretching over her slight body and sliding between her legs. 'And now I've got to wrestle you out of the blasted thing.'

Skye rolled away and sat up with a giggle. She tugged off the top and the bottoms with alacrity while he watched her with answering amusement.

'You missed me,' he commented with satisfaction.

'Of course, I did,' she muttered, recalling all those lonely nights of broken sleep in the children's room.

Enzo spread an appreciative hand over a small pouting breast and bent his head to capture the rosy nipple in his mouth. 'Never stop being that honest with me,' he urged.

'Why would I?' she framed, thoughts blurring as the tug of his lips sent an urgent shot of pure, naked craving down into her pelvis.

He kissed a haphazard line down over her body, found the heart of her and dallied there, long fingers toying with her tender entrance while he tormented her with his mouth and the tip of his tongue. She hit a peak so fast it left her breathless and, with an audible hiss of enthusiasm, he flipped her over, lifted her and drove into her from behind, punctuating that move with a revealing groan of deep satisfaction.

Excitement gripped her from head to toe because she

was so sensitive, his every thrust set her on fire. She couldn't get enough of him. He couldn't get enough of her. Perspiration filmed her skin and she careened into another breathtaking climax with the sound of his name on her lips. She collapsed on the bed and Enzo pulled her close.

'I like you screaming my name,' he said raggedly.

'I didn't scream!'

'You said my name with wonderful enthusiasm. I liked it,' Enzo rephrased smoothly, sitting up to lift her over him and wrapping both arms round her.

'I feel like a cuddly toy.' Skye pressed her lips against a bare brown shoulder, still intoxicated by the delicious sensations thrumming through her limp body.

'I'm working up to carrying you into the shower and then we'll explore the island and go waterskiing.'

'What if I don't like it?'

'We'll try something else. I'm very flexible.'

Two days passed in a whirl of activity. Skye preferred jet-skiing to waterskiing because she couldn't stay upright for long on the water. They went snorkelling and sailing in a catamaran. They also dined on the beach and went skinny dipping afterwards, sitting long into the night on the shore with drinks. Enzo gave her a beautiful gold watch and Skye picked a souvenir bauble for the Christmas tree back home. He confessed that he was missing Brodie and Shona, which touched her heart, and he bought a pile of toys for them.

They slept on the flight, Enzo up early, back in a sleek, sophisticated business suit. They had had so much fun, she reflected as she pulled on jeans and a sweater, prepared for the icy temperatures that awaited her back home. She had to pick Brodie up from his playgroup. She still felt dizzy with happiness after forty-eight hours of Enzo. She didn't feel that she should be so happy but Enzo was in excellent form as well.

Oh, who are you trying to kid? she asked herself in exasperation as she put on her ankle boots. Even though she had kept warning herself to keep her head in Enzo's vicinity because their marriage wasn't destined to last, she had still fallen for Enzo like a ton of bricks. How could she not have fallen for him? From the outset he had looked out for her in every way possible. He had cared for her, supported her and never once put her down. He made her feel special and he shared everything with her. Of course, she had fallen madly in love with him, but she wasn't planning to tell him and she wasn't going to make a fuss about it either.

Some day in the future, Enzo would announce that he was returning to Italy and she would have to deal with it. She wouldn't throw her feelings in his face. He didn't deserve that when he had been honest with her from the beginning. It wasn't a proper marriage. Enzo had never planned to stay with her and the children, she reminded herself. He would leave and she would have to make the best of the situation.

They parted at the airport. 'I'm catching a lift with my security team to the factory,' Enzo explained. 'I'll try not to be late tonight. I want to see the kids.'

When Skye got back to the house, eager to see Alana

and Shona, she was disappointed. Alana had left a note explaining that she had taken Shona out shopping with her. She then discovered that Mavis, her late mother's car, had a flat tyre. Already running late, she phoned Enzo.

'May I use your car? Mavis has got a flat and I haven't got time to change it.'

'Matteo can drive you. He's the best driver on my staff,' Enzo advised calmly.

'I'll change the tyre when we get back, *Signora*,' Matteo declared helpfully as she climbed into the SUV.

They were heading downhill into town when Matteo bit out something in anxious Italian. The big vehicle was jolting from side to side as the older man worked down through the gears. 'The brakes have gone!'

As they headed for a T-junction, Skye gripped the side of the seat as Matteo struggled to slow the car down and finally steered into the ditch.

'She's likely to tip over!' he warned her.

Her heart was in her mouth. There was a thunderous crash and the car juddered violently as it tipped into the ditch. She struck her head hard on the passenger window. Pain lanced through her temples and then blackness engulfed her and she knew no more...

CHAPTER TEN

SKYE WOKE SLOWLY. Her head hurt. She had the vaguest recollection of being sick, of medical staff fussing around her. Eyes opening in dismay, she started to sit up, realising that she was in bed, but her head swam so dizzily she flopped down flat again, struggling to overcome another bout of nausea.

'Thank goodness, you're back in the land of the living,' a familiar voice commented and she focused on her sister, who was standing beside the bed, clutching Shona on one hip. 'I came very close to strangling Enzo.'

'Why?' she whispered, stretching out her arms to her little sister, who was trying to break free of Alana's hold to reach her. 'Give her to me.'

Shona subsided into a clinging heap by her side, tucked between the bed bars and Skye's slight body.

'Where's Brodie?'

'He's with Enzo.'

'What happened? The car crashed, didn't it?' she whispered.

Alana sat down by the bed and sighed. 'It tipped over. Matteo actually did a very good job of saving you on that hill but you bashed your head and then the airbags went off and bruised you. You arrived in an ambulance. Matteo was a bit shaken up but he was all right and he phoned Enzo from the scene.'

Relieved that the older man was not hurt and that someone had remembered to pick up Brodie from his playgroup, Skye whispered, 'What did Enzo do?'

'Where do you want me to start?' Alana groaned. 'When he got a speeding ticket on the way to the hospital and got a police escort with sirens? When he created a scene in A & E and they threatened to throw him out? Nobody does drama like Enzo. If you'd been dead, Enzo would have thrown himself off the top floor.'

'Currently, your husband is fully occupied dealing with the police enquiry into the accident,' an older man in a white coat told her cheerfully as a nurse joined them to run through routine checks.

The consultant told her that she'd had a CT scan while unconscious and ran through her symptoms with her before asking her questions to check that she wasn't suffering from any mental confusion. Those completed, he remarked that the nausea and dizziness would take time to recede and that it would be best for her to spend the night in the hospital and once she got home she was to rest for a few days to aid her recovery. He added with a straight face that he didn't believe that the services of the top neurosurgeon on standby in London would be required. Skye rolled her eyes and even that small facial movement hurt.

The nurse was plumping her pillows to help her sit up when Enzo appeared in the doorway, Brodie clinging to his hand. Enzo had lost his tie and his lean dark features were taut and unusually pale but his strained dark eyes lit up like golden flames when he saw her awake. Her little brother tore free and raced up to the bed, only to be restrained by Alana. 'Careful, Brodie,' she said. 'Skye has a sore head.'

'Oopsie,' Skye confirmed, touching her fingers to her head and her face.

'Oopsie.' Brodie calmed as Alana lifted Shona from her side.

'Kiss better?'

'Sì...' Enzo breathed, striding forward to lift Brodie up so that he could kiss his big sister. 'Gentle, now.'

'You've taken ten years off my life,' Enzo told her unsteadily, brilliant dark eyes welded to her bruised and swollen face. 'Most people come round quickly after a concussion but you didn't and I was afraid that you would go into a coma.'

'And end up eternally asleep like the Sleeping Beauty,' Alana interposed with a hint of amusement. 'But you know what it took to wake *her* up and your husband was more than equal to the challenge.'

'I'm fine, Enzo.'

'You are many things right now but fine is not one of them. The airbags deployed and bruised you up because you're so small. When I saw you lying on that trolley in the emergency department, you were so white and still...' Enzo shook his tousled dark head to shake free of that recollection and visibly swallowed hard.

'I'll take the children back to the house,' Alana announced.

'The nanny will be staying on until Skye has recovered.'

Skye frowned at Enzo. 'I'll be right as rain by tomorrow.'

'You'll have to take it easy for a few days and you can't do that looking after Brodie and Shona. For once, *I'm* going to look after *you*,' Enzo proclaimed. 'I'll work from home for the rest of the week.'

'That's not necessary,' Skye began.

'Let him. It'll make him feel better,' Alana whispered as she gave her pale sister a gentle hug. 'See you soon.'

Silence fell as the room emptied.

'A *neurosurgeon* on standby?' Skye questioned in disbelief.

Enzo stood his ground and straightened his broad shoulders, not an ounce of embarrassment on his dark strong face. 'I was really worried about you.'

'What did the police want?'

'They want to check over the car. The arson at the factory has made them suspicious. It should have been me in that car,' he breathed tautly. 'I wish it had been.'

'Well, I don't. I'm grateful that you're all in one piece. Matteo did a great job coming down that hill. And amazingly, he stayed calm.'

'He was a special ops soldier when he was younger.'

'I'm sorry… I've messed up your whole day,' Skye murmured.

'Is that a joke?' Enzo asked tightly.

'No, of course it's not a joke. I know how busy you are right now. The last thing you needed was a—'

'A dead wife?' Enzo sliced in rawly. 'And it could have been *all* of you in that car!'

'Thankfully, it wasn't.'

'When I saw you lying there, I realised something very important. I almost lost you. The shock was good for me.' Enzo paced restively at the foot of the bed, his bronzed profile tense. 'We need to have a serious talk tomorrow.'

Skye swallowed thickly. 'About what?'

'About us…this marriage.' Enzo made a slashing motion with one lean hand in a gesture of frustration. A chilling quiver of alarm ran down her taut spine. 'I've made a hash of it and now I'm probably going to make an even bigger hash by breaking the rules…but this is not the moment to discuss all that.'

Rules? What rules? He insisted on staying with her and, try though she did to remain awake, she drifted off to sleep, only opening her eyes when a nurse came to do checks on her again and offer her something to eat.

'Go home, Enzo,' she urged then. 'You look exhausted. Have you even eaten since this morning?'

'I bought snacks in the cafeteria for Brodie and Alana.'

Her heart melted inside her chest because she was willing to bet that he had seen to everyone else's needs before his own. She knew how her self-proclaimed spoilt, selfish playboy operated and he was exactly the opposite of what he said he was. Her eyes stung like mad and she wanted to slap herself for getting so sentimental and overwhelmed by her emotions, but she couldn't help it when she loved him so much. And what did he intend to discuss about their marriage? *He* had broken the rules? *What* rules? Had he worked out that they had grown too close to easily separate? Did he feel the need to remind her that they were still on the road to an eventual divorce? Or, even worse, had she betrayed the strength of her own feelings?

'Why are you crying?' Enzo sprang out of his seat and settled down on the side of the bed.

'I'm not crying. I think it's just the aftermath of the accident, a bit of shock or whatever,' she framed jerkily. 'Just ignore me.'

A blunt forefinger traced the path of a tear down her cheek. 'I've never been able to ignore you. I did try at the beginning before I got in too deep.'

'Too deep?'

'We're not about to discuss that now. You're not fit,' Enzo asserted, vaulting upright again, glittering night-dark eyes locked to her troubled face. 'Get a good night's sleep and we'll talk tomorrow.'

'If you're planning to ditch me, do it now. I'm not that fragile!' Skye declared, squaring her slight shoulders.

Enzo surveyed her in wonderment. 'Why would I ditch you? You're my wife.' Revealingly, he hesitated for a moment before grudgingly adding the qualifier, 'Sort of my wife.'

'A sort of a wife isn't a real wife and we both know that,' Skye told him flatly, crushing down the jolt of pain that had pierced her when he'd chosen to be precise enough to make that distinction.

Enzo gave her an intense appraisal, something of his inner turmoil etched in his rigid features and the unalloyed darkness of his gaze. 'We'll talk tomorrow.'

He felt guilty about wanting out of their marriage, she

thought wretchedly. He was afraid of hurting or upsetting her and was determined not to do so when she was in a hospital bed, banged up from an accident. Or maybe he was planning to return sooner to Italy and was worried about how that would affect her adoption plans for Brodie and Shona. Could his attitude to her change so quickly? Enzo wasn't moody but he was volatile. He wasn't used to restrictions either, she acknowledged ruefully, and there were few living situations more restricted than that of a married man with young children. Well, whatever his decision, she would take it on the chin and stay strong.

The next day, when she was being discharged, Skye dressed with care in the clothes that she had specified by text that Enzo bring with him when he collected her. Only her hand emerged from behind the bathroom door to reach for the bag.

'You don't need to bother with make-up,' Enzo told her from his side of the door.

Oh, yes, I do. She had been horrified by the reflection that had met her in the mirror first thing. Her hair was a birds' nest and her face was puffy, her eyes pink. She looked awful and thought it would hardly be surprising if Enzo had looked at her the night before and wondered what he was doing with her. Dressed, with her hair tamed and a little cosmetic magic applied, she at least looked presentable.

'I just want to get you home,' Enzo told her, tucking her with care into a brand-new SUV. 'I think you should go straight to bed.'

'I'm already fed up with lying in bed. I'm not dizzy

or sick any more. Whatever you've got to say to me, just get it over with,' she urged tightly.

'Not in the car,' Enzo said stubbornly, lean brown hands flexing round the steering wheel. 'But I should mention that your ex may be behind the arson at the factory. Apparently, there's evidence that his car was parked nearby in the middle of the night. The police suspect that he has an axe to grind with me.'

'Oh, my word.' Skye covered her shaken face with spread hands.

'It's not your responsibility. Don't let him overshadow our lives. Put your ordeal with him behind you and don't look back.'

That was easier said than done, Skye reflected unhappily. Ritchie would never even have known of Enzo's existence had she not moved into his house and started working for him. Of course, she felt guilty.

The house was unusually quiet. 'Where are the children?'

'Isabel took the kids to that indoor playpark in town.'

Equipped with a cup of coffee, Skye sat down in the sitting room. Enzo hovered restlessly by the door. For a moment she simply feasted her eyes on him, the lean, strong face with the classic features that had mesmerised her from their very first meeting. Sexual awareness lurched low in her body and she was embarrassed by her susceptibility. She couldn't ever look at Enzo without thinking of how it felt when he kissed her and touched her or without noticing how the energy in the room flared in his highwire presence.

'I'll keep it brief,' Enzo promised tautly. 'When I first

mentioned marriage to you, I attached a lot of absurd conditions to the agreement but everything's changed—at least for me, it has. I want to keep you.'

Her brow indented. 'As in…?'

'I want it to be a proper marriage. I want us to be permanent.'

Skye swallowed with difficulty. *Permanent?* Her lilac eyes flew wide in her heart-shaped face because she was stunned by that announcement. 'But—'

'Obviously I'm in love with you. *Crazy* in love with you,' Enzo breathed in a roughened undertone, spreading his hands wide in emphasis. 'Everyone else saw it but me. I didn't realise. I didn't get it. I didn't understand why I couldn't wait to get back here to you and the children every night. I honestly believed I wouldn't ever fall for anyone again and then it happened without me registering it.' He winced at that acknowledgement.

'*Crazy* in love with me?' Skye repeated with an arrested expression on her flushed face.

'Perhaps I'm not very attuned to what goes on in my head when it comes to the emotional stuff. At the beginning, I genuinely believed that I only wanted to help you, but the more time I spent with you, the more I wanted you, the more I liked you and the more reasons I found to keep us together.'

Skye nodded with a dreamy smile now starting to dispel the once tense line of her mouth. 'So, my engagement ring isn't only window dressing?'

'No. I wanted a ring on your finger, a ring that told everyone that you were mine, but I didn't want to admit that because it went against the rules I set at the start. We were supposed to be like friends with benefits, practical, unemotional, no attachment.'

'You picked the wrong girl. I'm seriously attached to you,' Skye admitted chokily, the turmoil of her roused emotions bringing tears to her eyes. 'I was so scared of getting hurt but I couldn't stop myself feeling more and more for you every day...and when we were in the Maldives, well...' Skye plucked at her dress and evaded his gaze. 'You made me feel *so* special—'

'Are you saying you love me too?'

Skye rose from her seat and closed both arms round him. 'I was scared of losing you. I thought maybe you were panicking and you'd taken on too much with us all and that you wanted out of our marriage again. And last night you said we had to have a serious talk about us! How much sleep do you think I got after that?' She struck his shoulder weakly with her fist in punishment for that sleepless night. 'Sometimes you don't think stuff through, Enzo. Of course I assumed it was something bad and that I was going to lose you.'

'Always such a pessimist. You couldn't lose me if you tried. I will always be here for you. I have never felt like this before, so committed to one person that sometimes it's a struggle to stand you being out of my sight,' he confessed ruefully. 'I don't ever want to let you go. When you got hurt yesterday, it felt like my world had come crashing down. I attempted to picture my life without you and I *couldn't.*'

'But I'm OK,' she reminded him firmly, hands straying inside his jacket to the warmth of his chest, lingering over the muscles indented there, revelling in the warmth. And now she finally felt as though she had a proper right to touch him, to make her own moves without fear of what she might be revealing. 'I love you so much and tonight, I'm going to show you—'

Lining his fingers with hers, Enzo walked her towards the stairs. 'I'm out of bounds until you get medical clearance.'

'You can forget that. The way I see it, I got medical clearance the moment I left the hospital and this is a very special day and, right now, we're alone in the house.'

'Skye, I love you, but—'

'No buts. I don't want to wait until tonight.' On the landing, she kissed him with all the passion she had often tried to tone down.

Enzo lifted her off her feet with a groan. 'This is why I love you. You're stubborn and fiery and you stand up to me, so I suppose I have to compromise.'

'Compromise will be *so* worth your while,' Skye told him sunnily.

A wicked grin slashed Enzo's wide sensual mouth as he settled her down on their bed. 'You're mine now,' he said thickly.

Skye yanked him down on the bed by the edge of his jacket. 'You're mine too.'

Enzo doffed his jacket with enthusiasm and embarked on his shirt buttons. Skye shimmied out of her stretchy dress and he tugged her into his possessive arms and held her tight. 'I've got you.'

Skye buried her head in his shoulder, loving the smell of his skin and his hair, feeling like the luckiest woman in the world. He shifted lithely against her, acquainting her with his arousal, and excitement kindled. His lips connected with hers and the slow burn began in her pelvis, making her strain into even closer connection. And for a long time, there was mostly silence broken only by occasional gasps and sighs and mutterings until they both lay replete in each other's arms.

'I'll love you as long as I live,' Enzo swore hoarsely.

'So you have to live for ever.' Skye felt ecstatically happy for the first time ever, awash with emotion and hazy wonderful dreams of the future.

'Possibly a baby in a year or two?'

'Oh, definitely. Haven't Brodie and Shona turned you off in the slightest?'

'No, they taught me that I love having a family. We may move to Italy once the adoptions are finalised, but it's not set in stone,' Enzo murmured lazily. 'We'll see how we both feel when the time comes.'

EPILOGUE

SIX YEARS LATER, Skye twirled in front of the mirror in their bedroom. She had teamed a flimsy flirty skirt and a corset-type top in pale purple with sheer stockings and very high heels. It was Enzo's thirty-third birthday weekend. The evening before they had partied half the night away in an exclusive Roman club with their friends. But tonight, they were having a dinner party solely for two and she had given their staff the night off.

Donning a robe to cover the outfit because she didn't want the children asking tricky questions, she went to check on them. They lived in Tuscany in the midst of beautiful rolling countryside only a couple of miles from Enzo's grandparents and all the facilities of the town. Their home was an architect-designed contemporary house that was extremely spacious and comfortable. As soon as the adoption was granted, they had moved to Italy. Skye had wanted Brodie to have the time to become acclimatised to a new home and a new language before he started school. It had worked a treat because the children had initially picked up Italian much more easily than Skye, although she had since caught up.

Enzo had moved the headquarters of the Durante

Group to Florence and now based himself there. That year when he had first become involved in running his vast inheritance had been a very busy one, incorporating loads of travel as Enzo acquainted himself with the different sections of the business. For a little while she had worried that he would turn into a workaholic, but her multiple pregnancy had immediately centred Enzo's interest on staying closer to home and spending time with the children they already had before the challenging birth of another three babies.

Luka and Gaetano looked at her with identical Enzo-style grins and abandoned their Lego fight to climb into bed without even being told. She tucked them in. They had madly curly black hair and Enzo's eyes and they were four years old. Next door their sister, Gianna, was already cuddled up with half her cuddly-toy collection in her princess bed. Gianna had green eyes like Alana and straight black hair she liked to wear in braids.

When Skye and Enzo had finally decided to try for a baby, they had assumed it would take a while for her to conceive. In fact, it had happened within weeks and they had both sunk deep into shock when they'd learned that Skye was carrying triplets. The pregnancy had been trying and the triplets had arrived early by C-section and now, with Brodie pushing nine and Shona seven years old, they had agreed that their family was complete.

Brodie was reading in bed. Brodie was always reading and quite the swot at school. 'I'm nearly finished, Mum,' he mumbled absently, barely looking at her.

Her little brother had asked her and Enzo if he could call them Mum and Dad after he started school. He understood that he was Skye's brother and he knew all about his late parents but, like many children, he didn't want to be different from his peers.

Resisting the urge to laugh at his uninterest, Skye went in to see Shona, who was a very pretty little girl but a complete tomboy, who modelled her wardrobe on her brothers. 'Is Dad home yet?' she asked sleepily.

'Not yet.'

Removing the robe and giving herself a last check in the mirror, Skye was heading downstairs when she heard Enzo's car and she smiled. Enzo strode through the door, complaining about roadworks and hold-ups while fending off Sparky's bouncy enthusiasm. Age had yet to slow Sparky down. 'Dinner awaits,' she told him.

As she served his favourite meal, which his grand-mother had taught her how to cook, she was thinking about how happy she was. They saw a lot of Eduardo and Sophie Martelli, who had become as much Skye's family as they were Enzo's. Her relationship with Enzo and her self-esteem had gone from strength to strength after Ritchie had been found guilty and imprisoned. Once the arson attack, his part in it and his photograph had appeared in the newspapers, a couple of women had come forward to identify him to the police for assault-ing them. But before those charges could even come to court, Ritchie had been killed in a prison riot.

Skye hadn't wished her ex-boyfriend dead, yet there was no denying that knowing he was no longer around gave her a certain sense of relief because she was con-vinced that while they were getting married in Italy, in an attempt to kill or seriously injure Enzo, Ritchie had cut the brake line on the SUV that had crashed. Regrettably, however, the police had been unable to find enough evidence to charge him with that crime.

'That's some outfit,' Enzo commented as their wine was poured, wondering what she was up to because Skye generally wore classic fashion and there was nothing conservative about what she was wearing. The provocative garments clung to her every delicate curve and showed off her shapely legs. He settled back to enjoy his meal, dark eyes lingering on her with appreciation. Skye always liked to keep him guessing.

'If only you knew,' Skye teased with a secretive smile.

'When do I get my surprise?'

'After dinner when we go upstairs.'

Anticipation infiltrated Enzo and he ate fast. He had never stopped being grateful for having met Skye and her siblings in his twenty-seventh year. She had turned his life around, smoothed his reconciliation with his grandparents and given him five fabulous children. He knew he had been rewarded five times over for stopping to help her that night on the road.

'Go lie on the bed. Get comfortable,' Skye instructed him tautly as she locked the bedroom door behind her.

He raised a brow, removed his jacket, tie and shoes and reclined back in relaxed mode against the carved headboard.

'If you laugh, I'll kill you,' she warned him anxiously before disappearing into her spacious dressing room. Music sounded, and it wasn't her usual style either. 'Pour Some Sugar on Me' by Def Leppard filled the room with a loud, raunchy rock beat.

And then Skye reappeared and began to dance, a little jerkily at first because she was visibly nervous. She needn't have worried because Enzo was transfixed from her first movement. It was the very last thing he had expected. In fact, he had been expecting her to produce another present from the dressing room. His jaw almost dropped when she tugged at her top and it detached from her body and went flying off. It was a specially made stripper outfit, he realised as the pouting curves he adored were bared, revealing glittery pink nipple pasties with tassels attached. He adored the surprise because Skye, being naturally shy about her body, had moved out of her comfort zone purely for *his* benefit.

As the music clicked off, Skye was in the act of crawling across the bed and he grinned at her, loving her so much in that moment for the anxious light in her eyes.

'Best present ever,' Enzo growled, lifting her up onto him, shamelessly acquainting her with the hard, urgent thrust of his arousal.

'Was it?'

'How did you learn to dance like that?'

'Videos online. Do you remember once asking me when I was going to rip my clothes off for your benefit?' she prompted eagerly.

'And you said *never*...' A heartbreaking smile curved his wide sensual mouth as he laced long fingers into her curls. 'I have never loved you more than at this moment and it was the sexiest show I ever saw because it was specifically choreographed for me.'

'I was scared you'd laugh,' she confided.

He kissed her with devastating passion until she was

breathless. 'Never felt less like laughing. Much more in the mood for ravishing, *piccolo mio.*'

Skye beamed down at him, her insecurities vanquished, and her confidence restored because the smouldering glow in his dark golden eyes convinced her. 'I'm still crazy about you, Enzo.'

Enzo swung her down beside him and groaned. 'I'm besotted and sometimes I can't believe you're mine. We *have* to make the most of tonight because Alana is arriving on Monday and I'll be lucky to get five minutes with you for the first few days. You'll be gossiping morning, noon and night.'

'Yes,' she agreed sunnily as questing fingers played with the edge of her thong panties, and she gave an encouraging wriggle.

Before very long there was no further conversation and she lay afterwards in the circle of his arms, replete with joy and fulfilment.

* * * * *

UNVEILED AS THE ITALIAN'S BRIDE

CATHY WILLIAMS

MILLS & BOON

CHAPTER ONE

'DANTE, MY BOY, it is time for you to marry once again. The time has come.'

Antonio D'Agostino's hands fluttered, his eyes dampened, his mouth wobbled and he reached for the linen napkin at the side of his plate, which he pressed over his eyes for a few fraught seconds.

Summoned from Milan to his uncle's palace near Venice, Dante watched this emotional spectacle with an element of wry scepticism. Antonio had been circling round this thorny subject for years, delicately sidestepping any outright conversations on the matter, content to lob arrows over a wall and hope one of them landed.

Now Dante sat back, pushed his plate to one side, adjusted his chair and stretched his long legs.

He was quite accustomed to his uncle's emotionalism. Antonio D'Agostino could weep for Italy at the drop of a hat. He had shed tears over everything from the plight of displaced people to the fate of stray dogs. He was the polar opposite of Dante's parents and Dante loved him for that.

Growing up, Dante's uncle had been the one who had opened his eyes to the fact that life could actually be fun. Born into Italian nobility, both his parents had been the epitome of duty. Their aristocratic ancestry had come with obligations They had never allowed themselves to forget that and neither had they ever let *him* forget it. It was drummed into his DNA, embedded from the day he'd been born, invisible chains around his ankles from the very day he'd been old enough to walk.

Until the day they'd died—being driven to the opera on a rain-drenched, foggy evening, taking his ex-wife, Luciana, with them in an accident that had changed the course of Dante's life for ever—they had never once, strayed from what had been expected of them.

Vast estates were there to be managed… They had mixed with the right people, who all lived in the right places and had the right amount of blue blood running through their veins.

Anything else would have been unacceptable.

And for Dante, their only child, they had done their very best to position him on the same road down which they had spent their lives travelling. They had failed to factor in an irreverent, fun-loving, globe-trotting uncle who would probably have spent his lifetime living it up on his substantial inheritance had it not been for Efisio's and Sofia's deaths.

At this point, he had become the majority shareholder, thanks to Dante having relinquished much of his stake in the company years previously to focus on his own substantial holdings. Antonio had fed considerable money into the family empire and, in return, Dante had the freedom to hold the reins of his own holdings without having to split the very little time he always seemed to have at his disposal.

'You know how I feel about…marriage,' Dante said warily, but there was an undercurrent of warning in his voice, a reminder that this was a subject not open to discussion. 'And, Antonio, tears aren't going to get me to have a rethink on this. Marriage? It's a place I have no intention of ever revisiting.'

CATHY WILLIAMS   9

Antonio sniffed and rang the bell for their food to be taken away.

Dinner had been served in the smaller of the dining rooms, which was still a stunning marvel of chandeliers, frescoes and ornate turquoise-and-gold wallpaper, only interrupted by four sprawling paintings of the Venetian canals.

Dante had no idea where this conversation was going but fondness for his uncle prevented him from summarily dismissing the conversation out of hand. He would politely hear him out and *then* dismiss the conversation out of hand.

'We should have a brandy.' Antonio got to his feet as soon as the dishes had been cleared away.

'I have work to do before I retire.'

Antonio waved aside the objection.

'How often do you make it to Venice, Dante, to visit your frail, old uncle? Once a year?'

'Once every six weeks,' Dante returned drily. 'And let's not forget summer, when I'm here every week for at least a couple of days at a time, sweltering in the heat and battling the crowds every time I get up the courage to venture into the city.'

'Work, work, work.' Antonio waved dismissively, 'You'd better take my arm, Dante. I'm not a young man any more.'

'You're hardly ancient at seventy-two...' But Dante obligingly supported the much shorter man as they made their way out of the dining room and towards one of the sitting rooms, favoured by his uncle because it overlooked the finest of the manicured gardens to the side of the palace.

Was it his imagination or had his uncle shed some weight? If so, it would do him no harm. If Antonio was fond of passing dark judgement on his nephew's life choices, then Dante was equally outspoken about his uncle's penchant for rich food, every morsel of which seemed to settle around his waist.

'I am not going to be distracted this time, Dante. I mean what I say. It is time for you to marry. It is time for you to put Luciana behind you. I realise you still love her but she has been gone now for over four years and Angelina needs a mother.'

Dante stiffened. He was outraged and taken aback in equal measure by his uncle's full-frontal invasion of his privacy. Diplomacy had been jettisoned and there was not a single syllable in Antonio's remark that he didn't find offensive.

He remained silent.

Emotionalism might be his uncle's familiar terrain but it very much was not his. A rigorously unemotional upbringing had left no room inside him for that. That said, he was guarded and still as they entered the grand sitting room.

The palace might have been compact, compared to other grand Italian estates but it was still enormous and furnished with a level of ornateness beloved by his flamboyant uncle. Here, two of the walls were a dramatic red, and a lifetime of travelling the world was there for all to appreciate in the form of anything and everything that had been collected along the way. A statuesque African marble tribal priestess held court on a Persian rug of finest silk, framed by two exquisite watercolours from the Far East. Dante was pretty sure this was a one off, as the interior of palaces went.

'So...' He opened the conversation as he moved to sit on one of the deep chairs. 'Can I ask what's brought about this sudden urgency for me to find a wife?'

His eyes were drawn to a pair of curling, hand-crafted wooden snakes crawling along the wall, a souvenir from a trip to Mexico a million years ago.

He turned his attention back to his uncle, who had sunk into the chair facing Dante and was now fumbling in his trouser pocket to whip out a crumpled piece of paper, which he thrust into Dante's hand. His eyes, once more, were welling up.

'What's brought this on? I'm giving up running all this, Dante.' He waved to encompass the room, the palace and beyond. 'The land, the estates, the properties: all of it. Even this place—too big for an old man like me. I know Efisio respected your desire to step back from active participation in the family business, but I have reached the end of the line, and I need you now. I ran away from my duties as a boy and returned to them when I had to, as a man, when Efisio died. I have enjoyed the journey in my old age, but no more.'

He cleared his throat. 'And read the letter. Go on. It's from my consultant in Venice. I'm dying, Dante, so *that's* why you need to marry. Someone by your side when you take over. How can I face my maker knowing that you're still drifting? That Angelina is without a mother? That you remain in the grip of the past? Not to mention the fact that you will have to be more present in the running of the family empire, and you know as well as I do that they are all traditionalists. I have had to listen daily to your various relatives ask me when you're going to settle down once again.'

'Forget about my conservative relatives! I can handle their curiosity. But what's all this nonsense about meeting your maker? Since when are you dying? What the hell are you talking about?'

But Dante's hand was trembling as he unfolded the official letter and read it, then read it again, his panic only steadying when he began to decipher the glimmers of optimism in the diagnosis.

'You never told me that you were worried about your prostate, Antonio,' he admonished grimly.

'You're a busy man. Why would I worry you?'

'I will telephone this consultant first thing in the morning.'

'You will do no such thing! I can handle this.'

'You're spinning tales of meeting your maker and you haven't even heard what the prognosis is.'

'I need treatment. You read it! They've done tests. They need to do more!'

'No one seems to be panicking.'

'I'm panicking! My life is over and I want to leave it safe in the knowledge that my favourite nephew—'

'Your only nephew'

'Is married. You have lots of fine words about never marrying again, but I love Angelina, and what lies ahead of her without the guiding hand of a mother? The child is young now, but time marches on. I've kept my thoughts on this to myself but this death sentence...' His eyes welled up.

'You need to stop talking about death sentences, Antonio. This is not the time for high drama. What are these various tests you've been having?' But Dante's mind was in a whirl as he was forced to confront a situation he had known was hibernating in the shadows. Antonio, reluctant though he was to admit it, had a point. He didn't see enough of his daughter and, whilst she had everything that only vast wealth could buy, he really had no idea how to plait hair, pick out matching pink outfits or answer questions about nail polish. She was sweet-natured, gentle and undemanding, none of which made his guilt any less burdensome.

Antonio was scared, and fear had propelled him into voicing deep concerns to which he had previously only alluded, and those concerns were not entirely baseless. The bottom line was that his uncle felt that he was now facing his own mortality, and whether he was right or wrong on that front was immaterial.

'I can hardly conjure up a suitable wife from thin air,' Dante mused, folding the letter and setting it down on the table between them.

'But you can think about it—think about settling down.

There are many lovely young women out there, if you would open your eyes. It would make a dying old fool so happy...'

Dante reached for the handkerchief and handed it to his uncle. A steady supply of them was always a must when visiting. He watched in silence as Antonio dabbed his eyes, visibly more relaxed now that his worrying news had been imparted.

'You need to stop playing the death card, Antonio. I've read the letter and, yes, it's not a bad thing to be concerned. But if you filter through the technical terms and make your way past the medical terminology, you can see that this is not a terminal situation being described.'

He would reassure his uncle, but he could detect real anxiety on Antonio's face, and Dante loved his uncle. He loved him in ways he had never loved his own remote and aloof father. Loved him for the way he'd occasionally swept in to rescue him from his boarding school routine, whipping him out for a weekend to see a football match or a play, where afterwards they'd hobnobbed with the actors backstage, because Antonio seemed to know them all. Life in his gilded cage had been joyless. His uncle had been the only one occasionally to open the bars of that cage and show him what was possible outside.

So Antonio was after him to get married. Well, was there anything he wouldn't do for Antonio? He would oblige.

Dante relaxed. The sickening panic that had gripped him began to fade and he began to think as he always did: rationally; coolly; unemotionally. All things were possible when you eliminated emotion from the equation. Life had taught him that from a very young age. Rely on cold logic and you never lost your way. Yes, his uncle had opened pages in which life was painted in many different hues, a life of freedom and adventure.

But, for Dante, those pictures were snapshots of a life

anchored in the more serious, unrelenting business of hard work and duty. He loved Antonio but he had never been persuaded into emulating him. Perhaps, he often mused, DNA trumped everything. So now…marriage? He knew just the woman to walk down the aisle with him.

He smiled a slow, leisurely, obliging smile and gave just the slightest of shrugs.

'You win.' He held up both hands in a gesture of surrender and Antonio's eyebrows shot up.

'You will think about settling down? For my sake?'

'I will.' Dante tilted his head to one side. 'But there's no such thing as a free lunch, old man. I get to engage with your consultant, no holds barred, from tomorrow and there will be no decision made, no appointment taken without me by your side. Agreed?'

Antonio leant back in the chair, closed his eyes and smiled.

'Agreed…'

Kate was not expecting Dante to return for at least another three days. He had gone to Venice to see his uncle and would then be flying to New York on business.

Could she manage?

It had been one of those polite questions not in search of an answer, because she was very much used to managing in his absence. Wasn't she? She had smiled back with equal politeness and told him that of course she could manage.

She had now been working for him for over two years and she would have staked her life that she knew his eight-year-old daughter, Angelina, a darn sight better than he knew her himself because he was so seldom around.

He swept in when work allowed him and spent some quality time with his daughter—which usually took the form of collecting her from her prestigious day school in

Milan and treating her to a mega-expensive meal out somewhere before depositing her back at home base, job done.

At least twice a month, he had a formal briefing with Kate for updates on Angelina's schooling. Kate had no idea how he formatted the school holidays, when she was released from duties, free to do as she wished. But, from everything her little charge had told her, he just swapped one nanny for another—Kate, who was there for most of the year, and her replacement, for when she disappeared for the very generous holidays she'd been given as part of her package.

Angelina adored him. She clung to those little moments together and held them close like treasures. The year before, he had attended her nativity play and she had been unspeakably excited for him to be in the audience.

Yet, from Kate's point of view, he was cold, distant and far too absent from his daughter's life.

He was also way more good-looking than he had any right to be, and so eye-wateringly rich and crazily sophisticated that he always managed to make her feel self-conscious and deeply uncomfortable.

But every single criticism of the man was overshadowed by the handsome amount she was paid at the end of the month. Not only were the perks of the job staggering but there was no way she could ever have earned what she had over the past two years anywhere else in the world.

And she needed the money.

Still…

It was a little after eight in the evening. Kate was curled up on the sofa in the sitting area—just part of her suite of rooms in his vast mansion on the outskirts of Milan—and she wasn't expecting him back. She picked up her mobile, stomach clenching as she heard his accented, deep drawl down the end of the line, politely asking her whether it was too late for him to have a word with her.

'I—where?' Kate was confused. 'I thought you were—um—in New York…'

'It's unlikely I would be asking you to meet me if I were in New York. I'm in the kitchen. I've just arrived back in Milan.'

'Right.'

'I take it that Angelina is asleep? No, no need to answer that. I'll find out how her day has been when I see you. Fifteen minutes? Will that work for you?'

'Of course.'

No time to change. Her day uniform was always reasonably formal, not because there had ever been any restrictions on what she wore but because she felt it was appropriate. Right now, cold as it was with Milan fully in the grip of winter, her uniform comprised woollen skirts, tights and sensible jumpers.

She glanced down at the faded jeans and the old rugby shirt given to her by her father ages ago—although where on earth he could possibly have got it was a mystery—and hurriedly tidied her hair, pausing as she passed the ornate, full-length mirror by the door.

Twenty-four years old, five-seven, slight in build, straight, shoulder-length brown hair, regular features… She wondered if this was why he always made her feel so self-conscious. He was so ridiculously good-looking and next to him she always managed to end up feeling as exotic as a sparrow.

When she'd first come to work for him, the house had felt bewilderingly large. After two years, she was familiar with its layout, though all the marble, columns and swirling staircases that separated the various wings never failed to impress her.

She hurried down to the kitchen but, when she reached the door, she paused and took a few deep breaths.

She was composed as she pushed open the door and padded into the kitchen, hovering indecisively for a few seconds, waiting for him to look at her. He was staring out of the window at a bleak November night and, when he finally turned, his dark eyes were opaque, his expression unreadable.

Kate did her utmost to control the rush of heat that engulfed her. Every time she saw him, it was as though she was seeing him for the first time, captivated all over again by his swarthy beauty. He was well over six feet, his hair midnight-black and cropped short, his aristocratic features sharply, exquisitely perfect, his body lean and muscled.

'I hope I didn't interfere with your evening.' Dante nodded to a bottle of red on the marble kitchen counter but his dark eyes didn't stray from her face. 'Join me in a drink?'

'No. Thank you.'

'You can sit, Kate, and there's no need to look quite so nervous. You're not about to be reprimanded for something you may have forgotten you've done. How is Angelina? How were the tests she took two days ago?'

'Great. She's had some excellent results in her maths and English and, in fact, she was asked to read her essay out loud for the class. Her Christmas play is the week after next and I wonder if you've perhaps decided whether you can come or not…?'

'I see no reason why not. I'll get my PA to clear my diary for the day, although naturally I can't promise anything.' He swirled his glass and stared down into the deep red liquid for a few seconds, then looked at her in silence.

This woman had worked for him for a little over two years and he knew next to nothing about her personal life. Not that he had ever had much interest in digging deep. She was highly competent, Angelina adored her and she kept herself to herself. What else could possibly be relevant?

He was well trained when it came to drawing very clear lines between himself and his employees but, even so, there had always been something resting in the shadows that drew his reluctant eyes to places they didn't belong. To the slender gracefulness of her figure, to the smooth calm of her features and to barely-there hints of undercurrents that belied that calm exterior.

'She'll be thrilled.' Kate smiled and met his gaze. 'She's always very excited when you attend school events.'

Dante wondered, just fleetingly, whether there was an implied criticism there and then decided that there wasn't.

'I expect you must be wondering why I've asked to have a chat with you.'

'Well,' Kate returned cautiously, 'Not at all. I work for you and—and—naturally you're going to want to find out how Angelina is, how her day's been...'

'I've just been to see my uncle.'

'How is he?' This time Kate's smile was genuine. She was very fond of Antonio. She and Angelina would often visit, sometimes at the beginning of the summer holidays before Kate returned to England, sometimes during Angelina's half terms. How on earth he could be related to Dante was a mystery because, as personalities went, they couldn't have been more different.

'Not well, I'm afraid to say.'

'My word, what's the matter with him?'

'To be blunt, he's been diagnosed with possible cancer. Nothing's confirmed but the signs bear thinking about.' Dante held up one hand as though to stop a possible interruption even though Kate's mouth had dropped open in speechless, horrified silence. 'I personally don't think that it's nearly as serious as he seems to believe, but he's fairly frantic with worry. I've spent the past day and a half with him, going to see his consultant so that I can get a clear picture of what exactly is going on.'

'And...?'

'More tests need to be done. Things aren't as clear cut as they might have assumed, given all the physical symptoms, but there were certainly no murmurings of doom.' Dante stared at the drink, took a sip and sighed. 'Unfortunately, things aren't quite as straightforward in other areas as could be expected.'

'What do you mean?'

'Antonio seems to think that this diagnosis places him at death's door, despite reassurances from myself and from his consultant. He's managed to convince himself that the Grim Reaper is lurking around the corner and he's now in the process of putting his affairs in order.'

'What does that mean?'

'It means, firstly, that he's going to give up overall running of the family estates. Frankly, much of the business of running the estates is already extensively handled by people I put in place when my parents died, and before Antonio assumed full control, but it's a big deal for him. He's going to leave the palace and is making noises about retiring to the countryside, even though there's absolutely no need for such a drastic change.'

'I guess the palace *is* very big for a man on his own.'

Dante frowned.

'What does size have to do with it?'

'He might feel a little lonely, I guess...'

'This place is not much smaller. I've never felt lonely in it.'

Kate shrugged and gazed down at her fingers linked on her lap.

What a world Dante D'Agostino inhabited. One in which

palaces, castles, vineyards and villas were all just part and parcel of an accepted lifestyle. Was it even possible for him to stop and consider that an old man might just find a palace something of a handful, even if all his needs *were* catered for?

She thought of some of the places she had lived in with her parents, forever travelling across the country, dipping into Europe now and again, jumping from mobile home to canal boat to the occasional caravan thrown in for good measure. One of the most permanent places had been a commune in Scotland, where they had lived for over two years, during which time Kate had thrived, caught up on her schooling and enjoyed the temporary bliss of having roots in one place.

Her hippy parents had never contemplated the horror of settling down in one place. She couldn't remember a time when she had lived in any place bigger than a handful of rooms and where getting on top of one another had been part of the deal. Home tutoring had joined forces with conventional education now and again, and she had just had to make the best of it in all the weird and wacky places they had stayed in.

And here she was with a guy who couldn't see why a palace to house one person might be a bit over the top.

'Why are you smiling?'

'Was I?' Kate blinked and looked at Dante and, for a few seconds, the breath caught in her throat because he was so close to her, close enough for her to fall into the dark depths of his eyes which made her feel oxygen-deprived.

'He's considering bee-keeping as his new hobby,' Dante imparted with a frustrated gesture. 'I have no idea where that came from. I believe he watched a documentary a few days ago… Look, the point is, he's having a re-evaluation of his way forward and that seems to involve several…what can I say…?'

He defaulted into Italian and, fluent though Kate now was, she couldn't quite keep up with whatever he was trying to say. Whatever it was, he wasn't comfortable with it, and she felt just the slightest twinge of unease.

He'd told her that there was nothing to worry about, that she wasn't going to be reprimanded, but what if this impromptu meeting was to sack her? Or perhaps just *let her go*, maybe with a sympathetic golden handshake?

Kate was suddenly clammy with panic. She depended on this income and the prospect of having it whipped away filled her with fear. Two and a half years ago, her father had had an accident on his damned motorbike. He was in his fifties and yet still fancied himself a young buck, with his fast bike which always seemed to take precedence over the rusting old car her mother preferred to use.

It had been horrific. He had lost a leg in the accident and, at that point, the travelling days had come to an abrupt end. Her father, always the most genial of guys, always ready for a joke, a sweet-natured bear who'd have done anything for anyone, had plunged headlong into a crippling depression.

The change to their lifestyle, the intense months of physio, and the loss of all those occasional earnings that had kept them afloat had all been too much.

As well the shame. Her dad had had to face the lack of time and thought he had put into their future, always living in the moment. With little to fall back on, he had been overwhelmed by a sense of failure, and it had been heartbreaking.

At the time, Kate had just started teaching at a primary school in Windsor. Her parents had rented themselves a mobile home by the coast and had been planning to stay in one spot for the duration of summer.

Her mother would sell the jewellery she made at Christmas fairs and her dad would find work at one of the local nurseries. He was a talented landscape gardener with an encyclopaedic knowledge of plants.

The accident had put paid to everything.

Her mother had been strong and supportive but there was no way a mobile home was going to be sufficient. For the first time in their lives, they had been forced to face the prospect of bidding a permanent farewell to their travelling days.

They had no money saved to speak of, no pension set aside for a rainy day and an indefinite wait for the sort of intense physio her dad needed—and never mind his mental health, which had been in a sorry state.

Her wonderful, free-living parents had needed more than just cups of tea and sympathy. They had needed hard cash. They had needed money for a house that could be adapted, for a dedicated physiotherapist, for someone to help get her dad's head back in the right place and to take the stress and strain off her mother's shoulders.

And then this job had been advertised. Kate had applied on a whim because it had hinted at a good package. She had got it and the package was stupendous.

What the heck would she do without it?

There were still all sorts of things eating up the money she sent over every single month. She had been able to put down a deposit on a tiny place in Lancashire for them but there was still a mortgage to be paid off. Physically, her father's recovery had been all they could have hoped for, but he was still prone to bouts of depression, so still saw his lovely therapist once a week.

Then there was the business of them earning money. They were still relatively young. She had set up a cottage industry for her mother to pursue her jewellery-making on a bigger scale, which was going well. The house had a fair amount of land and, at some expense, Kate had developed an acre of it into crops that her father could harvest for their own consumption and to sell locally. Everything took money and, amongst all of this expenditure, she herself still had to save money for her own place at some point.

She whitened as a future scenario unravelled in her head, taking a wrecking ball to dreams and expectations she now knew she had been stupid to bank on. How long had she reasonably expected this job to last—for ever? How could she not have factored in the obvious, which was that everyone was expendable, and no more so than a young teacher who had landed the plum post through sheer luck—or something. She had never quite worked that one out.

She tucked her hair behind her ears and realised that her hands were shaking.

'I know what this is about,' she said, clearing her throat, determined to deal with the elephant in the room before it stampeded all over her. Circumstances had made her strong. A peripatetic lifestyle had toughened her, forged an independence in her, because she had never had the luxury of the same faces, the same friends, around her growing up. Her father's accident and everything that had happened subsequently had only served to make her stronger.

But right now she felt weak.

'I very much doubt that,' Dante murmured truthfully.

'When somebody close to you falls ill, everything changes. Your uncle is ill and you—you've had a rethink about Angelina and her future.'

'I have? Hmm…maybe so, in a manner of speaking…'

Kate chewed her lip and tried hard to summon up all that strength and energy she had always been able to fall back on but those reserves were proving hard to locate.

'You no longer need my services.'

She looked away because she was terrified of seeing

confirmation of that blunt statement in his eyes. The silence stretched.

'Interesting deduction, but you're very wide of the mark with that one,' Dante drawled eventually.

'What do you mean?'

'Perhaps you should have something to drink before I say what I have called you here to say.'

He didn't wait for her to respond, instead moving to fetch another wine glass and then proceeding to pour her some of the red wine, before sitting back and looking at her with deadly seriousness.

Kate smiled weakly. He was being so polite, so controlled, yet he was still so forbidding.

She gulped down a mouthful of the red and welcomed the rush of alcohol to her head.

'Along with the sudden desire to move house and the new-found interest in bee-keeping, my uncle…' He hesitated and then said on an exasperated sigh, 'Has got it into his head that it is time for me to find myself a wife and settle down.'

'Oh. Well…'

'Surprised?'

'It's not something that he's ever mentioned to me,' Kate said in confusion. 'And I have no thoughts on that one way or another.'

The man might be sinfully good-looking, and with a pedigree that would have every eligible woman in the country pulling tickets to join a queue for the role of *wife,* but Kate had no idea, because his private life had always been private. In all her time working for Dante, she had never known him bring back any woman or introduce his daughter to anyone who was potential wife material.

That said, he was away an extraordinary amount, and probably had a wild and raunchy life somewhere else.

The thought of which brought hectic colour to Kate's cheeks and, when she slid a look at him from under her lashes, it was to find him staring at her with his head tilted to one side. He didn't have to utter a word to press all sorts of crazy buttons inside her.

'At any rate, he's got it into his head that he's on the way out, and he can't possible depart this mortal coil without seeing me settled with a suitable woman.'

'And is there…er…a suitable woman around?' Kate asked while she busily wondered where this was heading.

'In actual fact, there is,' Dante murmured.

'Oh.'

'This is why you're here and why we're having this conversation, as it happens. The truth of the matter is I care very deeply for my uncle, and my fear is that stress and worry will propel him to the early grave he's convinced awaits him when there is no reason why he shouldn't outlive us all, with suitable treatment.'

'I understand,' Kate returned with heartfelt honesty as she thought of her own father and the depression that had consumed him after his accident.

Dante looked at her narrowly for a few seconds. 'Do you?' He paused and shrugged. 'No matter. Personally, I am utterly uninterested in marriage. I've been married once and it's an institution I have since resolved never to venture near again.'

Kate nodded. He'd loved and lost. In his office, a dramatic painting of the flamboyant, haughty beauty hung behind his desk, a testament to an irreplaceable love.

'But you said…'

'I don't *want* to marry, Kate. I *intend* to. Those are two quite separate propositions. And do I have a suitable candidate in mind? Yes, I do. She is sitting in this kitchen with me. I've asked you here, Kate, for your hand in marriage.'

CHAPTER TWO

FOR A FEW SECONDS, a crazy, dizzying thought spun through Kate's head. She'd *actually* thought that the guy sitting opposite her had asked her to marry him!

Since she had clearly misheard, she pinned a frozen, polite smile to her face and looked at him quizzically.

What was there to say? She blinked like a rabbit caught in headlights and waited for clarification.

'You're not following, are you?' Dante said drily. 'I don't blame you.'

'I'm sorry. I really don't understand what's going on.'

'My uncle...'

'I get the bit about your uncle. The bit I *don't* get is the bit that came afterwards.'

'It's simple. Antonio is in a fragile place. He's desperate for me to marry. He has been for some time, but only now has the suggestion broken the surface and been voiced outright. I did what I could over the past couple of days to reassure him that this is not the terminal situation he fears, but...'

Dante raked his fingers through his hair and, in that instant, Kate saw something she had never seen before—she saw his humanity and a love for his uncle that had been called to account and held up to scrutiny.

Which brought her no closer to understanding what was

going on. She eyed the bottle and wondered whether another glass was called for or whether a steady head was what was needed.

'If marriage is what he wants, if it can help him navigate this temporary setback, then marriage is what I will give him.'

'But *me?* Signor D'Agostino...'

'Dante.'

Kate skirted around that informality. 'Why me?'

Her head had not stopped spinning. She realised that she was leaning forward, every muscle tense with strain, her whole body in a state of shock.

'It's simple.'

'Simple?' She wondered whether they were on the same planet. She'd always known that this was a man who lived in a different realm from her and most other people. He breathed the rarefied air of someone who led a life of extreme wealth and privilege, accustomed to servitude and obedience, but surely their worlds were not so badly aligned that he could actually think that asking a perfect stranger for her hand in marriage was *simple?*

'Like I said, I've already been married.' His face darkened and he glanced down before raising cool, midnight-dark eyes back to her face. 'I will not be going there again in any way that is meaningful. I do not want a woman who thinks that there will be love involved, or anything else for that matter. All doors to any relationship along those lines were shut a long time ago.'

'Anything else?' Kate asked faintly, her brows knitted as she tried to keep pace with what he was telling her.

'Think hard about that one,' Dante drawled wryly, 'And I'm sure you'll get my drift.'

He sat back and sipped his wine while Kate absorbed exactly what that remark meant.

A marriage without love or sex for the sake of his uncle... The colour drained away from her face and her mouth fell open.

'I want a woman I can communicate with,' he said with deadly seriousness. 'And one who is guaranteed to get along with my daughter. Angelina is as central to this as my uncle is. I also want someone who knows exactly how the ground lies and will not complicate matters by thinking that there will ever be anything more to the arrangement than what's on the table.'

'And you think *I* fit the bill?' Kate queried incredulously. 'What you're proposing... Look, I'm sorry, but you're going to have to find someone else to fill the role...'

'Because this doesn't tally with your romantic vision of what a marriage should look like?'

'That amongst a thousand other reasons!'

Dante allowed the silence to fill the space between them. This was the first time any conversation between them had strayed out of safe territory.

He had regular face-to-face meetings with her, was always pleased with what she had to say about Angelina and even more pleased with what Angelina had to say about her. She maintained an excellent balance between discipline and fun, probably because she was young and lively. She and Angelina did a great deal together and, whenever he took his daughter out to lunch or dinner, he was always treated to enthusiastic reports of picnics had, galleries visited, concerts attended or biscuits baked.

But, for the first time, she was no longer in her comfort zone and he was seeing aspects to her that had not previously been apparent. The convenient image was shifting and what was swimming into focus was something different. He was seeing a fiery independence that didn't quite tally with the 'eyes down', reserved woman who sometimes answered his questions so quietly that he had to strain to hear her. The woman who never entered his office for their briefings without a uniform of neatly ironed skirts or trousers, and blouses that were invariably buttoned to the neck.

Shuttered eyes briefly took in what she was wearing now, old, worn clothes that did wonders for her slender, boyish figure and a face that was oddly appealing as she stared at him with flushed cheeks and defiant, glittering hazel eyes. He'd seen her before—of course he had—but he was *seeing* her now and something stirred inside him, a dangerous sizzle that he stamped down with ruthless efficiency so that it barely registered on his consciousness.

'Two years,' he said abruptly.

'I beg your pardon?'

'Marriage for two years—after which you will be free to go your own way.'

'Absolutely not!' Kate sprang to her feet and glared at him, furious that in the midst of this bizarre conversation he remained as cool as a cucumber.

But then the man was so cold—so chillingly contained. His interactions with his daughter were so formal compared to her own relationship with her parents. She knew that he loved Angelina as much as Angelina adored him and had seen flashes of it now and again when he had smiled at something or quizzed her about something she might have said. Who knew? Perhaps during those lunches and dinners, when the pair of them went out, he was a different man but Kate doubted it.

'Sit back down. Please. This conversation is far from over.'

'It is for me,' Kate told him quietly but her legs were wobbly and she remained where she was, hovering.

'I have not got to the crux of this.'

Naturally, she thought, she was not interested in the crux of anything. His proposition was insane. Perhaps this was how Italian nobility behaved, with complete disregard for the sort of basic codes of behaviour that most normal people adhered to.

'I'm really not interested.' Yet she still dithered on the spot, held captive by the cool, calm assurance in his eyes.

'Marriage will come with…some eye-watering advantages.'

'Really? I'm doubting that very much.'

'Two years and you leave with a fortune big enough to keep you in whatever lifestyle you desire for the rest of your life.'

'I'm not interested in…feathering my nest,' Kate stumbled.

'Sure about that? Because you were the only candidate interviewed for this job who was honest enough to tell my panel the real reason you were interested in taking it.'

Kate felt slow, burning colour scorch her cheeks. She could remember that interview as clearly as if it had been yesterday. Three interviewers sitting opposite her, very charming and very encouraging, each equipped with questions about her proficiency, her qualifications, her expectations and her willingness to live abroad.

They had quizzed her on possible scenarios and asked her how she would handle certain situations. She had been told that there would be a bodyguard present in certain instances. Was she comfortable with that?

Kate had been unfazed. She'd had too much on her mind just then to be nervous and had already predicted that she wouldn't get the job anyway. Had she cared? Her father had been in hospital, facing the prospect of his life being turned on its head. Neither he nor her mother had put down sufficient roots. Money was going to be an issue. Problems coming from all directions had piled up in droves, and her head was far too cloudy with anxiety and unhappiness for her worries over a job interview to find a foothold.

Their final question, delivered with the same inscrutable politeness, had been why she wanted the job and Kate had taken a deep breath and answered truthfully.

'The money.'

All three had glanced at one another with barely concealed expressions of shock, at which point she had weakly tacked on something more conciliatory about the challenges of dealing with a charge on a one-to-one basis, where input would be all the more essential, and the desire to improve her stumbling Italian.

She had got the job.

'You wanted the money,' Dante reminded her and then he allowed her to stew in her own mortified silence for a couple of minutes.

'I suppose that was faithfully reported back to you by the people who interviewed me?'

'I had transcripts and recordings of every word said.'

'I see. Why did you choose to give me the job, in that case? Can I ask?'

'Because I appreciated your honesty. You were the only one to mention the amount the job was going to be paying, even though I'd wager that every single one of your competitors was thinking the same thing. I like to know where people stand. No room for misunderstandings.'

'But...'

'I also liked the way you dealt with certain test cases presented to you. Plus, you were young—young enough for Angelina not to see you as a teacher, waiting for her to return from school to pick up where she had left off with the learning.'

'Why didn't you conduct the interviews yourself?'

'Because…' Dante leant forward and smiled slowly. It was a smile that sent a spiral of something hot and unexpected curling through her. 'It's my experience that, for better or for worse, I can sometimes have an effect on people, and that would have been detrimental to the interviewing process in my opinion.'

Kate knew exactly where he was going with that remark. Of course he would know just the sort of effect he risked having on any prospective candidates. He was a guy who scrambled brains. She had seen the way people jumped at his command, the way cool, self-assured people stumbled into speech when he addressed them, the way nerves seemed to paralyse their ability to think on the spot. Had he wanted the people being interviewed to lose the power of speech every time he asked a question?

Which brought her right back to his proposition, and to the twist in the conversation, because he had done his due diligence and had found her Achilles' heel.

'I have no idea why you need the money,' he admitted with an exotic gesture that spoke volumes. 'I could have dug a bit deeper, but how you choose to spend what you earn is your business. I had sufficient information at my disposal to offer you the position, including naturally a comprehensive criminal background check.'

Kate didn't care about background checks; they were standard procedure. She was, however, aghast that he might have investigated her private life which, as far as she was concerned, was beyond the pale.

'That's just awful,' she told him bluntly and Dante frowned.

'What?'

'Everything. This! All of it. A marriage proposal like this—putting money on the table as though it buys everything and everyone. The way you casually mention that you could have pried into my private life without my knowledge!'

Dante flushed darkly.

All the fire and passion that had been conspicuously absent on the many occasions when they had had their debriefings was in evidence now. Her eyes flashed and there was vivid colour staining her cheeks. That electric spark that had sizzled burst into life again, turning his preconceived notions about her on their head. It was disturbing and he didn't like it. He frowned and dragged his thoughts to heel.

She was... *Was she criticising him?*

For the first time in his life, Dante found himself on the back foot with no response readily available.

'Like I said, I respected your privacy.'

'But now you've decided to use what I said at that interview against me.'

'Kate, what I am offering is not exactly water torture. As my wife, you'll have a life in which everything you could possibly need or want will be at your disposal. In addition to that, you'll walk away from it a young woman with the world at her feet, able to do anything you want, no expense spared.

'Of course, a pre-nup will be necessary to avoid the possibility of greed trumping common sense but, that notwithstanding, you'll find me an exceptionally generous man. If you've been saving to buy your own house, pay off debts—hell, if you want to treat yourself to a yacht or a lifetime of holidays on exotic islands—then you'll be able to afford to do so! In return, I ask for two years of your life, during which we will share space as friends. This may not be the sort of marriage you dreamt of but you'll have nothing but my greatest respect for its duration.'

* * *

Kate opened her mouth to object, then she thought of her parents. When she had sat them down and laid bare the groundwork for the life they would lead, the one she would do her best to subsidise, her father had cried. She had never seen him cry before and it had stuck in her head, a permanent reminder of what they had gone and were still going through, and the hardships, tough times and pitfalls that still lay along the way.

Their place was tiny and cramped with belongings they had accumulated in their many travels, none of which they had been willing to dispose of. The therapist steadily continued to eat away at her salary and the farming her dad had insisted on—because he couldn't envisage himself ever doing anything that wasn't to do with the land—ate money and gave very little back in return. He had to have someone to help with the heavy stuff, and the equipment was astonishing, considering the small acreage being cultivated.

But would he stop? Absolutely not. He'd given up his beloved travelling, with each day an adventure, and there was no way he was going to suffocate doing something in front of a computer indoors. He needed to be outside, to feel the air on his face and breathe in nature.

Nature and fresh air didn't come cheap, especially when he was still in the floundering stages of small-time farming. But there was no way she would do anything to deter him because his mental health was the most important thing in the world to her.

As Dante's uncle's was to him—not to mention Angelina. As he had said, her well-being would be integral to the peculiar arrangement he was suggesting. The two people in the world he cared for the most were the beating heart of this deal...

'And what happens after two years?' she heard herself ask. 'Even though,' she hastened to add, 'It's all academic.'

'We part company.'

'And your uncle will be upset all over again,' she said quietly. 'Not to mention Angelina.'

'My uncle will be in a better place, and he will finally accept that marriage and I...no longer see eye to eye.' He smiled grimly. 'And Angelina will be nearly eleven. She will be maturing and will be able to handle the eventual break-up. And, of course, you will doubtless have a bond with her and so might wish to continue to communicate and visit...provide continuity. I would never prevent you from doing that. In truth, would it be so very different from what happens in very many families when a marriage breaks down?'

He leant towards her and she could breathe him in, a woody, clean smell that filled her nostrils and made her feel a little heady. 'Will you think about it at the very least?'

'And if I say no? What happens next? Do you cast me out?'

Dante's eyebrows shot up and he burst out laughing.

'Cast you out?' He was still amused when he finally looked at her. 'That's very melodramatic, isn't it? Where do you imagine I would cast you—into the dark wilderness? On the first ship back to England with just a crust of dry bread for the journey? To the local train station with no time for you to pack your bags?'

'Very funny,' Kate muttered *sotto voce* but, when she looked at him, something inside her did a little inexplicable flip because he suddenly looked *young*, temporarily shorn of the cold self-assurance that made him so intimidating.

'Of course I won't cast you out,' he said with wry amusement. 'I have proposed something to you, something no more or less than a business deal of sorts. I did it because I care deeply about my uncle and want to make him happy. Antonio is a good man—the best. He deserves it. But…'

He shrugged and looked at her levelly. 'If it's too much for you to consider, then so be it. Naturally your job here will not be affected in any way, shape or form and this matter will never be discussed again.'

'And you'll, I guess, find someone else suitable for the—er—role?'

'No.'

'No?'

'You are really the only one who fits the bill.' He looked at her pensively. 'I would never risk any woman getting the wrong message and that would be something very easy to do. I would also never risk anyone my daughter might not get along with, and she gets along with you. The stories she tells me… Her face lights up when she talks about you. No, you are the only one who would do—for this.'

He stood up, stretched and then rubbed the back of his neck. 'My apologies for interrupting your evening…'

'Signor D'Agostino… Dante…um, I'll think about it, about your proposal.' Their eyes collided but Kate didn't look away. 'I'm very fond of your uncle.' She smiled awkwardly. 'And the money would come in very handy. I'm just being honest.'

'I like that. As I mentioned, this would be a business proposition. We would have separate quarters, naturally, but should you accept the details would be hammered out between us and all the necessary legalities would be arranged. I have a team of extremely discreet lawyers.'

'*If* I accept…'

Dante smiled and Kate did her best to hold on to her composure because she could read triumph in that smile.

But it was a tempting proposition.

If it weren't for her dad, for the financial commitments

that made it so hard for her to put aside any money for her own future, then she would never be here now, considering his outrageous proposition.

But…

The thought of giving them the sort of lifestyle that might go some way to compensating for what they had lost—maybe even a little caravan so that they could sate some of the wanderlust that would never really desert them… The thought of the freedom to do this without the cold anxiety of how far any money she earned could ever go…

Temptation dangled in front of her like a banquet spread wide to tempt a starving beggar. Surely two years wasn't an eternity to put aside when the rewards were so tempting?

She would still be young, but she would be settled, with her parents' and her futures secure. And it wasn't as though he was asking her to do anything but share space under his roof. As he'd been keen to point out, they would have their separate quarters. She wondered if that was common anyway in his world, where the rules most people obeyed didn't seem to exist.

'I'll think about it.' She glanced away but, had he looked into her eyes, he surely would have seen capitulation.

She said yes.

Dante looked at her over the continental breakfast laid out on the table between them the following morning. With Angelina dropped off to school and all calls on hold for the next couple of hours, allowing him to discuss the details of their marriage, he seemed quietly satisfied.

'I'll arrange a meeting with my lawyers as quickly as possible,' he said in response. 'But first we have to go over the bare bones of this arrangement—make sure we're on the same page.' He nodded at the spread of breads and jams in front of them. 'And eat something, Kate. You're allowed.'

Oddly, and despite the fact that she had been working for him for over two years, this was the first time Kate had sat down and shared a meal with him without the presence of his daughter or other people around.

Kate's eyes skittered away from his but she was still very much aware of him in her peripheral vision as she reached for a croissant. He was dressed in black jeans and a heavy cream shirt rolled to the elbows with the top two buttons undone, revealing a sprinkling of dark hair. When she looked at him, she was struck by the notion that she had agreed to marry this man, a guy who sent her nervous system into freefall and with whom she had nothing in common.

'This feels strange,' she confessed.

'That's because it *is* strange. That said, I very much appreciate you agreeing to my proposal. I must ask you whether you are absolutely sure that you want to go ahead with this because, once the announcement is put out there, retracting it would be...somewhat awkward.'

'Two years isn't a long time in the grand scheme of things.'

'Especially given the financial incentive,' Dante murmured. For the first time, he found that he was intensely curious about why the money mattered so much to her. Was she saving for a fancy house in a fancy neighbourhood? Paying off a student loan and whatever debts she might have accumulated when she had been studying? Investing in gold bars—because who could ever go wrong with that?

Certainly, there was no significant other on the scene. That had been mentioned in passing only a couple of months ago, when he had had to ask her to work for three weeks over the summer holidays which she'd been due to have off to return to England.

'Of course, please tell me whether you have commit-

ments of a personal nature, in which case I can try and arrange a fill-in from the agency until Sara is well enough
to return after her operation.' He hadn't bothered to beat
about the bush.

Sara, the middle-aged woman who covered the holiday
period with Angelina, had been rushed to hospital with
appendicitis.

'Personal nature?'

'A boyfriend, perhaps?'

He had shrugged away the potential intrusiveness of the
question but his dark eyes had been watchful.

'I—no… I'm a free agent, as it happens…'

At the time, Kate had struggled not to laugh—boyfriend?
She had spent most of her life living in and out of suitcases
with her parents. Certainly, during her teenage years, when
most girls her age had been navigating their way through
the complex world of boys and first relationships, she had
been busy making sure she kept abreast with schoolwork.
With her in and out of various schools, there had simply
never been the opportunity to build any kind of relationship with any boy. Then, just when she had found stability,
settling into her career, the unexpected had happened with
her father's accident to sweep her back off her feet. Boys
were a luxury she had just never got round to sampling.

'We'll have to work out a timetable to break the news,
but I suggest telling Antonio first and then waiting for him
to digest it.'

'He's going to be a little surprised.'

'As understatements go, you could very well be right.'

'Is he actually going to believe that we're a couple?'

'People are always keen to believe what they want to
believe. At any rate, looked at logically, it would make a
lot more sense than were I to produce a brand-new fiancée

from nowhere, like a magician pulling a rabbit from a hat. But the truth is, my uncle knows you and likes you, and I doubt he's going to question our arrangement when he's made such a fuss of marrying me off.'

He flushed and then confessed, with just a trace of discomfort, 'I'm not sure he would be thrilled and impressed were I to show up with one of the women I usually date dangling on my arm with a diamond on her finger, anyway... He's met two of my past girlfriends and has been noisy in his disapproval.'

Kate's lips twitched. 'Noisy in his disapproval?'

'You'd be surprised,' Dante said drily, 'How much can be conveyed through a series of snorts, eye rolling, sighing heavily and head shaking.'

Kate threw her head back and laughed, a proper belly laugh that surprised her, because since when had Dante D'Agostino been the sort who encouraged hoots of laughter?

'What sort of women have you dated in the past?' The directness of the question surprised her as much as her laughter just had, and she saw him hesitate. But, more daringly, she added, 'If we're supposed to be a couple, then surely we'll need to know a few things about one another?' She blushed and ducked her gaze, dipping her finger into some of the crumbs on her plate and licking them off without looking at him. 'I only ask because I can't remember you ever...'

'I never have. I've always refused to allow Angelina to be witness to my love life. I...may not see my daughter as much as I know I should, but every decision taken has her at the very centre of it.'

Kate nodded approvingly and he continued in the voice of someone making a decision, but a decision that might not have come easily,

'Unchallenging,' he said. 'My girlfriends—fun, unchallenging...beautiful.'

Kate smiled and nodded, and wished she hadn't asked the question, because of course those were the sort of women this man would be attracted to. His wife had been shockingly beautiful and it was unlikely he would have strayed far from that benchmark.

'I'm guessing my uncle will have the champagne on tap when I break the news to him that you're going to be my wife,' Dante murmured with wry amusement.

'I expect he will.' Her smile felt stiff and painful. If his uncle had snorted with horror at a parade of sexy, unchallenging beauties, then of course he would approve of the dowdy nanny who looked after his beloved great-niece.

'But, before we say a word, I think it might be appropriate that he perhaps sees you in a slightly different light. He might have his own doubts about the speed with which I've suddenly become attached to you, but he can be persuaded into believing that I've simply woken up to the potential of someone who isn't quite what he thinks. He may very well like to imagine that what might have been an already existing loose relationship between us has crystallised into something more, thanks to his prompting.'

'What do you mean?'

'My uncle lives some distance away from my place in Milan,' Dante mused thoughtfully. 'It's fair to say that that lends itself to a romance happening behind the scenes, one of which he would be ignorant. That said...'

He looked at her carefully, handsome head tilted to one side, his stare unwavering until she had to control the urge to squirm.

'That said...?' she prompted, to move the conversation along.

He flushed and for the first time looked truly uncomfortable.

'Look, I wouldn't want you to take this the wrong way...'

'Take what the wrong way?' Kate asked, instantly suspicious.

'Eh, in keeping with your new role, it might be prudent... How do I put this...?'

'What? If you have something to say, then might I suggest that you just say it?'

She narrowed her eyes, pursed her lips and was undeterred when he said, 'Is this the stern-teacher face you pull out of the box when my back is turned?'

She folded her arms and waited and, grudgingly, he murmured, 'The small matter of your wardrobe.'

'What about my wardrobe?'

The lingering silence spoke volumes. He was allowing her to join the dots, and join the dots she did.

Her choice of clothing just wasn't going to cut it. Kate gritted her teeth together and did her best not to take it as a personal insult. She told herself that it was no more insulting than applying for any job that required a specific uniform. She had accepted an unusual job and she would be required to have a specific uniform.

'I see...'

'You find my remark offensive.'

'No, of course not. Why should I?'

'You want to say something. Say it. We're on a different footing now.' He relaxed back and stretched out his long legs to one side, crossing them at the ankles. His expression was cool and questioning, and that made her bristle. He was so composed, so assured, so controlled and basically so unperturbed by something that might not have been meant as a barb but had wounded like one.

If they were to embark on this different footing, then

maybe it would be a good time to lay down her own ground rules or else risk getting lost without a voice, agreeing to every condition laid down whether she wanted to or not.

'Fine. I get it,' she said curtly. 'If I am to play a convincing part, then it's important that I play the part well. And, sure, if I show up on your arm and I'm no longer the dowdy nanny he's accustomed to, he might get it into his head that perhaps the whole "overnight marriage" thing isn't quite as preposterous as it seems… But please don't think that you can give orders and expect instant obedience, *Dante*. How would you feel if *I* asked *you* to change elements of *your* wardrobe?'

'What elements?'

'Your…your shirts,' she said, waving vaguely at him and scowling. 'Maybe I don't really like shirts with monograms on the pockets. Maybe I find them stuffy.'

'Do you?'

'Possibly.' She was suddenly horrified at this change of role and disoriented by the speed with which everything was suddenly happening.

'What else?'

'I don't have a list at my disposal. I just want…' She sighed, 'I just want…'

'You won't be.'

'You don't know what I'm going to say.'

'You don't want to think that you're jumping into a fast-flowing current with no control over any riptides underneath that might drag you away.'

'How did you know?'

'My apologies for offending you by suggesting a rethink on your wardrobe. If you really want to stick with what you have, then of course I'm not going to force you into a shopping spree. But, aside from the business of enticing my uncle into believing our piece of fiction, there will be functions and galas you'll be required to attend...'

He grimaced and smiled. 'As few as humanly possible, if I have anything to do with it, but that aside there will undoubtedly be numerous occasions that call for...dressier outfits than you probably have. You might find that it's just a lot more comfortable if you choose to blend in by wearing them.

'And then my uncle... He might be a little sceptical, if I'm to be completely honest. It would certainly mark a seismic change for me to be suddenly seriously involved with a woman who can't relax in my company and shows up dressed for a day at the office when we go out together.' He grinned. 'And if, in return, you want me to put my monogrammed shirts into storage for the duration of our marriage, then consider it done.'

'I don't care about the shirts,' she said truthfully. 'Like you said, what I do care about is an arrangement where I feel I've relinquished control.'

'Trust me.' He leaned forward and his dark eyes were urgent and serious. 'This is a pact, and we each hold one half of the steering wheel. We'll adjust to move around one another in harmony. I would never ask you to do anything you wouldn't want to do. Of course, should you wish to have an...arrangement...with someone, then discretion would be imperative...'

Dante lowered his eyes and his thoughts flew with unerring speed to a scenario that made his senses stir. This woman, naked on a bed, her clothes discarded, wearing only a small, slow half-smile, beckoning with the promise of sexual gratification. He felt sudden heat pour through him and gritted his teeth in exasperation.

'When I have an arrangement with someone—by which

I guess you mean find a guy—then I won't be in a different kind of arrangement with someone else. When I choose
to have a relationship with someone, then I will do so as a
free person so I can have a meaningful relationship that's
actually going somewhere. Two years isn't exactly a lifetime to wait.'

'Have you ever had one of those meaningful relationships as a free person before?' Dante asked with genuine
curiosity, and Kate blushed and stammered.

'I'm still young. I've…been busy forging a career and of
course, being over here, working…'

'You know there were never restrictions imposed on how
you spent your free time here,' he returned quietly with
some consternation, and she smiled shyly.

'I know.' She wondered what he would have made of her
life lived on the move. Of her parents, happy to globe-trot
with her in tow. In many ways, he'd been right when he
said that she would be good in this role, because they were
so very different that there would never be any chance of
either of them being confused into thinking that what they
had might be more than it was.

Two people from different planets could never forge
bonds that were anything but superficial. She relaxed and
smiled with real warmth. They *would* move round one another in harmony, and it was fantastic of him to suggest that
she keep in touch with Angelina when it was all over—as
she would with Antonio, no doubt.

And, in the meantime, a frightened old man would feel
calm and content and able to deal with what the immediate future might have in store for him.

This would work, and the thought of not having to shoulder a future of potential financial problems, of her parents
being happy and her father's mental health getting back to

where it once used to be, filled her with sudden, soaring euphoria.

'I'm happy to have the Cinderella makeover,' she said with a tentative smile. 'Now that the pumpkin is going to become a carriage, and the dress code for a carriage is completely different...'

'Good! As long as you realise that I'll never be your Prince Charming...'

Kate's smile widened and she laughed.

'I think it's safe to say that you could never be my Prince Charming and, while I'm married to you, I won't be looking for one either. As for you...' She shrugged and, for a few heart-stopping seconds, their eyes met and held and the breath left her in a sudden, inexplicable whoosh.

But when she blinked that unsettling feeling was gone and her voice was amused and neutral. 'You're free to do as you please, and I know you'll be discreet.'

'Well.' He raised his cup of coffee to her. 'Here's to the perfect arrangement. Tomorrow, we can take step one...'

CHAPTER THREE

STEP ONE, in actual fact, came several days later when Dante informed her that they would be going to meet Antonio, staying there a couple of days.

In that time, life had moved at warp speed. Documents had been signed. Kate's hand had hovered over the final page, and she had reminded herself that this was simply a two-year contract during which she would still have duties, but of a different kind.

Although, in actual fact, her time with Angelina would remain the same. She had insisted on that. She might assume the mantle of wife, but she had no intention of assuming a change of lifestyle to the extent that she packed in the thing she loved doing and replaced it with the sort of thing she imagined wives and partners of very rich men did: shopped; lunched; spent crazy amounts of time having bits of their bodies tinkered with…

When she had explained that to Dante, he had burst out laughing and told her that she could do as she liked. Indeed, he'd said, he liked the idea that there would be continuity with his daughter, that she wouldn't have to endure the inconvenience of having a replacement nanny foisted onto her.

Kate had taken that to mean the less disruption to his daily routine, the better. She would also have ample time off to go and see her parents. That had been something else upon which she had insisted without going into any details about why it was so important to her.

'As you wish.' Dante had shrugged and she'd gathered that, when it came to the lives of rich, powerful, Italian nobility, evenings of bonding around the telly and walks together at the weekend throwing sticks for the dogs weren't things that were particularly valued. Or maybe they weren't of value *to him*. He had not batted an eyelid at the prospect of her being away from a couple of weeks at a time. She expected his ex-wife was the one he had cherished and, when she had died, so had the importance of the family values she had always taken as a given.

Things were in place. And so was her new, improved wardrobe. She had been handed several credit cards and instructed to spend as much as she wanted, wherever she wanted.

'I could accompany you,' he had said, glancing up from his computer as she had stood in front of the massive desk in the suite of rooms he occasionally used as his offices, when he wanted uninterrupted time to work. 'If you feel you may need input.'

Horrified by the thought of having Dante traipse from boutique to boutique with her, giving his verdict on the clothes she would be wearing, she'd shaken her head vigorously and told him that she was perfectly capable of doing a little clothes shopping on her own. It wasn't rocket science. She would take Angelina with her, which had made him smile—a smile that knocked years off him.

There would be a shared diary of events, updated by email daily so that she would know what was planned from one week to the next.

'Although,' he had told her, 'Most of my time will be spent working. If there are any invitations you feel a particular interest in attending, then naturally I'd be more than happy to oblige. But, like I said, I try and avoid those meet-and-greet social affairs.'

'Why?' Kate had asked and the look he'd thrown her had been part-surprise, part-disapproval.

Had she breached a boundary line? She was getting the feeling that he had a great deal of those in place, but he had said noncommittally, 'I usually can't quite see the point of them. I'm generous in my charity donations, so fundraising galas are an unnecessary indulgence, and if I want to mix with the elite, I can do so in my own time and at my own convenience.'

End of conversation.

Angelina had no idea that anything was remiss although, as Kate now paused to glance at her reflection in the floor-to-ceiling mirror in her sitting room, she could see the eight-year-old gazing at her with some surprise. They had had their shopping expedition, with Kate tactfully avoiding most of her little charge's outlandish suggestions of fur and sequins. Afterwards, Dante had unexpectedly surprised them both by taking his daughter off for some tea, a gesture which had been greeted with breathless excitement and yelps of pleasure.

But had she extrapolated anything from that shopping trip? Judging from the surprised expression on her face now, Kate wryly thought maybe not.

The casual, non-working uniform of jeans and a jumper had been replaced by pale-grey cashmere culottes, a grey cashmere jumper and some flat, black ankle boots. The outfit had cost the earth. The soft black coat which would accompany the outfit had also been eye-wateringly expensive. Her initial hesitation about buying stuff she would never have dreamt of buying, because frugality was part and parcel of her DNA, had been firmly squashed by reminding herself that *this was a job.*

Dante was as remote as he had been before, and would

remain that way. It would be up to her to play the game as coolly as he did. He would be irritated if she made a big deal every time she bought anything new, because money was no object to him and so henceforth should be no object to her. Indeed, she suspected that her off-the-peg clothes and second-hand vintage stuff she found in charity shops would have filled him with quiet horror and embarrassment, had she paraded them in front of his exclusive friends and family.

'We're going to see stay with your Uncle Antonio for a few days.'

'Is that some of the stuff we bought?'

'Er...yes.'

'You look pretty.'

'Thank you.' She caught Angelina's gaze in the mirror and smiled. 'Not too much grey?'

'I have that nice yellow and red scarf you could borrow.'

'If it's the one I'm thinking of, with the sequins and the sparkles and the ponies, then I'll say no.' She grinned. 'Much more suited to you than to me, I think.' She hesitated, then said in a rush, 'And your dad is going to be there as well.'

'Is he?'

Angelina, who had been sprawled on one of the chairs playing games on her tablet, sat up, alert and bristling with excitement.

'You never said! Naughty!'

'He only confirmed the timings last night. Are you pleased?'

'How long is he going to be there?'

'I'm not sure, darling. Hopefully, the whole time...' She felt the familiar tug on her heartstrings at Angelina's breathless, childish thrill at the thought of having her dad around for several days on end. He was so busy—he lived life in the fast lane, with time spent with his daughter precious and erratic, although in fairness, when he *was* with her, he was one hundred percent *with* her.

She watched as Angelina leapt off the chair and danced around the room for a couple of minutes.

She was a beautiful child with very, very long dark hair, soulful dark eyes and her father's smooth, olive complexion. Serious most of the time, when she laughed her face lit up, and she was laughing now. In that moment, a streak of rebelliousness shot through Kate like an injection of adrenaline.

It would be easy to fall into a routine of fading into the background, but she had made a start laying down her own rules, and she wasn't going to allow him to nod and agree and then proceed to do exactly as he wanted.

He was that kind of guy, from everything she had seen over time. He lived a charmed life surrounded by people who did as he told them to. She had never met his parents, but hanging in one of the many formal living areas was an imposing oil painting of them together and they looked formidable, as formidable as their only son.

In this mutually beneficial arrangement, however, he was no more in charge of her than she was of him and gut instinct told her that it was important to remember that.

His chauffeur would drive them from Milan to the outskirts of Venice, where Dante was already with his uncle. The next few hours were spent packing and then travelling in the luxury of Dante's car, one of his fleet of cars, and the least sporty but the most comfortable.

It was a shame they couldn't detour to see Lake Como or explore Verona, with its Roman amphitheatre. Kate had only ever read about Verona when she had had her head buried in Shakespeare's *Romeo and Juliet* and had been intrigued by the romance of a city she'd never previously heard of.

It was cold and dark, and the shadowy landscape that flashed by as the car ate up the miles only hinted at the splendid beauty of hills, valleys and the sprawling vineyards that produced the Prosecco for which the region was so famed.

Kate gazed out, her mind half on the retreating dark shapes of hills and mountains standing guard around the swirling dunes of the perfectly aligned vineyards. In summer the sight would be magnificent, a sea of green interrupted by glorious clutches of houses and churches, each small town worth seeing in its own right.

Nerves were kicking in. Next to her, Angelina was slumped, asleep. As plans went, this one made sense, and the end result would be worth every second. But, as Antonio's mansion drew closer, she wondered how easy it would be to coexist with Dante who was so cold, so intimidating, with those flashes of warmth and humanity so few and far between.

It was one thing laying down laws. It was another having the will power to follow through.

She had mentioned nothing to her parents and was toying with the idea of keeping it all under wraps. Her parents would be appalled and disappointed at anything that smacked of an arranged marriage. They had never spent a day apart, except for when her father had been in hospital. So what would be the point in breaking their hearts? She would be able to return to see them, perhaps not for entire weeks at a time, but certainly frequently. She could easily talk about loans, bonuses and her employer's generosity when it came to justifying the sums of money she would be spending on them.

Honestly, they were both naïve when it came to anything financial. Why else had they ended up as they had? The small deception would be simple enough to achieve. Only the discomfort of knowing that she was lying to them, or at the very least being incredibly economical with the truth, gave her pause for thought.

It was after eight by the time they finally made it to Antonio's palace, a frothy, wintry, extravagant concoction nestled in huge grounds and woodland. Half of it was lit like a Christmas tree, the other half in darkness. Antonio only used part of his grand house.

The car slowed as they eased up the tree-lined avenue and circled the courtyard before slowing to a stop. Before they could all emerge, the front door was open and Antonio was briefly silhouetted, before being quickly ushered inside by Dante, who towered over his uncle. Kate tensed, roused Angelina and was thankful for the distraction of her excitable chattering as they hurried inside and the front door closed against the bracing wintry weather outside.

And then the gravity of the road she was about to go down hit her. Antonio stooped to embrace Angelina; Dante looked at her with those dark, deep, cool eyes as he reached down to swing his daughter up into a bear hug. The overwhelming grandeur of the palace, with its pale marble floors and intricately sculpted ceilings, spoke to a life lived in a different world.

She wasn't just going to be playing a part for a limited period of time. She was going to be entering the world of one of Italy's most exalted families, moving amongst people she would otherwise never have met in a million years, and she was going to have to do it with credibility.

How on earth was that going to work out?

Apprehension and excitement hit her in equal measure. As she stepped towards Dante, she felt a momentary keening towards him as the one solid point in a world that had suddenly been turned on its head and, as though reading her mind, he steadied her, placing his arm around her shoulders.

'Are you all right?' he murmured, voice low as Antonio, still stooping, engaged with a suddenly lively Angelina.

'It's been a long day...'

'Of course.' He drew back and began ushering them towards the kitchen, while giving orders for the bags to be taken up to their respective quarters.

She looked amazing. How had he failed to pay attention to the clear-eyed beauty shyly hiding behind her dutiful subservience? There was nothing obvious about her but, dressed in that casually elegant outfit, she was somehow so intensely alluring that he was shocked at his own reaction. He didn't want to be sabotaged by his body, and had no intention of allowing that to happen, but he was still disconcerted enough to remove himself and put some distance between them.

'I should take Angelina up,' Kate offered. 'Is it the usual room?'

But she hesitated when Angelina stopped, folded her arms and demanded her dad do the bedtime routine. His being around for a bedtime ritual was rare, and it was only when she glanced across to see Antonio looking shrewdly at this sketch that she blushed, not quite knowing what to do. Did she tear Angelina away from her father, politely insist? Remind Dante what he was supposed to do when presented with his daughter's current book?

'Dante, I think your daughter demands that you settle her.' Antonio chuckled, removing the decision from her hands. His eyes were sharp. 'Kate, why not sit with me a while? It has been some time since we chatted.'

Kate met Dante's dark gaze and their eyes tangled and held for a few breathless seconds. Yes, Dante might have an idea of his daughter's bedtime ritual, but he was so very often back late. Bedtime rituals with young children were always evolving, sometimes on the back of something as small as what might have happened at school that day, some childish gossip far more important than whatever book happened to be on the go.

Kate lowered her eyes but her lips twitched, and she knew that Dante was very much aware of the sudden flash of amusement on her face, just as he knew exactly what she was thinking.

She turned to Antonio and smiled brightly, and was aware of Dante hovering uncertainly as they both left him to his own devices and headed towards the kitchen. She could hear Angelina's excited chatter fading in the background.

'No staff,' Antonio said, settling her and then fetching them both a glass of wine. 'Food has been prepared and is in the oven. Supper when Dante is back down. You may have noticed that much of the palace has been closed off. I confine myself to a few rooms. It is my health and my age. It is all too much. But what joy to have you all here, and let us not mention how heart-warming and unusual to see my nephew fulfilling his paternal duties...'

'Unusual?'

'As unusual as you all being here, visiting the invalid at the same time, my dear.'

'You're hardly an invalid,' Kate teased gently, although she could see lines of anxiety etched on his face that she couldn't recall being there before. Had Dante mentioned anything? They should have spoken, but too late now.

'That is very kind of you, my dear. But enough of me. It is good to have you all under my roof for the first time.'

'Hardly for the first time...'

'Ah, but not often enough, my dear. An old man comes to rely on these small pleasures. Seeing you together... I should take this opportunity to tell you a little of my beloved nephew, although I should also add that this is to remain between the two of us.'

'I—I'm not sure I want to be in a position, er...'

'In a position of hearing about my nephew? Now, now. At heart, are we all not curious about one another?'

Kate burst out laughing and Antonio smiled broadly.

'That's below the belt.' She was still laughing when she said that.

'But is it not the truth?' He gestured broadly, briefly reminding her of Dante, who often made the same exotic, expansive gestures when he talked. 'He is a product of his background. A harsh upbringing, my dear, will always breed a man who is unfamiliar with the gentler side of human nature.'

This was the first time Antonio had ever delved into any kind of personal commentary on his nephew. They had always got along famously. He adored Angelina, and was fun to be around, but confidences of this nature? Never in the past.

Something trickled through her but she couldn't pin it down. She was suddenly eaten up with curiosity. It swept through her like a tidal wave, making her wonder how long it had been there, like a pernicious weed waiting for an opportunity to push through the polite barriers she had always had in place–a month? Six months? A year? Ever since the first moment she had seen him and been rendered mute by the shock of his dark, dangerous beauty and his cold but stupidly charismatic remoteness?

That, too, sent a trickle of *something* through her.

'He's an incredibly kind man,' she heard herself say, meaning every word of it. 'And very fair. A *good* man.'

Antonio's bushy eyebrows shot up but he smiled and nodded approvingly. 'He is all those things and more—but his parents? My brother? They were strict, cold, did not believe in displays of emotion. Dante was reared to inherit the crown, so to speak. He was never allowed the little freedoms his friends enjoyed.'

Kate listened in silence but she felt the sting of sympathy prick the back of her eyes.

She could all too well picture a boy developing into a

man, his life conditioned to point in one direction, with the weight of his future duties resting heavily on his shoulders.

She knew what Antonio was telling her. He was telling her that there was a reason his nephew was so stilted with his daughter, and she was suddenly desperate to dig deeper, to find out if he had always been like that even when he had been married. Had he relied on his first wife to provide the things his upbringing had not equipped him to provide, such as spontaneity and a sense of playfulness? The ease of a physical connection?

She also wanted to ask him what had prompted his sudden urge to confide but, before she could work out how to broach that delicate subject, he leaned into her and confided, 'Old I may be, my dear, but far from an old fool. Not long ago, I told my nephew that it was time for him to leave the past behind, to marry, and now...' he sat back and spread his arms wide with a satisfied expression '...here you are. Both of you! What a happy occurrence!'

What had they done? Kate thought. Was he suspicious? Or did he think that she and Dante were—*what?* A happy couple in love? In some place of blissful courtship which had been simmering for months on the sly? Dante must have let something slip, given some hint of what was to come. This was all part of their arrangement, discussed in advance, and yet deceit carried its own rancid odour.

In that moment, she decided that she would spare her parents that deceit. In the meantime, she opened her mouth at least to try and quell some of his unrealistic expectations but, before she could say a word, the kitchen door was pushed open and Dante was with them.

She drew in a sharp breath, aware of him as never before and wondering whether it was because of what Antonio had told her.

'Dante...' She caught his eye and tried to signal something but he raised his eyebrows, smiled and told her that he had found it impossible to follow the plot in the ballerina book Angelina had insisted he read to her.

'You might want to make a habit of it,' Kate quipped, the sudden tension draining out of her, because he looked hassled but rather pleased with himself. Maybe also because he had assumed a three-dimensional aspect that he had been so determined to conceal, at least from her, a history that somehow pushed through all her preconceived notions of him. 'You'll soon realise that Daisy's unrealistic adventures are as nothing compared to some of the other classics she enjoys reading. Monty the Rat will leave you puzzled for many days.'

He flashed her a sudden smile that knocked her sideways and she blinked in confusion.

'Now, children…' Antonio clapped his hands, summoning them to order and snapping Kate out of her temporary feeling of dislocation.

'Is champagne called for?'

'Your uncle…' Kate cleared her throat. 'Has…er…'

'Pre-empted our announcement? I would have broken the news to you myself, Antonio, but I thought it best to wait until Kate got here with Angelina.' Dante smoothly relieved her of her stuttering attempt to steer the conversation.

'I expect Dante told you, my dear, about my health situation?'

'He did, Antonio, and honestly—I'm sure you're getting worked up over something that will be manageable. Times have moved on hugely when it comes to treatment for various cancers.'

'I prefer not to rely on the possibility of good fortune, my dear. There is nothing worse than misplaced optimism. I had no idea, when I expressed my desire that Dante marry, that you and he were, how should I put this, perhaps already an item?'

'We…we…er…'

'The tentative beginnings,' Dante said smoothly. 'No shouting from the rooftops, naturally, but as you know that isn't my style anyway.' He smiled at Kate, inviting her to step into the story he was spinning. 'But perhaps you hastened things…'

'Well, I cannot apologise for that, Dante.'

'You must be a little surprised,' Kate ventured as she felt the brush of Dante's arm against hers.

'I am too old for surprises and too close to meeting my maker to question them when they come. Now, let us enjoy the moment for what it is. A time to celebrate! The finest champagne is called for.'

'I take it there is no shortage in the fridge?'

'Ah, Dante, how well you know me…what is a man without champagne?'

He moved away from her, strolling towards Antonio. There had been no display of pseudo-affection. As he'd said, not his style.

It wouldn't be expected. Dante wasn't a guy who did public displays of affection, and for him to change tack would be astonishing. That hit her in a flash. This would truly be nothing more than a business arrangement and, although that should have lifted her spirits, she felt a twinge of disappointment.

Was it because, with Antonio's unexpected confidence, a box had been opened? Were opened boxes ever a good thing? Didn't they usually herald unpleasant surprises?

She had grown accustomed to the travelling life she had led with her parents. But she could remember a time when she had been very young—maybe Angelina's age—when her parents would sit her down, look at one another with barely contained excitement…and she would know, with a sinking feeling, that everything was about to change once again.

Time to move on. There'd be some weeks or months building up friendships, but then would come the call of the unknown, and the suitcases and boxes would be packed and onward bound they would go... While she had looked back through the window of whatever old car they had been driving at another disappearing view of what might have been.

Opened boxes weren't for her. She knew that she would do well to remember that.

Champagne was popped and she smiled until her jaw ached. Overjoyed, Antonio was unquestioning when it came to the details of their sudden romance. Dante tossed some vague crumbs out there and Antonio accepted them and moved on. Perhaps he preferred mystery over chapter and verse, or perhaps he was just relieved that his nephew was going to marry and settle down.

She allowed her eyes to wander to the man she would marry and she shivered. Her gaze drifted from the harsh, chiselled perfection of his aristocratic features to the brown column of his neck and the latent strength of his broad shoulders.

And then it drifted further down as she half-listened to them both talking about some of the various strands of the D'Agostino empire that would require Dante's input in preparation for his uncle fully retreating from all business concerns. This was the business end of their marriage, she thought: the way wealthy, powerful families operated. Giggly wedding planning wasn't for them.

Antonio began flagging shortly after dinner was eaten. He waved aside Kate's offer to tidy up. Staff would be back first thing and would be dismayed to find their job done for them.

Dante offered to accompany him to his quarters but was likewise waved away, and within minutes, he and Kate found themselves alone in the kitchen with the empty bottle of champagne on the table.

With a sharp tug of embarrassment, Kate banished from her head all wayward thoughts of the breath-taking physicality of Dante.

'I would say that went smoother than expected.' Dante raked his fingers through his hair and slanted her a glance. 'Of course, he started fishing as soon as I got here. The fact that we were both going to be here for no particular occasion had his antennae bristling. You've been shopping, I see.'

Kate blushed and nodded, and felt awkward as Dante's dark gaze rested briefly on her. 'You *did* suggest it...'

'Suits you,' he murmured. 'Subtle but elegant.' Yes, it was the first thing he had noticed when she and Angelina had hurried in, because it was the first time he'd seen her in anything other than the sort of background gear she seemed so fond of wearing.

But had he intended to say anything? He just hadn't been able to help himself in the face of her elegance...the slight gracefulness of her body... She might not have the careless, flamboyant confidence of a lot of the women he'd known, including his ex-wife, but there was a certain understated elegance about her that was equally *sexy.* More so, if anything. He dropped his gaze and felt his breathing quicken.

Kate fiddled nervously with the stem of her wine glass and sneaked a glance at Dante from under her lashes.

A white loose shirt emphasised the burnished tone of his skin and she was fascinated by the whorls of hair curling around the dull chrome metal band of his watch.

From this angle, she was offered a tantalising glimpse of muscular thighs spread apart encased in casual dark trousers that managed to look coolly elegant and wildly sexy at the same time.

Why was her focus suddenly drifting—because he'd made some offhand remark about the clothes she happened to be wearing?

'I'm surprised he wasn't more inquisitive,' she said, reverting to safer waters. 'But I suppose that's all for the good. One thing we haven't discussed is the actual business of the wedding. I realise you're a very important person over here and—'

'No need to worry on that score,' Dante interrupted. When she arched her eyebrows, he continued neutrally, 'I had the big deal when I married Angelina's mother. I have no intention of a repeat performance, whatever happens to be expected of me.'

'Oh. Good.'

'Any other questions or concerns?'

'I—I felt awful about deceiving your uncle,' she said quietly. 'I know this is a done deal, but I suppose being here... watching his face light up...'

Dante tilted his head to one side and gazed at her in silence for such a long time that she began to fidget.

'You're very sentimental, aren't you?'

'I—I've never really thought about it, to be honest.'

'When you're with Angelina, when you talk about her, your face is transformed and the same just then—you looked damp-eyed, imagining that we are in the process of committing a heinous crime by entering into this contract.'

Kate shrugged. 'I—I don't think I'm out of the ordinary in feeling a twinge of guilt. It's just that you—you're—'

'What? What am I?'

'I wouldn't want to offend you.'

'I wouldn't worry on that score,' Dante said gently. 'I don't offend easily.'

'Well, then, I guess you're so...*cold.* Do you ever really *laugh*? Have you ever let your hair down?' She shot him a helpless look from under her lashes. 'You—you're like a robot!' She instantly wished she could take those hurtful words back as a dark flush delineated his sharp cheekbones.

'I'm sorry,' she said in a rush.

'Why?' He shrugged. 'We're just very different people.'

'And, yet when you came back into the kitchen, I could see you really enjoyed that bedtime ritual with Angelina.'

Dante shifted and went to pour himself some more champagne, only to discover that they had finished the bottle, so drank some water instead. His flush deepened and he glanced at her.

'I... It was, yes... I enjoyed it. Doesn't happen often. My fault. I should...' He raked his fingers through his hair and frowned. He could hear the stiffness in his voice but knew he couldn't fight it. It was just who he was, for better or for worse, and yet, next to her open, transparent spontaneity, that stiffness made him feel a thousand years old.

'Should what?'

'Nothing. It is... Life's far too short for regrets.'

'But never too short for new beginnings,' Kate returned gently. 'We're here tomorrow. Why don't you take Angelina somewhere—out for the day? Not just an expensive meal somewhere.'

'I...'

'Is that a yes?'

'Yes,' he said, voice low. He shot her a look from under thick, sooty lashes. 'But...perhaps you would agree to come with us both...?'

'It's a deal.' She smiled and her heart fluttered when he slowly smiled back.

CHAPTER FOUR

OF COURSE THEY must go—and not to the local town! Venice and no less would do!

Antonio practically ushered them to the front door the following morning when Kate tentatively mooted the idea, making sure to dilute it with lots of apologies for leaving him, but he was having none of it.

'This old man has no intention of standing in the way of two lovebirds!' He had winked at them both while Angelina had been busy weighing up various breakfast options, all home-baked and spread on the vast marble-topped ten-seater which limply tried to pass itself off as a casual kitchen table. 'And no need to hurry back!' he had boomed, a far cry from the pallid, uncertain man of a day ago. 'I have things lined up.'

'Things?' Dante, in the middle helping himself to a bread roll and filling it with cheese, moved as he ate and half-peered at his laptop, which was open and blinking with emails. 'What things?'

Antonio huffed with a flush. 'As it happens, I remember I have an appointment with the consultant this morning.'

'What?' Dante slammed shut his computer, glanced at his watch and then at his uncle. 'Time?'

'I am not following you.' Antonio busied himself with breakfast, making a deal out of pouring himself some coffee and stirring sugar into it while avoiding eye contact with Dante.

'Time of your appointment?'

'You will be in Venice! Beautiful winter weather out there, and a lovely time of year to visit—fewer crowds! Did you know that there are over three hundred bridges in Venice? Staggering!'

Dante caught Kate's eye and she raised her eyebrows sympathetically.

'I feel it might be impossible to be in two places at once, Antonio.'

'If that is your way of telling me that I am not capable of making my way to see a doctor without having my hand held, son, then I will try not to take offence!'

'Antonio…!'

'Angelina, why don't we go and get changed to go out…?' This from Kate, who was vaguely wondering how it was that she and Dante had managed to morph into '*love birds*' when the picture they'd so far presented was of two people who barely knew one another and certainly weren't keeling over with loving looks.

'Stay!' Dante swung to look at her, adding in a gentler voice, that was nevertheless still thick with frustration, 'Please.' He looked at Angelina and smiled tersely. 'Angelina, perhaps you might go to your room and, eh, get ready, as Kate has suggested? We will be with you in a matter of minutes.'

Accustomed to doing as she was told, Angelina didn't utter a word of protest. She immediately headed to the door. For a few seconds Kate found it hard to recall that look on Dante's face the evening before, when there had been something there, something warm and a little uncertain, but quietly happy after he had settled his daughter. This was now the face of the distant father she was accustomed to. The man who had been raised to be as cold and remote as his own parents had been, as Antonio had explained.

Instead of pulling back, though, Kate had to bank down a peculiar surge of warmth and empathy towards this harsh, complex man who was suddenly fleshing out into a three-dimensional guy as compelling as he was good-looking. She didn't want or need *compelling*, however.

She slowly turned to look at them both as the door quietly closed behind Angelina. She sat at the table so that now she and Antonio were both sitting, while Dante stood towering above them. He radiated power and intent while Antonio bristled with pious self-defence.

'Do you really think I would let you face those demons on your own, Antonio?' Dante asked quietly, relenting sufficiently to pull up one of the chairs, which made him no less forbidding in Kate's opinion. 'You were frightened half to death when you summoned me here to tell me the news of your diagnosis. You were still frightened even after I'd spoken to your consultant myself, and tried to relay to you the optimism which you should have been feeling. And yet you sit here and tell me that it's somehow now offensive for me to insist on coming with you to your appointment?'

'Indeed I do!' Antonio countered robustly, which Kate personally found impressive.

'Indeed *you do*?'

'I had a little blip.' Antonio lifted his shoulders with elegant dismissal, although his eyes were a little shifty when he looked away after a couple of seconds. 'We all do. Tell me you have never had the occasional little blip in your life, Dante! I appreciate everything you have done, and…'

He half-smiled and shot Kate a sly, sideways glance. 'Perhaps the glad tidings of your marriage plans have fortified me.' He beamed, reaching across to pat Dante on the arm. 'Yes, indeed, I feel I have put my finger on it! I am a new man, son. A new man with renewed purpose, and one who would very much like to face down my own demons without anyone by my side giving me advice on how to do it!'

Dante flung himself back in the chair, raked his fingers through his hair and looked utterly bewildered for a few seconds.

Kate, watching him, was tempted to smile.

He had been deprived of doing the one thing he so badly wanted to do, which was to see his uncle through troubling times, and yet she knew from her own experience that everyone had to grope their way forward on their own terms.

'If you're sure, Antonio...'

Stepping in to fill the awkward, stretching silence, Kate smiled reassuringly, and Antonio visibly relaxed, although there was something still there, something ever so slightly *guilty* in his expression. She was probably way off target with that.

'Happy you understand an old man!' He rose to his feet and shuffled to the fridge to peer inside for a few seconds, before turning to look at them. 'You young things need to get out of this stuffy house and have some fun in the City of Canals!'

Stuffy house? The kitchen was big enough to fit in most of the places where she had ever lived when she and her parents had been on the road! But he was shooing them off and, with barely any words exchanged, they were at the front door half an hour later, ready for their day of sightseeing to commence.

Angelina, on cue, had unerringly known when to reappear. This time Dante took time to look down at his daughter and then, in a gesture so rarely seen, he stooped, tenderly stroked back her hair and smiled. For a few heart-stopping seconds, Kate's breath caught in her throat and she had the awkward feeling of being witness to an intensely personal moment.

Angelina smiled at Dante, a wise, young smile, and then he scooped her up and really hugged her tight. She riffled his hair right back before he put her back down.

'It'll be fun.' He turned to Kate and smiled. 'We've been effectively dismissed by a stubborn old man, so let's get out there and do some sightseeing.'

It took a couple of seconds to focus. She had been transported for a moment and seen the loving dad behind the stern man, but she blinked and gathered herself sufficiently to nod.

She had only managed to get to Venice a couple of times since she had started working for Dante. A combination of distance, responsibilities keeping her close to Milan and holidays back to the UK to visit her parents had clipped her wings when it came to exploring.

Then there had always been the question of money. It had never felt right to treat herself to anything frivolous when she knew that there were places the money should go to first. Her parents always did their best to encourage her to spend what she earned, to persuade her that they could manage on their own, that things would improve over time: when the land started yielding a bit more; when her mother's jewellery began selling into shops; when her father finally made it to the top of the waiting list for the prosthetic leg that would revolutionise his day-to-day life...

When...when...when...

She would see the gratitude and vulnerability underneath their generous, kind-hearted reassurances and would know that letting them down was never going to be an option.

But now... Now, with this arrangement in place, she would be able to achieve so much...*everything*.

Which, as she slid a sideways glance at the towering guy

striding confidently next to her, Angelina between them, set the agenda for her mood. Buoyed at the thought of what this brief inconvenience was going to achieve, Kate sidelined her natural inclination to keep Dante at arm's length and allowed herself to relax.

When was the last time she'd relaxed?

As they began to explore Venice, wrapped up against the biting cold, Kate realised that she had forgotten what it felt like to let life glide past her, to live in the moment and appreciate the things around her.

Dante was a surprisingly good guide and a fount of information, which he threw at them both, nodding and pointing at various landmarks to bolster what he was saying.

'The Doge's Palace took centuries to complete.'

He pointed out all the hallmarks of the Gothic architecture, squatting down so that Angelina could follow the sweep of his hand as he contoured the perfect symmetry of the building, and feigned astonishment that she couldn't rustle up facts and figures about one of the city's most famous landmarks.

Kate's eyes swept over him as he stooped and she was a little startled when he vaulted back to his feet to capture her gaze with a frown.

'She's eight,' he murmured as they strolled towards a café for a coffee break. 'What are they teaching her at school?' But he winked when he said that and gave Angelina's hand a little squeeze.

Kate grinned and then laughed.

'They're teaching her how to be a kid.' She joined in the moment, not looking at him as she reached into the backpack she had brought to extract a sketchpad and some graphite pencils. She handed them to Angelina along with a few light-hearted instructions on drawing, as best as she could, the square in which they had been seated and which was the biggest open space in the city. From here, they were treated to the spectacular view of the stunning, elegant buildings, as old as time, that made up the city.

'Use your imagination,' Kate urged Angelina. 'The Basilica is gorgeous and so is the bell tower...but you can draw them how you see them through your eyes.'

'I will do it for you, Papa!'

'I will frame it and keep it on my desk at work.'

It was there in the sudden flash of warmth in Dante's eyes—that fierce paternal love that could be hard easily to detect.

How sad, she thought, to have all that love trapped inside, to be a prisoner of a harsh, duty-bound childhood. Had his ex-wife been the only woman who had managed to break through that diamond-hard exterior?

Curiosity clawed inside her, sudden and overpowering, and for a few seconds, as she vaguely listened to Dante explain something of the history of the piazza to his daughter, she could feel the acceleration of her heartbeat thudding inside her, confusing, disorienting and a little scary.

She blinked and what she saw was no longer the forbidding guy she had agreed to marry but the man—living, breathing and crazily, inaccessibly, stupidly sexy...

Kate screeched to a panicked halt at the image that flared in her head of his powerful, muscular body in bed with her.

Husband and wife...

Except that was going to be a two-year fantasy! And beyond that the chasm between them was so great that ever to think about breaching it would risk being swept into its cavernous depths.

The mere thought was terrifying. A lifetime spent travelling from one place to another had bred in Kate a healthy respect for staying put, for a simple, quiet life. She adored her parents, but she was very well aware of the limitations their

nomadic lifestyle had conferred on them. It was one of the
reasons they were where they were now, for heaven's sake!

Dante, with his suffocating, overwhelming personality
and his dark, dangerous charisma was the very opposite of
simple and quiet. He was a raging volcano and the line between fascination and mortal peril was wafer-thin. Gut instinct told her that, just as gut instinct had protected her for
two years against the devastating sex appeal which lurked
underneath the cool, remote veneer.

By the time they were on their way back to Antonio's palace, with Angelina nodding off between them, she had still
not managed to quite shake the disturbing, niggling thought
that a gateway had opened up, inviting her to tread inside.

'What's wrong?'

'Sorry?' Kate blinked, her almond-brown eyes locking
onto his.

'You've gone quiet on me. I thought today went…well.
So, tell me what's wrong.' His voice was a silky murmur
that feathered through her body with the intimacy of a caress.

'Nothing's wrong,' Kate said on a sharp intake of breath,
gripped by a sudden hot pulsing in her veins that left her
breathless and alarmed. 'I guess I thought it might be a good
idea to just sit back and allow you to spend time with Angelina.' She cleared her throat and continued in a firmer voice,
even though she was still acutely aware of him in ways that
panicked her. 'It's great seeing the two of you interacting.'

'Thank you for joining us.'

'You honestly didn't need me there,' she countered huskily. 'Why did you ask me along?'

'Because…' He shifted and flushed. 'A day out with Angelina… It's not something I am accustomed to enjoying.
It's not familiar terrain.'

'You should do it a bit more. She loved having you with

her for the whole day.' Kate half-turned to look at him and stopped breathing for a few seconds as their eyes clashed in the darkness.

'I know,' he said huskily and then smiled with tentative warmth.

'And you should do *that* a bit more,' she added on impulse. Why not? If they were going to marry for convenience, then he would be around in her life, even if it *was* for a limited period of time. And the fastest way to kill these uneasy, uninvited stirrings of *awareness* would be to get onto another track altogether.

The *friendship* track was a safe one. She would be able to engage, to smile, to socialise at his side without this unwelcome and unexpected fluttering inside her just because their roles might be a little different. She didn't know what to do with the restless stirrings inside her. She just knew that they had to *go away*.

'Do what?'

'Smile.'

Dante gazed into almond-shaped eyes the colour of milk chocolate flecked with green, and for a few seconds was utterly taken aback. Disoriented and not knowing why, he found himself staring at her, deprived of speech. What was that about…this hot stirring in his blood, the familiar way it tracked through his veins, making him restless and edgy? No, he *knew*. An inconvenient attraction, one he would have to sideline, to subdue, and subdue it he would.

In work, at play, in all the corners and angles of his high-voltage life, he was always in control. It was the way he had been raised—to keep his feelings contained, always to know where his focus lay. Inconvenient attractions? No, there was no room for them or for his eyes straying, feeding his imagination, shifting his focus. He was strong—always had been, always would be. It was the way he was, a rock hewn from his life's experiences.

Distracted, Dante succumbed to thoughts of a past he always kept locked away.

The dramatic painting might hang behind his desk, a constant and everlasting reminder of the wife who had been perfect only on paper, and yet, despite that visual reminder, he had consigned her to a place that did not occupy a single scrap of his mind.

Luciana had been beautiful and as eligible as him. The match had been brokered by his parents and Dante had had no qualms about its suitability. Two great Italian houses would join forces. He was and never had been interested in romance. He had always known that marriage would be a simple matter of business and pragmatism, the continuity of the family line. Of course, he had had relationships with various women over the years, but he had never envisaged longevity with any of them, and in fact he had always been discerning when it came to those. Playing the field, like a kid without any parameters or sense of self-control, had never been his thing.

Had he expected his marriage to be the nightmare it had turned out to be?

Never.

He had entered into it in good faith but it had quickly become apparent that his stunning wife was utterly uninterested in him. Before the ink was dry on their marriage certificate, she'd announced she liked a varied sex life, and her assumption was that he would have no problem with that. Of course, she would provide him with an heir to the family empire, because that was part of the bargain, but that was it.

She'd done her own thing. He'd buried himself in work, gritted his teeth and wondered how long he would be able to put up with the men and women who entertained his wife. The tipping point had been reached the very second his daughter had been born, at which point he laid down some basic laws and resigned himself to a marriage in which Luciana did as she wished but with discretion, and so would he, should he so choose.

In fairness, he knew that it was a lifestyle not uncommon amongst many of his privileged acquaintances. The fact that she'd been rude to everyone she considered beneath her had been as repelling, in many ways, as her conscious philandering.

Would he have ended up pushed to the point of divorce? Or had his upbringing been so deeply ingrained that he would simply have shrugged it off and accepted the hand he'd been dealt? As many would have, and did, in the elevated circles in which they'd both moved. As far as his parents, and indeed his uncle, had been concerned, there'd been nothing amiss with the pairing.

It was a question Dante had never got to ask, because she had died in the very car crash that had taken his parents—an accident on a rainy road late at night after a trip to the opera. A distracted chauffeur. Seconds during which his future had changed for ever.

Dante frowned at the rush of memories crowding his brain and saw that the woman next to him—the woman who was to become his wife—was looking at him with something very much like empathy. As that was something he didn't need, he abruptly turned away, before moving the conversation onto more pedestrian ground.

Between them Angelina had shifted so that she was now resting against Dante's arm, gently snoring, oblivious to the hushed conversation around her.

'I meant to mention that your first social engagement is in the calendar.'

'Sorry?'

Better, Dante thought, annoyed with himself for being derailed by beguiling almond-shaped eyes and a heart-shaped face oozing just the sort of gentle understanding he was not in need of. Much safer being back in the arena of discussing practicalities.

'If you recall, part of the arrangement between us involved joint functions attended together?'

'I thought that was destined for after the big day.'

'The big day?'

'Yes. When we tie the knot and pledge undying love and devotion to one another.'

'Ah. *That* big day.' He smiled a slow, curling smile and looked at her with dark-eyed amusement. 'Remind me... does obedience feature alongside the love and devotion?'

Kate blushed. The ice-cold guy with the killer looks clearly had a sense of humour, and that unexpectedly brought a rush of colour to her cheeks and a sharp sexual awareness that forced dampness between her thighs and made her blush even redder.

'I think all those vows might have to be tweaked,' she returned, voice hitched, still feeling the heat in her cheeks. 'What is this function, exactly? Will I be there in the capacity of Angelina's nanny?'

'You will be there in the capacity of my future wife,' Dante asserted. 'Once the announcement is made and everything is official, we can jointly break the news to Angelina.'

'Announcement...'

'Don't tell me that you didn't give that any thought?'

'Well, yes, in a manner of speaking...' Had she? Not really. She'd considered the up sides and the ramifications, but the details had all been wrapped up in that pre-nup she had signed. All other considerations had been shoved to the back of the queue for further inspection at a later date.

'I'm guessing from your blank expression that the *manner of speaking* you refer to was somewhat on the vague side?'

'Somewhat,' Kate reluctantly agreed. She thought about the sort of people she would meet, and the reality of what she was about to do hit her with the force of a sledgehammer.

She would be catapulted into a level of wealth that would surpass anything she might ever have encountered—which truthfully wasn't much, given her background. She had only vaguely seen from a distance the glamorous, expensively dressed people who circled around Dante, like twinkling stars orbiting the sun. The prospect of actually having to mingle with them made her feel a little nauseous.

'It's going to be a little odd, isn't it?' she ventured, chewing her lip and staring off into the dark distance as the chauffeur-driven car noiselessly gobbled up the miles.

'Undoubtedly it will be for you, but that's a big subject to broach in the back of a car with a sleeping child between us. We can talk about this when we are back at my uncle's,' Dante said with surprising kindness. When Kate focused she could make out the approach of the palace, its splendid pale contours as magnificent as an intricate gossamer confection.

Antonio had retired to his quarters, even though it wasn't yet seven-thirty in the evening, and as Dante lifted Angelina out of the car and carried her into the house he looked at Kate and drawled with wry sarcasm, 'My suspicion is that that sly fox has chosen to avoid a discussion on how the appointment with his consultant went.'

Kate burst out laughing.

'Would he be that devious?'

'That old man takes devious to another level.' But he was smiling with genuine affection and warmth. and

Head tilted to one side, Kate smiled back at him, because for a guy whose smiles were as rare as hen's teeth his was oddly infectious. She said thoughtfully, 'You really adore him, don't you?'

She remembered what she had been told about his parents, but that had been told to her in the strictest of confidences, even though now, with him about to take Angelina up to bed, she was so tempted to give in to curiosity.

Braced for an abrupt halt to a conversation which felt so different from most of their interactions in the past, she was surprised when he hesitated. And even more surprised when he mused, 'Antonio…was the cool uncle, the uncle who blew in from adventures, filled with tales of excitement. For me? A breath of fresh air.'

'Why?'

As if she had no idea.

'Because…' He began to head up the stairs, as light on his feet as a panther, even though he was well over six feet. Kate followed alongside him, guiltily thrilled to be allowed into his thoughts and straining so that she could hang onto his every quietly murmured word. 'My own parents were very different. Austere, traditional, sights firmly fixed on the bigger picture…'

'Perhaps that allowed Antonio more wiggle room to take a different path,' Kate said, standing back as he nudged open Angelina's door with his shoulder and carried her to her bed. It was a frothy four-poster extravaganza, very much in keeping with the ornate, beautiful room, big enough so that she had her own separate play area and another room for doing her homework and relaxing.

'You're probably right. He certainly never had time for convention and so, between us, our bond was very strong.

He was expected to pick up the baton within the family empire once he left university, as my father dutifully had, but as soon as that degree was in his grasp he decided that the family interests weren't sufficiently stimulating. He once confided that sitting behind a desk was no comparison to checking out what was happening in the Amazon. I think he reckoned the bookkeeping could wait—until, of course, it couldn't wait any longer.' He chuckled softly, not looking at her.

Kate watched him as he gazed down at Angelina, his expression open and revealing, the simple love of a father for his daughter, quietly murmuring confidences that were hardly confidences really, but which still felt like secrets shared. No wonder that she had been picked out for this strange assignment, she thought. Not only was it about relieving his adored uncle of his anxiety, but she fitted the bill when it came to Angelina. She was probably the *only* one who fitted the bill. He trusted her. He trusted her to look for no more than what was on the table and he trusted her when it came to his daughter.

She made the perfect fake wife.

They exited the room quietly and returned downstairs, although at the back of her mind Kate wondered whether he actually expected her to follow him. Maybe he would veer off in the direction of one of the many rooms to work, but he didn't. Instead he turned to her to tell her that there would be food in the kitchen, stuff prepared for Antonio, and that they should eat and he would explain about the function he had earlier mentioned.

'Didn't your father feel as though he'd been left in the lurch?' she asked, picking up the conversation they had started.

Dante shrugged and looked at her and she reddened as

she stared back at him, their eyes tangling, neither breaking eye contact.

'I'm being nosy,' she eventually muttered. 'Of course your family history is none of my business.'

'Some might say that it very much is now that we're travelling down a different road. At any rate, it's no secret that there was some animosity between the two brothers and, yes, my guess would be as you say.

'There's chicken and pasta...but no one to do the honours.'

'You're very spoiled.' Kate smiled and took over. 'Do you know where anything is kept in this kitchen?'

'I'm familiar with the location of the wine.' He grinned back at her, and the room swam for a couple of seconds, but then she busied herself with the food that had been earlier prepared.

But she was so aware of him, alert to his presence in ways she never had been before, and keenly aware of that moment just then when they had stared at one another while an electric charge had built with agonising potency between them. Had he felt the same? she wondered.

'My theory is that Antonio, having had to take over running the family business after my parents died, is making up for everything he thinks he may have failed to do by wanting everything in place.'

'What do you mean?'

'Of course, what I say here does not leave this room...' He waited until she nodded and knew, with irrefutable certainty, that she was utterly trustworthy.

'Antonio wants me married for many reasons. The first is that he believes I need the stability of a woman because of Angelina and because, in some way, he's always been like a father to me, despite or perhaps because of his globe-trotting ways. He always knew what he felt I lacked, which was the simple business of having fun, and he considered himself essential in bringing that to my life.'

Dante smiled. 'In whatever devious ways and means possible. But beyond that, this house of D'Agostino, which I'll now inherit, running along with my ex-wife's concerns, is a deeply traditional family affair. My uncle wants to ensure an easy transition now that he foolishly considers himself on the way out, and part of that, he feels, would be maintained with a wife by my side. He thinks he's sparing me the daily discomfort of all those traditionalists clucking their tongues in despair at my daughter's plight. To do him credit, they've probably been whispering for months, if not years.'

'But not to you...'

'No one would dare. I'm excellent when it comes to putting down my boundaries and no one has ever challenged them.'

'And what when the wife bails ship in two years' time?'

'Then, at that juncture, all and sundry will have realised that I am my own man and will not question decisions I choose to make. To be frank, if it weren't for my uncle's concerns and my desire to abate them, I wouldn't be considering this option right now.'

'Because you don't care what people think?'

'That and the fact that I'm not on the market for a wife— as I've mentioned. You'll be my partner, Kate, but you'll never really be my wife.'

It was a casual remark but it still made Kate shiver at the thought of a personality so untouchable, so controlled. She needed to forget about those glimpses of someone else which had given her pause for thought, had offered her an insight into the man beneath the billionaire nobleman, and remember how cold he was.

'Thank you for sharing that with me,' she said quietly. 'This food smells delicious, doesn't it?'

'It does. Antonio's chef is excellent. And as an aside...' he raised his eyebrows with amusement '... I do happen to know my way around a kitchen beyond the location of the wine cellar.'

'Oh, really?' Kate warmed to the dark eyes resting on her and flashed him a similarly amused smile, relieved that the ground was no longer shifting underneath her feet. 'I'll try to ignore all the staff you have at your house in Milan who are there to cater to your every whim.'

'Now you're just making me sound like a spoiled brat.' But he burst out laughing and, when it settled on her, his gaze held hers for a fraction longer than necessary. 'I did go to university in your country.' He sat forward to help himself to some of the food Kate had laid out for him.

'You shared a house with other guys—like a regular person?' She tried to imagine that and failed.

'In a manner of speaking. Two friends, and the house belonged to me.'

'Of course it did.'

Dante burst out laughing again, a proper, sexy, full-throated laugh, and in that instant there was absolutely nothing cold or remote about him. In that instant, he was dangerously, thrillingly, all red-blooded male.

'So maybe you have a point.' He was still half-laughing as he spread his arms wide in a gesture of pious acceptance, 'I may be a little spoiled after all.'

'A *lot* spoiled. And I guess you also had a bunch of people waiting on you hand and foot?'

'Not in the last year of my residency,' he drawled. 'Too many bodies in the house when, at the time, I was only interested in one.'

It took her a few seconds but, when she understood what he was saying, she went beetroot-red and was lost for words, which made him chuckle.

'You have a very transparent face, Kate. I've embarrassed you.'

'Not at all. Uh…no…'

'We're both adults.' He shrugged. 'I just say it as it was. So, moving on…'

Kate was only too glad to move on. Those casually uttered words had filled her head with graphic images and made her break out in a sweat. Yes, they were both adults, but for her? No. Casual sexual experiences were not in her playbook and she had never been in any hurry to put them there.

'Yes,' she said breathlessly. 'This thing—this function—will it be big? When is it?'

'Not big, no. Just relatives, friends and then we can sit with Angelina, explain it to her and take our time doing so.' He half-smiled. 'We cannot expect a young child to keep such news to herself, and I'd rather her friends know after it's been announced to their parents, so to speak.'

Kate relaxed. She wondered whether he still harboured doubts about her commitment to this proposition, hence the necessity to formalise their agreement in the eyes of those close to him before he told his daughter. If he'd known how much the money would mean to her parents, then he'd certainly have known that backing out, for her, was not on the cards. And as for this little get together… Something small and contained would be manageable, surely? She could deal with that.

'It's been put together in some haste but—' he shrugged '—no matter. What I can tell you is that it's perhaps sooner than you might wish for, but I don't see the point in waiting, especially when I suspect my uncle isn't going to let the grass grow beneath his feet. He'll be spreading the news faster than a town crier.'

There was wry indulgence in his voice when he said that.

It made her think of him as he must have been all those years ago, leading a splendid and privileged life of duty and responsibility, with Antonio the carefree genie in the lamp bringing magic and stardust to his childhood.

From her point of view, the sooner the beginning, the faster the conclusion.

'Sooner? Sooner as in…when, exactly?'

'Tomorrow evening.'

Kate's eyes widened and she looked at him in consternation.

'I'm not sure I'll be…er…mentally equipped to deal with… That's *very* soon.'

'Would waiting another week change anything?'

'Maybe not, but—'

'Excellent!'

'And so, this event is going to be here? You'd better tell Antonio first thing in the morning so that he can prepare himself.' She glanced around her, as if trying to spot a concealed army of waiting staff and platters of food, along with other warning signs of a party in the process of being arranged.

'Not here, no. The less stress my uncle has to face, the better. I have a yacht moored at the mooring pile of La Salute. Excellent views.'

'You have a *yacht* moored?'

'Small. Nothing fancy, but I suspect the guests will shun jeans and sweaters.'

'So, formal—how formal?'

'More opera than cinema. You can shop tomorrow. I'll open an account for you. You'll find that there will always be an extremely healthy balance for you to dip into.'

'Signor D'Agostino…'

'Dante. I feel that it's essential you address me by my first name, bearing in mind we're going to be married.' He shot her a slow, crooked smile that had her pulses suddenly racing. 'The fewer eyebrows raised, the better.'

'So we're supposed to be… Er, do we have to pretend…? What I'm trying to say—'

'You're blushing again. I like it. Please feel free to make a habit of it. And to answer the question you're struggling to ask—no. We don't have to hold hands or gaze into one another's eyes. Such public displays of affection won't be expected of me.'

'Oh, good.' Kate breathed a sigh of heartfelt relief, and then added with a rush of honesty, 'Because when it comes to holding hands and gazing adoringly into a guy's eyes I would want to actually be involved with him.'

'Good. I like that. No room for misunderstandings. To-morrow, we'll leave at seven, with Antonio there a little earlier, as there are a number of relatives he hasn't seen in some time. It'll give him time to chat. And one last thing—leave the jewellery to me.'

'The jewellery?'

'You're about to enter a different world.' Dante smiled with a mixture of amusement and kindness. 'It's only fair that you have all the parts of the uniform you'll occasion-ally be required to wear…'

CHAPTER FIVE

NERVES KICKED IN roughly half an hour before Dante was supposed to meet Kate in the marble hall where they would be driven to the private water-taxi waiting to deliver them to his yacht.

Having relaxed the evening before at the thought of something small and contained, with just a handful of close friends and relatives to contend with, Kate had spent the day in a state of mounting nervous tension.

True to his word, Dante had opened a personal account for her, and the sum deposited had made her eyes bulge and her mouth go dry. He had texted her the name of a boutique located in one of the fashionable streets on the outskirts of the city and had informed her that she would be expected and would be looked after. She could choose whatever she wanted.

Kate took this to mean that she would be guided into the right sort of formal dress for the occasion, just in case her lack of relevant experience somehow made her go rogue and end up buying something unsuitable.

In truth, she didn't care. This was not a case of standing up for herself and demanding the right to wear whatever she saw fit. This was not any kind of relationship in any way, shape or form. This was a business arrangement—frankly, he called the shots, and why would what she wore matter to her when he was no more than a means to an end?

If she had felt the occasional, unexpected frisson in his company, then that was to be expected, because she was on a different footing with him from she had been in the past.

His choice was high-end, haute couture with no price tags on any of the garments. The implication was, presumably, that if you had to check the price, then you couldn't afford to shop there.

She was treated with bowing and scraping subservience. She was put through her paces by two terrifyingly elegant women—which she found horribly uncomfortable—before being made to try on a dizzying number of elegant dresses and make a choice.

'Perhaps,' one of the women suggested in Italian, 'You might find it helpful to take several with you, in case Signor D'Agostino has a preference?'

To which Kate burst out laughing and said, with a shake of her head, that he had already had quite sufficient input into the whole exercise, thank you very much. She didn't think they quite understood her broken Italian.

Then there was her nails, her hair, the accessories...

Several hours later, buffed and polished, Kate looked at her reflection in the full-length mirror in her bedroom suite. The girl staring back at her bore no resemblance to the one who had started the day in jeans, jumper and thick waterproof coat, eschewing the expensive purchases in favour of comfort.

That girl had been fresh-faced, make-up-free and hardly worth a second glance, as far as Kate was concerned.

This one looked five years older and was elegant, sophisticated and, frankly, unrecognisable. Her hair had been highlighted and was a rich mix of chestnut and gold, and swept up and expertly kept in place, save for some tendrils artfully framing her face. It emphasised the length of her neck. The dress, a simple cream and black silk affair, fell straight to the floor, fitted her like a glove and accentuated her slender build. It was cold, and she would wear a shawl and her cashmere coat.

Heart beating fast, Kate was captivated by the image staring back at her. She marvelled at how a simple change of outfit and a few clever tweaks to her hair could turn the nanny into...someone who was still a nanny but now appeared fit for the nobleman Dante was. Or at least, more fit now than she had been twenty-four hours ago.

She had never paid any attention to her appearance. When much of her life had been spent travelling, basking in sun one minute and huddling under the awning of a caravan in a different county the next, stuff such as gazing into mirrors and wondering what shade of lip gloss to wear to the prom were weird luxuries that had never really featured.

So now, mouth half-open, she could scarcely believe the transformation. If her parents could have seen her now, they wouldn't have believed their eyes. She suspected that they probably wouldn't have approved either. They had always subscribed to the hippy way of thinking, that *au naturel* was always best, and that the best things in life were free.

Kate breathed in sharply and her eyelids fluttered. At least, she thought, the best things in life had always been free until her father had had his accident—at which point they had all discovered that the best things in life came at a hefty price.

Hence the reason she was here, gaping at this new version of herself, with her stomach in knots.

She grabbed the clutch she had bought—one of the many expensive accessories—along with the strappy sandals which were silly, given the cold weather outside, hooked the shawl and coat over her arm and took to the stairs.

Angelina was in her room, in the safe care of one of the young members of staff who had babysat in the past, watching television. Kate had popped in earlier, making sure to keep all mention of the party to herself, as per Dante's instructions. She had hugged her tightly, tighter than usual, and had thought how odd it was that in the blink of an eye she would be a *stepmother* to this adorable little girl with her contained, sweet-natured personality. A little confused at first, Angelina had squeezed her right back and kissed her forehead in a curiously grown-up way.

Kate would be pleased to get past this tiny element of subterfuge.

She made it to the bottom of the stairs at the very moment Dante was emerging from the wing of the palace he had been using for his office.

She saw him before he saw her because he was distracted, reading something on his mobile, and because she had raced down the stairs barefoot and so had barely made a sound.

He looked…breath-taking.

His raven-black hair was swept back, accentuating the harsh, chiselled angles of his face, and he was dressed formally in a dark, bespoke suit, a white shirt open at the neck and no tie, which was the only concession to casual dress. He looked every inch exactly what he was: an aristocrat; a man who lived on a different planet from her, looked at the world through different eyes and had always, from the day he'd been born, breathed in the rarefied air afforded to the uber-elite.

No wonder this was a match that suited him, she thought, tearing her eyes away and bending to put on the sandals. She would never pose a threat, would never try and outstay her welcome, would always recognise the vast chasm between them and would never be tempted to breach it.

To all intents and purposes, she was a temporary asset that would always be invisible, and therefore in no danger of ruffling the calm surface of his day-to-day life.

Dante had not been aware of Kate soundlessly descending the sweeping staircase. He'd been too busy checking his emails, and scanning communications from the various people who had hurriedly organised the function he had set in motion. It was something that had to be done, so he might as well get it over with.

Why wait? An announcement would have to be made, and any thought of communicating the situation on the down-low was out of the question. He was a D'Agostino, after all. He could have waited a while and taken his time with the invitation list but, as far as Dante was concerned, the people he actually cared about enough to want on that prized list were few and far between. If it was all very last minute, then he was not unduly bothered about who could make it or not. In all events, not a single invitation had been turned down, such was the scope of his power and influence.

Glancing at his watch, and half-turning to the staircase, he saw Kate just as she was bending to see to her sandals... and for a few seconds the breath left him in a whoosh.

She was fiddling with the straps and his eyes followed the graceful curve of her pale neck and the slender delicacy of her arms. She was maybe five-six, and so slightly built that he felt a strong breeze could whip her off her feet. He heard her click in tongue in annoyance and snapped out of his momentary trance to walk towards her.

'Allow me.'

She smelled of fresh flowers and the scent filled his nostrils, pausing him as he knelt to attend to the sandals that had been giving her trouble.

It was an intimate gesture, touching her, kneeling at her feet, the dominant male yielding to a beautiful woman. Her ankles were narrow enough for him to circle with his fingers and her skin was soft and silky-smooth. She was wearing pale-pink polish on her toenails and it seemed ultra-feminine on her.

The straps were fiddly and he had big hands. Was that why he was having a hard time doing the things up? He was hyper-aware of her hand lightly on his back as he knelt in front of her. Eventually, job done, Dante vaulted to his feet, making sure to step back a few paces so that he didn't invade her space.

Knockout.

That was the only word for the complete picture that hit him square in the face as he looked at her full lips, small, straight nose and a heart-shaped face that lent her a look of disingenuous innocence. He felt a surge of hot blood rush through him, insistent, unwelcome and reminding him that this was not the first time his body had broken its leash and done its own thing in her presence. Everything inside him stirred in sudden hot arousal and, for a few seconds, it was such a shocking reaction that he barely recognised it. This was not part of his rigid, orderly approach to life. This was wild and uncontrolled, and he rejected it at speed, but in its wake he was left shaken and grittily confused.

'I have the jewellery,' he said abruptly, reaching into his pocket and pulling out a deep-purple velvet box.

'Okay.'

Kate had likewise stepped back, eyes wide, breathing shallow as she looked at him.

'Wow.' Her mouth fell open at the intricate, ornate diamond-encrusted necklace he held up. It cascaded between his lean, brown fingers like a tinkling, glittering waterfall of precious gems. She reached out and hesitantly touched the necklace with the tip of a finger.

'It won't bite.'

'Tell me this isn't real.'

'Not real?'

'These diamonds!'

'Why would it not be real?'

'Dante, I couldn't possibly wear this.'

'What are you talking about?'

She gazed at him and sighed at the bewildered frown on his face. Then she touched the necklace again, another quick, light touch, and he smiled, suddenly relaxed and amused at her tentative response.

'Turn around, Kate, and let me put it around your neck.'

'What if I lose it?'

'You won't lose it.'

'What if it…falls…breaks? It must be worth a fortune.'

'It's insured,' Dante said kindly. 'But it won't fall, and where will you lose it?'

'Anywhere! I might be leaning over the side of your yacht! I've never in my entire life been on a yacht before. What if I'm seasick?'

'Over the side of the yacht? I'm not seeing it, personally. If you feel nauseous, then I'll be right by your side—no problem. I'll deliver you in one piece to the rest room. Probably a better bet than running for the side of the boat. Besides—and small point of order—it's going to be stationary.'

'You're being sarcastic.'

'You're making it hard for me not to laugh.'

'I'm not used to all of this!'

'I'll be right there by you. We're in this together. I'm not going to abandon you to whatever fate has in store, trust me. Now, turn around and let's get this done or we'll be late.' He leant into her and whispered with amusement, his breath warm against her neck, 'Although, I'm guessing you wouldn't say no to buying time...'

Nerves shredding at the feel of his warm breath on her, Kate hastily spun round to feel his cool fingers on her neck as he expertly clasped the priceless necklace securely. Then he walked her over to the gilt mirror on the wall and stood behind her, watching her as she gazed at the diamonds encircling her neck, tentatively touching it in disbelief.

Oddly, this simple gesture made Dante's heart swell with a certain amount of pride.

'It's a family heirloom,' he said, his eyes briefly dropping to a tiny mole on the back of her neck before meeting and holding her gaze in the mirror. 'Belonged to the family on my mother's side. It wasn't quite ornate enough for my ex-wife's taste, so it's remained vaulted until now. It suits you—your outfit—perfectly.'

He stood back but it was suddenly an effort to look away. 'We should go.' He cleared his throat and spun round on his heels, breaking the fragile connection between them and striding towards the front door.

Caught up in a magical moment for a few seconds, Kate briskly walked towards him, allowed him to help her with the shawl and then shoved her arms into the sleeves of the coat before hurriedly tightening it around herself. She could still see the image of his dark head as he had knelt at her feet, fiddling with the thin straps of the sandals while she had done her best not to pass out.

It was cool in the night air and—in keeping with a phoney relationship, with no effort being necessary unless there were witnesses around—Dante spent much of the drive on the phone, switching languages as he discussed business, while Kate stared out of the window as the sleek car ate up the miles towards Venice.

She didn't quite know what to expect. The one thing she did know, however, was that she had to play it as cool as he did. It hadn't escaped her notice that, while she had been in a state of nervous freefall when he had stepped close to her, when his fingers had brushed the back of her neck and feathered against her foot, he had remained as cool as a cucumber.

Nor had it escaped her that he had, in passing, paid a compliment about her dress, but had he told her that she looked okay? Not a bit of it. She looked the part, and that was the key thing.

And why was that? Because he didn't *see* her—not really. Not in the way her treacherous eyes saw *him*. Not in the stupid, crazy ways that made her shiver, gave her goose bumps, made her go weak and sparked a tingle between her legs that was shameful but pleasurable.

Venice at night was stunning, a kaleidoscope of light reflecting off water, shifting and changing so that the elegant ancient buildings gazing into the canals looked otherworldly and mysterious. A city of possibilities, drenched in romance. The air was still and cold.

They were delivered to a water-taxi that was waiting for them. As she stepped out of the car, sliding past Dante's driver, who had whipped round to open the door for her, Kate felt very much like the woman that she had never imagined being. She felt like Cinderella, with the pumpkin banished to the shadows, replaced with a carriage. And gone were the chain-store clothes, swapped for the finery of a princess: the diamonds; the silk and cashmere... Borrowed clothes for a borrowed person who would, in due course, be returned to her own world, where she belonged.

But for now…? He was right. She had entered a different world—*his* world—and this was her new uniform.

Until the time came for her to give it all back.

The canals were so much calmer by night, and the bridges looking down at the waterways were so softly lit that it made Kate think of how it must have looked centuries ago, filled with dark corners and intrigue.

She could feel the warm weight of Dante's thigh against hers as they were taken to where his yacht was moored.

'There.'

Lost in thought and absorbed by the dark, shifting scenery, Kate started at his warm breath against her cheek and followed to where he was gazing.

'Your yacht.'

'Does it live up to expectation?' Dante glanced across to her, taking in her soft, delicate profile, and feeling her nerves, even though she hadn't said a word. He had worked in the car on the way but he had been aware of her next to him, gazing out of the window, and he would be lying if he didn't admit that he'd wondered what was going through her head.

He felt a twinge of guilt. Yes, this was a business arrangement, but she was young and she would be nervous. She would not have his reserves of self-discipline and cold, hard, focused inner strength. His upbringing had made him tough and the personal experiences that had followed—his ice-cold marriage to a woman for whom he had not, by the end, had a shred of affection or respect—had made him even tougher.

But beyond that, whilst this woman sent off all the right vibes of being strong and self-contained, he sensed an oddly vulnerable side to her.

Certainly, he doubted she'd ever had any first-hand, lived experience of the world she was about to enter. The women he knew would be familiar with this life. His ex, who had grown up with a similar level of privilege, would barely have glanced in the direction of the yacht. Nor would she have trembled at the touch of that diamond necklace around her neck. She would have been storing up complaints for the staff, already assuming oversights would be made. Dante had invited her parents out of politeness and had been relieved when they had made their excuses.

'Are you still nervous?' he asked, tilting her chin so that she was looking at him, trying to glean what was going through her head although, in the darkness, he couldn't make out a thing.

Kate shrugged. 'I'll get through it. As we both know, it's just part of the job.'

Dante frowned, for some reason disconcerted by that, even though he knew it was absolutely the response he should have been looking for.

'Surely there are some aspects of this that you enjoy?' His finger was still resting lightly on her chin. 'What about the shopping?'

'It's…an experience.'

'A good one?'

'A different one.'

'Can I ask you something?'

'Of course.'

'Can I ask why the money is so important to you?'

'You can ask,' Kate said evenly. 'But actually it's none of your business.'

Dante stared, rendered speechless by a response no one had ever before delivered to him in his life.

Kate belatedly shot him a placatory smile. 'You're lost for words.'

'I…' Dante raked his fingers through his hair and gazed

at her. 'I admit,' he conceded with an expressive gesture of defeat, 'No one has ever spoken to me like that before.'

'*Never?*'

'Never.'

'That's probably because people are too intimidated to say what they really think when they're with you.'

'You find me intimidating?'

'*I* don't,' Kate said thoughtfully and honestly. 'But I'm guessing most people do.'

'I'll keep a close watch on how many people curtsy and bow to me when we're on the yacht,' Dante said pensively, his dark eyes glinting with amusement. 'That would be the litmus test, I guess. What do you think?'

What did she want, or more probably need, the money for?

The question lodged in his head like a burr, to be pulled out and inspected at a future time, if only to satisfy his curiosity.

'I think you're making fun of me, and I'm also beginning to think that that's something you enjoy doing,' Kate returned, but lightly. Her heart skipped a beat as their eyes tangled and held before he looked away, and she realised that they were approaching his yacht. It was huge, now that they were up close to it, warmly lit and reflecting on the sheet-calm water like an oil painting.

'The question is…' Dante was seduced into teasing her back '…do *you* enjoy it as much as I do? And, for the record, I'm not making fun of you. I respect you too much for that.'

'Then what are you doing?'

Dante remained silent for a heartbeat.

'I'm…'

What was he doing? Was he flirting with her? He wasn't a flirt. No. No way.

'I'm breaking the ice between us,' he told her with a brisk smile.

'I should have asked,' Kate said stiltedly after a few seconds, nerves kicking in big time, 'Whether your friends and relatives know what this sudden party invitation is all about.'

'Not in so many words.'

'What does that mean?'

'They'll suspect an announcement of some sort, I'm sure. Gathering all these people together at short notice…? Not something I would normally do.' He raised his eyebrows with a wry grin. 'Italian tongues have a habit of wagging.'

If he was lightening the conversation to ease her nerves, then he was succeeding. She smiled back at him and thought how good he was at this, how cool and collected at steering them into a zone where emotions were absent.

'I don't think Italians have the monopoly on wagging tongues. But what about Antonio…?'

'Has been requested to say nothing. I'd rather deliver the glad tidings myself.'

'They're going to be shocked,' Kate muttered with a grimace. 'I don't suppose anyone would have predicted that Dante D'Agostino might have picked the nanny to wed, when the line of suitable candidates probably stretched from here right back to Milan.'

'They'll accept it.' Dante's answer was unequivocal. 'And there will be congratulations all round.'

'Yes, but they're going to be horrified.' Kate chewed her lip and imagined the scenario, which was reassuring on absolutely no level. 'They'll think I'm after your money.'

'It is possible they may have a point, looking at it in the cold light of day...' Dante mused wryly.

'I'm not a gold-digger!'

'I know that.' He smiled and in passing appreciated the heated colour in her cheeks.

They had arrived but he wasn't ready for his own party just yet. The conversation was stimulating, and of course the driver of the water-taxi would be content to wait for however long it took.

'I— There's no way on earth I would ever go after anyone just because they had money!'

'Repeat—I know.'

'This is a completely different situation.'

'Kate...' his voice was gentle '... I *know.* You've been working for me for over two years. Not once have you ever been anything but professional in your dealings. I realise that you are no more a gold-digger than I am a ballet dancer.' Without thinking, he rested his finger on her chin and then absently outlined her lip before pulling back, startled at that brief, physical caress.

'We have an arrangement.' He looked away to the yacht he rarely used. 'It's one that suits us both. Don't waste time and energy worrying about what the people you are about to meet might think of you or your motives.' He smiled a warm, reassuring smile. 'You might actually find,' he murmured, 'That some of them are actually rather pleasant and accepting.'

'You would say that,' Kate muttered. 'You're not in my shoes.'

'They'd never fit. Smile at me, Kate. It'll be just fine. I won't leave you to the mercy of strangers.'

'There's no need to stick to me like glue. I mean, they're your friends and relatives. Of course you're going to want to circulate…' she protested awkwardly, but the thought of him being next to her was warmly reassuring. He was a cold, forbidding man and yet…there was a strength inside him and a natural moral compass that anchored her and brought her fizzing anxieties under control.

'Ready?'

'As ready as I'll ever be.'

'I want you to understand something, Kate.'

'What?' On the verge of rising to her feet, unthinkingly supporting herself from the gentle rocking of the water-taxi by holding onto his shoulder, she paused and looked at him.

In the darkness, his eyes glittered and his handsome face was all shadows and angles. When she inhaled, she could breathe in the woody, intensely masculine scent of whatever aftershave he was wearing.

'I would never have suggested this…arrangement…if I didn't have the utmost respect for you. Not only have you excelled with Angelina, for which I am immensely grateful, but you frankly haven't put a foot wrong. So when it comes to this…situation…you have my assurances that I consider you perfect for the role.'

He shot her a slow, crooked smile. 'I owe my uncle a debt of gratitude,' he murmured. 'And it's my dearest wish that he is healthy and happy. But I would never go so far as to wed a woman I didn't respect in order to achieve that. Self-sacrifice only goes so far.'

Respect…for an excellent employee, one who had a good relationship with his daughter…

Every complimentary word that passed his lips was a reminder that never in her life had she contemplated a marriage like this—one shorn of real emotion, one in which love was a word that would never been uttered. Her wish had always been for all the dreamy, fairy-tale stuff, for the joy of love, passion, hopes and dreams shared.

But the up sides had been too tantalising to reject. So much could be done with the money and how selfish would she have been to walk away from that?

'That's…er…very kind of you to say that,' Kate said politely.

Dante shook his head in frustration.

What was it about her? He meant every word he'd just said about respecting her. There was no way he would have contemplated this escapade—if it could be called that—with anyone *but* her, when he thought about it.

But that polite tone of voice, with just a hint of indifference to him underlying it…

For some reason, it got under his skin.

'Shall we?'

She straightened, balancing as the boat rocked, and Dante nodded, instantly killing confusing thoughts that had no place in the scheme of things.

As the last to board, they were assured the complete attention of everyone there.

Kate knew to expect that and yet, as they stepped onto the massive yacht and walked down the stunted bank of wooden steps into the privacy of the gleaming wood, leather and polished chrome of the reception area, she felt her heart begin to gallop inside her.

She wanted to pause to appreciate her surroundings. Out of the corner of her eye, she was aware of the rich turquoise of the carpet, the polished patina of wood, the staircase to the left winding up to another deck and the twin sunken living areas with their arrangement of leather sofas.

Those things on the periphery of her vision were, however, all overwhelmed by the faces that turned to them just as soon as they were ushered inside.

The faces of a dazzling array of bejewelled, extravagantly dressed women and expensive-looking men of various ages, statures and doubtless of bank balances.

There was a hushed silence as they stood silhouetted at the entrance. Kate was vaguely aware of glass doors sliding softly shut behind them and of her cashmere coat and shawl being eased off her. In the periphery of her vision, she could see the darkness beyond the glass wrapped around the yacht, a black sky studded with distant stars like tiny diamonds and the secretive stillness of water, interrupted by reflected light from ancient buildings and bridges.

Somewhere in the crowd was Antonio and, as she searched out his familiar face, she felt Dante's arm circle her waist, drawing her closer to him.

She half-tumbled against him and felt the hardness of his body alongside hers. While she was busy trying to steel herself from going a little weak at the knees, she heard him say, in a lazy drawl and with a smile in his voice, how pleased he was that everyone could make it to his impromptu gathering.

'We all lead busy lives.' He spoke with velvety self-assurance, a man at ease addressing an audience. 'And I realise that this has been sprung on many of you. My gratitude for the effort you've all made in clearing your calendars.'

Kate recognised a platitude when she heard one. Grateful for clear calendars? This was a man for whom calendars would routinely be swept clean because no one would want to miss out on the golden ticket of a private invitation from him.

'I expect some of you may well be speculating about what I'm about to say next...' He allowed a moment's loaded silence as his dark eyes roved over a sea of curious faces. Kate, meanwhile, was toeing a thin line between rigid self-control and total nervous freefall.

'I would like to announce my engagement to this beautiful woman who has kindly agreed to be my wife.'

There was an audible gasp.

Surprise... Disbelief... Utter and absolute shock... Would anyone faint? Kate forced herself to smile, but her body was rigid with tension and she knew that she was transmitting that tension to the guy standing next to her. But how could she not be tense as a bowstring? She frantically wondered what was going through his guests' heads, all of whom would surely have known Dante's beautiful ex-wife with the impeccable pedigree.

They were standing here, confronted by Angelina's nanny—although not that many of them had even set eyes on her before. A mystery woman, she thought with shrinking self-confidence, had blown in from nowhere and nabbed the most eligible bachelor in town—or, rather, *country.*

And, just when those thoughts were swirling in her head like a swarm of angry wasps determined to cause maximum mischief, she felt Dante manoeuvre her so that she turned away from those curious eyes, turned towards him and then...

Her eyelids fluttered and suddenly she felt as though she were being dropped from a great height, so great that everything inside her was jumbled up, a swooping, diving, dancing jumble that made breathing difficult.

She was scarcely aware of raising her hands, resting her palms flat against his chest or of the way her eyes widened as he lowered his head towards her. She just felt the taste of cool lips against hers, soft and slow, and the flick of his tongue meshing with hers, wetness sliding against wetness.

It was the most erotic experience she had ever had in her life. Time stood still. Everything stood still. Everything but the rush and race of blood through her veins and the heady beating of her pulse. Hot liquid pooled between her

legs until she wanted to pass out. Her body closed the small
distance between them and she could feel his heat searing
against her, burning a dangerous path through the cool distance she dimly knew she had to hang onto.

She breathed in deeply, and geared up to push him away
gently but firmly, but he beat her to it. And in that moment
she knew just how important that cherished distance between them had to be, how vital it was that she never let
herself forget that this was a business arrangement and
nothing more.

Still trembling, she heard him murmur with a smile in
his voice, 'I knew you were nervous. I think that kiss should
convince everyone that this is the real deal. Agreed?'

'Of course. Yes.'

A kiss for show...to cement this deal in the eyes of the
world. No more, no less. Yet how her body had ignited.
Shame flared inside her.

'Something else,' he said huskily, and then he slipped
a hand into a pocket and pulled out a small, deep-purple
velvet box.

Kate looked down at it numbly.

What else but a fake engagement ring for a fake engagement? she thought.

He opened the box and murmured that he hadn't been
sure of the size, but there had been no time for measure-
ments.

But, as he slipped it onto her finger, she could see that
it fitted perfectly.

An oval diamond, glittering and sparkling on a slender
white-gold band. There was nothing garish about it. It was
the ultimate in good taste and refinement, and a thing of
beauty. A searing gesture of what should have been a deeply
personal and romantic moment between two people who
loved one another.

'Perfect fit,' Kate murmured, raising her eyes to his, seething with resentment at the bewildering emotional response that well-timed kiss had roused in her.

She stood back and with a cool, controlled smile turned to face the mesmerised gathering, holding up her hand so that they could all admire the ring glinting on her finger.

His hand had moved to her waist—another well-timed gesture of affection. She slipped out of the casual embrace, fortified by the distance between them that kiss had put, by the ice-cold reality check it had produced.

She could see Antonio beaming and she headed towards him, pausing en route so that the diamond could be admired, and making sure she didn't look over her shoulder at the guy who had almost managed to turn her world on its axis.

CHAPTER SIX

ALMOST, BUT NOT QUITE.

Kate had had her wake-up call, and had had a few moments of utter disorientation when he had kissed her. But now…? That had been three days ago and she had had time to put that kiss into perspective.

That kiss, those casual, fleeting touches, the whole business of a ring on her finger and a life not so straightforward for the next couple of years would be a good life, as things went, she'd told herself. The joy of knowing that her parents would be taken care of the way they deserved to be in exchange for Kate leading a life of privilege that most women would give their eye teeth for. Nothing more than attendance at some functions would be required of her.

That, and of course presenting the right front to Antonio so that he had the peace of mind he needed to get stronger. She could do that. The times spent in Dante's company would be limited, although it had to be said they might very well end up doing stuff with Angelina. But would that be a hardship? No. She loved Angelina and she would set herself a mission to bring father and daughter together on slightly less forbidding and formal terms.

In fairness, as though obeying the change in their circumstances, Dante had been more present with his daughter in little but important ways. Angelina had shown her text messages on her mobile phone, which Kate had come close to suggesting might be a little too much for a child that young. She had composed responses, littered with loving emojis, and had giggled the day before when Dante had returned the favour but had got several wrong.

She had received the news of their engagement with the excitable, unquestioning acceptance of a child—no probing, no discussions. Presented with an odd and surprising development, for which there had been less than zero advance warning, Angelina had accepted Kate's new role as though it was the most natural development in the world.

'That's the best news *ever*!' She had smiled, her dark, serious eyes shimmering with earnestness. And then she had given them both huge hugs while she and Dante had looked at one another and smiled in a moment of perfectly unified compatibility.

A date hadn't been set for the wedding and Kate preferred not to think about that. It would happen and it would be the first step on a road that would reap much-needed benefits for her family.

Beyond that, she was happy to shove any unease over the arrangement to the back of her mind. What was the point in dwelling on the down sides? She had to look at the bigger picture.

The only change to her routine, at the moment, was a move from her quarters to a rather splendid suite of rooms that adjoined Dante's. The interconnecting door would remain firmly locked between them.

'Isn't that going to lead to speculation?' she had ventured the evening before, as she had turned full circle to inspect her magnificent new accommodation. When she had finally swivelled to a stop to look at him, it was to see that he was half-smiling, eyebrows raised.

'Explain.'

'We're not married yet...'

'It would no longer be appropriate for you to be in the nanny quarters now that we're engaged to be married. *That* would lead to speculation. I may have loyal staff working for me, but they might question why you're still in the servants' quarters when my ring is on your finger.'

'Servants' quarters?'

'It's a loose statement.' Dante had shrugged, unfazed by the cool criticism in her eyes.

'Is that what you've thought of me all the time I've been working for you?'

'You just said it, Kate. You were my employee. I didn't categorise you at all, if you must know. You did an invaluable job with my daughter and that was the sum total of it. Why are you offended?'

'Aren't you embarrassed to be engaged to an employee?'

'Why is this suddenly becoming an issue?'

'Stop answering a question with a question,' Kate had ground out in frustration.

'No, I'm not,' he'd said equably, which she'd found even more frustrating.

'Is that because this isn't really an engagement at all? Because it's meaningless?'

'We're past the stage of getting cold feet.' Dante's voice had been low and cool.

'I'm not getting cold feet. I just...'

'You need to stop getting lost in detail,' he'd advised smoothly but not unkindly. 'Whether you worked for me or not is irrelevant. I'm not *embarrassed* to be seen to be engaged to an employee. That's denigrating yourself. We're moving forward with this arrangement and everything is settling nicely into place. Moving quarters is just the next step. Are you...?' he had raked his fingers through his hair and looked at her with his dark head tilted to the side '...

comfortable with that? I assure you, the interconnecting door will remain locked. You needn't fear that there will ever be any intrusion of your privacy.'

Kate had reddened. How much clearer could he advertise the fact that she wasn't his type? That he wasn't attracted to her?

'We should discuss…er…'

'Timings? The business of when the knot gets tied?'

'Yes.'

'Tomorrow,' he had said. 'I have a series of meetings until five. I can be back by six and we can either have the discussion here or I can get my PA to book us a table at whatever restaurant you would like.' He had looked at her with sudden curiosity. 'What sort of food do you enjoy?'

She had met his dark, interested gaze with thoughtful eyes. It had occurred to her that this pretty much summed up the strange situation—she would be tying the knot with a guy who didn't know any of her likes or dislikes, her hopes and dreams or her moments of sadness and despair.

Then she'd thought of her chequered background. Restaurants had been few and far between. She'd smiled with genuine amusement.

'All food.'

He'd burst out laughing, which had made the breath catch in her throat, because just for a split second he had no longer been the cold, forbidding guy with the enticing proposition. He'd been a normal, sexy *human being*, a stupidly good-looking guy with a sense of humour and a laugh that made her lips twitch and had made her want to laugh out loud as well.

A guy, something inside had told her, she could like.

Confused, she had pulled back and told him that anywhere would be fine.

So here she was now, staring in the mirror before heading downstairs to meet Dante, who would be taking her to one of the most exclusive restaurants in the city.

She looked around at the exquisite suite of rooms that would now be her home for the next couple of years. The backdrop was gold and marble for rich Persian rugs and priceless antique furniture, polished so that she could see her reflection in the grain of the wood. Beyond the living area was a bedroom dominated by a four-poster bed overlooking the landscaped gardens to the back.

Kate wondered whether his wife had slept in this very room, but then dismissed that idea, because of course he would have had her close to him, next to him, sharing his space. He might have implied that separate quarters was perfectly acceptable between a married couple of a certain elevated status, but she was sure he and his beautiful wife had not succumbed to that tradition.

He had brought her closer, in keeping with her promotion from nanny to fiancée, but she would never make it past that locked interconnecting door.

For the first time, she wondered about the woman she was replacing. What must it have been like for him to have loved and lost the way he had? To still be so enamoured of a woman that he kept a portrait of her where he could always see it?

What must it have been like for his beautiful wife to have held this powerful and sexy guy in the palm of her hand?

Kate inspected her own reflection now. She'd changed. She looked the part. Her hair was nicely layered, and expertly highlighted and glossy, and her new and ever-expanding wardrobe seemed designed to do wonders for her slender figure.

The long-sleeved, deep-blue dress was of the softest cashmere and loosely belted at the waist. Her knee-high boots were bespoke. When she wiggled her hand, the diamond glittered and sparkled. She slipped on a jacket of butter-soft leather that matched the boots and headed downstairs at a brisk trot.

She hit the bottom of the stairs just as her phone beeped with a message from Dante that he would meet her at the restaurant. His meetings had over-run.

Disappointment flooded through her, which was puzzling, because it wasn't as though she had actually been looking forward to spending time with him in the back of his chauffeur-driven car! On the occasions when they had found themselves confined in the restrictive space of a car, he had barely spoken a word to her, instead choosing to work while she passed her time gazing through the window, frantically trying to marshal runaway thoughts.

There was a moment of self-consciousness as she reached the restaurant, was ushered inside and relieved of her coat. She had heard of this place. It was an intimate space cleverly partitioned by arrangements of various ferns and palms on dramatic pedestals. Nestled between these arrangements were cosy chairs and sofas, all upholstered in vivid royal-blue. The lighting was mellow and, although the place was packed to the rafters, it still managed to convey the impression of not being busy. There was a library-like hush—no loud roars of laughter or the clatter of voices competing to be heard.

She was shown to Dante's table with deference, and there he was, sprawled in one of the chairs with a glass of whisky in front of him, scrolling through his phone, which he dropped the second he realised she had arrived.

She looked spectacular—that was the punch-in-the-gut thought that hit him as soon as he spotted her dithering by the entrance. He could sense her awkwardness, just as he could understand it, although no one looking from the outside would have seen anything but cool, sophisticated elegance. She had chosen her wardrobe thoughtfully. Everything he had seen her in was streamlined and simple, and this dress was no exception. It made the most of a slender frame that was no less sexy because of her lack of curves.

There was a delicate, uber-feminine prettiness about her that only now seemed to reveal itself, although maybe, for the first time and in these extraordinary circumstances, he was seeing beyond the image she had always striven to project.

He frowned, shifted and half-stood as she approached the table.

'My apologies for the change of plan,' he murmured, watching her with brooding intensity as she settled into the chair and immediately fiddled with her hair, tucking it behind her ears and not quite meeting his gaze for a few seconds.

'That's okay.'

'Drink?'

'Water would be fine.'

'Surely not?' Dante shot her a crooked smile. 'Not when we're engaged and having a relaxed evening out...'

'Do you think people are looking at us?'

'This is a very private place, and no, despite what you may think, we haven't suddenly turned into show ponies required to go through hoops and gallop over obstacles,' Dante returned wryly. 'Forget about an audience. Why not try and relax, Kate?'

He signalled to a waiter, ordered a bottle of wine then relaxed back in the chair and looked at her for a couple of seconds. 'How are you...dealing with all of this? You've moved from the sidelines to take centre stage and I want to make sure that you're dealing with the sudden shift comfortably. Are you?'

'It's early days…'

'And the attention is only going to become more focused, I must warn you.'

'I understand that,' Kate said quietly. 'And it's worth it.' She sat back, allowing the waiter to pour them both some red wine, which he did with suitable flourish.

Dante nodded. The money… He lowered his eyes and was suddenly keen to move the situation to a different footing.

But what footing? And why?

Dante was aware of his shortcomings. He knew only too well that his austere upbringing had prepared him for a life of success, achievement and duty but had left him without any capacity for emotional generosity. His only access to what he expected was a normal childhood had been via his uncle, whom he had adored. But Antonio's occasional visits had left him gazing through a window at what love, *joie de vivre* and physical closeness might look like, unable to get past that barrier to sample those things first-hand. That just wasn't him. Perhaps, if Antonio had been more of a constant, then his influence might have been greater, but he hadn't been. He had dipped in and out.

And so Dante had long ago accepted the man that he was. It was why he had not flinched at his arranged marriage to Luciana and, whilst disappointed with the outcome, had been prepared to suffer through it, with rules laid down once Angelina had been born. He might have found her antics distasteful but, on a basic, emotional level, he had remained unscathed.

So this arrangement, this distance between them, the politeness of two strangers…why the sudden urge to change that dynamic?

'So…' He cleared his throat. 'Our wedding.'

'Yes. The wedding.'

'How does it sound that we proceed within the month?'

'Sure.'

'I've already deposited a substantial amount of money into your account. Perhaps you've checked?'

'Thank you.'

'Once we are married, I will continue to give you a generous monthly allowance, which will be independent of whatever you need for your daily requirements as my wife. But of course, that's already been confirmed in our pre-nup agreement.'

'We don't need to go over the money thing,' Kate mumbled. 'It's all perfectly fine. If you could tell me what sort of things I need to…er…do before the wedding.'

'What sort of things?'

She sighed. 'Normally a wedding is a big deal. The mother of the bride gets involved. Flowers need to be chosen, menus tasted and bridesmaids' dresses picked out.' Her breath caught in her throat and she looked away hurriedly. That was not going to be on the cards for her.

'I understand.' Dante flushed.

'What was it like first time round for you?'

'Come again?'

'Luciana… It must have been splendid.'

'It was a—a noteworthy event in the calendar for many important and influential people in Italy,' Dante said roughly. 'But that's by the by. Unless you have a particular wish to get involved in the detail, there will be a team of professionals more than capable of handling it all. Naturally, should you have any preferences with regard to flowers or decoration…'

'No.' Kate lowered her eyes.

Dante hesitated. 'Of course,' he expanded a little awkwardly, 'If your mother—your parents—would enjoy some contribution to the arrangements…?'

'What?'

'Your mother. You mentioned that there is usually in-
volvement from the mother of the bride. I can tell you that
Luciana's mother was quite detached from the arrangements
for my previous wedding. It was all left satisfactorily to the
army of people employed to ensure the smooth running of
the event. But, naturally, in this instance—'

'No!'

Kate gulped down a fortifying mouthful of her wine and
stared at him with alarm.

Dante's eyebrows shot up, to which she offered a weak
smile in return.

'I'm not following you. Why the extreme reaction?' He
frowned. 'Anything you feel I ought to know?'

'Anything, like what?'

'Your parents—is there a problem with them travelling
here for the wedding?'

'They won't be coming, I'm afraid.'

'Why would that be?'

'Because...' She drew those two syllables out until she
ran out of breath while Dante looked at her in expectant
silence. 'Okay. I haven't told them.'

'You haven't *told* them?'

'I... I didn't really see the point.'

'No point...'

'It's not as though it's the real thing.' Kate rushed into
hurried speech. 'And they would be disappointed.'

'Disappointed?'

'I honestly don't want to talk about this.'

'I'm sorry but I do.' He looked at her in silence and then
said, in the voice of someone making up his mind, 'Indeed,
I insist upon it. Arrangement this may very well be, but I

don't believe in a cloak-and-dagger approach. I would also like to meet your parents.'

'No!'

'Why not? Are you ashamed of them? Of me?'

'I...' Kate tried to imagine her free-spirited parents confronted by Dante and her mind hit an immediate roadblock. They would be aghast. They would be shocked and incredulous that she had somehow fallen for the sort of guy they would privately have scorned. 'No!'

'What would happen should your parents discover at a later date that we are married? That it was kept a secret from them?'

'Why would that happen?' Kate asked uneasily. 'They don't live in this country.'

'Work with me on this one, Kate. They will find out in due course that we're married, and naturally I will be in the firing line. Perhaps they'll think that I've somehow taken advantage of you. My reputation could very well be at stake. You know from first-hand experience the importance placed on tradition and reputation in my family. I will not see that jeopardised for reasons I cannot begin to understand.'

'Yes, but...'

'I'm prepared,' Dante said quietly, 'To call the whole thing off rather than risk complications occurring later down the line. It would be inconvenient and awkward but I won't have sordid revelations rearing ugly heads at some point in the future.'

Kate gaped. She realised that in her head she had already begun to spend the money on so many things her parents needed, things that she would never have been able to help them with in a million years without it. Practical help for her father— a house which would cater to all his needs. Giving them a lifetime without guilt and fear for the future. Maybe, in time, a specially adapted caravan so that they could continue with their travels—maybe not quite as they had done in the past, but at least free from the worry that pennies spent today were pennies they might need tomorrow...

Was she prepared to derail all those dreams for the sake of a meeting? She could deal with this.

Certainly, she wouldn't be able to get them over here, but perhaps Dante and her could go and visit them for a couple of days on neutral territory—a hotel somewhere. She would have control over the situation, would make sure to steer them away from any hint that this was not a love match. They believed in love. It was what they would want for her—the very thing that they themselves shared.

She would pretend. She would waffle something and nothing about opposites attracting and then, in the blink of an eye, the charade would be over and they would understand that not all relationships lasted for ever and that opposites attracting was a recipe for disaster. That, at any rate, was a bridge to be crossed as and when in the distant future. There was plenty of time for a suitable build-up to the inevitable parting of ways, by which time their futures would be assured.

'Well, if you insist, then I suppose...although I still don't think...'

Dante wondered whether she knew that the more she protested, the more curious he was. He gazed at her in brooding silence till she ran out of steam. All the while, like a persistent undertow stirring beneath the surface, was the vague feeling that, since he had embarked on this scheme, every second spent in this woman's company revealed sides to her that were a lot more compelling than he could ever have predicted.

'Good.' He wrapped up her stammering, doubtful agree-

ment with a brief nod. 'Overjoyed that we're finally on the
same page. I'll arrange suitable cover for Angelina. I think
it would benefit her to stay with my uncle outside Venice.'
He half-smiled. 'They can talk weddings. Angelina can
show him her bridal Barbie which she was keen to show
me yesterday.'

His smile warmed, like sun melting the cool of snow. 'In
due course, your parents, I'm sure, will meet her. But for
now perhaps this situation would warrant just the two of
us there to break the news. I suggest we leave day after tomorrow?'

'Uh…'

'Do I detect the sound of more objections being raised?'
he queried with just a hint of impatience.

Kate could think of several, starting with the fact that,
at such short notice, there was no way she would be able
to sort out neutral territory for this meeting to take place.

'No. Not at all. I'll try and, er, find a nice hotel nearby,
somewhere we can stay for—how long? A day or two?'

'I do think,' Dante offered pensively, 'That a day might
be cutting things a bit short, wouldn't you agree? Even if
we take my private jet, travelling that distance for a brief
cup of tea seems a little excessive.'

'I'll…' Kate sighed as all exits closed. The 'brief cup of
tea' would have worked, as far as she was concerned. 'I'll
let them know that I'll be coming to visit, and I'll surprise
them with the announcement when we get there.'

'Excellent idea.'

'Maybe,' she suggested thoughtfully, 'I could go ahead?
Have a chance to, er, brief them ahead of the big reveal?'

'If that works for you.' He paused. 'Although I have to
tell you that I've never found any woman so reluctant to
introduce me to the people close to her. I'm presuming you

have a close relationship with your family—your parents and your siblings?'

'I'm an only child,' Kate admitted.

'We have that in common.'

'That's about all.'

Dante grinned. 'Maybe we just need to dig a bit deeper...'

Kate tingled inside at the velvety smoothness of his voice. 'And, to answer part two of your question, yes, I'm very close with my parents.'

'Hence the dread of disappointing them by not presenting them with the fairy-tale dream. It'll happen for you one day. I get it. As for your closeness to them? We part ways on that front.'

Their eyes tangled and she felt heat flood through her. There was a moment of disturbing intimacy in that rare admission and it felt exciting.

'I'll confirm arrangements with you by mid-afternoon tomorrow,' he stated, flatly breaking whatever temporary spell he had put her under and she, in turn, replied with equal cool restraint,

'Okay—and, just for the record, if my uniform here is to dress up, then your uniform will be to dress *down*.'

'Is that a challenge?' Dante murmured, lazing back, looking as if he was enjoying himself.

'Maybe,' Kate murmured, lowering her gaze. 'Maybe we both have to accept challenges when it comes to this... arrangement.'

Which didn't help when, three days later, Kate found herself at the small station that serviced the nearest town to where her parents lived.

It was bitterly cold. Light snow was falling, an ominous scattering of flurries, like an appetiser for what was to come.

She wondered what might be going through Dante's head. His original plan had been to follow her out and allow her some breathing space to set the scene with her parents. Vital breathing space, as far as she was concerned, because she would be able to use that brief window to assuage potential apprehension about the speed of her mysterious engagement...whilst simultaneously planting a few useful seeds about having her head in the clouds and barely being able to think straight. She hoped that would generate dark forebodings about marrying in haste and repenting at leisure.

As it happened, everything had changed at the last minute. A series of urgent meetings with the board members of the family empire had been expedited by two weeks because of unrest in the ranks following Antonio's announcement that he would be stepping down. As the successor to the proverbial throne, Dante had informed those fractious elements within the various companies that he would be giving them a fortnight to get their heads together and table whatever questions they might have about the way forward.

'So I'll come out with you,' he had informed her hours before she'd been due to leave, thereby putting paid to any hopes for a relaxing trip back. 'It will give me an extra two days out there and I can return earlier, get prepared for a lively board meeting. You, of course, may stay on as you wish.'

'I...maybe...' Kate had prevaricated, as she had wondered what else could go awry.

The weather, she thought now, gazing worriedly at the heavens. The weather could go awry. It often did in this part of the world, where fields, mountains and rivers met the open blank canvas of a horizon only intermittently interrupted with towns and small villages.

She had hummed and hawed and in the end told him very little about her parents. When she thought about him meeting them and the inevitable awkwardness, she felt sick. Part of her expected her parents to be quiet and overwhelmed, saving their disapproval for when she was on her own, and that would be fine. A couple of days of stilted politeness would be bearable.

'It might have been a better idea to be driven here, wouldn't you agree?' Dante murmured from next to her and she snapped her attention to him. He was dressed for the cold but in the manner of someone not accustomed to having to put up with it too much—overcoat, dark jeans, a dark polo and some shoes that were not recommended for tramping through slush.

The station was busy and she could see people glancing at him with curiosity. He stuck out like a sore thumb. She had dumped the fancy gear in exchange for the clothes she normally wore in this part of the world and was sensibly dressed in various layers with a waterproof and heavy-duty, *faux*-fur-lined boots. It was late January, and she had known that winter here would not be nearly as polite and cheerful as winter in Italy.

Even in the first-class compartment, the train had not been a luxurious experience, especially when she compared it to their last luxurious joint experience, which had been on his yacht.

'Certainly not,' she said stoutly and, when his eyebrows shot up, she added for good measure, 'This is what travel is like here.'

'Really?' Dante murmured drily. 'And so nothing to do with the "dressing down" instructions you issued before we left...'

'Which,' Kate countered sarcastically, 'I note you didn't take on board.'

'If you look, you'll see that I'm wearing boots and jeans.'

'They're designer,' she scoffed and Dante grinned.

'Was that not allowed? I can't quite remember.'

'We should go get a taxi.'

'Will there be a rank of them?'

'Possibly not *a rank*,' Kate admitted, leading the way and huddling into her waterproof as the snow began to gather pace.

'Kate,' Dante said gently, slowing her down so that she reluctantly turned to him. 'Why not let me to handle this?'

'What?'

'Let me get someone to collect us from…remind me what this station is called?'

She told him and then said sceptically, 'How are you going to materialise a driver from thin air?'

'You'd be surprised what I can achieve.'

He pulled out his phone, spoke for a few minutes in rapid Italian and then looked at her smugly.

'That's very unattractive.' She tilted her chin and out-stared him, and his grin broadened into a laugh, which continued as they walked through the small, bustling station out into the forecourt.

'What is?'

'No one likes a know-it-all.'

'That being the case…shall I take the chauffeur-driven limo and let you arrange your own transport to your parents' house?'

But he was looking around as he said that and there was amusement in his voice.

Naturally, there were no taxis outside, and their wait for the car he had ordered was short, a matter of twenty minutes before a sleek, black car pulled up.

'How on earth did you manage that?' she asked, impressed.

'Easier than you probably think,' Dante admitted, ushering her into the back of the car. 'I have extensive contacts with various driver services across many continents. I telephoned my PA and asked her to arrange for us to be collected here. The car would simply have to come from the nearest city. It was far speedier than I anticipated, so it's likely they had finished a trip somewhere relatively close. Why are you so jumpy about this?'

The car was warm and comfortable and Kate turned to find him gazing at her with an inscrutable expression.

She opened her mouth and then hissed a sigh. 'We have this…arrangement,' she said with a helpless gesture. 'I just didn't want to… I wanted to keep it over there…'

'So you said,' Dante drawled, settling back against the cream leather and gazing at her thoughtfully. 'What other little surprises are lying in store for me, I wonder?'

Here they were and, like an onion, the layers peeled off revealed yet more layers underneath.

Was this what he had anticipated?

No. In his world, women had always been remarkably straightforward, including his ex-wife, despite her outrageous and distasteful behaviour.

He had vaguely seen this as travelling down the same road with a woman who would be as predictable in her likes and dislikes as the many who had preceded her.

He had offered an arrangement that included more money than anyone could wish for and had closed the door on any unforeseen complications. It would be a simple trade-off— a huge sum of money, which she clearly wanted or needed, in exchange for a marriage in which no demands would be made on her. There'd be nothing beyond some public engagements and behind-the-scenes, mutual politeness and respect. His uncle would be happy, the traditionalists who sat on the family board would be happy. Angelina would be happy. Everyone would be happy and for him—there would be relatively little change in his life.

'I never expected you to actually meet my parents.'

'That would seem naïve to me, considering we're about to embark on two years of wedded bliss.'

'Two years being the operative words...'

'Generally speaking,' Dante murmured, 'I would never have expected my role as husband-in-waiting to be heralded with so much trepidation and alarm. I'm thinking that many parents would not have slammed the door in my face.'

'That's because you live in a world where you're surrounded by people who would do anything to be in your company.' But he was right—he was the ultimate catch. 'My mum and dad...'

'I'm listening.'

'Well, you'll have to wait and see, but please don't be offended if the welcome isn't as effusive as you probably think it's going to be.'

'Thank you for the words of warning.' Dante smiled and rested his eyes on her, taking her in, from the delicate pink of her cheeks to the sweet fullness of her parted mouth, and liking what he saw.

'Just keep quiet,' she said. 'And leave the talking to me.'

His smile broadened and she blushed beetroot-red as he looked at her with lazy, leisurely interest.

'Why not?' Dante agreed, amused. 'I can't remember the last time I was given orders by a woman. But I am certainly willing to let you take the lead, Kate, and discover where it will go...'

CHAPTER SEVEN

THE SNOW HAD been a graceful reminder to Kate of what winters could look like in Lancashire, in the tiny, off-the-beaten-track town on the outskirts of which her parents lived. It had gathered pace by the time the houses, shops and lights of the small town centre had been left behind.

It was slow going—always was. From the chaos and adventure of a life spent travelling, her parents had ended up living in the most secluded and remote spot they could possibly have found, their only link to the place a tenuous connection via Kate's mother's side of the family. Her aunt and cousin still lived there and, in fact, had been very kind over the long weeks and months. That said, they lived in one of the busier parts of the county, and it was a trek visiting her parents.

Sitting next to Dante in the back of the cab, Kate wondered what was going through his head. She didn't want to look at him. He came from the very upper echelons of Italian society and was accustomed to a life of sophistication and luxury—a life filled with people waiting on him hand and foot, moving from one exciting city to another, always surrounded by bright lights and the very best that money and influence could buy. What on earth must he make of this slow and tortuous trip from a tiny provincial station where, at this time of the year, he could be forgiven for thinking that the majority of the population had upped sticks and left because everywhere was shrouded in darkness?

His prolonged silence was saying it all, as far as Kate was concerned. 'It doesn't usually take so long,' she eventually blurted out, turning to look at him, and then past him into swirls of snow rushing against the windows.

'Is this where you grew up?'

'I... Not exactly.'

'It's difficult to see what the place is like,' Dante confessed. 'It's very—quiet. Is it always this quiet? Is it somewhere that comes alive in summer?'

He sounded dubious.

'I know it probably seems dull in comparison to what you're used to,' Kate said defensively, 'But it's beautiful here. As beautiful as Venice, in fact. A different kind of beauty, but equally stunning. The greens of the trees in summer and the colours of the hills in autumn are spectacular. Out here, in this part of the world, it's all open spaces and you can breathe—really breathe.'

'Kate,' Dante said softly, 'What I say is not meant as a criticism. And, for the record, why do you imagine that I would find it dull out here?'

'Because...' She was ensnared by the glitter of his dark, dark eyes resting thoughtfully on her face. For a while she forgot all about the snow outside and the silent, slow progress of the car through the unlit side roads bordered with fields and open space.

'Because?'

'Because you grew up with everything.' Kate breathed, held captive by his gaze and with her heart picking up pace until she began to feel faint. 'You've lived a life wrapped up in luxury. I should warn you that you might not find the living standard out here quite the same.'

'You are telling me that I am a snob?'

'Of course you are, Dante. Why wouldn't you be?' She was genuinely perplexed that he might see himself as an ordinary human being. When she looked at him, he was so obviously offended that she blushed madly and smiled.

'If you knew half the people I knew growing up, then you would probably redefine your description of a snob,' Dante said wryly.

'What do you mean?'

'To be a snob is to consider yourself superior to other people, to put yourself on a pedestal above other people. You're very much mistaken if you think that this is the man that I am.'

Dante paused, considering yet another plunge into confidences he was not accustomed to sharing. 'I—I was raised to be the very person you describe,' he continued slowly. 'And maybe Antonio was my saviour. He escaped the constraints of birth by denouncing everything and he brought that taste of freedom into my life when I was growing up. Yes, I grew up surrounded by everything money could buy, but would I describe my life as a happy one? Possibly not.'

'What do you mean?'

'It was a cold upbringing, you might say ...' He looked at her in brooding silence for a few seconds and was suddenly disoriented—by the snow and the darkness, or by her? By those calm, intelligent eyes resting on him, not pressing him for confidences and yet luring him into giving them. 'And then there was my marriage.'

A first for everything, Dante thought. A first for him. He had never spoken to anyone about Luciana. He had never been tempted to. But now, here, it felt pretty good just to utter those words, a prelude to a confidence he might regret. Who knew?

He was staring down from a great height, not sure why he was so willing to break with the script, and that uncertainty was also a first for him.

* * *

'I'm so very sorry,' Kate murmured quietly, reaching out on impulse to cover his hand with hers and barely conscious of the gesture. 'Sorry for you and sorry for Angelina. She was a very beautiful woman and you must have loved her very much. You have that wonderful painting hanging where you can see her, be reminded of her, all the time. If you'd rather not talk about it, then I'll fully understand. I know we're here and doing this—*thing*—but that doesn't mean we have to breach whatever boundaries we have.'

'This *thing*...' He raised his eyebrows. 'You have a very special talent when it comes to denting my ego.'

'Maybe that's healthy for you,' Kate returned without pause for thought and then she laughed at herself. 'Now I sound like the teacher I am.' She expected the conversation to swerve away from the intensely personal road it had travelled down, and was already waving goodbye to a million and one unanswered questions buzzing in her head, but he looked at her seriously after a short while and raked his fingers through his dark hair.

'It was an arranged marriage,' Dante said thoughtfully. 'Two dynasties uniting—expected and welcomed.'

'You agreed to that?'

'It may seem alien to you but—' Dante shrugged '—in my world, it's the done thing. It was an arrangement that worked well enough with my own parents. Unfortunately...' his lips thinned '... Luciana was not the sort of woman willing to do anything whatsoever for the greater good.'

'What do you mean?'

'I mean my ex-wife was a sensationally beautiful woman who knew not just the power of her own looks but the immense control that came when money was aligned to that beauty. She inhabited a world in which the only person worthy of consideration was herself.'

Kate remained silent. Many things suddenly fell into place, starting with Angelina's lack of interest in talking about the mother she had lost, and ending with her absolute devotion to her father, even though he could be so remote and so engrossed with his work. Angelina had never bonded with a woman who had probably never bonded with her. On the rare occasion when Kate had asked her about her mother in passing, she had not been so much angry, upset or tearful as indifferent.

'But you have a portrait of her...'

'It always makes sense to be reminded of mistakes made. How else do we learn?'

'But that's so...so extreme.'

'For you, perhaps. For me, it's practical. We learn and we move on.'

And *that* was why he was an island, why he would never allow himself to give his heart or his emotions to any woman: why this situation made complete sense to him. Not only had he been raised to put duty first but his one and only foray into marriage had been a disaster. So now, with her, he had nothing to lose. They were on the same page, she thought, except...

She frowned and thought of her own misgivings and was uneasily aware that things might not be quite so straightforward for her.

'You must have had your own learning curves in your life?' Dante murmured.

'None as dramatic as yours. Thank you for telling me about her. We're in this together and it helps knowing a bit about each other.' She thought of her parents and was less hesitant about him meeting them now. A little bit shared had put things into perspective. His perfect life hadn't been quite as perfect as she'd expected and hers... Well, he would discover soon enough that hers contained its own twists, turns and unexpected corners.

She could see a way to them having something of a friendship. Maybe it wouldn't be marriage the way *she* understood marriage, but they would mug along until the time came for them to go their separate ways.

She took a sidelong look at his dark, handsome face and wondered about those women he would take—discreet dalliances to sate a physical appetite...

She shivered, tingled and suppressed a surge of inappropriate curiosity.

That kiss—she could still taste it on her mouth and when she thought about that she felt faint. A proper relationship with this man, she thought—the touch of his mouth on her for real and the heat of genuine passion leaving him weak with want—what would that be like?

It was such a silly, a fleeting moment of disorientation, that she almost laughed out loud.

'Indeed,' Dante murmured.

Still half-wrapped up in inappropriate thoughts, she projected to the sleeping arrangements awaiting them and knew that at least there was no need to worry on that front. The bedroom was so small she couldn't have swung a cat in it and the bed was a single, just big enough for her to sleep in if she didn't move around too much. He would be on the pull-out sofa in the living room, and when she thought about what awaited him she wondered whether she should warn him in advance. What if he clocked where he was going to sleep and collapsed on the spot? She couldn't resist a smirk; paramedics weren't exactly a dime a dozen out in this neck of the woods.

'We're nearly here.'

'How can you tell? Everywhere looks the same.'

'Maybe in the snow,' she admitted, 'But I've been here

a thousand times. I recognise the landmarks even when the weather's like this.'

'There are a lot of questions I should have asked,' he said ruefully.

'Too late. Like I said, if you let me carry the conversation, then it'll be fine. It's not as though you're going to be sticking around for long anyway.'

'Just time enough for me to break the news before I disappear on urgent business.'

'You're a very important person,' Kate said, and her heart sped up a little as their eyes tangled in shared amusement.

'So I am,' Dante agreed.

'You should tell the driver to take it easy up the lane,' she warned as the trees closed in around them, shadowy silhouettes buffeted by the snow, which was now falling thick and fast. When she looked at him, he was staring out of the window, oblivious to her.

Her parents' tiny house loomed into view, ablaze with lights, which was a useful guide to the driver, because everywhere else surrounding it was plunged in snow and blizzard-dark. The car pulled to a slow stop and, as it did, Kate saw the front door open and there was her mum, huddling in a cardigan, her long hair swept to one side. For a few seconds, she was overwhelmed with love and affection.

'We're here.' She turned to Dante but then scrambled out of the car without giving him an opportunity to respond.

Dante hesitated.

He didn't know what he had expected, and he wished he'd asked a few more questions, although events had happened more speedily than he had anticipated. He had also been lazy. Lazy in assuming that it would be straightforward to present this as a business deal of sorts, that he would be dealing with a woman with no hidden corners and no particular story to tell.

He'd been lazy and locked up in an ivory tower which he had built around himself over the years, from childhood. He seldom thought of his childhood, because acceptance of his destiny had been bred into him but just for a second he recalled the lack of physical affection from his parents as something solid, sad and tangible. He remembered childhood anxiety at always having to show a certain face, to maintain a certain stance from the day he could walk and talk. He had grown up tough, hard and self-contained. But as he looked at his wife-to-be rush out of the car, hurtling like a kid towards the slender woman framed in the doorway, and watched the loving embrace between them, something inside him hurt.

He quickly stifled that and swept out of the car, knowing that the driver would follow with the bags, including the very expensive, hand-blown glass vase he had brought with him as a gift.

He was swept inside in a tide of warmth and welcome, swept into a house that was smaller than his bedroom, in which a tiny entrance hall gave way to a small sitting room on the right. Beyond that, he guessed, was a couple of bedrooms and a kitchen.

From behind the vibrant, youthful woman with the smiling face shuffled an equally smiling middle-aged guy with a greying ponytail. Then more hugs, embraces and questions came at them from every angle.

'Amanda and George... Come in! So cold outside... So, so pleased to meet you... The minute Katie said she was bringing someone to meet us, we knew...'

Her father had lost a leg but was speedy with a crutch. Dante wondered when that had happened. Neither could get enough of their beloved daughter. Honestly, he had never experienced anything like this in his life before; he had never felt such effusive love and affection, in which he was unquestioningly and generously included.

This was family life at its very best, he realised with a sense of wonder and a wrenching feeling of loss.

It was everything he had never had.

It was as well that he had been instructed to leave the talking to Kate, because for once he found that he was lost for appropriate words.

He gleaned some things in passing. He watched the inter-action between parents and daughter with intense, brooding interest, and responded with charm to the questions asked, while wondering what spin Kate would put on this manu-factured relationship.

And a conscience that had not bothered him at all before kicked into gear and gathered pace, even as the evening drew to a close after a magnificent meal and Prosecco to celebrate the news they had clearly been expecting.

'So, we have a little surprise of our own for you two love birds!' Amanda carolled, bringing them into a warm huddle while George watched from the sidelines with a broad grin.

Tuned in to every nuance of the woman by his side, his wife-to-be, Dante could sense her apprehension and he shifted closer to her and swung his arm over her shoulders, instinctively protective.

'A surprise?' Kate ventured fearfully and her mother burst out laughing.

'Couldn't talk the woman out of it!' Her father growled. 'But it made sense.'

'What? What made sense?'

Dante's arm around her was reassuring. The evening had been as she had expected. Her parents had correctly sec-ond-guessed the surprise she'd had in store for them when she'd told them she was bringing a guy for them to meet, and that they might need to sit down for the news. She'd never brought any guy back for them to meet, so joining the dots hadn't been too difficult.

The only surprise was the lack of judgement. They must have guessed how rich Dante was. That mega-expensive vase had said it all, not to mention the designer stuff unceremoniously dumped on the coat hooks by the front door as soon as they'd blown in from the snow outside. Yet neither of her parents had said anything remotely snide or derogatory about '*people who have more money than sense*'.

Kate wondered uneasily whether they were keener than she'd expected at her bringing some guy home. She was still young, but had she missed little signs that they were anxious about the effect of their peripatetic lifestyle on her? Were they just so relieved that she was '*doing what girls her age should be doing*' that they were happy to overlook Dante's exclusive background?

And, wow, had Dante played the part! Not that he had had to do much at all—just be there, so damned solid, oozing sincerity and charming the socks off both of them.

That he was rich was something they must have gleaned but she doubted either of them had any idea just how rich. Their darling daughter had fallen in love with a guy they liked, and with that all other concerns had been dusted off and stored for some later date.

'You'll find out soon enough.' Her dad winked and she quailed.

'We might not have much, Katie, darling,' her mother said, watery-eyed. 'But the minute you told us that you were bringing a chap home for us to meet, we knew it was the real deal, and your surprise... Well, grab your bags, kids, and head out to the cabbage patch! But you'd better run. This snow's getting heavier by the moment!'

* * *

'I'm sorry.'

Kate was appalled. Not ashamed, but appalled, because *now* what happened next? And what on earth had possessed her parents to present them with *this*?

Of course, she knew. They had presented her with her own private space—at great cost, because they just couldn't afford to rent one of these things.

Kate looked around at just the sort of thing she remembered from her childhood—a tight space with a fold-down double bed, a little kitchenette, a compact bathroom and somewhere to sit and relax, a pair of grey sofas that faced one another. In actual fact, it was huge compared to some she could remember.

'Why?'

'I wasn't expecting this.' Her eyes welled up at her parents' kindness allied to the nightmare of trying to work out how the sleeping arrangements would work. The howling blizzard was almost strong enough to buffet the caravan.

'You were nervous.' Dante looked around him, spied the fridge and opened it to find it fully stocked. 'I could sense it.'

'Can you blame me?'

'No. Let me pour you a glass of wine.'

'How could you sense it?' She took the glass he poured out and offered. She needed it. Nerves had stopped her from drinking all but a single glass of Prosecco earlier, but now she needed this.

She sat and waited as he perched opposite her, so close that their knees were practically touching.

'It puzzles me,' Dante admitted truthfully. 'There seemed to be some sixth sense at work.'

'Well, you were right,' Kate said glumly. 'They're so excited for me. For *us*.'

For a few seconds, their eyes tangled before he lowered his lush lashes, concealing his expression.

She realised that she'd been so anxious that she had almost forgotten how beautiful he was, how darkly, dangerously handsome. But she remembered at pace as she breathed him in and noted the confined bedroom space just behind.

Even casually dressed and dishevelled after travelling he remained drop-dead gorgeous, his raven-black hair spiky and a little damp, his harsh, arrogant features softened as he looked at her curiously. If she was going to put money on establishing a firm friendship with this guy, then she was going to be down by her life savings if she carried on staring at him like this. But her eyes were glued to his face and it was an effort to tear them away.

'I see that. It was…unexpected.'

'I bet you think that everything about today has been unexpected. Starting with the weather and ending with us spending two nights in a caravan. Unless… Would you consider rushing back to Italy tonight for an emergency?'

'An emergency what?'

'Meeting? They understand that you work hard.'

'Not hard enough to risk life and limb, and at any rate the driver has decamped to the nearest hotel for the next couple of days. It would be unfair to have him risk *his* life and limb to fetch me for a non-existent meeting. The money… is it to help your family?'

Kate cradled the wine glass and stared down into the deep claret liquid. 'There was an accident,' she said softly, 'Some years ago. My dad was thrown from his motorbike and he lost his leg. I should explain that my life has been… unconventional. A lot of travelling.'

She breathed in deep and retraced her past, realising that it was the first time she had ever really spoken about it to anyone. She told him there had been no steady friendships along the way, that she had not remained in one place next to anyone long enough for her to consider them an anchor or a soul mate.

It was strange that she would choose this man to open up to but it felt good—dangerously good. And he made a terrific listener, not interrupting, just hearing her out with his head tilted to one side and his eyes thoughtful, sipping red wine and settling into his surroundings without a hint of condescension or snobbery. The snow swirled outside but in there the portable heaters were winning a battle to keep the small space warm.

'And yet you found time to study? To get qualifications?'

'I enjoyed it.'

Dante looked at her for a while in silence, then he drained the wine, glanced around him and wondered aloud whether she might give him a tour of their new surroundings.

'Not only can I do that, but I can do that without moving from where I am.' She eyed the sleeping area which was partitioned off with a gaily printed curtain. 'You'll have to take the sofa, I'm afraid. It should have been the sofa in the house, which might have been a bit more comfortable...'

'Was that the plan for the happily engaged couple?'

'I only have a single bed in my room. It could never have fitted both of us.' She blushed.

'What are your plans for the money?'

'I...' Kate lowered her eyes 'I... There's a mortgage on this house which I've been servicing. My parents, like I've just said, never really planned for their future. I want to make sure they're okay. More than that—I want to make sure they have the best kind of life they can have, after what's happened, and that means no money worries. There are so many things I want to get for them, too many to quantify on the spur of the moment.'

'Can I tell you something?'

'What?' Kate asked cautiously.

'Had you simply asked me for the money to do as you have just explained, I would happily have lent it to you or given it to you. Immaterial.'

'I would never have done that! Are you crazy?'

'It's an offer not many would have refused.'

'As I've already told you,' Kate said with a shaky laugh, 'You mix with all the wrong people.'

Dante smiled back at her and her heart skipped a couple of beats. 'In which case, I'm a lucky man to have found you,' he murmured, then he added quickly, 'I'd like to say that, if you want to renege on this arrangement, then I'll honour the pre-nup agreement we made without hesitation.'

Kate burst out laughing. 'Again, you're being crazy.' She sobered up and looked at him thoughtfully. 'I could never accept anything from you without knowing that my half of the bargain had been met.'

'Up to you,' Dante murmured half to himself but his dark eyes were shrewd and watchful. He slapped his hands on his thighs and stood up, which instantly made the caravan shrink to the size of a matchbox. 'So I get the sofa,' he said, eyeing it with scepticism.

'I'm afraid so.'

The logistics threatened to overwhelm her but then she decided that there were sufficient partitions to make the awkwardness bearable, and if need be she could always decamp to her own bed on some flimsy excuse or other. Developing a nasty cold and not wanting to spread it might be weak as excuses went but it could very well do.

She hesitated but was grateful when he seemed to take everything in his stride, moving to take the glasses to the sink. He told her that she should head into the house for a shower and by the time she returned he would be on the sofa, and they could both get as good a night's sleep as possible given the circumstances.

'You can say that I have a couple of urgent calls to make,' he instructed. 'As a workaholic, I am sure they won't be too surprised that I've dispatched you for a short while so that I can complete them.'

And he was true to his word.

When Kate returned forty minutes later, in her flannel pyjamas with a thick waterproof to hold off the snow, it was to find that he had hunkered down on the sofa. There was one lamp on and his shape was a dark bulk, half-hanging off. He was far too big for it, and guilt slammed into her, because the bed was a double, nicely done up for them both. Her mum had scattered petals on the duvet in anticipation of the glad tidings.

This was a decent and generous guy with a good heart, whatever her misconceptions about him had once been. Yes, he could be cold and remote, but he could also be considerate and kind.

She might get goose bumps because he was just so stupidly good-looking—and she was, after all, only human—but he didn't fancy her, so why should she refuse to share a bed with him? Why should she force him to try and sleep on a sofa that was too short and too narrow to accommodate anyone of average build?

Why should she act weird?

She quietly slipped off the waterproof, breathed in deep and nudged him on an arm.

'Problem?'

'It's stupid for you to sleep on this sofa.'

She watched as he propped himself up on his elbows. He was wearing a black tee-shirt which, as items of harmless clothing went, somehow managed to emphasise his muscled arms and the sinewy strength of his forearms, turning it from a harmless item of clothing to a flimsy garment highly dangerous to her peace of mind.

Her mouth dried and she hesitated. 'Don't worry about it. I'm fine.'

'No, you're not.' His polite reassurance made her stubbornly more determined to do what was right. 'You'll wake up with cramp in every part of your body if you sleep on the sofa. You can use the bed. It's big enough for both of us. We're adults, and we both know what the deal is even if no one else does. Besides, we'll be playing this game for a while to come. What if we get invited somewhere overnight as a couple and we're stuck in the same bedroom? What then?'

'You make a valid point.'

She spun round, padded towards the bed and slipped under the duvet, pleased that her pyjamas couldn't have covered more of her body, and if she happened to be braless under the top then it was hardly as though she was endowed with breasts the size of cantaloupes. Often enough she skipped wearing a bra.

She sneaked a glance at him as he followed in her wake in the black tee-shirt, black boxers…and a body that was designed for salacious flights of fancy.

But this was the pact they had made, and this situation was one that had to be navigated, because she was certain that it would occur again at some point in time. Best get it over and done with.

But she still felt the weight of him on the mattress and the way she had to tighten up to stop herself from sliding towards him, and she was horribly aware of the snow falling outside like a silent, white, all-concealing veil.

And, in her head, she still had the image of him in that black tee-shirt and those black boxers, lean, brown and powerfully built.

His soft breathing was as intrusive as a foghorn and she was conscious of every slight shift of weight until, at last, she managed to fall asleep.

CHAPTER EIGHT

KATE WOKE TO something unfamiliar, and it took her a few
seconds for her brain to engage sufficiently to work out what
that something unfamiliar was—arms around her, heavy
and hot, and her head resting against a hard, male torso.

She froze and with each passing second it became evident
that at some point during the night they had slid together.
Maybe the cold had kicked in and they had gravitated towards one another in an unconscious attempt to stay warm.
Or maybe his weight had ended up drawing her towards
him despite her best efforts to cling to the side of the bed.

Did it matter?

She was here, with him pressed against her, and she
was beginning to break out in a light, fine perspiration.
She began gently easing herself away. The thickness of her
prim and proper flannelette pyjamas, which would have
made any Victorian maiden aunt proud, was scant protection against an imagination that was running wild. It was
stampeding through all that nonsense she had preached to
herself about it being no big deal to share a bed with the guy
when she would probably end up having to do it at some
point in the future.

She had somehow concluded that his ridiculous sex appeal was something she could acknowledge but essentially
remain unaffected by because, in her head, the real power

of attraction could only work if it was harnessed to genuine emotion. And, in the case of Dante, she had no feelings towards him. She was involved with him because of a suitable arrangement but that was about the extent of it.

She'd been wrong.

Every nerve in her body was ablaze with something powerful and frightening as she continued to quietly wriggle away from his heavy embrace.

She had no idea what the time was but the snow was still falling and it was inky-black through the windows.

She felt his arm tighten around her and, when she inched her head to take a look, she started because he was looking right back at her.

'Where are you going?'

Dante, who slept as lightly as a cat, had awakened before Kate had even begun her tentative withdrawal. But, instead of pulling back from the highly unnatural position in which he'd found himself, he had stayed put, enjoying the feel of her against him, as slight as a reed and as delicate as an orchid.

She smelled fragrant. Half-asleep, half-awake, he had breathed her in, enjoying the flowery, clean scent and absently linking it to her absolute lack of artifice.

Dante did not share his bed with anyone. Even when he'd been married, Luciana had had her own quarters. Twenty-four-seven intimacy had never been on his agenda. Towards the end of their short, disastrous marriage, intimacy had become an abstract concept bearing no relation to real life, because the very sight and sound of his ex had made him grind his teeth in frustration and despair.

'Dante, this isn't working.'

She flipped over and he drew back, although it was a

small bed and he was still so close that she could feel the warmth of his body. He also still had his arm lightly draped over her, resting in the dip of her waist. She tapped it with her finger and then nudged it away.

'It's a small bed. Some physical contact is probably going to happen. Are you bothered by it?'

'No! But…'

'Then why do you say it isn't working?' He paused and, in a voice thick with pseudo concern, asked, 'Have I unconsciously done anything during the night to provoke your concern? I haven't made a pass at you, have I?'

'No!'

'Good! I thought that perhaps, in the dead of night and half-asleep, I might have…'

'Nothing of the sort!' Kate was wildly flustered and fast regretting that she had opened the conversation at all when she could simply have shifted away from him and fallen back asleep.

'That's a relief although, as I've already assured you, I'm an intensely disciplined man. Plus, as you've quite rightly pointed out, we're destined to share a bed at some point in time. It's inevitable, and foolishly something I hadn't factored in.'

'Yes…'

'There will be work-related events…family situations… Something as straightforward as staying with my uncle might very well require us to share a bedroom, and not all those bedrooms will have sofas large enough for me to occupy. I don't think it's going to be feasible to issue a short questionnaire on the contents of other people's guest quarters every time we accept an invitation that requires an overnight stay.'

'Granted, but…'

'The key question I feel I must be asking is whether I

make you nervous. Do I? I wouldn't want you to feel un-safe with me lying here next to you.'

His voice was low and soft with the dark, velvety smooth-ness of the finest chocolate and it brought her out in a de-licious cold sweat.

'*Unsafe?*' Kate was swamped by images of him lying next to her with those sexy boxers and tee-shirt off, im-ages of her hands scrabbling over his chest, her body hot and willing, opening up to him like a flower slowly unfurl-ing. 'Of course I don't! You've been the perfect gentleman.'

Because you don't find me attractive...

Why, oh why, had she embarked on this excruciatingly awkward conversation?

'Good. Because you might be a very desirable woman but, as you've correctly pointed out, I'm the perfect gentleman.'

'Desirable?' Kate squeaked.

'I hope I haven't embarrassed you but honesty, I feel, at all costs.'

'That's...ridiculous.'

'Interesting way to respond to a compliment...'

His voice was a husky murmur, burning through her com-posure. Dante could feel it. He liked it and he was frustrated with himself for liking it, was keen to get things back on solid ground. He loathed the way this woman made things shift under his feet and he couldn't help thinking that it must be the novelty of her, her freshness, aligned to the peculiar situation they'd found themselves in.

'I would never have guessed at your background.' He moved the conversation along even though he knew that he should be ending it. Ending it would have been easy enough—he would have just had to briskly remind her of the hour, fake a yawn and turn his back to her. 'Must have been difficult, making friends, seeing things through.'

'What do you mean by that?'

'Boyfriends… I got the feeling during the course of the evening that your parents worried that they might have been depriving you of a social life they felt you deserved.'

Kate cringed. He'd been listening intently during dinner, head tilted to one side, charming but not dominating the conversation, allowing her parents to confide all sorts of things, because they had absolutely loved him. If she had hoped that he might not be paying attention, that he might have his thoughts focused elsewhere—rather than on what she imagined must have been a boring litany of childhood highlights from her devoted parents—then it seemed she'd been mistaken.

'It's—it's late,' Kate stammered. 'We should get some sleep. I'm sorry I—'

'But we're up now, and I don't know about you, but I'm wide awake. It's going to be a little awkward if we both now lie here in silence pretending to be asleep, don't you think? Besides, where's the harm in a little conversation? All those questions I should have thought to ask?'

Kate's head was spinning from his accidental compliment. *Desirable?* No one had ever called her that before— ever. She contemplated the awkwardness of them both lying next to one another feigning sleep, both knowing the other was wide awake. Had there been any need to point that out? Now it was all she could think about.

'I suppose now that we're up…'

'My point exactly. Of course, if you'd rather we get dressed and sit on the sofa to chat…'

'No. I'm perfectly…comfortable right here.'

'Sure? Earlier, you seemed to…'

'I may have overreacted.'

'So tell me about your parents. I'm getting the impression you thought this meeting might have been slightly different.'

Kate gave in. The more skittish she was, the more ridiculous she felt. The harder she tried and failed to keep her cool, the more she realised how essential it was to do so. 'Okay. I guess I never thought that they would... I'm not sure how to put this, Dante, without sounding rude...'

'Hesitant about speaking your mind? Once upon a time I thought that might have been the person you were. I was wrong. Shall I pre-empt you? You didn't think that your parents would approve of me. Maybe you thought they'd be polite and then wait for the right moment to ask you what the hell was going on? You didn't expect the photo albums and the scrapbooks. Also, maybe you thought that I might disapprove of *them*.'

So he was on a bed with her—big deal.

And what if he said that he thought she was desirable?

That little throwaway remark, so softly murmured, was the spanner in the works. But there was no need for him to know how she felt about him, was there? That would be to open a Pandora's box filled with all sorts of danger.

Her heart sped up at the thought of it. She wondered what that sort of *danger* might feel like. What it might taste like. She'd spent so many years knowing that security was the thing she wanted most. Why did the notion of playing with fire now feather through her, stirring excitement?

'Well?' Dante prompted and she blinked, surfaced and groped her way back to reality.

'I thought they'd have trouble accepting you,' she confessed, voice hitching as she shifted her gaze to stare beyond him to the shadows and angles of the space they were sharing. 'They've been hippies all their lives. They've never placed any importance on material stuff. You're the complete opposite of them and it never occurred to me that—'

'That they might actually find me likeable?'

'I warned you I might sound rude,' Kate said uncomfortably. 'And, yes, if you must know,' she added a little defensively, 'I was also afraid that *you* wouldn't get along with them.'

'Because…?'

'Because, when two worlds collide, it can sometimes be difficult.'

'You might say that about us,' Dante murmured. 'Although *collision* seems a dramatic interpretation. We're in this but you still can't get past finding difficulties everywhere. Relax.'

'I couldn't be more relaxed!' Kate protested tensely.

'Liar.' His voice was soft and amused.

His dark, velvety, accented voice made her shiver.

'You don't understand.' Kate detected an edge of desperation in her voice and cleared her throat, badly wanting to leap out of the bed, but well aware that to do so would bring up more tricky questions and rouse more curiosity than she could deal with.

'Understand this—instead of focusing on all the differences between us….and, yes, there are differences…try focusing on the positives.'

Dante shot her a brooding look from under his lashes. He had said all the right things but the feel of her on the bed next to him…not relaxing. Not at all. He'd never been ruled by his body and cold logic told him that he wasn't going to allow that to happen now. One of them had to take charge, had to be cool and composed, and it fell to him to be that person. The fewer complications that were introduced into this arrangement, the better, and any sort of sexual undercurrent was a complication.

But never had Dante wanted complications more than

he did right now. Never had he just wanted to give in to the demands of his body—to go with the flow. Should he have told her that he found her desirable? Too late to retract that statement.

'I guess…'

'We get along,' he expanded huskily. 'We'll learn how to circle one another and deal with situations like this, which are trivial.'

'Trivial…'

'And when it comes to the fact that we're from different backgrounds? Just remember that that doesn't mean that I'm cut off from the reality of what other lives might look like. Like I've explained to you, my life hasn't exactly been a bed of roses. We both bring different things to the table, but none of that affects the practicalities of this deal. It works on a lot of levels and let's put that at the forefront instead of undermining it with potential pitfalls. Make sense?'

'Perfect sense.'

Well, that told her.

How many times did one person need to have cold water thrown over their head before they got the message?

And Dante's message was loud and clear. Bypass the occasional flattering observation, and any casual shows of intimacy purely driven by a need to keep up appearances, and what she was left with was a guy reminding her that this was a business proposition. So why the constant analysing, the *ifs, buts* and *whys*? In the big scheme of things, as he'd said, this was trivial.

She'd edged away from him, and of course he had immediately done the same, but the bed was small. She could breathe him in. Her eyelids fluttered, her nostrils flared and her eyes locked with his.

And still…she wanted to return to what he had said,

when he'd let slip that he found her desirable. Why? Was it a case of flattery going to her head? She was so inexperienced. Was that it—that she just didn't know how to deal with this particular unknown? A sexy guy found her attractive and she just couldn't let it go, but wanted to worry away at it as though it were a shaky tooth?

The silence settled between them and Dante fidgeted. He was picking something up and, while he didn't quite know what exactly that *something* was, he was damned sure he didn't want to deal with it. Did he? No! He had shut the door on having to deal with emotions in any woman after his marriage. He had become adept at steering liaisons in just the direction he wanted, out of harm's way. He didn't need complications!

'What you said earlier...' Kate breathed.

Dante caught on fast to where she was going with this and killed it dead before it could develop roots and start growing. 'No need to tread over old ground. I was being honest with you for a reason.'

'I know,' she said on a deep breath and in pursuit of an honest clearing of the air between them. 'You must think that I'm very disingenuous but—'

'There's honestly no need for us to go down this particular road.'

'But there is. I think so. We can skirt round stuff but—'

'I didn't see the point in pretending that I was immune to your appeal,' Dante told her bluntly. 'You're an attractive woman. You just have to look in the mirror to see that.'

'You've never said anything like that before.'

'I have strict codes of behaviour when it comes to people who work for me,' Dante said shakily. He cleared his throat. 'I don't see an attractive woman and find myself compelled to pursue.'

'Well, I actually *do* still work for you in a manner of speaking...'

'Slightly different job title. Look, maybe I'm noticing things about you now because—'

'Because?'

Dante was fast realising that her directness wasn't confined to asking him questions about himself that he signalled he'd rather not answer. She dug in her heels and, it would seem, was happy to brave his displeasure over any and every matter she wanted to clarify.

'Novelty? Who knows, Kate?'

'Novelty...'

She had no idea what sort of women he really found desirable but she imagined that they wouldn't be slight and unremarkable with barely-there breasts and no hips or curves to speak of. So, yes, she got the novelty value aspect, but it hurt.

'And, if there's any kind of reciprocal situation with you...'

'Reciprocal situation?'

'You get where I'm going with this.'

'Ah. Yes, I do. I may be a little uncomfortable around you, Dante, but I think that's understandable. I don't have your level of experience. For a start, I'm a lot younger and I haven't been married. It would be unnatural if it was all water off a duck's back, wouldn't you agree? So, if I seem a little gauche, then that's why—and not because I'm suddenly finding you attractive because of the novelty of it all. That's not the person I am.'

'No?'

'Not at all,' she said stoutly. 'Anyway, I'm fully awake now.' She slipped off the bed. It was cold with the heaters off and the lack of body warmth hit her. 'I'll go read for a while, and in a bit I'll go to the house—let them know that you won't be here for long...'

*   *   *

Over the next day and a half, Kate realised that she knew less about her parents than she'd thought.

How could she ever have thought that they would disapprove of Dante? Because he was mega-rich, mega-powerful, uber-traditional and they were completely the opposite?

Had they actually been waiting for a suitable guy to appear in her life, a man with whom her father could bond? Because that was how it felt to Kate.

Her dad ignored all her dismayed protests that Dante really probably didn't have time to have lessons on self-sufficiency, to be shown every square inch of the land her parents were cultivating or to be treated to an hour's worth of prime viewing of the innumerable photos of the beloved motorbike that was no more.

He was a busy guy and had to leave to return to Milan, she had said more than once the evening before, but Dante had just turned to her with a smile and said that he could spare the time. Angelina was having a fantastic time with his uncle and a couple more days there wouldn't hurt her. He was chatting to them both every day, doing video calls. Angelina was unspeakably excited and preparing some kind of surprise for them when they returned—what it was, he knew not what, but hints were that it was of a culinary nature.

'It's important to get to know the parents of my future wife,' he had said sanctimoniously—which Kate had felt made her sound mealy-mouthed and petty, wanting him to leave when he was happy to stay on for a short while longer, especially given the weather.

Her nomadic, unconventional parents were far more conventional than she had ever given them credit for, Kate realised.

Her mother excitedly pulled her to one side so that they could discuss wedding dresses.

'We always wished we'd done it properly,' she confided, which was news to Kate. 'But we were young, and in a hurry, and both sets of parents were making noises about going to university and getting jobs like everyone else, and we just wanted to escape and have fun and see the world.'

Dante was oblivious to her concerns. He was the perfect fiancé and loving the role. If he was bored by her father's reminiscing, and by all the detailed plans afoot for growing what was at the moment just a cottage industry, then he gave no indication of it.

Not only that, but in the quiet of their quarters he was also the perfect gentleman. He'd taken the sofa, even though she'd assured him that there was no need. It had become quite clear that her novelty value on the desirability front had run its course and that what was being established now was a pattern of friendship that she knew she should welcome.

But, in some strange way, she felt as though she'd been outmanoeuvred and she hunkered down under the duvet, fulminating, while he quietly caught up on work in the tiny living area. The snow had gone from blizzard to a steady, thin fall and she could hear a stiff wind outside blowing it against the windows.

'Why are you sulking?'

Wrapped up in her thoughts, Kate started at the sound of Dante's voice, because she hadn't heard him pad across the floor to the bed.

She flipped onto her side and then wriggled up as he sat on the bed with her.

His gentle voice said he was about to dispense some friendly, anodyne words of wisdom and she didn't want any of it. She was fed up with the Mr Nice Guy image.

'You've taken over,' she said bluntly.

'What are you talking about?'

'This isn't how it was supposed to go.'

'What did you have in mind?'

'It doesn't matter. I don't want to talk about it.'

'I want you to.'

'Why?'

'Because I don't like the thought of you being unhappy. If you have a problem, then spit it out. I can't stand feminine wiles.'

'I'm not unhappy, Dante, and I'm not the sort of person who has feminine wiles! Which is very sexist, as it happens.'

'You're disappointed that your parents like me?'

'I'm disappointed that they've obviously been desperate to see me married off. I always thought they'd want me to be as free-spirited as they'd been.'

'They said so?'

'Not in so many words.'

'You're not your parents, Kate. Their dream was to see the world. Was that your dream?'

'No.' She sighed with frustration, half-resenting his kind voice, which was getting on her nerves the more she heard it. 'It was never my dream. Why are you being so nice to be, Dante?'

'I like you. I like your parents.' He shrugged. 'Is there a problem with that?'

'No problem.'

'Talk to me.'

'Isn't that what I'm doing?'

'I'm not your type,' Dante heard himself say in a roughened undertone. 'And what's the big deal if I'm being nice? Since when was being nice a crime?'

He raked his fingers through his hair and felt the silence pulse between them like a heartbeat. It was cold inside, even though the portable oil heaters were still doing their duty. This was the most basic place he had ever stayed in in his life, and yet the love that had obviously gone into preparing it for them had managed to turn it into one of the best.

He had anticipated a day or two of making a polite effort to advance the fiction of their love story but he hadn't anticipated the feeling of utter relaxation that had overwhelmed him in this small, back-of-beyond place where the bad weather never seemed to end.

This was the feeling he'd used to get as a kid when Antonio had breezed in from one of his adventures—a feeling of playing truant from the daily grind of doing his duty.

'Well?' he challenged. 'If you don't like me being nice, then what would you rather?'

'Nothing.'

'Would you like me to fit into the category you feel safest with—maybe be cold and remote, robot-like? Isn't that a description you once used?'

'Dante…'

'If I stop being *nice*,' he ground out in a driven undertone, 'Then you might not like the person you end up having to deal with.'

'What person is that?'

'A man who can't get you out of his head. A man who still finds you incredibly attractive and is finding it harder and harder not to touch you.'

'You—you don't mean that,' Kate stammered. She rested her hand flat on his chest. He was still wearing his jumper and jeans, and she was fully clothed in her thick pyjamas, but she could still feel the hot burn of his skin against her hand. He covered her hand with his. Somehow he was lying next to her and they were facing one another. She wasn't too sure how they had reached that position, but it felt natural, a feeling of calm after turbulence.

'Trust me. I never say anything I don't mean.'

'But you're not my type.' Kate clung desperately to a familiar mantra. 'And I'm just a novelty to you. You said that! This is just something that suits us both.'

'You're right on all those counts.'

Kate caught her breath in sharp, gut-wrenching disappointment.

'But...?' She found that she was hoping for a '*but*'.

'What would you like me to say? And you still haven't answered my question. If you don't want *nice,* then what would you rather?'

'But being attracted to one another...that's not what this is about.'

'If I touch you, would you still say the same thing?'

Kate's eyelids fluttered. She thought she heard herself whimper, because his words were so provocative and filled her with such crazy yearning that her whole body seemed to go up in flames.

She felt she should stand firm, but instead she clung to him, fingers curling into his jumper, a hand seeking the hardness pressing against her. With no experience at all, her body just seemed to know how to behave and what to do, propelled by a craving she had never had before, had never suspected existed.

'I don't know what I'd say! It's not a good idea... None of this is a good idea...'

'You're the one who started this conversation, so why isn't it a good idea?' He talked as his hands began a slow exploration of her, taking his time to feel the outline of her slight body under the heavy-duty pyjamas. He drew in a sharp breath as he slipped one hand under the top and felt the silky smoothness of bare skin.

'I can't think when you're doing that.'

'That's good.' He buried his face into her fragrant hair

and got high on the scent of her, then nuzzled her ear lobe before trailing kisses along the side of her cheek and covering her mouth with his. 'I want you so badly right now, I feel as though I'm going to explode, and if that's what novelty does to both of us, then what's wrong with trying it out for size? Sometimes doing something that doesn't make sense can feel very, very good…can turn out to make the most sense in the world…' He pulled back.

'Convince me,' Kate breathed, eyes dark with desire as she pushed her hands under his jumper.

'We both know the score. I'm not cut out for the emotional business of loving anyone. I don't have it in me, and maybe I never did, but you're the opposite. You want the real deal. But in between both those opposing poles, my darling, is a world of enjoyment to be had because there will be no strings attached.'

'No strings attached…' Kate liked the sound of that and he was right. She wanted love, kids and a 'for ever' commitment, but why not enjoy this blip on the horizon? What would be the point in being a martyr? Wouldn't it be all the more dangerous to deny this crazy attraction? Wouldn't that just feed it?

She was a novelty to him, but wasn't he exactly the same for her? He certainly didn't fit the image she had for any guy she would ever spend her life with. In her mind, her 'for ever' partner would be calm and steady as a rock; a nice, reliable guy who'd make her feel comfortable; a guy who wouldn't send her nervous system into freefall every time he looked her way. Why shouldn't she enjoy the thing that was not destined to last?

'Fun,' Dante murmured, his voice oozing honeyed temptation. 'We could have fun. Nothing lasts, and the great thing is that neither of us has a problem with that.'

Nothing lasts...

For them both, no, not this. This wouldn't last. That was all part of the deal.

'I want fun,' she said simply.

She lay back and breathed in deeply, her body an open invitation, and Dante was overwhelmed by a swoop of pure passion that made him tremble.

Nothing had ever felt better. He touched her gently under the top, then slowly unbuttoned it, then reared up to gaze down at her. Her small, exquisite breasts were tipped with nipples that were perfect tan discs. The thin light filtering through from the living room cast shadows over her and he felt he'd never seen anything so perfect before.

He braced himself on one arm to unzip his trousers but everything was moving too slowly. Shorn of his usual grace, Dante vaulted upright and realised that he was so excited that he could barely get off his clothes. He stripped jerkily, tossing them on the ground, and feeling the pinch of cold in the air. His brain was telling him to slow down but his body was accelerating at a pace he couldn't control.

He clenched his jaw hard and reminded himself that he was a guy with years of self-control bred into him. But when he subsided onto the mattress, and when his eyes caught the hot, drowsy gaze of hers, those years of self-control were washed away and he fumbled to undress her like a horny teenager, stumbling in his efforts and stopping to touch.

He couldn't get enough. He tugged down the pyjama bottoms and she wriggled in a frantic effort to free herself, as hungry for him as he was for her.

'I want to go slow,' Dante muttered shakily, half to himself. He breathed in deeply and touched her gently. He circled her nipple with the tip of his finger, round and round, until the stiffened bud throbbed against his fingertip. He kissed her—not hungrily, even though he wanted to, but gently and tenderly, taking his time and trying hard to ignore the demanding pulse of his erection.

Every touch was a thrill that was wondrous to Kate. Her body was alive for the first time in her life, opening up for this man, leaving her no time to think about anything but the pleasure of sensation.

He stroked the length of her body and she shuddered and clung to him, her nails digging into his shoulders and her legs splaying apart. Between her thighs was a dampness that made her restless and impatient for him to take her…to fill her.

How would that feel? Would it hurt? In the dim recesses of her mind, she knew that her virginity might be a stumbling block, but there was no way she was going to start a conversation about it, not when she was on fire and desperate for him.

Why would he find out anyway?

He covered her nipple with his mouth and suckled on it, drawing it in and firing her up even more as he licked it with his tongue until she was breathing fast and moaning, soft little moans she barely recognised.

Touching her, Dante felt attuned to her every move and every small whimper. Her body was slight, responsive and as delicate as a gazelle's; her thighs opening for him were slender and silky and, when he cupped her mound with his hand, he felt the wetness of her arousal.

'I can't believe how turned on I am right now.' He groaned, blindly reaching for his wallet, feeling for protection without moving away from her heated body.

'Me too,' Kate admitted. 'I just want you to keep touching me. I… Is this okay for you? I mean… I don't have a lot of…'

'Shh... Perfect. Couldn't be more so.'

He set himself the pleasurable task of exploring every inch of her body with his hands, fingers and mouth.

On an unbelievable high, Dante delayed what his body longed to do. He parted her slick opening and dipped his tongue to swirl it around the sensitive bud of her clitoris, and she squirmed against him, angling her body to take full advantage of what he was doing.

When he finally tore open the little packet and sheathed himself with a shaky hand, he was no longer a man in control of his body. He entered her with one long, hard and supremely satisfying thrust. Through a haze of soaring sensation, and even as her own body took flight with his, he was aware of her brief flinch and the sharp little exclamation that accompanied it. But all that was lost in a tide of utter satisfaction and he came with a long shudder, rearing up and swearing with pleasure under his breath, feeling her own body arching up to match his.

Dante fell back, spent. He couldn't remember a more satisfying experience but, then again, it *had* been a while. He'd never been a guy who lived at the behest of his libido. The last time he had slept with a woman had been over three months ago.

'What was that all about?' He flipped onto his side to look at her and manoeuvred her so that she was facing him. He brushed back her hair, enjoying the silky length sifting through his fingers, and patiently waited for her to answer. 'And don't try and pretend that you don't know what I'm talking about.'

'I told you I wasn't experienced,' Kate mumbled as colour climbed into her cheeks.

'That's a little different from being a virgin, wouldn't you agree?' Dante questioned gently. 'Why didn't you warn me?'

'Because I didn't want you to get cold feet,' Kate blurted

out. 'You…you're so experienced, Dante. I knew that if I said anything you'd be turned off.'

'Are you mad, woman?'

'I don't expect you fancy yourself a teacher when it comes to sex.' Kate was lost in defence of her decision, unaware of the soft stroking of her arm or the sudden stirring of his arousal against her belly. 'I expect your days of that are long gone and I was just so… I…'

'You were so hot for me that the thought of me retreating before I could satisfy you was too much to bear?'

'Something like that. Maybe. Yes. I guess…'

'I've never slept with a virgin before. Kate, in all your years travelling with your parents, growing up in a liberal environment, how is it that you never became involved with a guy?'

'Mum and Dad might have led an unconventional life,' she returned honestly, 'But it was never a case of "anything goes". I guess it's a bit like Antonio. He might have travelled around and chosen adventure over duty but look at where we are now… In his soul, he's as conventional as my parents. He was happy enough to let you get on with things but, the minute he thought he was facing his own mortality, all those traditional traits in him came out and he couldn't face the thought of you not settling down.'

'Touché,' Dante acknowledged thoughtfully.

'But, aside from that, it was difficult. Difficult hanging onto friends and difficult experimenting with boys.' She smiled and grimaced at the same time.

'And here we are,' Dante murmured with a lusty, satisfied smile. 'And believe me when I tell you, you being a virgin? Not a problem.'

Why did that feel so good? he asked himself. *So oddly good but also…so oddly dangerous.*

Because she was soft and romantic, with no hard edges to protect her from people like him—tough guys with no illusions, cynical on the subject of love.

Drifting this way and that, replete and foolishly contented, Dante pulled himself up short and reminded himself that fun often came at a price. The last thing he needed was for her to find out down the line that the price was too steep to pay. Her reasons for doing this were hard-headed, but that wasn't *her*.

No illusions—that had been the deal. Was there any need to remind her? How often did she have to have it confirmed that love was not in his repertoire?

Why over-egg the pudding? Too much thinking about precautionary measures would be self-defeating.

'In fact,' he ground out, 'It's so much not a problem that I'm already getting hard for you in record-breaking time.'

'Me too.' Kate sighed and curled into him, nudging her thigh between his legs, already heady for an encore, but he smiled, kissed the tip of her nose and edged back.

'Not yet.' He cupped the nape of her neck. 'Too soon to have me in you again…but, if you like, I can think of many ways to pleasure you without penetration. Would you care to sample what's on offer?' He swept his hand over her breast and oh, so gently, stroked her nipple. She moved closer, her heat melding and matching his.

'Yes, Dante. I rather think I would.'

CHAPTER NINE

DANTE LOOKED AT his wife-to-be with brooding intensity. This was a sight he never failed to enjoy and, ever since they had made love, he had been enjoying it solidly for three weeks.

She was getting dressed. The way she moved, with such grace, never failed to arouse him and that was something he had only just about got used to. He was a man who was easily bored, and that was something he no longer bothered to question, but he wasn't bored now, not nearly.

'You should come back to bed,' he drawled, propping himself on one elbow and looking at her with intense interest. He patted the mattress and watched as she ignored him, searching for clothes which had been scattered in haste on the ground.

She was grinning. He could make that out in the shadowy darkness of the bedroom. It was a little after eight, and the shutters and heavy voile panels only allowed slivers of light through, even though outside the day had already begun.

He couldn't believe that he was here, in a luxury riad in Morocco for three nights. Since when had Morocco ever been on his list of desired holiday destinations? Actually, when had he ever had a list of desired holiday destinations anyway?

But Kate had laughingly mentioned Morocco, had mentioned that it had always sounded so glamorous when she had been travelling around with her parents, absorbing information like a sponge and dreaming of seeing places without the headache of living in and out of boxes.

And, without bothering to think, he had got his PA to book the most luxurious place in the foothills of the Atlas Mountains, nestled in Berber territory. Every stick of furniture and every artefact in the spacious suite had been hand-sourced from Indonesia, India and North Africa. They had had a veritable sermon on the subject the evening before, when they had been shown to their over-the-top luxurious quarters. There was an infinity pool and they had their own magnificent plunge-pool.

Dante had been tempted to tell the enthusiastic lad that the marvels of the décor and the hand-picked furnishings were irrelevant, when his eyes were only programmed to linger on the woman standing next to him, quivering with excitement.

'Do you ever think about anything but sex, Dante?' she said lightly, slinging a tee-shirt over her head and slipping into some discarded knickers.

'It's very hard when I'm around you.'

'There's a ton of things we can do.'

'I'll bet you can't interest me in any of them. Or maybe just one...'

'We can go hiking. It's stunning here—breath-taking. The mountains...the greenery... Do you know there are even peacocks in the grounds? It's amazing.'

'How do you know all that?'

'I read the blurb in the information pack in one of the drawers. There's the hiking, there are day excursions to explore the area, there are cooking courses...'

'You can forget that particular one,' Dante said drily,

reluctantly abandoning the bed but not bothering to get dressed. 'I'm not interested in doing something other people are so much better at doing for me.'

'Lazy.' But her eyes darkened and she stood still, appreciating the raw, masculine appeal of the guy strolling towards her, totally uninhibited and at ease with his nakedness.

He smiled slowly and she blushed and tried to unscramble her whirring mind. 'You are *not* going to distract me,' she said in a muffled voice, but the closer he came the faster her body revved into fifth gear and, when he stopped in front of her, breathing had become a challenge.

'Sure about that?' He eased her towards him, their bodies pressed close, and guided her hand to his erection.

He pushed off the clothes, just. The tee shirt was half-on, half-off, one shoulder exposed, pulling against the soft smallness of her breast. As she caressed him, he played with her nipple, teasing it until she was moaning, head thrown back, eyelids fluttering.

She was definitely distracted.

'Wait…' he murmured. 'I think you're distracting me more than I promised to distract you. That wasn't part of the deal…'

He lowered himself and knelt at her feet, easing down the underwear, which she stepped out of and then gently parted her legs and surrendered on a sigh of utter bliss as he dipped his tongue…

Her whole body quivered under the devastating impact of that hot caress. Her fingers curled into his dark hair and her mind went blank. Each flick of his tongue carried her higher and higher until she was tipping over the edge, flooded with pleasure and ecstasy, and then slowly coming down from that high to a glorious feeling of contentment.

When she opened her eyes and looked down at him,

gazing at his dark head, never had she felt so at peace in her life before.

A wave of confusion rolled over her.

She knew excitement when she was around him, a feeling of living life on the edge and trying out stuff for the first time. Being *alive* for the first time as a woman.

But this peace? Her heart was thumping as she drew back with a wobbly smile.

'That was very bad of you,' she teased shakily. She cleared the fog in her head and things settled back into place.

'In which case,' Dante murmured silkily into her ear, 'Maybe you'd like to punish me later…?'

He heard the ping of his phone with another work message and ignored it.

He was getting good at doing that. He had another couple of days here, and so what if he took some time out and temporarily put work on hold?

'So we've agreed to scrap the boring cookery class,' he drawled. 'I'm amenable to an excursion but only if it's followed by a dip in our plunge pool, dinner served in our rooms and all sorts of fun afterwards. Deal?'

Kate burst out laughing. 'Deal.'

'Have you missed Angelina? Milan?' Kate sneaked a teasing sideways glance at him as they were settled into their first-class seats, ready to leave paradise behind and return to pick up where they had left off. 'Your work?'

He was staring at his laptop and she wondered whether she was already losing him as he returned to his punishing schedule. She didn't want that.

He glanced at her, shut the laptop and looked at her for a few silent seconds.

'Of course.' He paused. 'There's only so much time a person can take off work before the backlog piles up.'

'Don't you have people you can delegate things to?'

'In times of emergency, I have things that can be put in place.'

Those times of emergency had yet to materialise. He'd always been the guy in charge, first of his own affairs, and now the affairs of the family empire. He only casually supervised it, leaving the nitty-gritty to his uncle and the comprehensive bank of CEOs who worked alongside him. They were paid enough, after all—too much to be relieved of the majority of their duties because he was a workaholic who hated to delegate.

He had spent so much of his life harnessed to doing what had to be done. Was that freedom? In the process, he had drifted away from his daughter, always too busy to be emotionally and physically available.

He had this window to set things straight on that front, and why shouldn't he take it? The window wasn't going to remain open for ever. There was a limited offer on this particular deal.

Dante didn't believe in any sort of long-term relationship. He had once hoped for something that would at least offer functionality and a certain amount of predictable calm, but he had been wrong on all counts with Luciana.

He wasn't cut out for the hype and he liked the woman sitting next to him. He liked her, respected her and fancied her. She deserved a lot more than a guy who could never give her the life she dreamt of. But he could give her huge sums of money with which to help her parents, and he could give her hot sex until the time came when that side of things fizzled out.

As it would. When he couldn't emotionally attach,

there would be nothing to replace the first flare of heat. It wouldn't turn into anything deeper. It would just disappear. He was sure that, when that happened, they would be on the same page.

By then he would have lost this peculiar craving.

'That said...' he murmured, his voice inviting her to lean into him, which she did.

'That said...?'

'I'll be perfectly honest with you, Kate. I feel closer to Angelina than I ever have and I see a chance for me to spend more time with her.' He sighed. 'You've somehow managed to broker a valuable meeting ground between us and I don't want to lose that.' He shrugged. 'I suppose I've been victim to the cliché that it's way too easy to get involved in work to the exclusion of everything else.'

'That would be really great, Dante.'

'So, when it comes to my lifestyle of working all hours and snatching a bit of leisure time whenever and wherever I can? That, at least for the while, will be a thing of the past.'

'Angelina will really love that.'

'Of course, nothing is set in stone. There will be times when I have no choice but to go abroad, to work into the early hours...'

'Of course.' The loose, carefree feeling of drifting on a cloud was beginning to seep away. This sounded like the sort of formal speech a boss might give his secretary at her annual appraisal. She'd feasted her eyes on him in shorts, tee-shirts and loafers on their glorious escape to Morocco. Now, although he wasn't in a suit, he was in dark trousers and dark jumper and he already looked every inch the aristocrat he was.

She didn't know what she'd been expecting and was disappointed that she was disappointed.

'And then there's us,' he murmured in a lazy drawl, his dark eyes roving over her in a lingering inspection.

On cue, her eyes got slumberous with heat and her thoughts turned to the sinfully erotic. Despite the busyness of boarding going on around them, she still had to fight the urge to touch him. It was as though her newly awakened body knew no limits, was greedy for more, like a beggar at a banquet.

She also knew that he could see exactly what sort of effect he had on her, and yet she was helpless to prevent her body from responding.

He shifted so that their heads were together in intimate dialogue. 'When you look at me like that, I feel like getting off this plane right now and heading for the nearest hotel, motel or frankly anywhere where there's a bed and a door I can lock...'

He drew his finger over her parted mouth and looked at her with amusement. 'You have such a transparent face,' he said with a slow smile.

'I'm not sure that's a good thing,' Kate returned with heartfelt honesty. In fact, she was uneasily aware that it very much was *not* a good thing. '"*And then there's us*". What did you mean by that?'

Dante drew back but his eyes were still pinned to her face. He patted her leg and said crisply, 'I hadn't planned on this situation happening but, now that it has, I don't see any reason why we can't carry on having fun until—we're no longer having fun. At least, until we're no longer having fun between the sheets. We're both adults, we've discovered that we want one another...*a lot*...and we're going to be husband and wife.'

'Or we could just put the whole thing behind us as a... blip.'

'A blip?'

'Something that shouldn't have happened. Something that should be nipped in the bud because of complications that could arise.'

'What sort of complications?'

'Things have a way of turning messy,' Kate said vaguely. 'Don't they?'

'They won't turn messy. We both know the lay of the land.'

Dante marvelled at the rapid turnaround from when he had first laid down the rules of engagement. Then, the thought of sleeping with this woman had not featured on his horizon. Even when he had curiously begun to toy with the notion that she was a heck of a lot more attractive than he'd originally thought—when his thoughts had gone from '*no way*' to '*what if*?'—he had *still* been resolute in his stance. No sex and no muddying of the water.

Now? A three-hundred-and-sixty-degree turn.

'Besides…' He picked up his argument because he was intent on persuading her out of whatever doubts she seemed to have. 'Do you honestly believe that it'll be easy for us to lock the doors between us and pretend that nothing happened? Don't you think that there might be just the tiniest amount of awkwardness? Worse, has it crossed your mind that, the harder we try to fight this, the more it'll grow until it becomes an obsession?'

'I never knew you were so dramatic, Dante.' But she was frowning and what he said took root and mushroomed into various scenarios, all of which had poor outcomes.

Guiltily, she knew that she was also tempted to listen and agree because she wanted him so badly.

'You do that to me,' he said huskily and she sighed and lay back, eyes fluttering shut. She didn't pull away when he raised her hand to tenderly kiss the sensitive underside of her wrist and, when she slid her eyes to meet his, they both knew that she would be his.

With plans swiftly moving forward for a wedding that was getting increasingly close, Kate should have been in a place of relative calm.

They were getting along. They were finding that they had a lot in common, despite their very different backgrounds. The once remote, cold and forbidding man was now a guy who was witty, thoughtful and way too clever for his own good. He liked the way she argued with him and she enjoyed the way he listened and then pulled so many facts and figures out of the bag that she usually ended up scrambling to even up the debate.

And, of course, the sex—it was red-hot.

So why was she uneasy as the date for the nuptials was set and preparations put into motion?

Everything was straightforward. Wasn't it?

Standing in front of a floor mirror she was putting the finishing touches to her hair. When she looked over her shoulder, she caught Dante's gaze and smiled.

'Where's Angelina?'

'Flower arranging,' he returned wryly. 'She went out in the garden with Lorenzo and persuaded him to cut a dozen flowers for her to present to the invalid, although, from the sounds of it, the invalid is in remarkably good form.'

'He still hasn't said what's going on with his tests.' She looked at Dante. They were in his suite and she could see his reflection in the bank of mirrors to one side as he did up the buttons of his shirt. 'Why on earth is he being so secretive? Do you think he's concealing something from us?'

'He would never be as jolly as he's been for the past couple of weeks if there were clouds on the horizon,' Dante mused, reaching for a black cashmere V-neck jumper and slinging it over the white shirt.

He was idly appreciating the curve of her slender body as she angled her head to put on some earrings, tear-shaped diamonds he had given her a handful of days ago, personally chosen.

'Let me help,' he murmured.

He felt the silken softness of her skin against his knuckle as he fiddled with the earring, and he felt something else— the steady drumbeat of the unfamiliar. Was this what domesticity felt like? Was this what hope felt like? The familiarity between them was so easy that words were almost superfluous. Was this what *normality* felt like?

His mouth tightened. Once, briefly, he'd hoped for normality. Marriage to Luciana might have been arranged, and he might have approached it with acceptance of the inevitable, but underneath the cynicism hadn't there been *hope*? Hope that he might find something beyond what his parents had had? She had been a beautiful woman and, at least in the initial stages, vibrant and fun.

It had been an illusion and the hope he'd briefly nurtured had withered and died fast enough. Whatever small shred of optimism he'd ever had, about having a wife who might be more than a woman with the right pedigree, programmed to fulfil the duties into which she had been born like his own mother, had disappeared. That was not for him, and it was better that way, because there was nothing more painful than the loss of hope.

He didn't like the taste in his mouth now and, thinking about it, neither did he like the urgency of his body whenever he was near this woman.

Did she make him weak? Maybe not, but it felt like it, and he loathed that and rejected it out of hand because he knew what it could spell—a loss of control, a dismantling of barriers.

'The dress suits you.' He spun round on his heels and sauntered over for his wallet and the keys to his car, which he had intended to drive himself rather than use a car with a driver. Now, though, the romantic, exhilarating trip felt over the top and unnecessary. He needed to recover his perspective and romantic, exhilarating car trips, even with a mini chaperone in the back seat, weren't exactly a great starting point.

He needed a breather, by which time everything would have fallen right back into place and this moment would be lost to reality.

'I think I'll get Paolo.'

'Your driver? But I thought you wanted to take your car out for a spin?' Kate smiled. 'Weren't you the guy who made a big deal about never having enough opportunity to drive the cars you own?'

She had turned to look at him and he returned her laughing, open gaze with a shuttered expression.

'I've suddenly remembered I've got work to do,' he said abruptly. He scrolled down his phone without looking at her, but *feeling her*, and hating the thought that he might be hurting her with his sudden change of attitude. However, more pressing was his urgency to get back onto solid ground.

When he finally did raise his eyes, something inside him clenched because there was confusion in her gaze, although she was still smiling, her fingers fiddling with the diamond necklace round her neck.

'Okay.'

'I've taken a hell of a lot of time off.'

'I know.'

'Companies don't run themselves.'

'You don't have to justify working in the car, Dante,'

Kate said gently. 'I don't expect you to give up the day job because playing truant suddenly looks more appealing. I *know* you have work to do. Besides, when Angelina gets tired—and I'm sure she will on the trip there—she gets fractious and enjoys playing games and being entertained, so I expect I'll be busy doing that.'

'Good.' He wasn't sure how much better he felt but so be it. He waited politely by the door, still scrolling through his phone while she hurried to get all her various bits together, and when he did finally rest his dark gaze on her he swiftly stifled the rush of adrenaline at the sight.

She was as dainty as a fairy and as graceful as a ballerina. Expensive clothes suited her, made her look even more feminine and ethereal than she already was. He felt the sluggish heat in his veins and the stirring of a libido he found so hard to keep in check when he was near her.

'We should get going.' He turned, opened the bedroom door and stood aside for her to waft past him, brushing against him in a way that was unconsciously provocative.

Then he put distance between them, which was easy, because when they got outside Angelina was skipping and waiting, half-hidden behind a massive bouquet of flowers, while behind her Dante's head gardener smiled and lifted his shoulders in a resigned, indulgent gesture.

And in the car he sat in the front seat, opened his laptop, closed the partition between front and back and waited for feelings he couldn't fathom—but needed to banish— to subside.

CHAPTER TEN

WHAT WAS GOING ON?

Kate wasn't sure. Dante worked for the duration of the long car trip to Antonio's palace while she half-focused on an exuberant Angelina, who had an exhaustive supply of car games she wanted to play.

Had she said something? Done something?

Or was it just her imagination playing tricks on her? The truth was that the past few weeks had been utter bliss. She had never thought that they could blend so seamlessly, that their personalities could be so complementary. How could she ever have put him down as someone as chilling as winter sun?

She desperately wanted to find out but it was only after they'd finally arrived, after coats had been removed and discreetly taken away, and Angelina disappeared with Antonio and the flowers, which she insisted required immediate attention, that Kate was able to tug Dante to one side.

'What's wrong?'

'Wrong?'

'Have I said something?'

Their eyes met, hers anxious, his cool and unreadable.

'Not that I can think of,' Dante told her, moving out of the hall and heading for the sitting room, where pre-dinner drinks were being served.

Kate hesitated and tugged him to a stop, and felt the way he stiffened with a sinking heart.

Panic clawed inside her.

And hot on the heels of panic came the appalling realisation that she was hurt. She felt the gentle shove of being pushed aside and that *hurt*.

No, more than *hurt*. It sent her into a dizzying, frightening tailspin because somewhere and somehow she had been stripped of her defences.

Being in control—an adult having fun with no strings attached and no expectations—had been washed away under an onslaught of emotions, desires and wants that she had never predicted.

She had done well to recognise her own limitations, to acknowledge her lack of experience, so why on earth hadn't she made the logical leap to realise that those very limitations would leave her horrendously exposed when it came to dealing with a guy like Dante—would leave her *heart* horrendously exposed?

They had slept together, and she had been foolishly infected by his assurances that it was all some fun which would run its course, leaving no one hurt.

So what happened now?

She fixed a smile on her face while her thoughts continued pelting along on the runaway train.

'Good. And did you get much work done?'

'Enough.'

'Enough for what?'

Dante met that soft, sexy, questioning gaze and resolve slammed into place—no misunderstandings, no blurred lines. They'd slept together and he wanted to carry on sleeping with her. It was unthinkable that they wouldn't, because they enjoyed one another way too much to walk away from the physical side of the arrangement.

Unforeseen, but now impossible to ignore.

That said, ground had to be recovered. He'd wavered, found himself over-thinking the whole situation, and now was the perfect moment to gather himself and get the splayed deck of cards back in a stack, ready to be shuffled and dealt, but this time with him firmly in control.

He growled, stepping towards her, invading her space and breathing her in, her scent the headiest of aphrodisiacs. 'Enough for me to spend some undiluted time in bed with you later. No distractions. Just me and you, and me doing all sorts of sexy things to you.'

'Dante…'

'Shh…' He traced her lower lip with his finger. 'Let's not get wrapped up thinking too hard about this.'

'What do you mean?' Kate whispered.

'I mean, you were upset because I had to work in the car.' He pulled back and watched her with steady, cool eyes.

'I wasn't upset.'

'I'm not in the business of putting work to one side to cater for any kind of relationship.'

'We talked about this! I know that.'

'Do you?'

'Of course I do.' She drew in a deep, shaky breath. 'I know the limits of this situation.'

'That's good.'

'You've repeated the rules and regulations often enough to make sure I don't forget.' Her voice was terse, her body rigid with tension.

'Yet sometimes amnesia can kick in when the rules get a little tweaked, and us sleeping together comes under that category, wouldn't you agree?

Kate lowered her eyes. Her heart was beating wildly inside her as the cold ramifications of her misjudgement coalesced.

She fallen in love with a guy who was only capable of

lust. She'd given herself to him hook, line and sinker and now she felt sick at the prospect of the future yawning ahead of her. She saw a slow-motion scenario of Dante losing interest: turning his back on her because she'd outlived her novelty value; having discreet liaisons, which was what she had foolishly agreed to when everything had seemed clear cut.

'I suppose so,' she said faintly.

'But now we've cleared the air.' Dante pulled back. 'We'd better see what's happening with my daughter and my uncle and the flowers.'

'Which looked a little tired after the car journey here,' Kate chipped in, because a chirpy remark seemed to be expected of her. Sure enough, Dante nodded with an approving smile and turned, and she edged a little away but kept pace as they headed to the sitting room.

They could hear voices before they entered—Antonio and Angelina. She would have to keep up the front. Could she? She smiled all the way through a long early evening and then, when Angelina was in bed, through an even longer dinner. It was just the three of them, with a menu that never seemed to stop, and every delicious course tasting like cardboard.

Thank the lord, Dante knew how to hold court. If she hadn't been so tense, she would have been amused at the way Antonio bristled at every question to do with his health, which he'd repeatedly done ever since they'd returned to Italy, until Dante was forced into retreat. She would have been amused at the way this big, powerful, aggressively dominant male could be manoeuvred into a position he obviously didn't much like.

She would have stared in rapt fascination at the guy she had fallen in love with, would have hung onto every word and would have been utterly involved in every aspect of the conversation, because that was just what happened when you loved someone.

And, most of all, her head would have been filled with thoughts of what was going to happen when they headed upstairs, when the clothes came off and desire took over.

'Are you feeling all right, my dear?'

Kate blinked. Somehow the drinks had disappeared. Where? Had she actually drunk the glass of dessert wine that had been pressed on her? She hated dessert wine. And where was Dante?

'Sorry?'

'You're a million miles away. Have been all evening.'

'Where's Dante?' Kate blinked, owl-like. Antonio's eyes were narrowed, watching her shrewdly.

'Sent him off.'

'Sorry?' Conscious that she was repeating herself, Kate tried to get a grip. How on earth could she have been thinking of Dante and the sudden mess she was in all evening and yet literally not even have noticed when he left the room? 'Where?'

'Work.' Antonio shrugged. 'Told him I had unearthed some problems in the shipping sector of the company. Looked thorny. Urgently needed him to cast an eye. He seemed pleased enough to take the bait.'

'Bait?' Kate frowned, but she found it impossible to join the dots in the conversation because her brain felt foggy.

'You do not look like a radiant bride-to-be, my dear. Ever since you returned from seeing your parents, you'd been bursting with happiness. But now...?'

'No, no. Not me,' Kate said with dismay. 'I've been my usual self.'

'So what is going on here?' Antonio waved aside her feeble response. 'Have you and my nephew had an argument? To be expected. These things happen. Pre-wedding nerves, I believe it is called, although, having never been in that place myself, I can only speculate.'

'Antonio...'

Yes, she'd been brimming over with happiness, she thought miserably. She'd been floating on cloud nine but now she had crashed back down to earth and without any safety gear to cushion the fall. Every part of her was hurting and underneath the hurt was the dreadful fear for what the future might hold.

It would be fine because it would have to be. Her eyes started to well up and she looked away, but she didn't trust herself to speak, and into the telling silence Antonio prodded gently, moving to sit closer to her and covering her hand with his.

'I have seen it all,' he murmured in a voice that could have melted ice. 'You can tell me anything. Are you pregnant? Is that it?'

'No!' That managed to bring a smile to her lips. 'Now that *really* would be a disaster,' she murmured to herself. The smile didn't last. It faded when she thought of how Dante would greet an accident like that—with horror. His worst nightmare.

'Ah.'

Antonio rose unsteadily to his feet to move to the door, brushing away her helping hand, but then turned back round and reached for his phone.

'I see how the land lies, my dear,' he said sadly.

'I don't think you do, Antonio.'

'As I said, nothing comes as a surprise to me any longer, but perhaps there are things left to surprise *you*. You and my nephew. Who will be here in a minute—I have texted him. Told him I need to see him urgently.'

'Why?'

Antonio shrugged. 'Perhaps it is time for an old man to stop causing mischief...'

* * *

He sat them down.

Out of the corner of her eye, Kate noted Dante's wary expression. She wanted to reach out and squeeze his hand, share amusement at his uncle's dramatic antics, but everything had changed and that sort of spontaneous gesture no longer seemed carefree and innocent.

'I am afraid I have been guilty,' he said heavily, 'Of a small amount of well-intentioned deceit.'

'Meaning?' This from Dante, sitting next to her on the sofa and maintaining just enough distance to remind her that they were not the loved-up couple she had ended up deluding herself into believing they were, but two people who had simply enjoyed having sex within a relationship in which they'd both given themselves permission to do so without over-analysing.

'I *did* have a genuine scare.' Antonio huffed defensively.

'Meaning?' Dante repeated, voice considerably cooler, while Kate blinked and did her best to follow the trajectory of what Antonio was saying.

'I *thought* I was at death's door— that was perfectly understandable, and I will not have anyone say otherwise!'

Dante got there before her and flung himself back with a groan that was somewhere between frustration and despair.

It took Kate a little bit longer. She had to hear a bit more of the explanation before she got the gist of what Antonio was actually saying and then, just in case either of them had missed the glaringly obvious, he stated in defiant summary, 'Can anyone blame an old man for wanting to leave his house in order before he meets the Grim Reaper? Can anyone blame me for trying to steer my beloved Dante into a relationship that would benefit both him and Angelina— incidentally, the apple of this old man's eye? If it happened that I exaggerated the health crisis facing me, then could anyone blame me?'

He made a show of mopping his brow. 'I suppose, if we are all going to have a Spanish Inquisition about the whole thing, I would admit that I could have said sooner that my cancer scare turned out to be an infection, happily taken care of with the right medication.'

He flapped his hand dismissively while Kate digested this startling announcement. 'That's good,' she ventured faintly into the ever-increasing silence.

'But,' Antonio continued as implacably as a steamroller now that he had embarked on his comprehensive confession, 'I felt in my gut that you two…would work.'

He gestured with Italian eloquence but his eyes were sad. 'I admit that I knew it was a contrived relationship to keep an old man happy. I do not know, and nor do I wish to know, what sort of agreement you reached, but I was very happy to encourage you both. I was so certain, you see, that love would follow in the footsteps of convenience.'

He shot Kate a sidelong, knowing look.

'Things have not, however, lived up to expectation.' Another elaborate shrug as he rose to his feet. 'To conclude, there is no need for you to continue this pretence. I am fine, and it would be better to break it off before time and fate decide to cause even more mischief than I have.'

Kate was hardly aware of him shuffling out of the sitting room. The revelation had struck her like a blast of freezing air and had given her a choice in what happened next.

She was free to walk away without a guilty conscience and, more to the point, so was Dante.

She half-turned to look at him and met dark, inscrutable eyes before he vaulted upright to pour himself a whisky from the bottle that was sitting on a silver tray on one of the coffee tables.

'So,' he drawled. 'An evening to remember.'

He remained where he was, standing, sipping the whisky and looking at her over the rim of his glass. 'But it's a good thing that he isn't as seriously ill as we thought…'

Her head was swirling. She couldn't meet the brooding intensity of his gaze but things were getting clearer in her mind. Antonio had said what he had said for a reason. He had seen right through her to the love that had grown out of nothing, thriving on promises of happiness that had never been made.

She was at a crossroads now.

Give it all up—the money and the hopes for her family, because there was no way she would accept a hand-out for duties unfulfilled—and know that at least she would be walking away from slow, painful heartbreak before she served out her two-year contract.

Or breathe in deeply, keep her fingers crossed that she could maintain a front and look at the bigger picture, which was the very thing that had inspired her in the first place.

Or another option…

'Agreed.' She cleared her throat. 'Dante…'

'I'm not entirely sure what my uncle was hoping to achieve with his extraordinary confession, aside from the very important purpose of putting our minds to rest on the health front. Certainly, from my point of view, it's business as usual.' He shot her a devastating, wolfish smile that made her blood grow hot.

'Perhaps for you,' Kate said quietly. 'But not for me.'

'What are you talking about?'

'This isn't going to work. I should be able to get back to where we started, get back to where *I* started, but I can't.'

'Let's not over-think this,' Dante said roughly, strolling towards her and swamping her with his proximity as he sat next to her and reached to lace his fingers through hers. 'My uncle may have dropped a bombshell, but nothing has to change, and this situation still makes good sense. The traditional members of my family are appeased and, far more importantly, my daughter has a guiding hand for the next two crucial years of her life before she moves on to boarding school.'

'I'm in love with you.'

The silence that met this bald statement was deafening. His face had become a closed book and he moved his hand and sat back in stunned silence, giving her ample time to feel queasy.

'If I could be on the sex-with-no-strings-attached page, if I could think about what we have ending and turning into something else until the expiry date comes up, then I *could* carry on. Because I do need and want the money and will never accept any of it if we part company...'

'*If...*'

Going for broke, Kate breathed in deeply and said huskily in a rush, 'We get along so well, and I don't just mean in bed. As two people, we laugh and chat, and sometimes it feels as though we're *one*. Do you feel any of that? Do you feel that we might make a go of this?'

'What are you talking about?'

'We could...really see what happens, Dante. I know you've been burnt in the past and I... I've never thought that you were the kind of guy I could ever go for, but we could both be brave...see where this takes us for real.'

She saw his answer in the way he sprang to his feet and the speed with which he put distance between them until he was staring at her, narrow-eyed, from across the width of the room.

'That is not an option,' he said with unyielding ferocity. 'It never was and it never will be. You knew the rules of this...arrangement.'

'So I did,' Kate said sadly, rising to her feet, thankfully more steadily than she'd feared.

And also...relieved.

'Of course, I won't take anything that came with this deal,' she said, tilting her chin. When he brusquely told her not to be ridiculous, and to expect him to pay her exactly what he'd promised whether or not the contract had been fulfilled, she replied as hard as glass, 'I won't be accepting a penny from you. If you make the mistake of sending money to me, expect it to be returned to you immediately.'

She walked towards the door and paused, then she glanced over her shoulder at the drop-dead gorgeous guy who hadn't budged from where he had fled on the opposite side of the sitting room. 'It's been fun. I'll pack as soon as I head up, and perhaps you could get your driver to return me to Milan. I'll be gone by the time you get there. And say goodbye to Angelina. She's very precious and, just for the record, you'd be a complete idiot to ever think about sending her to boarding school.'

Final piece said, she let herself out, and within forty-five minutes she was on her way to pick up the pieces of a life she'd spent the past two years building.

She left a pool of cold behind her.

Dante hadn't budged as she'd shut the door behind her. He'd remained as still as a marble statue, his body wired and rigid, knowing that she was upstairs getting ready to go.

And of course there was no option! On cue, he had called his driver and ensured that his car would be ready and waiting to return her to Milan.

She was right—she would be gone by the time he got back there. Indeed, he knew that he could stay on for longer in Venice with his uncle, giving her ample time to clear off before he returned.

Love? No. Hadn't he made it perfectly clear that that wasn't on his agenda? Hadn't he told her more than once that theirs was a working relationship and nothing more, even if sex had been introduced into the equation, an addition that neither could have foreseen when their plans had been made?

He wanted his life run on clear-cut lines. His marriage had been a failure and had shown him the nature of his limitations which, deep down, he had already known. Emotions and the messiness that accompanied them were not for him.

Hadn't he told her that, more than once?

If she had chosen not to listen, then so be it, but now that the pact between them had been broken, and an impossible gauntlet thrown down, he had no choice but to let her go. Disentangling the whole business would be annoying and inconvenient but not beyond the wit of man.

Angelina would be bitterly disappointed, but she would recover, because children did that—they recovered.

All those thoughts raced through Dante's head as he eventually got moving and sat on one of the chairs, nursing a glass of whisky and scowling at a turn of events he hadn't anticipated.

Was this his fault? Had he led her on? Taken his eye off the ball and given her hope for something more where there was none?

He'd said all the right things…

But had he *done* all the right things?

He stared down into the amber liquid, swirling it in his glass, trying to think, but it was suddenly like wading through treacle.

His thoughts wanted to go somewhere but he could no longer direct them, and they drifted in his head, disconnected and just out of reach of interpretation.

Time would sort this edginess out, he decided. And he

would send the money to her. What she chose to do with it would be up to her but, having met her parents and bonded with them, it was the very least he could do.

It was several hours later before he fell asleep, half a bottle of whisky to the good.

Kate knew that she was dithering. She'd been so tired after that drive back to Milan. Dante's driver had been waiting for her, not that she'd needed reminding of how keen Dante was to see the back of her now that she'd become too hot to handle with her declaration of love.

She should have slept in the back of the car but her head had been buzzing. One minute, she'd been as high as a kite and elated that she had been brave enough to tell him how she felt, and them immediately after plunged into the cold depths of misery as a future without him had loomed ahead of her in all its cold reality.

Which meant that she'd been exhausted by the time she made it back to his villa in Milan. Exhausted enough to have fallen asleep, fully clothed, on her bed.

Not *his* bed, which she had shared for so many glorious nights, but hers, the bed she should have stuck to before adventure had beckoned and she had thrown caution to the winds.

She woke with a fuzzy head, disoriented, and for a few seconds wondered where the heck she was and what was going on. Weak sunlight was streaming through the windows because she hadn't bothered to draw the curtains.

Realisation of what had happened hit home with the force of a sledgehammer, galvanising her into action.

What an unholy mess. That was all she could think as she flung things into the suitcases she had brought with her from England.

She didn't want to think about Dante. She didn't want

to think about anything. She couldn't begin to contemplate the nightmare she had left him to deal with when it came to retracting the engagement they had only just announced.

She had to sift through the finery to pull out all her old stuff, depressingly shabby and cheap in comparison, with her head all over the place. It was only when she had dragged her cases down and was about to head to the kitchen to grab some coffee that she heard the thunderous sound of a helicopter.

Dante's helicopter.

She recognised it from those rare occasions he had landed on the specially designed bit of land at the back of the villa. Like many uber-wealthy Italian aristocrats, he had helicopters at his disposal, although he seldom used them because of environmental reasons.

What the heck was he doing back here?

She needed time to run away!

But, if she couldn't have that, then she needed time to gather her forces. He would have been called back on urgent business and with any luck she could avoid him altogether. She couldn't imagine he wanted to say anything to her or even see her.

But as she lay low in the kitchen, aware that he would spot her bags by the front door when he entered, she was braced for a confrontation as she heard the sound of his footsteps on the marble floor.

And then there he was.

So tall, so impossibly handsome. She struggled to breathe and had to make her way to one of the leather chairs by the table and sink into it whilst dragging her eyes away and focusing on her coffee.

He looked terrible. Good. Maybe he'd at least reflected on the road ahead that would involve him wriggling like a worm on a hook when he was forced to explain away the vanished engagement.

She couldn't imagine him wriggling like a worm on a hook.

'I'm sorry.' She broke the silence to look at him as he remained standing in the doorway. 'I didn't expect you to return so quickly or else I would have left earlier. I've already packed, as you've probably seen. My suitcases are by the front door. I'll finish my coffee and be on my way.'

'Kate…'

'No!'

'No what?'

His voice was haggard. 'Have you been drinking?'

'Maybe a little.'

'And you *flew* the helicopter?'

'Would that worry you?'

Sudden rage consumed her. How could he just show up here and have this devastating effect on her? Yes, she knew, of course she did, but she still resented the love that made her vulnerable.

'It would worry me if anyone was stupid enough to do anything that could endanger their life and other people's lives while under the influence of drink.' Her voice was cool.

'My pilot got me here.'

'I'm going to go now.' She pulled her phone out to call the cab company she always used, and when she next glanced up it was to find that he had covered the distance between them and was standing in front of her, his hands resting on the back of the chair which he had pulled out. 'I don't want you here,' she whispered shakily.

'I know you don't but… What you said…'

'No! I refuse to discuss that. I said what I said and I'm not going to go over it. Why would I? You've made yourself abundantly clear on the subject of not wanting me in your life.'

'Can I sit down?'

'It's your house.' But as she began to stand, a response to him sitting down, she froze because he reached out to circle her wrist and memories of his touch flooded through her with blistering force.

'You told me you love me,' he rasped. 'I was a fool to push you away.'

Kate glanced at him, torn between dragging her hand away and listening, and then hating herself for being tempted to listen.

'I'm not listening.'

'Please.'

She hesitated. He was the last man on the planet to beg for anything but there was a plea in his dark eyes that cut through all her defences.

'You have five minutes.' She shrugged off his hand, folded her arms and stared at him in unwelcoming silence.

'That'll do.' He raked his fingers through his hair. 'You know so much about me. More than anyone ever has. I never realised how much I'd told you over time about myself or how comfortable I'd become in your presence until—until suddenly our familiarity with one another hit me, winded me, scared me.'

He sighed. 'I'd never had that before. Even with my parents there was a formality that we never managed to breach. I think somewhere, somehow, I'd hoped that I might find *normality* with Luciana, find that elusive thing that seemed to make marriages tick…' He smiled sadly. 'And, when my marriage ended in disaster, I shut the door on those hopes for ever.'

'Yes,' Kate acknowledged with painful honesty.

'I concluded that I wasn't capable of love, and more importantly would never again delude myself into believing that it might exist for me, for someone like me.'

He gazed at her with such tenderness that she was disoriented. Even in the depths of their passion, when real life had disappeared under an onslaught of wild craving, she had never seen what she saw now.

She wanted to talk. She remained silent.

'I never knew that it would sneak up on me like a thief in the night, steal all my ramparts and leave me exposed. Kate, my darling, when you told me how you felt, I obeyed the instincts that had been driving me for most of my life. I pushed you away. And then I drank too much whisky for my own good and pretended that, when it had done its work, I'd open my eyes and find that nothing in my life had changed. Find that you were gone, but I'd be on track, because no one had ever thrown me off-course before.'

'And?'

'I thought of you coming back here…packing your things just like you've done…and the thought was so unbearable, I couldn't sit still. I couldn't breathe. I felt like I was suffocating under the weight of thinking that I might have lost you for ever.'

He paused and shot her a crooked smile that was filled with so much emotion, her heart felt fit to burst. 'So here I am. Begging your forgiveness and telling you that the thing I want most in life is to be with you, to share my dreams with you and…most importantly…to not feel scared of a future of giving my heart to the woman I love. So…will you marry me, my darling? For real?'

Moments like this, Kate thought in a daze, were made to be bottled.

'There's nothing in the world I would like more, my love…'

* * * * *

COMING SOON!

We really hope you enjoyed reading this book. If you're looking for more romance be sure to head to the shops when new books are available on

Thursday 3rd August

To see which titles are coming soon, please visit

millsandboon.co.uk/nextmonth

MILLS & BOON

MILLS & BOON®

Coming next month

INNOCENT'S WEDDING DAY WITH THE ITALIAN
Michelle Smart

"Do you, Enzo Alessandro Beresi, take Rebecca Emily Foley to be your wife?"

He looked her in the eye adoringly and without any hesitation said, "I do."

And now it was her turn.

"Do you, Rebecca Emily Foley, take Enzo Alessandro Beresi..."

She breathed in, looked Enzo straight in the eye and, in the strongest voice she could muster, loud enough for the entire congregation to clearly hear, said, "No. I. Do. Not."

Enzo's head jerked back as if she'd slapped him. A half smile froze on his tanned face, which was now drained of colour. His mouth opened but nothing came out.

The only thing that had kept Rebecca together since she'd opened the package that morning was imagining this moment and inflicting an iota of the pain and humiliation racking her on him. There was none of the satisfaction she'd longed for. The speech she'd prepared in her head died in her choked throat.

Unable to look at him a second longer, she wrenched her hands from his and walked back down the aisle, leaving a stunned silence in her wake.

Continue reading
INNOCENT'S WEDDING DAY WITH THE ITALIAN
Michelle Smart

Available next month
www.millsandboon.co.uk

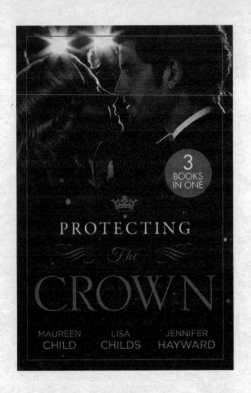

MILLS & BOON

THE HEART OF ROMANCE

A ROMANCE FOR EVERY READER

MODERN

Prepare to be swept off your feet by sophisticated, sexy and seductive heroes, in some of the world's most glamourous and romantic locations, where power and passion collide.

HISTORICAL

Escape with historical heroes from time gone by. Whether your passion is for wicked Regency Rakes, muscled Vikings or rugged Highlanders, awaken the romance of the past.

MEDICAL

Set your pulse racing with dedicated, delectable doctors in the high-pressure world of medicine, where emotions run high and passion, comfort and love are the best medicine.

True Love

Celebrate true love with tender stories of heartfelt romance, from the rush of falling in love to the joy a new baby can bring, and a focus on the emotional heart of a relationship.

Desire

Indulge in secrets and scandal, intense drama and sizzling hot action with heroes who have it all: wealth, status, good looks…everything but the right woman.

HEROES

The excitement of a gripping thriller, with intense romance at its heart. Resourceful, true-to-life women and strong, fearless men face danger and desire - a killer combination!

To see which titles are coming soon, please visit

millsandboon.co.uk/nextmonth